Old Mountain
Cassie

The Three Lessons

TONYA PENROSE

ISBN 978-1-64079-922-6 (paperback)
ISBN 978-1-64079-924-0 (hardcover)
ISBN 978-1-64079-923-3 (digital)

Copyright © 2018 by Tonya Penrose

All rights reserved. No part of this publication may be reproduced, distributed, or transmitted in any form or by any means, including photocopying, recording, or other electronic or mechanical methods without the prior written permission of the publisher. For permission requests, solicit the publisher via the address below.

Christian Faith Publishing, Inc.
832 Park Avenue
Meadville, PA 16335
www.christianfaithpublishing.com

This is a work of fiction. As such, names, characters, businesses, places, events and incidents are either the products of the author's imagination or used in a fictitious manner. Any resemblance to actual persons, living or dead, or actual events is purely coincidental.

Printed in the United States of America

"Sow a thought and you reap an action; sow an act and you reap a habit; sow a habit and you reap a character; sow a character and you reap a destiny."
—Ralph Waldo Emerson

For Lindsay, Karen, and Tom, as without them, *Old Mountain Cassie* would still be living in three spiral notebooks.

Chapter 1

IN THE QUAINT APPALACHIAN VILLAGE of Divine, brooms swept their shop owners outside to trade tales of the latest sighting of Old Mountain Cassie. Local lore claimed Cassie held the secret to a prosperous and joyous life for those so destined. Outside Holsom Market, Lacey Jordan stood admiring the baskets of fresh blueberries. Her growing fascination to meet the reclusive mountain sage intensified as she eavesdropped on the latest Cassie chatter swirling around her.

The ding of a text intruded, calling her back to the morning's upset. "What a weasel!"

"Who's a weasel?" her approaching friend, Serene, asked, glancing around for anyone weasel-like nearby.

"Oh, hi, Serene. You startled me. My boss, Don Mitchell, of course. How could you even ask after me sharing this guy's ongoing stunts?" Lacey released a pent-up sigh, daring her eyes to shed a tear over her current dilemma. She took the elastic from her wrist and tied corn silk hair away from her petite face. At the moment, her thirty-something self felt warrior-like just thinking about her boss... now ex-boss.

"Well, one person's weasel is another person's lion." Serene allowed a grin to show.

"Weasel, the man's no lion," Lacey stated emphatically, clearly not ready to share in any of her friend's attempt at humor. "Listen, I'm heading to the woods. I need a hike after my morning."

"You got the day off or something?" asked Serene.

"Yeah, I got something, all right. I e-mailed you my news, and no, I don't want to discuss it here on the sidewalk surrounded by the display of blueberries and listening ears. You coming?"

"Can't. I've got a full afternoon of clients, and obviously an e-mail to read explaining why you're not at work, but instead standing here all fiery with another Don exclamation." Serene's raven-colored hair cascaded around her shoulders, framing a willowy figure. Discerning, brown eyes didn't match her thirty-six years of age. Serene glanced at her friend's SUV parked a few yards away. "Go. I can tell you need the solitude. Just promise me you won't go looking again for Old Mountain Cassie's place."

"Come on, Serene. In two years of being in the forest, I've never come close to discovering anything Cassie-like. There's no point in looking according to Charlie at Holsom Market. Besides, he told me only those meant to have an encounter will find her. By the way, he's gotten in some beautiful yellow tomatoes, if you're interested," Lacey added, hoping to distract her friend from any more discussion around her obsession with Old Mountain Cassie. "Here's an idea, why don't you come by later and we can go for pizza?"

Serene studied her friend for a few seconds. "Hear you, but not sure I believe you about Cassie, though pizza sounds good. Who knows, maybe I will have a contract to celebrate." A wave punctuated her friend's retreat to the world of real estate sales.

Lacey got into her small SUV parked in front of Charlie's market and, with a nod his way, closed the vehicle's door. No need to lock your doors in Divine. The locals took offense to anyone doing such a thing. Pleased her weathered hiking boots waited in the front seat, Lacey headed to the trails. The sooner she got into nature, the sooner she could release her anger at Don, the weak-witted weasel.

Lacey had to admit her fascination with Old Mountain Cassie was growing. She kept sensing that meeting Cassie held some unknown significance for her. She'd heard tales of Cassie's doings ever since moving to the quaint mountain retreat that boasted more than its share of "interesting folks." Local color didn't come close to describing life in Divine. One day, she'd ask Charlie how the town got its name since he acted as the town's unofficial historian.

Lacey found a clearing and parked. She checked the backpack kept ready for hikes. Water bottle, granola bars, adhesive bandages, notebook, and a pen. She tossed in the cell phone to please the common-sense part of her.

The day still held promise, Lacey thought as she moved toward a blaze-marked trail. The sun's rays added warmth to the sixty-degree day's pleasure. Clouds were few but, upon examination, put on a show of shapes that could hold a person's attention for a stretched-out afternoon. She'd told no one of her recent heightened senses and appreciation of nature's friendliness. How could she? She didn't understand these odd occurrences herself.

A bird flew by, dipping low to catch a current singing a robin's song to Lacey. The trail head narrowed to a path well-worn, welcoming a solo hiker. That was her, all right. Plenty solo. No mate. Now no longer employed.

She replayed the parting scene one last time in her mind, knowing the woods would accept her rant…would take her tears falling on the carpet of mosses. Yep, Don had called her into his office all smiles and good morning chatter meant to set a tone of rare civility. Lacey knew what was coming before he changed the subject. The board of directors for Stardust Jewelry, Inc. had issued a directive for yet more staff cutbacks. Don had made his choices, and she was one.

It didn't matter that Lacey had been his award-winning senior gemstone buyer and had brought in new accounts even during escalating gold prices. No, what mattered to the portly Don was keeping happy his young junior buyer, Ginger, who also happened to be his latest girlfriend. Much to the distress of Lacey's coworkers, Ginger would be moving to Lacey's expansive corner office, clueless to the job's demands and rigors. She felt sorry for those left depending on Ginger to save the company's second quarter sales. She truly hoped Stardust could survive despite the weasel's decisions.

And how like her worrying mind to choose now to bring painful memories forward. Hadn't it only been two years since she exchanged her coveted position with a diamond syndicate in New York for a simpler life in the little Appalachian village? Lacey had craved this change after losing both of her parents to a freak sailing accident off Nantucket. Being an only child intensified the emptiness left by loving parents. Back then, she'd decided to write a new chapter for herself, and she'd been making a pretty good success of it until today's surprise.

Lacey escaped to the woods, granting her anxious mind permission to take stock of her current situation. First, she gratefully acknowledged her money market account held the twelve months' reserve for living expenses that her parents had always encouraged her to maintain for a rainy day. Her retirement account didn't factor into this mental review. Okay, she reasoned, so money worries didn't top the list of concerns…yet. Figuring out what work she truly wanted to do next surely did. Maybe losing her job would provide the catalyst she needed to plot a different course, and may it present soon. Taking a fresh look at her surroundings, Lacey let go a breath, realizing her changing lot asked her to figure out some things she'd been ignoring for a long time, starting with her life lacking passion and joy.

A group of squirrels chattering over a stray acorn brought her back to the present. They looked at her as if to say, "You decide which one of us is the most deserving." Lacey's legs moved her closer, while her mind watched in awe. She glanced down at five, furry faces and the lone, tasty acorn. Her hand snatched up the brown nut. Their protesting screeches increased as if each squirrel was making his case for the acorn. Lacey offered it to the scrawny, little fellow closest to her. He scampered over gently, accepting the nut from her extended hand. She could have sworn the critter grinned at her. His buddies took off in search of food, while he remained by her side acting like a hiking companion. "You're strange but cute." Lacey tossed him some granola, reveling once again in another friendly forest exchange.

Unaware she'd been observed, Lacey continued her meditative hike, noting the sun's face had dropped behind Hemlock Mountain. The forest creatures began their callout to end the day. Normally, her gold wristwatch determined her movements but not today. Today she felt timed with all of nature. How was it that this afternoon she'd heard and sensed so much around her? She'd been asleep to the abundant beauty of nature's rhythms and voice.

A red cardinal fluttered by, his chirp interrupting her musings. He landed on a low branch, eye-to-eye with her, his head dipping in a nod.

Lacey stood, smiling at his courage. A sense of feeling connected to everything in some unknown way took hold. She inhaled a cleansing breath, returning her awareness to the waiting bird. "I must say I prefer your company to that ex-boss of mine. Trust me, you'd not care for the weasel either." Great, now she was conversing with a male cardinal while her mind and life were unraveling. She needed her vehicle to take her to something based in reality…pizza.

Chapter 2

HIDDEN BY A STAND OF rhododendrons, Old Mountain Cassie watched through wise eyes, a smile dressing her face. She'd seen Lacey on hikes often and had been witnessing a change in the young woman. The forest dwellers amplified this shift as they announced Lacey's visits and moved closer to make their introductions known.

Cassie knew a Seeker when she saw one, and this pretty little gal had just begun the desired awakening. The older woman secretly studied the younger one. Confidence on the outside hid Lacey's confusion churning on the inside. "Yep, Seekers have to find their truth once nudged…their special gifts in the proper time," Cassie whispered to her dog, Lickety Split.

Cassie had made the same journey long years past to understanding the ancient truths…The Three Lessons on how to live life amazing. It'd been easier for her than it would be for Lacey. The path toward finding her gift was nurtured easy-like by the women in her family. Each took the knowledge and grew it in their special way…in their special time. The gift manifested in ways that were unique for each Seeker, ways that were often vexing too.

True, Lacey hadn't met the older woman studying her from behind the green thicket, nor could she know that Old Mountain Cassie would soon become her teacher. Cassie had helped other Seekers gain understanding to discover their unique abilities. Cassie knew God sent a Seeker only when she felt ready for the undertaking, but the time wasn't right this day.

Old Mountain Cassie grew her patience with a deep breath, trusting that the joy of gaining a new student wouldn't cause her to reveal herself yet. This Lacey would be a challenge no doubt. The younger woman had grown many years grounded in her society. Parting with those known ways to blossom boundless toward a fresh way of living would not come easy at first.

    Two young deer emerged from the thickets to join Cassie, their velvet noses pushing her departure. "Okay, okay, I understand. Guess it's time I be moseying home." With one final glance at Lacey chatting to her companion cardinal, Old Mountain Cassie and her dog slipped away.

Chapter 3

Lacey entered her cottage. She exchanged her hiking boots for a pair of navy flats and caught a glimpse of her puzzled face in the hall mirror. The day had left her changed and full of questions. Serene's familiar knock told her the quest for understanding the job loss and forest encounters needed to be postponed.

Serene flew past the open door. "Hey, listen, I've been thinking about this whole job loss thing. I can only imagine how hard this has hit you. All I'm going to say on the matter is that something grand will present itself and make you glad you're not in that pressure cooker job. The stress has been enormous on you, and I think—"

Lacey raised her hand to protest.

"Won't say another word. Nope, not even a syllable." Serene grinned as proof she'd left the serious talk behind. "So, tell me, how did the hike treat you? You didn't go looking for Old Mountain Cassie?" She paused. "Did you?"

Lacey started to object.

"I know. I know. You can't help being obsessed to hear any village chatter about our recluse, not to mention the constant hope for a Cassie sighting." Serene studied her friend's face, waiting for a reply.

"Okay, I admit to still feeling a smidge intrigued—"

"A smidge?" Serene rolled her eyes. "Oh, never mind. Let's go. I'm so hungry that I could eat squirrel." Serene snagged her friend's purse, propelling them out the door.

"Funny you mentioned squirrel. I met a cute one today, but alas, no sighting of Old Mountain Cassie." She gave an exaggerated sigh and then winked. "Let's walk the few blocks to Paulie's Pizza Palace, and you can share the news if you sold any Divine real estate this afternoon. That's far more interesting." Lacey led the way, setting a quick pace for her hungry friend.

Paulie's wasn't much of a palace, more a converted stone house with a quirky roof and a narrow walking bridge that crossed a noisy stream. Only if Lacey drank enough of Paulie's Chianti and squinted did she glimpse something castle-like in the design.

Paulie could turn a pizza even better than her old favorite haunt, Mama Leone's in Brooklyn, which Lacey had discovered thankfully just blocks away from her apartment. Mama fed her weekly, and now she had Paulie filling that need with his crust that was buttery delicious with a savory crispness, making it as unique as Paulie. "My pies once tasted, make yous' mine for life," Paulie liked to tell new customers.

"Wonder what our Pizza Man Extraordinaire has in store for us tonight?" Serene asked, bringing Lacey back to the present. They stood inside the entrance with their hunger, waiting for Paulie to seat them.

"I feel like something veggie...no animals." Lacey wrinkled her nose, thinking of her forest friends she'd met earlier.

"What? You love his jerk chicken pizza."

"Ugh. No feathers either. Not tonight," Lacey muttered, feeling queasy at the thought.

"Well, well, ladies, come on here. I've got a booth right in the corner, so yous' can chat it up like always." Paulie's flushed round face meant he'd enjoyed a busy night. His stocky shape was easy to ignore when his caring, brown eyes settled on anyone in his midst.

The two sat, smiling up at the hardworking guy whom everyone liked as much as they did his food. None of his regulars got a menu. Instead, Paulie served his "special customers" the pizza he felt matched his read on them.

"So, what yous' want to drink this lovely spring night? Serene, I have you a nice cold brew in a frosted mug. Am I right?" he asked with a wink.

"You know me, Paulie." Serene tucked the napkin under her chin and started making friends with the wooden bowl of buttery pretzels.

"Lacey sweetheart, I think you want a drink other than your usual. I got my ears on. Speak." Paulie's proud Italian upbringing was captured in every phrase.

"You're right as rain. I think hot tea would be lovely."

"Hear that, Serene? Tea. No fizzy water. I sensed she wasn't feeling it for the usual," he replied, having fun with the girls.

With her mouth full of pretzels, Serene could only manage a nod.

"Well, okay then. You, two fine ladies, just relax now. I know just the pie to bring each of yous' tonight." Paulie departed, stopping at each table to see if things were "copasetic." He prided himself each week on learning a new word and didn't mind sharing it with his patrons. Satisfied that everything was indeed copasetic, Paulie went back to the kitchen to place the orders.

"Paulie's something. I bet he gets lonely." Lacey dug into the pretzels with gusto.

"Him lonely? You're kidding. Paulie lives at his Pizza Palace. People are here all the time."

"Yeah, but he's closed two days each week. Wait a minute here, are you wanting to date Paulie?" Lacey latched onto the idea of Serene and Paulie 'mingling.'

"No, of course not, but I was just thinking whom we might fix Paulie up with, you know, an evening out and maybe a movie. Nothing intense."

"Count me out of matchmaking. Barbie's still not speaking to me. And she's my hairstylist, so not good." Serene reminded Lacey.

"Well, honestly, how could you know the guy you hooked her up with had a huge spider collection?"

"On every wall. Very creepy. He seemed so nice." Serene ended with a sigh.

"Like I said, your motives were well intentioned."

"You're right. How did I know he was president of the Ardent Arachnology Club? Good that I didn't find him a property to buy. He's staying put in the nearby town." Serene sat back, done pleading her case. She eyed the empty pretzel bowl with disappointment.

They looked at each other and burst out laughing. The two friends spent the next twenty minutes chatting about various doings in the quaint mountain village. They shifted the conversation to the season's favorite topic... the always anticipated Divine Day Festival. Planning it always brought everyone out of winter hibernation. And Divine did love its celebrations. The pizzas arrived, staving off any more talk until the first bite could be savored.

"Paulie takes personal pizza to a whole new level." Lacey stared down at her pan. The crispy crust lay covered in cheese but topped with the surprise of pine nuts. She grinned, recalling her squirrel friend earlier, and fell in love not with Paulie but with his concoction. Now, this pie was indeed copasetic.

"Good grief. You actually like that squirrel and bird topping? Give me my beloved pepperoni and Italian sausage any day. Yummy!" Serene snagged a slice.

"Yous', gals, all happy...copasetic-like?" asked Paulie, making another round.

"Oh, man, I love you for giving me my dose of Italian heaven tonight. The flavor of the sausage is spectacular." Serene looked up at Paulie, giving a wide-tooth grin to her "pie pleaser."

He returned her smile that said more than "cheese" to a surprised Serene.

"Paulie, I've never had pine nuts on pizza before. I absolutely adore this. I won't dare ask how you knew."

"Babe, Paulie has senses others don't," he replied, though his brown eyes never left Serene's face.

Lacey took in the bonus of observing her two friends. *Maybe... just maybe*, she thought.

Lacey picked back up on discussing the mayor's idea for a new theme for Divine Day Festival. That topic carried them through to the end of the meal. Standing outside the restaurant, the two friends hugged good night and turned in opposite directions.

Lacey set a slower pace during the few blocks back to her cottage. She glanced up at the night sky. How the universe spoke to her spirit when she paused to connect. She walked up her sidewalk, thinking the rocker on her front porch looked lonely and decided to keep it company. What better place to review the day's events and watch the stars travel. Funny how the loss of her job wasn't a part of the look back. No, it revolved around the encounters in the woods and Paulie making her the strange but delicious pizza. Embracing the cool evening air, Lacey realized she'd forgotten to share any of the hike's details with Serene.

She and her rocker found a rhythm. A shooting star traveled across the sky as if connecting the dots of one star with another. Was that maybe what life was about? Connecting the dots each day to form a picture of a life lived? Then what did the dots show about her time so far? Nothing out of the ordinary, and for the first time, that awareness left her feeling…unsettled.

Chapter 4

OLD MOUNTAIN CASSIE WATCHED THE dying embers inside the stone fireplace as her thoughts returned to the young woman who had visited her woods. She knew Lacey wasn't a local, but she did fit easily with the townsfolk. Cassie had no doubt that Lacey belonged in Divine. The Heavenly Scrolls declared that fact, and today Cassie was focused on one Lacey Jade Jordan. Jade. The name honored the family lineage and Lacey's grandmother Violet Jade… who happened to be Cassie's eldest sister.

A young Cassie hadn't spent much time in her older sister's company. Violet had been twelve years ahead of Cassie on life's journey. Each woman in Old Mountain Cassie's family had known about "their gift" and was free to discover how the gift manifested. Yet the beautiful and frivolous Violet had succumbed to society's charms, abandoning her special "gift" at their parents' front door. She had chosen with her free will to ride off in Kenneth Morton's fancy wedding carriage to become his affected wife. Violet sent her family an occasional letter and returned home only once to attend their mother's funeral.

Violet's only daughter, Rachel, stayed behind in their antebellum home in Natchez. Cassie's older sister didn't dare chance any of the family questioning whether Rachel had discovered and put to service her own rare gift.

As a grown woman, Cassie devoted her life to large doses of solitude. She'd inherited a tract of land outside Divine that included a mountain and a generous sum of money to be used for her life's calling. She'd learned quickly that gifts came with a personal price, a price Cassie paid with a glad heart, for in the giving lived joy.

Cassie always felt the pull of these mountains, rich with their vibrant vegetation and unique beckoning. Among the plants and trees, her gift stirred. Here she'd received God's guidance and tools to unlock her true purpose for being.

Her eyes looked toward the window where a familiar sound gathered in decibels. She gave a nod to Lickety Split, the mixed mutt that claimed her when a mama skunk chased him onto her porch. He'd just about licked her plumb into the next county with his gratitude of being welcomed.

"Lickety, let's you and me take a gander."

She opened the heavy planked door. The dog, aptly named for his quickness to retrieve and the generous use of his tongue, bolted outside. Cassie and he had an understanding. Lickety could stay as long as he kept the critters out of her house. The front porch allowed furry visitors, but Lickety and Chakra, the calico cat, were the only ones invited indoors.

"I hear ya. I hear ya," Cassie shouted back to the ruckus going on in her critter garden. Each spring, she planted a carrot patch for the bunnies to come enjoy. Two feisty hares were into a fuss over the first carrot ready for harvesting. "You at it again? Never seen two girls always chasin' after the same thing. Today it's a carrot, isn't it?"

The rabbits paused, hearing Cassie's admonitions.

"Well, give it here." Old Mountain Cassie shook her finger at them.

Showing some age but no shortage of agility, she whisked the carrot up and snapped it in two. She bent down to settle the squabble by rewarding half to each expecting furry face. The pair sat side by side munching the treat.

"Back to friends, is it? Well, how about next time settlin' this yourselves? Me and Lickety Split got herbs to tend." Cassie and the dog returned to finish their breakfast before moving to the herb shed and gardens.

"Lick, we gotta get the sets of ginseng sorted for starters. Need you to do a bit of toting."

Lickety answered with a few barks and one cool slap of his tongue against Cassie's ankle.

"I don't care what Chakra thinks about you bein' a suck-up, you'll do. You'll do." She leaned down to pat her companion's head.

The dog stood with uncharacteristic patience as Cassie placed the empty carry pack on his broad back. "Good fella, let's be off. We've got some harvestin' to do I'd be thinkin'. Yep. Got a little gal payin' us a visit one day soon who will be needin' something special to help with her learnin'."

Lickety offered his support with a few deep ruffs.

"Good to know you approve of our plan," Cassie said. She stopped to greet a new mother and her offspring. "Well, well, Tilly, I do believe that's the best-lookin' pair of Lil Toms I've seen in a spell." The turkey nudged her babies to stand up for Cassie's admiration. "Yes, handsome fellows aren't they, Lickety? Take good care of them now," Cassie continued on, picking up the pace upon seeing the early afternoon sun drop behind the trees.

Once inside with her plants, the mountain woman busied herself pinching drying leaves and caressing the new shoots, all the while encouraging the herbs to enliven their energy-giving abilities even more. Shelves lined each side of the shed with abundant natural light pouring in from fixed panes of glass. She'd designed every inch of the building, careful to bring in southern light with the sun's morning rays. As an herbalist, she understood the sun's powers and let her plants take full advantage of the gratuity.

The building's design was a perfect square measuring forty by forty, a size she could manage and still produce what was needed. Money might exchange hands, but often as not, it could be a bushel of apples or a peck of roasting ears. No matter, she had everything she desired.

A long table ran down the center of the largest room where the herbs were sorted and prayerfully dedicated to their mission. Special sacks with burlap and wax paper lay spread. Colored string and labels declared contents and use. Two rinsing sinks on each side assured cleanliness was blessed. Gooseneck faucets brought in the energizing water from the spring outside. Touched by Cassie's unique tending, the plants glowed with a rare vibrancy.

Cassie glanced over to see Lickety napping in his "shed bed." Satisfied, she continued her ministering.

The day slipped away, time ignored. "Well, pooch, what do you think of this little tote of ginseng?" Cassie held up a few bags. "Let's see. It weighs about seven pounds. Easy enough for you to carry, don't ya think?"

Lickety stood up and stretched. "Ruff."

"I hear you, boy. I'm ready to go too."

The setting sun warmed Cassie's back as she walked the path home. It had been a steering kind of day like she'd been nudged along. No doubt a Lacey meeting would be orchestrated. A fresh excitement ignited Cassie's spirit. She gave one of her characteristic solemn nods while her wise eyes glowed with a vitality usually reserved for the young. The shift within her had begun.

Chapter 5

Lacey awoke the next morning long before the songbirds hastened another day. She padded in her favorite mint green slippers to the compact kitchen clearly designed for someone with low expectations of producing any culinary delights. Assorted tea bags competed for attention in a wicker basket. "Let's see, what does this morning feel like?" she muttered aloud as her bright coral painted fingernails searched. "Ah, a warming cinnamon tea." She hesitated. Maybe raspberry, nice and fruity. Perhaps that could count as a fruit in her food group. Lacey's spirits lightened as she freed the tea bag from the envelope.

Her cat, Topaz, sauntered by, no doubt his hopes high as he checked out the food bowl. Finding it still empty, he sat down to wait. Lacey knew meows were soon to follow if she didn't awaken the can opener to the tin of his favorite mackerel. "Yuck! How can you eat this so early?" she questioned a moment later, scooping the contents in the bowl labeled "cat's meow."

"Topaz, I've been thinking. I hope you enjoy having me around because I'm not feeling like a job search is my next step just yet. I need a change, to what I haven't a clue, but no more jewelry companies for me. Nope, however, I may need a reminder as soon as the recruiters start calling, so stand ready." She pointed her index finger toward her feline friend and gave him a wink.

The normally aloof Topaz shadowed her all morning. "What's with you fur-and-feather types being so friendly of late?" Lacy asked, trying to navigate around the cat and the laundry basket. She felt like she'd turned into a critter magnet. Too bad she wasn't having the same effect on some great guy. Except for a few tepid dates, romance had been absent since moving to Divine. Mostly she tried to ignore that vacancy, but the reminder would creep in on a rare blue day.

The bell rang outside her cottage door, interrupting her musings. Straightening her pastel blue sweater over her jeans, she went to greet the visitor.

"Sorry to intrude on your morning, but Serene let it slip that your job had been eliminated. And, well, I thought…" Jane Ann shoved a basket of sweet-smelling treats into Lacey's arms. The older woman stood, smiling, pleased at being able to chalk up another good deed. Jane Ann, with her motherly countenance, prided herself on being the first at a door when a need arose for one of Divine's folks.

"You are so kind to make these for me. Thank you, Jane Ann."

"It's not that much really."

"Serene and her lip slips." Lacey chuckled while lifting the red checkered cloth napkin to peer inside the wicker basket.

"Yes, well, I was out walking Rascal last night and ran into Serene and Paulie heading toward her place. Now, isn't that some fine news?" Jane Ann grabbed a short breath of air. "I baked you a chess pie and some applesauce cookies," she said, hurrying on with her chatter.

"Looks delish, my kind of comfort food. This is one time Serene's yap brought me good stuff." Lacey bit into a warm chewy cookie. "Very yum."

"Glad you like my sweeties. It's hard to know what to bake for folks. I mean what they'll enjoy and all. You look like a sweetie kind of girl so…stop that, Rascal." The matron bent down to untangle her beagle's leash from around the porch rocker.

"So, you said Serene and Paulie were out last night, huh?" Lacey's amusement threatened to break through her serious expression.

"My stars, yes. I think I may even have spied them holding hands, though I can't swear to it."

"Interesting for sure, Jane Ann."

"Mind you, they acted like it meant nothing. One of those happenstance meetings, but they kept eyeing each other somethin' silly."

Lacey planned to have plenty of fun with her friend over this particular sighting. Granted, it wasn't near as good as spotting Old Mountain Cassie, but it would do…for now."

"They're moonstruck, I'd be guessing. Anyway, I gotta be going now, heading over to Charlie's with some apple muffins. The old geezer has finally agreed to carry them in his market," Jane Ann stated with a serving of pride.

"Why, Jane Ann, that's wonderful news. I can enjoy those muffins now and not have to wait for the summer sidewalk festivals."

"Aren't you the sweetest thing? You be sure and share that thought with Charlie. It'll help my cause." Jane Ann gave a wave.

Lacey took her basket of goodies inside, thanking God for leading her to Divine and the warm, caring people that defined the mountain community. She couldn't imagine spending her days anywhere else. Her elusive man, the love of her life, would just have to get his stars aligned to find her here. She made a solemn vow to find a way to remain in Divine and sealed it by having another cookie.

Driving toward Asheville, Lacey glanced at her watch. She and three empty cardboard boxes had an appointment with her old office and the task of carrying personal items back to her home's den. She reflected on the fact that some of her close work friendships would continue. She smiled, remembering the e-mail invitation for her going away party at Detective Dagger's Mystery Dinner Theatre. At least, that was something to look forward to.

And she made a mental note to call that sneaky Serene her first free moment and get her to fess up to some serious hanky-panky with Divine's Paulie. "Imagine her holding out on me," Lacey muttered to the vehicle's windshield. The spring day felt refreshingly cool as she made the forty-five-minute drive to the city.

Downtown Asheville was a city caressed by mountains on all sides. It had been given the name "The Paris of the South." Quaint shops with signs promising enlightenment were scattered along the sidewalks. Restaurants proudly displayed their menus, offering organic fare to inspire health. An eclectic mix of people dotted the city's landscape. Stardust's five-story building contributed to the downtown skyline. Lacey felt gloominess encompass her as she entered the atrium's elevator.

Lacey admitted there were lots of people she'd miss seeing, but surely there was a bigger plan to be revealed. Yes, this door was closing, and even though she didn't yet see the next door to walk through, she needed to believe it waited out there…somewhere. It must. Lacey stepped out of the elevator, plenty puzzled why she wasn't feeling frantic about trying to create a plan of action, for that had always been her way of dealing with the unexpected.

Chapter 6

Cassie whiled away the morning in her cabin. She liked to piddle more and more nowadays. It rested her mind. She needed that, especially when a new Seeker was being presented. She always stored up extra energy knowing her reservoir must be full. This day she'd chosen a particular herb, elderberry root, to be brewed in her favorite flowered teapot.

She sipped her energy brew and let a little fall from her cup into Lickety's water bowl. Chakra came nosing to see what he'd gotten that she'd missed. "I see your 'me too' radar is turned on, Miss Chakra. Last time I offered you a sample of my recipe, you pretended to cover it up." Cassie chuckled knowing well her cat's behavior. She had another potion for Chakra that catered to her persnickety ways. She'd mix up a batch later.

Cassie's farm did a good job of meeting most of her needs. Her hens laid enough eggs without much fuss, and she put up garden vegetables each summer to keep through the winters. The fruit trees scattered on her land satisfied her sweet tooth. She liked to dedicate a week each season to drying her apples and peaches. And her own health-infusing herbs and mountain spring water kept everything harmonious within her body. Beans and rice from Charlie's stocked her pantry, and Bud's Sweet Clover Dairy offerings made her bones extra strong. But the most pleasing part of her diet came from living simply alongside nature and partaking of her bounty.

Cassie's truck headed toward Divine with Lickety Split riding proud in the truck's bed. His black nose turned to catch every smell passing by. Cassie's hair, plaited and wound into a tight coil, didn't suffer the wind blowing in the truck's windows. A flowered shirt and denim overalls captured her spirit and original nature. This was Cassie's civilized go-to-town garb and, truth be told, her wardrobe most days, except for when her female wiles were awakened every blue moon.

The pickup chugged down a Divine side street. The few locals possessing grit hollered a greeting Cassie's way. Most steered clear, rather allowing the yarns to spin up a character that even Cassie admitted would take some doing to live into.

It's not that the wise sage couldn't be friendly, more she didn't see the need to waste her time passing the time. Small talk was just that…small in the giving and more in the taking. She had always spoken her mind, choosing an economy of words with such "time wasters." That choice served her well but did fuel the tales.

Cassie entered Mable and Frank Mercer's store. She'd ordered some new overalls and shirts so as to look fresh for Lacey's tutelage. No need setting any lazy examples as a great aunt. She handed Mable her pickup slip with a friendly Cassie nod and ambled down the aisles to see if anything caught her fancy and became a want.

Frank came out of the stockroom carrying an armful of shoe boxes. "Well, well, Miss Cassie, it's always a real pleasure having you visit our store. See anything you cotton to?"

"Appreciate that. I did spy those red boots on display over yonder." Cassie pointed at the item, eyeing their sass. The female in her showed up whenever a pair of fancy new boots caught her eye.

"These here?" Frank held up the shoes so Cassie could examine them closer.

"Yep. Got a size six? I might…just might I say, take a pair off your hands, if the price sounds right."

Frank handed over the shoe box. "Here you go, Miss Cassie. Brand-new style. Just got them in yesterday."

Cassie's hands were quick to grab the box and disappear around the aisle to a chair.

Frank grinned at the elusive woman. Anyone who spent a moment in the mountain woman's presence couldn't help but admire her spirit.

"What about that price?" Cassie's voice came from further away now.

"Why, for you, Miss Cassie, let's call it an even two hundred," Frank hollered back. He discovered her standing in front of the mirror kicking up a fuss. Red boots flashed on her feet like a fire truck's lights. Yep, Cassie sure defined special.

"Here's one eighty-five cash. You made yourself an easy sale." Cassie plopped the bills in Frank's outstretched palm.

Mable wouldn't be happy with his bad bargaining, but Cassie had her ways. She got him on something just about every visit. Good thing he could count on two hands the visits Cassie made to their store each year. He couldn't afford her as a regular. Frank pocketed the money. "Miss Cassie, I gotta say you sure look mighty pretty in those red boots."

"Oh, you hush. You got a fine wife. Save your flirty ways for her," Cassie replied in good spirits. She walked her sassy red boots up to the counter to settle her other bill with Mable and claim her packages.

Within minutes, she'd loaded her purchases in the truck's bed for Lickety to watch while she bought a newspaper.

A tuckered-out Cassie felt the call of her peaceful woods and home. The boots needed a rest, and so did the woman wearing them.

Chapter 7

Lacey made her farewells to her coworkers at Stardust, promising to see them at Detective Dagger's. They were a caring and talented bunch; however, the numbers of employees had dwindled considerably in the last year. Many of them had to scatter around the country to land new positions. Jobs in the jewelry industry were highly competitive, even in the best of times. She willed her mind to let her be and not send her into a jobless panic. Deep inside, Lacey knew the void was around her lack of direction and joy.

A fine mist of rain covered the windshield as Lacey steered the SUV toward Divine. The silence wasn't kind. She knew her mind craved a replay of her current situation, but she resisted. Instead, she selected a jazz station and waited for the lead singer to engage her for the journey home. And a stop at Serene's should provide some needed laughs and keep her mind distracted.

"Hey, Lace, come on in. I just tried calling you." Serene scurried back to her kitchen.

"Sorry to interrupt. You're having dinner." Lacey threw her purse on the chair, following her friend.

"It's just a BLT, but I'm not stopping till I eat this bad boy." Serene shrugged and piled the bacon even higher. "Want one?" She offered, pointing to the makings left on the counter.

"No thanks." Lacey's eyes trailed around the open room, always adoring Serene's place. It was decorated like a model home. Show ready, as Serene liked to say. The style was purely her with lots of eco-friendly choices like bamboo floors and reclaimed stone for her fireplace surround. The fern green and ivory color scheme gave it a Zen feel like you were at one with nature. "I really love the look of the new décor."

"I do too. As a real estate agent, I need to be able to reflect to my clients what Divine symbolizes and offers. You know…earth-friendly people who care on a deeper level." Sometimes she struggled to convey that meaning to others. Her words had to be chosen carefully to fit the audience.

"So, is Paulie…an earth-friendly fellow?" Lacey tossed out, watching with amusement when surprise colored her friend's face.

Serene tried to buy time by chewing her next bite more slowly than a turtle crossing the road. "Paulie…Paulie? Why ask me that? He's not a client." Serene quickly took another giant bite, eyeing Lacey suspiciously.

"Oh, well, it's just that Jane Ann saw you both last evening. And come on, spill it. Don't make me beg. I'm not good at it." Lacey went over to the vine-printed sofa and patted the cushion next to her.

Serene followed, bringing her last bite of sandwich. She took her time settling down. "Okay, okay, I'd planned on telling you."

Lacey raised an eyebrow and smiled. "Still waiting here."

"Yeah, yeah. Let me just say Jane Ann gets around way too much. She needs to stay home and bake more."

"Stop stalling."

"Fine. So, after I got home, nothing was on television but those ridiculous reality shows." Serene placed the empty plate on the slate coffee table.

"Keep talking."

"So, I thought I'd take a walk up to Sweet Treat's and get a cone. I'd been craving their pistachio mint ice cream all the live long day."

"Skip the craving part. Get to the juicy stuff." Lacey begged, holding her smile in place.

"It's not juicy. Come on. So, I'm about a block from my cone when Paulie is locking up the Palace. He's, you know, walking my way and all friendly. You know how he acts. He starts his flirt up asking why a pretty girl like me is walking alone."

"Funny, Paulie's never flirted with me. Point of fact, Paulie doesn't flirt except with you, dear Serene. He's just friendly Paulie to the rest of us. Please continue."

"Whatever. I tell him I had this day-long craving for pistachio mint, and he's, like, telling me that it's his favorite too."

"Imagine that," Lacey added.

"Do you want to hear this or not?"

"If you will hurry and get to the good part."

"So, he asks if he might escort me the rest of the way and stuff." Serene leaned back against the sofa cushions and picked up a nail file.

"Serene, best friend of mine, you're leaving out the good parts on purpose." Lacey snagged the file and put it back on the table.

"I want to hear about your visit to Stardust. That's enough about me," Serene volleyed back, trying to gain the upper hand.

"My story can wait. Your stuff is on the front burner and heating up."

"Oh, fine. He bought me an ice cream cone, and we 'chatted it up' like Paulie says. Got to know each other a little better. You know, he's really an interesting man. I didn't realize how much went into making pizza dough."

"Do tell." Lacey waited.

"Aren't you the funny girl? Turned out to be a nice evening. Paulie is warm and caring, and he takes his gift of feeding all of us very seriously."

"Yes, he does. He has a good spirit. And it's clear you are leaving out the parts about how you really feel about our Pizza Man," Lacey interjected.

Serene gave an impish grin. "For now, yes. That's all you're getting from me tonight." Serene's tone grew serious. She grabbed her empty plate, taking it back to the kitchen, sending a clear signal the subject was closed.

Even though they loved to banter, Lacey respected her friend's privacy. Serene would share more when she figured out her feelings.

Lacey's curiosity over this possible budding romance needed only a small dose of patience.

Serene returned with a pan of blond brownies and napkins. "Here you go. Consider it chum food. Your turn to share now. And for your information, I've been sending you good vibes all day."

"They helped because the whole Stardust pack-up experience turned out to be almost pleasant, absent of any drama. These brownies are so yum not to be chocolate," Lacey said, licking her fingers and eyeing a second bar. "Not much to report, really. I'm still worried about the company's health. Cleaned out my office and doled out my account files to the junior buyers to handle for the time being. Accepted a gazillion hugs, ate myself silly off a tray of cookies, savored some coffee toasts for future luck, and promised to attend my farewell party at Detective Dagger's Mystery Theater. Oh, and the weasel was thankfully out of town, and of course, Ginger was hiding who knows where. That's pretty much it. The end of my career at Stardust, Inc. all tied up in a nice parting and with me still not having a clue what I want to do next." Lacey felt sadness seep in with the recounting. She had to admit there were aspects to her work at Stardust that had felt gratifying, and she already missed some of her coworkers.

"The karmic wheel does turn," Serene interjected. She handed Lacey another brownie.

"Thanks. This really is an excellent recipe."

"Yeah, these bars are delish, if I do say so myself. Serene polished off number four. I did change the recipe and used fresh milk and butter from Sweet Clover Dairy."

"That must be the magic because I can't stop eating them either. Get that pan away from us and back to the kitchen." Lacey begged, swallowing her last morsel.

Serene rose with the pan, eating crumbs as she returned them to the counter. "I can't believe we have polished off all but three."

"I know. We're shameful. I'd better head home and work off those office cookies, a waffle, hash browns, and now your crazy good dessert. I'll be up till two in the morning on the treadmill," Lacey moaned as she moved toward the front door.

"Maybe I'd better take a walk myself," Serene added. She reached for her sweater while opening the door to the surprise of Paulie's smiling face. He stood waving a pint of pistachio mint ice cream in the air.

"Paulie, you just scared the pudding out of me." Serene opened the door wider.

"Yo, Serene, I'm sorry. I still had my craving and thought I'd see if you did too. I bought us a quart. Figured we'd be all 'harmonious' sharing. Am I right?" Paulie's eyes shone with happiness finding her home.

Serene stood in the door frame with her mouth wearing an enormous smile. Her head bobbed up and down. No words escaped, but Paulie seemed pleased with her body language.

Lacey came back from a quick U-turn to the kitchen. "Excuse me. I'll just take these last brownies with me, Serene. Seems you've got ice cream to share." With a wave to the distracted couple, she knew there would be more "stuff" coming about Paulie. Lacey laughed, doubting the two even noticed her leaving.

Weariness claimed Lacey as she turned into her driveway. No treadmill tonight, she thought feeling guilty, but the upside was her frets wouldn't claim her attention. A quick shower and her book by a favorite self-help author waited on her nightstand. Maybe her answer to what next waited in the book?

Chapter 8

OLD MOUNTAIN CASSIE AWOKE FROM one of her educatin' dreams. When they visited her, it meant only one thing to the sage—her new Seeker was in preparation, and it wouldn't be long before they were introduced in God's way. Today, she planned to unearth some old family photos. Lacey would surely need some proof of their connection. Having a Seeker who also happened to be her great niece made this assignment her most cherished reward. And finding the jade box had to be on her get-ready list.

Cassie paused, recalling how the box came to her. Violet had shoved the green inlaid jade box into Cassie's young arms before the Morton's carriage whisked her away and said, "You keep it. I don't want to tap into my special gifts. Never have. I just want to be like everyone who is normal in the world. There's a letter inside the box explaining."

Cassie felt sure Violet tried to live normal but never made a real success of it. She was only a success at pretending their mother always said to the family. Cassie reckoned her older sister had done just okay acting normal and raising Lacey's mom to be like others in their society.

"Lickety, we'll need every provin' tool for our Lacey. She's a questionin' one, all right, and won't take our word about things. Yep, the days are about to get mighty interesting. We best work up some powerful preparations." Old Mountain Cassie stood outside the open closet with her red boots dressing her feet.

The dog answered with his characteristic deep bark.

"First preparation, the way I see it, is a Cassie-style breakfast and an extra helpin' of Lickety Split mush for you." Cassie reached down to give her companion a scratch behind his ear.

The dog helped his cause by lifting a paw to shut the closet door with a resounding thud.

"I see what you mean. Eat first. Search and find later," Cassie said, heading toward her kitchen. The room had an eccentric look, not unlike the cook. Her favorite iron skillet waited by a six-burner red enamel stove. The solid hickory cabinets and golden quartz countertops supported the surprise of Cassie's kitchen possessing a modern stainless-steel refrigerator and dishwasher. A white antique style sink was dressed in a red checked skirt, giving the past a chance to be represented. Cassie flicked on the switch, showing off the stained-glass pendant lighting. It all worked together perfectly, mirroring Cassie's unique style.

The skillet came to life as soon as Cassie dropped a hunk of the local dairy's butter into it. Thick slices of home-baked bread got a bath of egg, thanks to Cassie's hens' contribution. A sprinkling of her special spices completed the dressing of each slice. The skillet did its part browning each piece to rightness under Cassie's discerning watch. Fresh fruit and cream waited in a purple pottery crock. Lickety sat next to his bowl with plenty of hope.

"Well, Lick, my Cassie Toast is about ready. Let's get your dish looking good too. What do you say?"

The dog planted a couple of wet kisses to Cassie's cheek as she bent over pouring his favorite breakfast into the container. His tail wagged faster as he watched her fill his bowl.

"You lover, you. Now I gotta go wash my face again. The red boots disappeared down the hall a little faster than normal. Moments later, a flushed Cassie and her tail-thumping dog tucked into a hearty meal together in a most companionable silence. It was their way.

Black overalls came out of the closet, along with a purple pinstriped shirt and jacket. Cassie looked down at her red boots peeking out from her chenille robe. A pout appeared on her face as she reached down to remove them in lieu of the trusty hiking boots that had seen her safely home on many a trail. She looked around the bedroom for the felt hat but saw only a tidy room with everything in its place.

"Lick, you seen my hat?" she hollered with impatience.

An answering bark sounded, followed by four feet galloping toward the great room.

Cassie entered to see the dog jumping in the air and trying in vain to snag the hat resting on the coat hook. "Good boy. Thanks for savin' me a hunt." Cassie placed the hat on her head and straightened the brim before bending down to reward Lickety with some extra love pats. "Listen here, Lick, before I hunt for the photos and jade box, I crave a bit of outdoor God time. You comin'?"

The dog streaked out the door and looked back at Cassie with the big chew hanging from his mouth. He grinned back, signaling he was accompanying her.

Mystic Rock Park didn't belong to anyone. It belonged to everyone. The slice of heaven resided on dedicated land where rocks came together to provide seats for anyone desiring to gaze upon the awe-inspiring gorge and take in some serious splendor. Cassie visited whenever her spirit felt like soaring. She could sit a long spell on her favorite rock, ignoring time and its constraints. She fancied others came there to have similar experiences and still others just to appreciate God's majestic beauty.

The day appeared glorious with the temperature touching fifty degrees. The sun's rays made a light show in the woods. Lickety entertained himself by chasing the moving shadows and biting at the mountain breezes. The two companions stopped near noon for their snacks.

"Come on, Lick, let's not dilly-dally. We're not far from a real sit-down."

Mystic Rock opened her arms quickly from the path in the woods. The view still awed Cassie with a breathtaking show guaranteed to greet all the senses. God liked to visit her spirit here.

"Something, isn't it?" Cassie asked her dog.

"Excuse me?" A voice came from behind a group of blooming mountain laurel.

Cassie rounded the corner to see the person to whom the voice belonged. Surprised, she quickly recovered. "I was talkin' to my dog there. His name's Lickety Split." She stopped herself from rambling on.

"Well, I have to agree Mystic Rock sure is something, all right. I've only recently been coming to this spot. If you're from here, I bet you know tons about its history." Lacey studied the older woman and, instead of being leery, felt a peaceful presence envelop her.

Cassie gave a curt nod. "Yep, I've been to this park more than a few times." She gave a little chuckle. "Pardon us. We'll be settlin' over yonder." Cassie moved hastily away to avoid more familiarity with Lacey. If Lacey answered, it got lost on the wind.

Cassie closed her eyes and took a deep cleansing breath trying to ignore Lacey's nearness. Another breath followed, but relaxation didn't. *Drat it all*, she thought. This isn't working. She took a peep. Everything seemed comfortable, except her insides. Cassie tried her breathing ritual once more…sending the crisp mountain air to her lungs to help her slip into the meditative state.

"Excuse me again, but I was wondering if you'd happen to have an adhesive bandage? I seem to have cut my leg on a sharp rock." Lacey's too-pale face looked down at Cassie.

Cassie eyed the cut and saw it wasn't deep, just messy. The pale face wasn't from blood loss but fear. "Hold on, gal. I've got what you need in my pack." Cassie rose to the occasion and walked over to retrieve her special kind of bandage.

"I normally carry something in my backpack, but for some reason, it's gone missing. Sorry to be such trouble," Lacey offered, trying to appear more responsible.

"No trouble at all. Here you go. Just rub this on the cut." Cassie handed her ball of what looked like mosses.

Lacey eyed the offering, trying not to show her concerns over the glob of God knew what. It didn't look like any bandage she'd ever bought from a drugstore.

"Go on. It's safe." Cassie encouraged.

A still skeptical Lacey took the ball and rubbed her bleeding cut. Within seconds, the oozing stopped, and the pain vanished, along with Lacey's doubt.

"Wow, that's something." She glanced at the woman standing a few feet away. Her mind interrupted, asking her to wonder if, somehow, she might be conversing with Old Mountain Cassie. Lacey dismissed the thought as fanciful, allowing that this woman didn't appear all that old.

"Always works too. See you won't need any adhesive strip now. They're not good for you no ways," she added, sharing more wisdom.

"Yeah, you're right. The cut looks like it's closing up already." Lacey studied the healing ball and her blood on it. She couldn't very well hand the magical sphere back in that state.

"You keep it. Rinse it off good, and it'll be ready for the next time." Cassie nodded, turning back toward her spot.

"Wait, thank you again. Guess I'll be going now." Lacey stood, testing her leg and amazed at the absence of pain. "It's been lovely meeting you." She tossed the words out, realizing they sounded too formal.

Cassie slowed her walk but didn't reply.

"My name's Lacey."

"Good name," Cassie said as she disappeared behind a thicket.

Chapter 9

The evening found Lacey and Serene munching buttered popcorn at the Cinema & Pub, Divine's only theater. Comfortable blue upholstered chairs encircled oak tables in the quaint dimly lit cinema. They'd intentionally arrived early to ensure a seat and to have time to chat.

Why don't you tell me about your day?" Lacey turned her chair to face Serene and waited.

"How about this? I finally wrote a contract with that young couple from Greenville. Yep, I sure did." Serene's head bobbed up and down as she stuffed another handful of popcorn into her mouth.

"Wonderful! Aren't they the couple who were all stressed out with job pressures and looking for a weekend getaway?" Lacey recalled.

"The very same. Hard to believe it's been a month since they showed up wanting an acre to build a cabin. One wanted a mountain view, and the other kept insisting on a noisy stream." Serene shook her head, remembering.

"I do so marvel at how much energy you give to conflicting couples. Don't you ever get two people who want the same thing?" Lacey asked, feeling sympathy for her friend.

"Where's the challenge in that? No joke. Sometimes I do get buyers that agree on how much to spend, but still, there's always some kind of conflict. My job is to help them find 'a piece of heaven' to call home."

"Yeah, 'a piece of heaven.' That sounds nice. And you know what?" asked Lacey.

"Tell me."

"You do exactly that for just about every client. I don't know how you find the places, but you do. Sister, you've got the touch." Lacey smiled back.

"Hmm…the touch. Yeah, I like that. Thanks." Serene sat taller in her chair.

"So, tell me which won? Was it the view or the stream?"

Serene's face beamed with joy. "Both. I found both. The only hitch was they had to buy five acres instead of one. The owner didn't have the land on the market. I'd run into him last week at Charlie's market. He mentioned about wanting to start a trout farm but needed more funds to accomplish the goal." Serene paused to wave to a familiar face.

"And so?" Lacey prompted.

"And so, I remembered that earlier conversation and that he had fifty acres of lovely land having streams and views. I called and asked him if he could spare five acres in return for the dollars to make his trout farm dream a reality."

"Very synchronistic, I'd say." Lacey nodded.

"Oh yes, but it gets even better. Once I told the young couple I had something loaded with charm to show them, they got excited before we even left the office. So cute. Anyway, I drove them out to see the land. The mountain views were especially magnificent today, and the stream was extra chatty from an earlier rain shower." Serene stopped.

"And…" Lacey encouraged, wanting to hear the best part.

"And when we got out of the SUV, there smack down in front of us was this glorious rainbow. The colors were incredible, Lacey." Serene still couldn't believe the vision.

I love rainbows," Lacey said wistfully. It's the colors you know, all combined in this beautiful harmony. Never mind, so what happened next?" Lacey asked, returning to the story.

"Well, they both started hooping, hollering, and hugging, carrying on like two kids on a hot summer day playing in a sprinkler. They kept saying how the land was the prettiest and most magical spot they'd ever laid eyes on. The two declared it theirs at that moment, and all conflict just evaporated into the mountain air."

"How wonderful for everyone involved. Truly," Lacey said, enjoying the happy ending.

"I agree. I love my work," Serene said with a sigh. She folded her hands in prayer and relaxed back in her chair. "Okay, your turn. What did you, the free spirit, do today?"

Lacey's response got interrupted by the screen's coming to life and the lights dimming. The music's somber notes caused Serene's eyebrow to raise as she glanced over at Lacey.

"Give it a chance," Lacey whispered, already sensing her movie-picking days looked *finito*.

The stabbing happened to the main character within the first five minutes. Serene groaned. Lacey slipped lower in her seat.

The two friends exited the theater, discussing the endearing qualities of the sleuth. They agreed the movie rated five stars, and Lacey felt redeemed.

"I love British sleuths. Don't you?" asked Lacey.

"I do. I especially enjoyed the female sleuth's quirky sense of humor," Serene added, adjusting her shoulder bag back into place.

Both turned the corner, walking the last blocks to Lacey's home. They passed a few neighbors chatting about blooms on azaleas, while a teenage boy and girl said a sweet good night on a front porch.

"What do you have to snack on at your abode? I know, always food with us." Serene gave a chuckle. "I still want to hear about your day before I head home and finish some paperwork," Serene added.

Lacey nodded in agreement. "Umm, let's see. I can make us some super tasty fruit smoothies."

Serene wrinkled her nose. "That's it? Smoothies? When I made those delish brownies and, I might add, let you pilfer the last three? Smoothies?" Serene stopped walking as her hands settled on each hip.

"Smoothies are very healthy." Lacey defended in mock sternness.

"Well, let me tell you, they don't sit right on top of root beer and heavily buttered popcorn. What else you got, sister? Or I'm heading on home to where my kind of snacks reside."

"Okay, Miss Picky, how about some mini frozen tacos?" Lacey didn't wait but started walking again. She knew her friend's tastes well.

"Now you're talking my food. Smoothies. Really. Pick up the pace, will ya?"

In less than thirty minutes, the two friends sat on Lacey's sofa with a tray separating them. Tacos rested on a plate, and glasses of cold lemonade offered fire control from the accompanying hot sauce.

"You know, these are really quite good for frozen. Where did you buy them? Charlie's?" Serene asked. She added even more sauce, letting it drip off onto her napkin.

"Actually, I found them at Earth's Bounty," answered Lacey, taking another bite.

"Wait a minute here, are you feeding me some of that—"?

"Natural grains instead of animal meat. Why, yes, I am, and you've been delighting in every bite," Lacey stated clearly, enjoying the emotions playing across Serene's face.

Serene carefully returned the remaining half of her taco to the plate. She stared at the appetizer and then at Lacey and then back again. Lacey waited, amused by her friend's inner struggles.

Reconciled, Serene picked up her taco and took another large bite. Her eyes dared Lacey to utter a word. "Tell me about your day. Anything noteworthy to share besides this taco tale?"

"I drove over to Mystic Rock to sit and ponder about my career being stalled and, of course, me as well."

Serene nodded. "That's the perfect place to go too. So what insights came? By the way, good lemonade. Please don't tell me where you bought it or what's really in it." Serene pleaded.

"Wouldn't dream of it. Just keep sipping while I tell you about a strange encounter. The insights I'll keep to myself, for now anyway."

"I'm listening."

"Well, I was sitting on a rock, taking in the vistas, when this older woman, actually quite a character, and her dog ambled by. We did share a brief exchange about the park, and I could tell she wanted to be alone, which, of course, I respected." Lacey stared off.

"So, what happened next?" Serene felt curiosity take hold.

"She disappeared to find her sitting place. I decided a bit later to take a short walk on the nearby trail. You know, sorta to gather my thoughts, only I stumbled right off, and a rock gashed my shin."

Serene's eyes darted to Lacey's legs, which were covered in jeans. "Are you all right?"

"Yeah, but just listen to this next part. I looked for a bandage but realized they were missing from my backpack, and I still can't explain that fact, but anyway, I digress. I go in search of the woman to see if she might have something I could use. The bleeding started up again as I walked in the direction of where I saw her go. I confess that I felt a tad worried about the cut." Lacey paused and took a sip from her glass.

"Did you find her?"

"I did. She was sitting on a rock with her dog nearby. I apologized for invading her serenity and told her of my mishap. She didn't have an adhesive bandage. In fact, she said they weren't good to use. How about that?" Lacey asked.

"Great. So here you are bleeding while some hiker gives a dissertation on the cons of adhesive bandages," Serene said, waving her arm.

"Listen, this is the crazy part of the story. She takes out this brown mossy ball and tells me to rub the thing on my cut. For real." Lacey watched for her friend's first reaction.

"Oh goodness. Seriously?" asked Serene, her level of interest piqued.

"Yeah, I kinda had the same reaction. She insisted, though. I don't know how to explain it, but I felt this instant trust of her."

"Then?" asked Serene.

"Then I rubbed this earth-smelling ball over the cut." Lacey grabbed a deep breath before continuing. "Serene, I swear to you I stopped bleeding immediately. Yes and get this. The cut closed up liked you'd expect after days of healing time."

"I believe you. Really, I do. What happened next?"

"Well, I stood there trying to decide what to do with this magic ball of whatever it was. I mean blood on it and all. I didn't want to hand it back to her all gross. She read my mind, I tell you. Told me to keep the healing ball. Of course, I thanked her for the help and tried to introduce myself properly." Lacey paused.

"What do you mean tried?"

"I gave her my name and expected her to tell me hers. Instead, she walked away and hollered back something like 'nice name.'" So, I left bringing my souvenir and story down the mountain. I can't stop thinking about this unconventional woman and, well, this whole encounter today with her. I can tell you it's taken the focus off my worries."

Serene sat quietly, something she didn't normally do. She had little doubt now of the older woman's identity. Her struggle was whether to tell Lacey. Serene settled on her answer. "I can see why you'd react this way. The mountains, like the rain forest, have many healing plants and trees."

"It's more than the crazy healing moss ball. It's the woman. I felt familiar with her. I can't explain it, but there's more to this meeting… another level or something. Oh, forget it. Clearly, I'm not myself since losing my job." Lacey stood gathering the empty glasses and tray.

Serene followed Lacey into the kitchen. "Look, I've got to go, but try to put these mixed feelings to the side. I've learned the important things return, so don't fret. I'm just happy you're okay and nothing serious happened to you out in the woods alone. Sometimes I worry about your solo hikes." Serene smiled gently.

Serene walked home with her relief. She couldn't be the one to tell Lacey she'd finally had her Old Mountain Cassie encounter. She was schooled enough to know a better way of introduction would be orchestrated.

Chapter 10

Lacey heard the phone ringing. The day was cold and damp, and her warm shower won out over a dash to answer. She glanced down at her cut, still amazed to see only a sliver of a mark remaining. Lacey wondered how the mossy ball would respond to the fine lines beginning to show around her eyes.

She dressed in comfortable stretch jeans and blouse with spring flowers, hoping the cheerful print would elevate her mood. There had to be some secret to happiness that those around her seemed to tap into. She wanted to feel that way too. And why was this melancholy feeling shadowing her? The question punctuated by a heavy sigh propelled Lacey into the den where her cell phone and message waited. Aunt Gabby's all too familiar voice trespassed heavily into her morning.

"Lacey dear one, I didn't hear back from you. I left a message with someone named Ginger at your office. So, I figured a follow-up call to your home was necessary. I hope this call doesn't catch you up short, but you've always been such an adaptable girl."

Lacey groaned and then paused the message. Aunt Gabby. Just who she needed to hear from at this point in her life. Lacey hit the resume button.

"So, I'm taking you up on the offer to stop by if I'm ever in the area. I'll be flying into Asheville tomorrow around three in the afternoon. Now, please don't you worry about getting me from the airport. I'll rent a car and will have no trouble finding you in that mountain holler you've taken up residence with. Ta-ta for now." The message ended, and so did her coveted tranquility.

Lacey stood statue still with her mouth open as big as a cave's. Her mind kicked into gear. Her dad's sister was arriving in little more than twenty-four hours. This couldn't be good. And, that spiteful Ginger had managed to deliver a final zinger by keeping Aunt Gabby's message to herself. She would hold tight to the hope the visit would be a brief stopover. Yes, she'd cling to a drop-by visit and a quick getaway from the holler by her aunt. Aunt Gabby was coming. Just swell. Things could get worse after all.

Lacey didn't hesitate a moment to plan her day of unexpected cleaning and grocery shopping. Her aunt's reputation as impossible to please only added to her growing stress. Since her parents died, Aunt Gabby had assumed the role of matriarch for Lacey and her two grown cousins. Recently widowed and lonely no doubt, Aunt Gabby surprised everyone when she bought a condo on Miami Beach. Lacey and her cousins hoped Gabby would make new friends and be much too busy to expend energy seeing about them. Aunt Gabby…tomorrow…here in her peaceful town. "Just swell," she muttered again, aloud this time.

The vacuum came out of the closet first and did a turn with her around the small cottage. Lacey looked at the futon in her den and contemplated putting her aunt on that and padlocking the den's door. Feeling guilty, she and the fresh sheets went to make the guest room seem inviting, but not too much so. After all, there had to be limits to hospitality, even Divine style.

Serene showed up at dinner time waving a bag of sub sandwiches and dragged a weary Lacey to the table. Both women enjoyed sharing meals.

"What's with you? That face tells me you're plenty riled. In fact, you looked the same at the library meeting earlier." Serene stopped unwrapping the sandwich and stared.

"I know," Lacey said, sitting down.

Serene realized they needed beverages to drink, and her friend was too distracted to even notice. She slipped from the wooden chair to grab something cold from the refrigerator.

"How did you know I needed a dinner delivery?" Lacey removed the wrap from her sub sandwich to see salami and pepperoni staring back. She shoved it over to Serene's placemat and hoped the other one wasn't a mate.

"Just felt the nudge, I guess. Hey, all I see in your refrigerator are kiwi smoothies. Tell me we finally have other choices."

"Of course, you can have cold, clean Divine water from the tap or a tasty smoothie," replied Lacey. She felt beyond grateful to her friend bringing much-needed laughs and food.

"Well, how about wine? Anything stashed for a celebration?" Serene still wasn't giving up.

"No wine, sorry, and even if I did, believe me, I've nothing to celebrate tonight," said Lacey, feeling depressed and depleted.

"Like I said, the kiwi smoothie sounds perfect with my spicy Italian hero sandwich." Serene laughed and plopped two glass bottles down on the table.

"I'm going to the store tomorrow morning, so what do you want me to stock for you? I'm willing to make exceptions and bring home your toxic beverages," Lacey asked, relieved to see a veggie sub now in front of her. She took a big bite.

"Normal drinks…come on, like cola, root beer, ginger ale. Finally, someone put enough peppers on this for me. How's yours?"

"Good. Really good. What's the cheese?" Lacey asked, mouth full.

"Got me. I just told the girl to put the best on." Serene looked up and grinned.

"So, okay, I'll get you more drinks tomorrow, especially after your bringing dinner. You do realize that you named only sodas and that they're not good for you? Toxic liquid like I said."

"Yes, they are good for me. They sparkle me right up." Serene looked around the room. "Speaking of sparkle, what's up with the spit and polish? This place looks like it's ready for inspection by a drill sergeant."

"That's exactly what's going to happen in less than twenty-four hours from now. I've got my Aunt Gabby passing through, and I quote, 'this mountain holler' where she's no doubt planning to inspect my digs and me too."

"The Aunt Gabby who drives you nuts talking and bossing nonstop?" That explained Lacey's long face. Serene sat up straighter and put the napkin in her lap, feeling Gabby's eyes on her already.

"The very one. I can't believe my luck. I'm telling you this has the makings of a genuine calamity. Let's see… I lost my job, don't have a clue what I want to do next, and the cherry on top… a visit from Gabby." Lacey gave a heavy sigh. She'd been full of those breaths lately.

"Well, you can handle a few hours and at worse an overnighter. How can I help?" Serene asked, feeling sorry for her friend.

"You already have by showing up with food and listening to my whining."

"Hey, do you want me to stop by tomorrow and check on things? Make sure it's not a crime scene," Serene offered, trying to interject some needed humor into the moment.

"Thanks, but I should be able to hold my sanity with only a few hours in Aunt Gabby's company. Don't you think?" Lacey asked, doubt creeping back.

Serene shrugged but kept the smile on her face.

"Okay, just call me day after tomorrow. I'm pretty confident in promising you an entertaining story about my time with Aunt Gabby," Lacey allowed a grin.

"Then I'll be looking forward to some prized comic relief."

Serene stood clearing the table on her side. "Gotta dash."

"You're leaving so soon?" asked Lacey.

"Yeah, sorry. I've got some things to do myself tonight…not near as fun as your housekeeping, so don't be jealous. Besides, I think I spy a dull spot on the hall floor," she said, hustling to the front door before Lacey figured out she was teasing.

"You're kidding?" Lacey yelled.

Serene laughed harder seeing Lacey drop down on her hands and knees searching for the missed mopped spot. "Poor Lacey. This aunt must really be something. Too bad I don't get to meet her," Serene said, looking back from the screen door.

"You come back here. I don't see the spot. You've got to show me." All Lacey heard in response was more laughter.

"I'll get you back. Just you wait," Lacey fired back, closing the door, grinning. She'd go polish the dining room table for the second time before calling her cleaning day finite.

Chapter 11

Lacey was locked in war with weeds showing their superiority in her flower beds. The cherry-red wheelbarrow held a full load of the season's uninvited guests and the other uninvited one would be arriving in the afternoon by auto.

She wiped her dirty hands on her jeans, while her smudged face testified to her labors. Finished, Lacey turned to gather up her gardening tools when her eye caught a black luxury sedan moving slowly down her street. Panic washed over her, enhancing her disheveled appearance. The car slowed in front of the cottage.

Red hair shone through the car's open window. "Lacey...Lacey, I've found you, darling girl."

Lacey stood shocked as her aunt's rental car pulled into her driveway too early. There wasn't any time to make herself presentable. The yellow cashmere sweater and cream-colored pants lay waiting on her bed, ready to garner aunt approval. She pasted on a smile and walked over to Gabby who stood waiting for a proper greeting.

"Aunt Gabby, it's so wonderful to see you." Lacey gave a peck to the rouged cheek. "I thought you were arriving this afternoon. Sorry that I'm such a mess."

Gabby chose to ignore Lacey's appearance for the moment. "A most fortuitous happening, dear girl, brought me to you earlier. My layover in Charlotte was cut short by an empty first-class seat becoming available on an earlier flight." Gabby examined Lacey's face more closely. "My goodness, Niece, you positively resemble some scrawny waif."

"Oh, Aunt Gabby, I've been gardening, you see. Come on inside, and I'll make us both a glass of fresh fruit punch, and I'll clean up." Lacey started moving forward but sensed her aunt hadn't followed. She pivoted around to see the car's back door open.

"Dear girl, please come fetch my bags, won't you now?"

"Bags, Aunt Gabby?" she asked, hoping her ears had failed. Sighing, she turned, retracing her steps.

"Why, yes. Didn't you get my last message?" Gabby replied, exasperated.

Lacey shook her head.

"Dear, oh dear, could I have left it on someone else's cell phone? How utterly embarrassing for a stranger to know my plans." Gabby massaged her temples.

"Yes, you must have dialed a wrong number. Tell me now, please, what did I miss hearing?"

"Well, just that my condo renovations were going to take a tiny bit longer, and that meant I could turn my drop-by into an extended visit with my precious niece." Gabby's hand failed to fluff her lacquered auburn hair.

"Umm…condo renovation?" Lacey's voice rose to meet her growing panic.

"Yes, dearest heart. Didn't I already explain that I'm redecorating? I simply couldn't abide the dated color scheme another moment. Turquoise and flamingo…so tacky." Gabby raised her nose a bit closer to the sky.

"Well, I can see those colors might not speak to your style, but tell me, how long will I be enjoying your visit?" Resigned to her plight, Lacey began removing the two-piece designer luggage set.

"A week is my best guess, but I brought extra just in case, sweet girl." Aunt Gabby turned toward the cottage.

"A week…how lovely," Lacey said to her aunt's retreating backside.

"You'll need to make another trip to the car," instructed Gabby.

"Another trip?"

"Precious, you sound like a parrot. The trunk has a few more of my necessaries, as I like to say."

"More, more necessaries?" Lacey's mind refused to accept.

"Do stop that chatter. I'll just let myself in. Well, well, this little cottage is so very quaint. I hope the inside is not disappointing." The coral-colored designer suit disappeared behind the front door.

Lacey released the trunk lid to gaze at three garment bags and another suitcase. "Necessaries," she mumbled. She could leave the trunk open and hope some passerby without a conscience might snag the lot. Fat chance…more likely they'd leave them at her front door. Thieves and Divine didn't keep company. Lacey and her fresh frets followed her father's sister through the open front door.

"Thank you, sweetheart. You can put them in my room, and we can get me settled after luncheon." Gabby's head turned, assessing the living area.

Lacey maneuvered down the narrow hall to the guest room. She stacked the cases in a corner, hung the garment bags, and gave the space one last check before going to wash up. Her hostess duties awaited.

Minutes later, Lacey entered the room where Gabby had found a seat. "Aunt, I'm sorry, but I didn't expect you—"

"Lacey, this cottage is almost…charming. My timing, as usual, is impeccable because I see some changes that we simply must make once I've settled. Gabby turned her focus back to Lacey. "What were you saying, dear one?"

"Just that lunch will be a sandwich since I didn't expect you this early."

"Oh, don't go to any extra effort for me. I'll fit right in with your routine…you'll see. No special treatment expected out here in this mountain hootenanny." Gabby flicked a stray hair from her shoulder.

Lacey swallowed the unflattering reference to her town and moved to discuss sandwich options. "Aunt Gabby, I can offer you a grilled cheese and tomato soup. I've some delicious cheese from our local dairy that I'm sure you'll love." Lacey moved toward the kitchen.

"No cheese…too binding. I do adore cucumber and watercress finger sandwiches," Gabby replied.

"Sorry, those makings aren't in my fridge. How about a peanut butter and banana sandwich?" Lacey loved them best.

"Are you expecting children this afternoon?"

"Excuse me?" Lacey asked, frowning.

"Never mind. Toast with honey will be fine and a lovely pot of tea. I'll just look forward to a nice dinner. I'm sure you've planned that meal out sufficiently." Gabby settled deeper into the chair, tugging at a crease that had the courage to appear on her skirt.

"Tea and toast sound perfect. I'll get the tea kettle going. Please just relax and be comfortable," Lacey said, forcing her mouth to let the agreeable words out.

"Yes, I'll try, Niece. I'll certainly try," said Gabby, running her index finger along the table's edge, satisfied with the absence of dust. She glanced around the room, giving the furniture her trademark discerning look. Her hazel eyes locked on a pair of golden ones sitting in the opposite chair.

Topaz watched, acting aloof, but his swishing tail gave his mood away to anyone who understood the feline nature.

"Lacey, there's an animal in here crouched on the chair," Gabby cried out.

"Oh, that's Topaz. I forgot to introduce you two. Isn't he beautiful?" Lacey answered. She'd forgotten all about her aunt's distinctive dislike of pets. Any pet.

"Must he stay inside while I'm here for my short sojourn?" Gabby wrinkled her bobbed nose crafted by a renowned Miami plastic surgeon.

"Aunt, he's a love. Give him a chance. I bet the two of you will become inseparable."

Gabby noted the pleading undertones of her niece's words and attempted to understand the lonely girl's need for a domestic pet. "I'm sure you're right," she said, sending the cat vibes to steer a wide berth from her.

Over lunch, the two women exchanged bits of news. Lacey gave a cursory explanation about her job being eliminated and how she'd spent the last days trying to get in touch with her joy and talents in hopes of attracting a fulfilling kind of work. Lacey knew her aunt was incapable of understanding, so she kept the telling simplistic and lighthearted. No point in inviting more judgment on her life. She elected to avoid detailing why she had chosen Divine to call home too. Better to give her aunt a chance to see more of the town first.

Aunt Gabby entertained Lacey with tales of her social escapades on Miami Beach with her friends. Most of the ladies were widowed and chose to focus their energies on staying active in each other's business. To Lacey, their outings to the theater and shopping sounded pleasurable but not very nurturing to the spirit.

Lacey surmised the decorating outlet served as her Aunt Gabby's attempt to breathe life into her days. She really hoped that happened, but with growing inner awareness, Lacey suspected what Gabby sought resided inside her and not on the outside.

"Would you mind terribly if I excused myself for a short respite?" Aunt Gabby implored.

"Of course not, Auntie," Lacey said, unable to control her teasing ways.

"Auntie?" Gabby huffed. "I've never been an auntie and don't have any desire to become one now, dear Lacey. I can abide Aunt Gabby, so let's not have another utterance of that low country noun." Gabby's chin lifted to amplify her words.

"Aunt Gabby, truly I meant it as term of endearment." Great, now she sounded like a character straight out of an 18th-century romance novel. Her aunt's demeanor was already rubbing off on her.

Gabby's temper cooled. "I'm sure you're right. Let's go see my accommodations. Shall we?" Gabby forced a smile.

The two walked in silence down the hallway. Lacey stood aside to let her aunt enter.

Aunt Gabby preened at the respect shown and nodded approval of her niece's returning manners. "My, such an abundance of natural light."

"I know. I love the sunlight too." Lacey always thought the room extra cheerful with the two large windows.

"How does one ever nap under such illumination?" Gabby took in the small twin bed with the bright floral quilt dressing it.

"I have an eye mask that I can loan you. That should do the trick," Lacey offered, hiding her hurt.

"By all means, go and claim it. This quilt's loud pattern is giving me the beginnings of a migraine." Gabby's fingers touched her temple.

Lacey disappeared to look for the eye mask and a pillow to scream into. How would she survive a week with Aunt Gabby under her roof? *Stop*, she admonished herself for dwelling on the length of time. "Take it one day at a time. One day at a time," she chanted softly while hunting for the mask. Her own problems would need to simmer on a back-burner until Gabby departed.

"Lacey dear, please bring me an aspirin too. My head is splitting. Wherever did you find such a coverlet? Must be a relic from Haight Ashbury days. Oh, my poor head. Do hurry."

Serene stood gazing out her office window, feeling the push to call Lacey. The aunt was due in town soon, and a call to show support might help. She walked back to her desk and dialed her friend's number.

Lacey had just closed the guest room door, wishing she could nail it shut for a week, when the phone rang.

"What now?" she asked of the unknown caller.

"Whoa. What's happening? Are you spiffed and ready?" Serene asked with a playful lilt to her voice.

"She's here…early," Lacey whispered into the phone. "And she's going to stay an entire week. Seven days. How's that for starters?" Lacey escaped to the porch.

"Wow! Not what you expected. What else? I'm done for the day, so spill it." Serene sat down feeling compassion for her friend's situation. The timing for this visit seemed plain lousy.

"Well, there's a growing list of unacceptable food, speech, and décor. I like you too much, so I'll spare you the details of my last two hours with her."

"Kind friend, what are you doing about dinner?"

"Dinner? I've made baked spaghetti, salad, and crusty bread. Everyone likes spaghetti, right?" Lacey's confidence evaporated as she remembered the tons of mozzarella cheese "binding" the casserole in the refrigerator.

"She's clearly not everyone, though. Your aunt sounds like the queen of preferences."

"Maybe I exaggerated," Lacey replied, her better nature trying to return.

"Knowing you, I bet you're exaggerating her to be a whole lot more agreeable than she is."

"You're right. She'll refuse the spaghetti…it's got cheese. Lots of nice cheese," Lacey added with more despair.

"Ah…she's suffering from intestinal issues," Serene, the nutrition expert, answered.

"Issues are one way of saying it. What am I going to do now? She'll probably hate the salad I made too." Lacey began her characteristic nervous pacing.

"Stop pacing."

"Okay, okay, I've stopped. I swear I don't know how you—"

"Listen. I've got yous covered. Let me handle dinner, and I'm officially inviting myself for an evening of free entertainment at your place. Set the table. I'll be there by six." Serene rang off before Lacey could voice any protest.

Topaz jumped into Lacey's lap to offer needed affection.

Did she just hear Serene say yous? No way. Maybe she could use an aspirin too. Maybe half a bottle.

Chapter 12

Cassie entered the cabin, taking time to appreciate its welcoming nature. She'd called on her intuition over the years to assist her in creating the ideal environment for her feeling, thinking, and being. Before calling the night done, she'd find that jade box.

She loved the warm feeling the wood floors and beams gave to the space. She had chosen her comforts carefully over the years. Living alone meant she needed to spoil herself with kind places to relax and renew. Her rockers were her first love, for they were her transportation to visit the existing levels on the Other Side…heaven. The sofa and cushiony chairs were always inviting. The shelves flanking the fireplace contained her earthly entertainment…books, music, and a radio for listening to the outer world's doings. The openness of the living area, eating and cooking areas pleased Cassie, especially when a guest came calling. The balcony seating area upstairs looked down on the common area with two bedrooms sharing the space. She, like her niece, loved color and so used all seven of the spectrum colors lavishly in her décor. Somehow a sense of harmony existed in every space. A log cabin her home might be but one with ample square footage to share her life and welcome her home this night.

After enjoying a soak in her claw-footed tub, Cassie padded down the hall to a room she called jambalaya. Some might not see the space that way. If a body spent time within the four walls, they'd come to see an order and theme to what at first glance looked like chaos. Cassie went over to an overstuffed tweed chair and plopped down with a sigh.

Her eyes settled on the wall of shelves displaying treasures freely given to her over a lifetime. Old Mountain Cassie acknowledged the totem bestowed by an elder Cherokee chief. A framed picture of a smiling younger Cassie boarding a fighter jet with a four-star general sat on the shelf next to a photo of her teaching The Three Lessons to a Fortune 100 CEO while they communed on the front porch. She smiled lovingly at the prima ballerina trying to teach Cassie's body the basic five positions. The mountain woman could allow her mind to recollect the joy each of these Seekers brought her, but no doubt it would cost the evening. She blocked the desire to remember, ignored the other photographs, and accepted the bookcase didn't house the jade box.

In the corner sat an old whiskey barrel that Cassie used as a lamp table and inside the keeper of some precious items not meant for showing. Carefully, she moved the original Tiffany lamp over to the nearby desk. At first, the lid resisted being set free, forcing Cassie to grab her letter opener to pry it loose. The overhead light shone inside the barrel's few pieces wrapped in tissue paper. Old Mountain Cassie lifted the first bundle, pulling the paper away.

"Finally," she said aloud. An aged photo of Violet and Cassie sharing a sled ride was chosen to be shared at the right moment. And at the bottom of the barrel peeking from tissue paper, the green jade box glistened. It came to life and light in her hands. An agile Cassie sat on the wood floor cross-legged and placed the box in front of her to better admire its beauty. She decided to move the box to a shelf in her great room, where she could keep an eye on it. "Now I'm ready to meet Miss Lacey and share The Lessons."

Chapter 13

Lacey heard Aunt Gabby stirring from her nap and glanced at the clock on her mantle. Her aunt had only been in the house a few hours, yet it felt like an eternity. *Five-thirty and all is not well*, she thought, bracing for the guest room door to open at any moment. Sweet Serene would be arriving soon, bringing them dinner for the second night. Lacey conceded some serious payback was due for her friend's devotion.

"Lacey dear?" came the voice from the room.

"Yes, Aunt Gabby? I'm here."

"Be a love and draw my bath, won't you? I need a bit of freshening from my nap before dinner."

Topaz waited by Gabby's door. Lacey scooped him up and tossed the ball of fur on her bed. She didn't need him stirring her aunt's anger this early in the evening.

"I've got the water running. I'll just go set the table." Lacey found her nicest placemats and cloth napkins. Their sage and cream color showed off her more informal style dinnerware. An arrangement of lilies and ferns flanked by two ivory candles made for a table setting surely, even her aunt would approve. Lacey decided to wait to select the wine until Serene's rescue dinner arrived.

"Ready for my bath. See how easy I am to please?" the voice said, breaking the last moment's peace.

"Bath's waiting," Lacey hollered back, leaving the bathroom. You might want to leave the door cracked. The room steams up something fierce."

"Very well."

Lacey relaxed, hearing her aunt enter the bathroom. A few more minutes of solitude to relish, she thought.

"Where are the bubbles? I always have bubbles."

Lacey returned to the room to see a robed Gabby staring into the crystal-clear bathwater. "Oh, how about some lovely scented oils? Lacey quickly poured some jasmine bath beads into the tub.

"Is that jasmine? I must say—"

"Yes, enjoy your soak. I have to get back to the kitchen." Lacey knew whatever her aunt was about to say had to be yet another objection. She scurried out, leaving the door cracked about as wide as the loose floor plank she'd like to use to wallop her aunt into the world of please and thank-you. Only Serene would appreciate her twisted humor. The doorbell brought Lacey back into reality.

Chapter 14

"Here I am with a dinner that a chef in Tuscany would approve." Serene lifted the cardboard box and waved it under Lacey's nose.

"Do I smell garlic and herbs?" Lacey gave her rescuer a hug and took the box into the kitchen.

Serene removed her sweater and threw it across the sofa's back before following Lacey's path. "How about this for a menu—shrimp scampi, rice pilaf, roasted vegetables, and tomato basil salad? Oh, and spumoni for dessert. Here, put it in the freezer, will yous, Lace?"

Lacey caught the "yous" for sure this time but decided best to let the slip pass since Serene saved her behind with another meal. She'd be patient and pick the opportune time to confirm Paulie's imprinting on her best friend.

"So, my menu?" Serene asked, reminding Lacey a question waited for an answer.

"Sorry. Sounds scrumptious. You're terrific. However, did you get this prepared after working all day?" Lacey sampled the rice, giving a thumbs-up.

"I know an elf. No more questions," Serene answered, wanting to deflect that question. She got spared.

"Get out of here, you flea-bitten creature! No, no, don't you dare!" screamed Aunt Gabby.

Lacey and Serene both heard the splash followed by a throaty meow and Gabby bellowing Lacey's name.

A dripping cat ran past them with a gold fish-shaped sponge hanging from his mouth.

"Oh no," Lacey wailed to Serene, hurrying down the hall.

"Oh yeah," Serene replied, holding back her laughter at the scene playing out. She followed close on her friend's heels.

"Aunt Gabby, are you all right?" Lacey remained outside the door.

"I most certainly am not all right. That varmint jumped into my bath and has run off with my Italian designer sponge!"

The two friends could hear Gabby stepping out of the tub, fussing about such trying accommodations and how creatures belonged outdoors.

Lacey dared to interrupt her aunt's rant. "I'll be glad to order you a new sponge, but in the meantime, my friend, Serene has brought us a wonderful meal to share tonight. Please come and join us when you're recovered," Lacey said sweetly.

"Dare I risk leaving my cell for more escapades? Maybe I should have a tray in my room," Aunt Gabby stated, feigning weariness.

"Well, of course, Aunt Gabby, if that's what you want."

Serene took control. "Hi, Gabby. Serene here. Please reconsider. My lovely feast will be so much more pleasurable for your delicate digestion if you sup with us and not in your room alone."

Lacey's shocked face looked at her friend, who just so effortlessly spoke Gabby's language to the impossible woman on the other side of the door.

Serene winked.

"Well, obviously, you're a girl of refinement, and that quilt on my bed is positively nauseating me. Maybe you're right." The door opened, and a silk-robed Gabby hurried across the hall to her room, giving a curt nod to Lacey as she passed.

"Wonderful," Serene called back. She poked Lacey.

"Yes, wonderful, Aunt Gabby. Dinner's ready when you are."

"I'll be just a moment," came the muffled reply.

"Where did you learn to talk like that?" whispered Lacey as they emptied the containers' contents into bowls and a serving platter.

"I've many hidden talents, I'm told." Serene shrugged and lit the candles.

Topaz peeked around the corner and, seeing Lacey's glare, disappeared to lick himself dry.

"Oh yeah? Says who for instance?" Lacey's good mood briefly returned to match Serene's.

"Lacey dear? Do introduce me to this lovely young woman, won't you?" asked Gabby, putting an end to their banter.

"Of course, Aunt Gabby, I'd like for you to meet my friend, Serene, who simply couldn't wait to greet you. Serene, this is my Aunt Gabby."

Gabby put out her hand, showing off her perfect manicure. Serene grasped the hand gently, the gesture clearly impressing Gabby's uppity nature.

"I'm sure it's a pleasure." Gabby seated herself on the nearest dining room chair and unfolded her napkin.

"Equally mine," responded the chameleon Serene as she claimed the seat next to Gabby.

Lacey shook her head to clear the vision of these two vying for the best manners. "Aunt Gabby, I've opened a bottle of chilled Chablis. Would you care for a glass?"

"Just the tiniest of taste, dear." Gabby held up her index finger to indicate how much a taste looked like in her glass.

Serene and Lacey made eye contact when the finger finally dropped after the goblet was filled to the rim.

Lacey glanced at the half-full wine bottle and longed to put a straw in it and take to her bed for the rest of the week. Instead, she served her aunt a generous portion of somebody's shrimp scampi meal that had Paulie's recipe imprint on each bite, but Lacey kept mute. Her gratitude to both Serene and him trumped her desire to state the obvious.

The serving pieces made their rounds and returned empty, a sure sign Serene had successfully turned the day around for Lacey and Gabby. Her aunt, now mellowing from the wine, spent the rest of the meal either lavishing compliments on practically every morsel touching her lips or sharing details of her busy life on Miami Beach. Serene and Lacey interjected appropriate responses when called upon. Aunt Gabby had no problem carrying the conversation for the next two hours.

"Well, dears, this has been a most surprisingly pleasant evening. However, I must ask to be excused. I find myself suddenly quite weary." Gabby's hand came up to cover an escaping yawn.

"We understand, don't we, Serene?"

"Yes, of course, we do. By all means, Gabby, you retire. No doubt we'll be seeing each other again soon," Serene added, smiling.

"Precious, do come by tomorrow if you can. I'll tell you all about my last real estate purchase. I'm sure I can add to your knowledge of the business."

"Sure, Serene, you trot on back here." Lacey winked, enjoying sucking her friend back in for another performance.

"I've got a better idea, ladies. Let's meet for ice cream at Sweet Treats and then have a little stroll afterward."

"The stroll is for calorie guilt," Lacey explained.

"Sounds sublime. Lacey, you must escort me first thing in the morning to shop for the proper attire. Night, ladies." Gabby swayed down the hall toward her... cell.

"Sleep well," Lacey replied.

"Night, Aunt Gabby," added Serene.

"Whew. Call yourself spectacular, and I'll agree. Start making a list of ways I can repay you." Lacey followed her friend to the front door.

Serene put on her sweater and gave Lacey a fast hug. "I already have, made a list that is. Ice cream is on you for starters."

"Check that one off. I've got it covered. Serene, thank you again. What would I do without you?"

"Starve." Serene laughed and walked into the night, humming.

Six more days to go, Lacey thought, leaning against the closed door.

Topaz stuck his head around the corner to see if it was safe to make an appearance.

"You! No more misbehaving, or you'll be spending some cold and lonely nights in the laundry room, and that's if you're lucky."

The cat rubbed against her leg.

"Not working. Where's Aunt Gabby's goldfish sponge?" Lacey went in search of the stolen article and to prepare for bed. She could hear soft snores coming from the guest room. She made a mental note to serve wine at every meal starting with tomorrow's breakfast.

Chapter 15

AFTER SAVORING A TASTY SUPPER of brown belly gravy pot roast and roasted root vegetables, Cassie realized a sweet taste had been missed at her meal. Her answer to that hankering accompanied her to the porch. Cassie kept the wood porch swing moving as she polished off the last of the dark Belgian chocolate candy bar. She looked around before licking her fingers. Her good manners were her constant companion, but melting chocolate was too good to waste on a paper napkin.

Interrupting the evening's peace, Lickety Split came running from the back of the house with a mad rooster on his tail.

"Heavens, Lick, why did you go and get Roy riled up?" Cassie scurried into the front yard to cut the rooster off before he had a chance to punish Lickety for no doubt some hen annoyance.

The bird flapped his wings, screeched, and strutted around the yard, letting off steam and never taking his eyes off Lickety.

Lick cozied to Old Mountain Cassie's side, taking comfort in her protective maneuvers. He kept his barks to himself to avoid further trouble with the agitated red rooster.

"Dog, get yourself on that porch and don't you dare move... not even your tail. I'll be there as soon as I get some things out of my truck."

Lickety Split dashed for the porch and, with one quick leap, landed where he was told. Head hung low, he crouched down so the rooster couldn't see him and better where he couldn't see the rooster.

Satisfied the ruckus had ended, Cassie headed to her truck. She hoped her Seeker would like the new floral teacups she purchased and the special brew Cassie had concocted for Lacey's first visit to her home. She needed to prepare her teaching plan before calling the night done. The Three Lessons message was customized for each Seeker, for everyone digested truths differently. Cassie gave a sigh and trudged back, taking her Lacey anticipation with her.

Chapter 16

Lacey waited until almost ten o'clock for her aunt to appear for breakfast. Homemade hot cinnamon buns and coffee separated the two women.

Bored with any breakfast topic, Gabby asked, "Could we do a bit of shopping, dear? I do so need some suitable mountain fashions."

"Yes, of course. I have time right after I put these plates and cups in the dishwasher if you'd like to visit our nicest clothing store in Divine," Lacey offered.

"Well, I suppose for time's sake I could, at least, look here. I can always drive into the city another day if need be." Gabby rose from her stool. "I'll be ready in a flutter."

"Great. The temperature is already in the fifties, so a light sweater should do you fine for our outing."

"A sweater?" Gabby turned. Her left eyebrow raised in disbelief.

"Yes, didn't you bring one? No matter. You can borrow one of mine. I've all colors and sizes," Lacey went on to explain.

"Dear girl, I don't wear yarn knits. They're simply not my style. I've a navy blazer that should do nicely but thank you…I suppose."

"Sure. No problem. Is there something else before I finish cleaning up in here?" As soon as the words were out, Lacey wished she might fetch them back. Her aunt's eyes spoke before she did.

"Why, yes, darling Lacey, I couldn't help but wonder if we shouldn't do a tad of redecorating today. That window begs for a table with a lovely crystal vase."

Lacey jumped in before any more helpful ideas could be voiced. "Aunt Gabby, I so appreciate you wanting to offer your no doubt exquisite decorating skills, but alas, I've got some calls to make this afternoon before we meet Serene. Let's put our attention on you today. I don't want you expending energy on my place while you're supposed to be getting a vacation from interior design." Lacey didn't add that her savings needed to support her and not her aunt's decorating addiction. She clenched her jaw, waiting for the coming reaction.

Aunt Gabby noticed the worried frown playing across her niece's face. Intuition told her there was indeed more to the refusal. "You're such a considerate niece. You simply must tell me later more about your life in this backwater town," said a concerned Gabby. She retreated to her room.

Lacey overheard her tell the quilt it must be flipped over to its more tolerable beige side for the duration of her visit. The rustling sound assured her of Gabby's success. Lacey sighed and wondered what instructions her aunt might have for the morning sun shining brightly through her pair of windows.

Lacey parked her SUV in front of the more upscale shop. "Here we are, Petunia's Patch."

"Petunia's, umm, Patch? Please, not more vivid colors I beg of you." Gabby touched her temples. "I might as well tie that hideous quilt around me and call it a day."

"Now, Aunt, give Petunia's a chance, at least." At this rate, Gabby would be the talk of Divine by lunch.

"Please, Petunia's, don't fail me." Gabby pleaded as she followed Lacey into the tiny boutique.

"Good morning, ladies." Petunia's eyes traveled to Lacey and next to Gabby. "Lacey, how nice you look today."

"Thank you, Miss Petunia. A compliment is just what I needed to hear. Listen, my aunt is visiting and needs a few things. Gabby this is—"

"Yes," said Gabby, interrupting the introductions, deciding this woman might understand her finer ways. "Do you have anything that is remotely classy-casual?"

Petunia smiled politely. "I think I know of a couple of ensembles that might suit your fine figure and style to perfection," Petunia said, signaling a relieved Lacey she'd sized up her aunt in more ways than one.

"You, dear lady, are a breath of fresh air. Lead on." Gabby held her head higher.

"Lacey, if you have any errands, why don't you leave your aunt in my hands?"

"Oh, please, do call me Gabriela, or Gabby, if you must."

Petunia gave a nod of understanding.

"Well…" Lacey hesitated, not trusting how Gabby might behave.

"Darling Niece, you know me. I don't want to be a burden. You go right ahead. I'll visit with Petunia until you return."

"All right then. I do need to stop by the bank, along with a few other errands," said Lacey.

"Gabriela, why don't you go to the fitting room and let me bring you some garments to try? I've a few pieces tucked away for my discerning ladies."

"Sounds lovely. This is exactly the way my boutiques in Miami Beach please me."

The two women disappeared to the back of the store.

Lacey cast her eyes heavenward in gratitude. She'd savor her small taste of freedom. She wondered if there were any laws against abandoning a tiresome aunt. The punishment might not be all that bad in comparison.

A more relaxed Lacey entered Petunia's not knowing what to expect. Petunia sat next to her aunt in a wingback chair, chatting pleasantly. Five shopping bags lined the counter by the cash register, giving testament to Petunia's selling abilities.

"Back so soon, Niece? Petunia and I have been enjoying getting to know one another," Aunt Gabby said, clearly in her element.

"Yes, that's true. Your aunt and I have found we have quite a few things in common." Petunia winked.

Lacey's mind absorbed the words but held to the feeling of amazement. "How nice, I'm ready if you are, Aunt Gabby. I see we have a few shopping bags to load."

"Dearest Niece, would it be an imposition if you took the packages and left me with Petunia awhile longer?"

"I guess—"

"Yes, that's a wonderful plan, Gabriella. My part-time girl arrives any minute. You must come home with me, and I'll serve us a light lunch of cream cheese and olive finger sandwiches," said Petunia, warming to her subject. "We can even eat out on my veranda," Petunia offered with her usual generosity to others.

"Finger sandwiches, you say? I simply cannot refuse such a delicate repast. Lacey, you understand." Gabby tucked a stray curl that had the nerve to touch her forehead.

"Of course. I know how much you love a lady's luncheon." Lacey mouthed, "Bless you," to a smiling Petunia.

"Lovely. Then it's all settled. Your aunt and I will have an afternoon to learn more about each other. I'll bring her to your cottage later if that's agreeable?" Petunia had a fondness for Lacey and felt genuinely happy to be able to help the girl out.

"Thank you so much, Petunia, for your kindness. I'll just grab these bags and be on my way." *Before you come to your senses and change your mind*, Lacey thought.

Lacey made the final trip to retrieve the remaining two shopping bags and to say good-bye. She heard Gabby clapping her hands when Petunia asked if she'd care to play bridge tomorrow. Petunia appeared to be a real, honest-to-goodness, God-sent sitter for Gabby in the making. Lacey would offer to sweep and dust Petunia's boutique for a month if she kept her aunt occupied again tomorrow.

A free unexpected afternoon to do what she wanted loomed ahead. Dare she allow herself an escape to the woods for a hike? Why not? The baked spaghetti might be tolerated by her aunt's improving mood by tonight, thanks to precious Petunia. Yes, a hike sounded perfect after she completed a few more chores.

Lacey's mood lightened as she left a note to her aunt stating she'd be home in time to prepare their dinner. She even took the time to write the menu out, hoping to give Gabby a chance to mellow with the mozzarella while she tried to mellow herself in the woods.

Lacey felt a pull to return to the magical place where the animals and birds had been so engaging. The closer her vehicle came, the more peace descended on her weary mind. She stepped out of her SUV transformed by the forest's beauty that always provided all manner of abundance.

Chapter 17

CASSIE AND LICKETY SAT AT the water's edge. They allowed the stream's hypnotic chatter to lull them into deep relaxation while the afternoon slipped away. Old Mountain Cassie felt compelled to remain seated on the soft carpet of mosses. She knew the herb orders waited back at the plant shed, but Cassie also knew she was where she needed to be.

The birds told her before her eyes did that her Seeker was approaching. Minutes passed before Cassie's ears captured the sound of footsteps on the path leading to the stream. She waited along with the unusually quiet Lickety for the hiker to emerge.

Cassie saw her first, and joy washed over the older woman. Finally, the real meeting she'd anticipated for so many years was unfolding this day. This time, Cassie's manner would offer warmth to the younger woman. She smiled at Lacey, a smile that had been locked away for a long spell and finally set free.

A surprised Lacey caught sight of the woman she'd remembered from Mystic Rock Park. A coincidence, she thought. She offered a wave to the friendly face directed her way.

"Well, well, we meet again at another magical spot." Old Mountain Cassie's eyes twinkled with inner happiness.

"Talk about coincidences," said Lacey, voicing her thoughts.

Cassie's expression changed to a more serious one though still open and friendly. "Lacey, there are no coincidences. How's the cut?" Cassie paused, giving her pupil time to grow in trust.

Lacey glanced down at her leg, holding Cassie's statement inside. "It's healing nicely. Thank you again for coming to my rescue the other day. And how nice that you remembered my name too."

"Of course, such a pretty name, like I told you. Lickety Split and I have been whiling away an afternoon with the creek. Care to sit a spell with us?" Cassie walked back to her spot and sat down, never doubting Lacey would follow.

Lacey joined Old Mountain Cassie and took in a deep breath. "Everything smells so alive here. I've only recently discovered these hidden trails. How about you?"

"Who? Me? I've been around here an age, maybe two. "Your senses are tellin' you right, and you'll experience more and more of 'nature's enchantments' each time you pay a visit, if you're of a mind, that is." Cassie stretched out her legs and looked down at the water and decided not to tell Lacey she'd ventured onto her land.

"I plan to keep coming. How could I not when the birds and squirrels have made me feel so…welcome?" Lacey said, testing. Surprise flushing her face, she leaned over and plucked a five-leaf clover, twirling it between her fingers like a parasol.

Old Mountain Cassie's wise eyes saw the gift. "Nature's enchantments," she stated again.

"I've never seen a five-leaf clover before. This is special." Lacey took out a piece of paper from her backpack and carefully wrapped her treasure.

"A sign of something special…yes, ma'am, clovers can be most special. I have quite a fondness for them." Cassie gave a nod.

Lickety scooted closer to Lacey and rested his chin on her lap. His big brown eyes asked for attention.

Lacey reached over and rubbed his velvety ears.

"Well, I'll be switched. Never seen Lick take to someone newly met who didn't offer a bone first. That clover's already workin'," Cassie added with a chuckle. She pulled the fallen strap from her overalls back in place. She needed to keep this encounter easy.

"I confess I've been attracting animals like crazy lately. Sadly, no single men, just animals. Must be my new perfume they like." What made her say that about men? Geez, what would the woman think of her spouting some shallow chatter?

Lickety gave her a wet lick.

Cassie laughed at them. "May be the perfume, but as for your fellow, he'll be along directly to ask for your heart. I'm bettin'."

Shocked to hear Cassie's words, Lacey could only tuck the prediction away. "You know, I never caught your name. I mean you know mine, and I know Lickety Split's." Lacey grinned. "So tell me, wise woman of the woods, what do people call you?" she asked, making sure to keep her tone light. She'd already met the woman's skittish side.

"No, I don't suppose I gave it at Mystic Rock. You're right. Name's Cassie, though I hear most around these parts call me Old Mountain Cassie." Her eyes stayed on Lacey.

An empty minute ticked by the two women.

Lacey's brain struggled to grasp the words just spoken. "Oh, my stars! I mean no kidding? Really? You're Old Mountain Cassie?" she questioned, sounding like some dimwit. She couldn't help herself. There seated next to her was Divine's one illustrious woman she'd been hoping to meet. "You're Old Mountain Cassie?" Lacey's words came around again.

Amused but a heap more pleased, Cassie answered, "Yep. Like I just said I was. Why? Shouldn't I be?" She gave a chuckle, appreciating Lacey's reaction. She'd experienced it before.

"Of course, you should be." Lacey gave a nervous laugh. "It's just that, well, I have always, well, not always, but certainly since I've been—"

"Hold up, Missy. Take a breath and gather those feelings into clean words and then speak them. Try it." Cassie felt gladness that the younger woman acted excited to meet her.

Lacey drew in a breath and collected herself as Cassie had instructed. "Thank you. I'm better. What I meant to say is it's so nice to meet you at last." Lacey exhaled, relieved she could form a simple sentence again.

"At last?"

"Yes, well, I must admit I've been intrigued and captivated by Divine's fascination with all things Old Mountain Cassie. You sounded like this amazing woman, and I wanted to know someone…like you. You see, I've been hoping that on a hike one day, our paths might cross." Lacey prayed the woman would take her words as a compliment and not some weird obsession.

Cassie sat quietly for a moment. "Guess your hope has been granted. As for me being amazing, I'd probably say it a little differently, somethin' like Cassie's gifts can be amazin' on a good day. Yep, that's my closer truth, Miss Lacey."

"I'll take your word, Cassie, but the woman who gave me the healing moss is pretty extraordinary. You knew its healing properties," Lacey said, feeling relieved they'd moved past the awkward moment.

Old Mountain Cassie gave a nod. "Yes, plants and I do speak the same language. They share their gifts, and I give thanks and pass them on where they're needed."

"So, plants are your work?" Lacey asked, wanting to learn more about this woman.

"My work? Maybe more like we're coworkers." Cassie gave one more nod. She needed to make her exit before more questions came calling. "Lickety, you and I best tell our new friend so long. We've got some things to tend this day."

Lickety Split's tail wagged a couple of times. He stood up but not before laying a warm, wet lick on Lacey's cheek.

"That kiss certainly felt generous of you, Mr. Lickety." Disappointment that the meeting was ending so soon washed over Lacey. She smiled at the dog to hide her emotions. Lacey's legs brought her to stand. "Would it be all right with you if I 'hoped' we might meet again?"

Old Mountain Cassie tucked her braid back into place and adjusted her overalls. "Lacey, I expect another meetin' will happen one of these days real soon. Yep and Lickety and me will be glad of that, won't we, boy?"

The dog answered by putting his paws to Lacey's waist and giving a loud howl.

Lacey chuckled. "Lickety, I'll take that to mean yes. Tell you what, I'll see about having a bone with me for next time."

Cassie had turned away, walking toward a narrow path that Lacey hadn't noticed. "Be seein' you." And once again, she disappeared into the woods.

Lacey stared at the stand of trees that had welcomed Old Mountain Cassie back…the woman she'd been hoping to meet. What is it about the forests and mountains here that draw such fascinating people? And dare she ponder if she could become one?

What made them special? She needed to understand. Lacey thought about Serene and her unusual abilities with helping others find their piece of heaven around Divine and Paulie's talent for serving food to energize the body and make a person feel happy inside. Then she thought of Bud and his dairy producing such delectable products. Yes, some of Divine's folks had uncommon abilities, maybe even a little magical.

Lacey hoped future visits with Old Mountain Cassie might shed light on these ponderings and bring greater understanding. How to ask? That would prove the challenge she feared but one she felt charged to take on given the chance. She'd just spent time with the one and only Old Mountain Cassie…unbelievable.

Lacey's runaway thoughts continued to keep her engaged. She questioned if she really possessed any gift that might bring such good feelings to others. How enlivening to be able to touch someone's life in a positive manner and make a difference, even at subtle levels.

She continued to give her mind free rein on her walk toward the vehicle. The forest creatures scurried about accepting, but not including her this day. Her watch reminded her of a waiting and most likely hungry Aunt Gabby. Lacey picked up the pace to her hostess duties and to share her Cassie visit with Serene. She'd gotten much more than a Cassie sighting.

Chapter 18

The day found Cassie in her shed's workroom. She'd completed assigning herbs to their waiting packets and now brought her attention to the final and most important step—instilling prayer energy to each box going out.

She took the boxes with their open lids into her special sanctuary. Cassie lit the gold and white candles and entered into prayer. With her energy-filled spirit, she bestowed a gentle blessing on each box. The aura containing all of the colors of the rainbow came down and infused each plant offering in the boxes. She took in the vision and rested in the healing light, accepting God's cherished gift to all who understood.

Cassie's body remained as still as her dog on point. The earth connection needed this from her, as she acted as the bridge for the "jubilation" to take place. It had become her word for the transference of the power in service to those waiting to receive her herbs.

Slowly, the aura receded, leaving sparklers floating in the sanctuary. Still, Cassie sat watching, being the observer, the silent witness to the majesty of vitality's movement. Seconds became minutes until the energy dance ceased. Cassie drew in some clearing breaths. She'd merged with the light, feeling a powerful connection.

Back home and tucked into her feather bed, Cassie's gentle snore settled in the room, allowing her devoted pet companions to relax into their slumber as well. The moon cast its glow through Cassie's large picture window, illuminating them all in a protective veil of white energy sent to renew and restore.

Chapter 19

Lacey's day couldn't have been more different than the wise woman she now knew as Cassie. She arrived home to a gabby aunt wanting to fill her in on her "most exquisite" day with Petunia. Lacey made her best effort to listen to the details while she hurried to get dinner for them on the table.

"And her luncheon, dear one, has my mouth still watering," Gabby prattled on.

"Well, that's good because the baked spaghetti is ready. Would you mind tossing the salad, Aunt Gabby?" Lacey placed the olive oil and red wine vinegar next to the bowl.

"Yes, the baked spaghetti." Gabby sighed, ignoring her assignment and scurrying over to cast a doubtful eye on the casserole.

"I'm happy to try and dish you a serving without the fresh mozzarella if you like?" Lacey anticipated the critical words forming on her aunt's lips. She moved to get a dinner plate and serving utensil.

"Fresh mozzarella, you say?"

"Yes, a very fine cheese from Divine's own Sweet Clover Dairy," Lacey replied, covering a smile.

"Well, in that case, I'm sure my delicate system can partake of quality cheese. It's just that packaged grocery store kind that I simply cannot abide." Gabby took a fork and tasted the mozzarella. Her characteristic smacking sounds returned to a grateful Lacey.

"Is it good?"

"Give me that spatula. I'll serve myself while you toss the greens."

Lacey watched her aunt pile the pasta on her plate with enough gusto to please Paulie. *What an unpredictable day*, Lacey thought, filling the salad bowls.

Gabby took her salad and entrée to the table. She did manage to pause for Lacey to be seated before twirling an enormous amount of spaghetti on her fork. She chewed and smacked for a lifetime before adding, "I must say this is surprisingly good. You made it?" She took another mouthful followed by a second filling of her wine glass.

"I did, and especially for you," answered Lacey, amused at the zest Gabby was showing the meal. "Don't forget to save room for an ice cream with Serene and me."

"Hmm," was all Gabby's mouth could offer.

Serene entered the front door, calling, "Let's go, you two. I've been dieting all day so I could have a large caramel nut sundae with extra whipped cream."

"Ooh, caramel sounds sinfully intoxicating, but I'm in the mood for an old-fashioned banana split. Do you happen to know if your little ice cream place makes them?" Gabby asked, gathering one of her new shawls around her shoulders.

"Absolutely," replied Serene.

"Decadent ones," Lacey added.

"I declare this mountain air sure gives one a robust appetite. You'd never believe all that I've taken in today. Your calorie counter would positively go up in smoke," Gabby said, directing this declaration to Serene.

Lacey winked at Serene. "She's telling the truth too. Come on, ladies. I need a hot fudge with pecans myself."

Back home later, a weary and talked-out Aunt Gabby didn't bother to sit down. "Ladies, if you'll excuse me, I think my munchkin bed is calling me. I'm so tired from my delightfully Divine day I don't even think I'll mind that quilt." She hugged Serene and Lacey and disappeared down the hall.

Serene and Lacey both signaled thumbs-up and dropped down on the sofa.

"Well, she seems to be settling in and, dare I say, developing a sense of humor," Serene said. She crossed her legs and snuggled into the comfortable cushions before giving Lacey her full attention.

"I think I owe Petunia huge. I'm convinced Petunia cast some spell on her before bringing her back here." Lacey grabbed a gold throw and covered her legs, getting comfy too.

"Let's hope the spell lasts a few more days until your aunt motors on down the mountain holler." Serene cracked a grin. "Tell me how you spent your few free hours, not having to do Gabby's bidding."

"The only part of my afternoon you might find interesting is my hike. In fact, I'm willing to bet you're not going to believe what I'm about to tell you."

"I'm listening. Full focus on you. And don't you dare make me try and guess either."

"Okay, okay." Lacey smiled, eyes dancing. "I met Old Mountain Cassie on my hike. I did. I met her. Up close and personal. The real deal. In the flesh. Hello? Did you hear me?"

Serene sat quiet, allowing her lighthearted mood to shift thoughtfully. "That's incredible. I bet you found her pretty fascinating. Tell me." She hoped Lacey didn't pick up on her shift and instead stayed with her excitement.

"She's fascinating, all right, but there's something much more moving inside of her. We only chatted a few minutes, really. I think she's a kind of sage."

"You think?"

"I do. She sees things differently. It's like Old Mountain Cassie has a secret, the kind of secret that can change your life if she'll tell you. All I can say is my obsession to meet her got justified a whole big bunch today. Do I sound like a loon? I still can't believe I actually talked to her. I am a loon, aren't I?" Lacey shook her head.

Serene bestowed a smile on her friend, understanding well the Cassie experience. "Not a loon at all." Serene didn't add any more words after that statement but rather kept the channel open for Lacey to continue her discovery. She'd learned this listening skill from Old Mountain Cassie not that long ago.

"Well, I'm relieved you don't think me nutso. I mean you know how I've had this fascination with her ever since I first heard her name from Charlie standing next to his display of canned cling peaches." Lacey grew thoughtful. "After that, I felt a tug to watch for a Cassie sighting each time I hiked."

"Yes, and your tugging proved true, didn't it?" Serene turned to face Lacey so that she could be even more present for this powerful sharing.

The position change gave Lacey a chance to study Serene's face to be sure she really did understand. "You're right. This Cassie encounter feels like some dream now, and yet I have a souvenir of my first meeting."

"First meeting?" Serene wanted Lacey to connect the pieces for her.

"Oh yeah, that other day at Mystic, remember the woman I met that gave me this healing moss thingy?"

Serene nodded.

"Well, that was Old Mountain Cassie, only she didn't introduce herself, so I didn't realize until today. Wonder why she did that."

"Now that you've met her, why do you think?"

"Maybe she wasn't in the frame of mind to be friendly. Sometimes I get that way."

"I think that's a simple answer."

Serene's reply went over Lacey's head. "Or maybe the time wasn't right," Lacey offered, connecting to a stream of knowledge she hadn't even realized. She frowned at Topaz, who jumped up on the sofa.

"Another choice that makes sense." Serene knew that answer came from Lacey's spirit and not her mind. Truth always resided there. She'd wait and see how long her friend might hold on to this newer stream of intuition she'd tapped into.

Lacey stared at the ceiling. "Yes, the time felt right today. I'm open now and want to know her. Before I was just fixated on anything Cassie, without any depth of purpose, just me having a shallow human thought."

"And now?"

"Now that I've spent time with her, I sense she has the wisdom to share, something I don't yet understand or can explain but compelling to me just the same." Lacey paused, reflecting on her words. "Did I just say all of that?"

"I'm your witness, and for the record, I think you're on to something," Serene added a dash of encouragement to keep Lacey in the flow.

She looked at Serene once again, making a connection. "I feel different having met Cassie. It's like I sense an opening to a gateway…maybe. Gateway? I don't know what made me choose that word." Lacey struggled to find more words to explain the novel feelings. It's like there's an excitement anticipating the next meeting like it's my destiny or something." Lacey took a breath. She wondered what aspect of her was carrying on this conversation. Wasn't Old Mountain Cassie some recluse in the woods? *No*, she argued with her mind. Serene's voice called her back to the present.

"Listen, Lace, I can certainly perceive a change in you, and your words are doing a remarkable job of capturing the experience. Is there more you'd like to share about your time with Old Mountain Cassie?"

Lacey's mind strived to recall any more tidbits about Cassie. "She works with her herbs and plants, or as she described, they are coworkers of sorts." Lacey looked up from stroking Topaz's ears and smiled.

"Coworkers, huh? What a unique perspective."

"That's exactly what I thought too. And I forgot to tell you more about Lickety Split." Lacey chuckled, remembering his friendly nature.

"Well, you know me. I'm not a huge fan of big dogs. What did you find special about the fellow?"

"How did you know he's a large dog?"

"Ugh…I…well, with that name, I just assumed he must be a good size." Serene wanted to slap her big yap. She'd been so careful in choosing her words. She could only hope Lacey's active mind would carry her to other thoughts.

Lacey's desire to share more trumped her need to question Serene's answer. "If you say so. You're pretty astute. And yes, he's a big dog and a love. He's all into licking as his favorite way to show affection. Lots of licking. He and Cassie have some unusual understanding that's quite something to behold."

"For a short encounter, you surely gleaned a lot, I'd say."

"Until you said that, I didn't realize how rich the exchange was for me." Lacey sat back, replaying her time with the incredible woman. She wanted to cherish and remember every moment.

"Why don't I slip out and let you have some quiet time?"

An absent Lacey nodded with her eyes already closing.

Serene closed the front door and let out a trapped sigh. Except for almost giving away her knowledge of Lickety, she felt satisfied by her performance tonight. She'd been fully present, checking her bantering ways at the door. Serene turned for home, wondering what Cassie's next move might be and trusting The Three Lessons would soon be gifted to her friend.

Chapter 20

THE REST OF THE WEEK passed for Old Mountain Cassie in an expected manner. She'd devoted extra hours to her plants so that she'd be more available for Lacey. Her clients understood that orders needed to be placed or risk delays as Cassie's time shifted to her new Seeker. Most of her customers had been with her long enough to anticipate these shifts. Adaptability became a trait they all shared and reveled in for their own personal growth. Those evolved understood her relationship with plants and herbs as something sacred.

She felt genuine pleasure seeing her customers not act with baser emotions of the typical business people populating the planet. There wasn't any struggle to rush, no frustration, just trust and acceptance that things were as they needed to be. And the flow of the plants' energies continued to provide proof for all who were in tune and receiving.

"Wonder what our Lacey has been up to? I'm thinkin' we'll be laying our eyes on her pretty soon, Lickety."

Her companion came over to Cassie and gave one of his rare grins. His mouth stretched back, and white front teeth gleamed.

Cassie made a decision. The day looked way too glorious to waste inside. She grabbed her fishing pole and other necessaries for someone who felt confident they'd be bringing home dinner. Her cast iron skillet had been lonely during her last week of hard work. Time to give it something to sizzle over.

"Come on, Lick. The plants need a break from me, and the trout have waited too long for this tasty fly. How does cornmeal-fried trout and green tomatoes sound for dinner?"

The dog sprinted outside, barking enthusiastically.

Cassie caught her first fish within minutes of casting her line in the cool mountain water. "Fish, take your time. Don't send me home so soon," she said, looking into the clear stream rushing along the rocks to eventually find the sea.

Lickety Split abandoned the stick he'd been tossing in the air to inspect Cassie's catch before it slipped into her basket.

She cast her line back, willing one more trout to come home with her but not just yet. "See what a hurry that water is in? We're not like that. Are we, Lick?"

Chapter 21

THE LAST DAYS HAD BEEN mostly tolerable for Lacey with her aunt filling every space in her small cottage. Bless Petunia for taking Gabby as her new pet project. She found time each day to escort Gabby on some kind of outing. Lacey could buy out Petunia's entire inventory, and still, that wouldn't be enough to repay her. She sat at her desk when she heard Aunt Gabby welcoming Petunia inside.

"Darling Pet, you're as punctual as Lacey's annoying cuckoo clock. Do come in, won't you?"

"Hello, Gabriella. I've got the most wonderful jaunt planned for us."

"Splendid. Splendid. Shall you tell me, or do you wish it to be a surprise? I adore surprises…nice ones, of course," rambled Gabby while looking for her Italian designer handbag.

"Well, I suppose I could treat this as a surprise plan if you're willing to take some direction from me. Oh, hello, Lacey," Petunia said, seeing Lacey enter the room.

"Hi, Petunia. I heard you both chatting away." Lacey squeezed the smiling woman's hand and mouthed yet another thanks.

"You are my consummate guide. I defer to your excellent social skills, darling Pet. Such an enjoyable week."

"Well, I'll just get back to my desk. You two don't pick up any stray guys," Lacey added teasingly.

"Oh, posh. There aren't any men for me in this holler…I mean Divine, Pet, are we ready?" Gabby asked, quickly recovering her manners.

"We are. Bye, Lacey." Petunia ushered Gabby out the door with a final wave and turned her attention to showing her new friend a surprise good time.

Petunia and Gabby enjoyed a conversation en route to the destination.

"Petunia, I have the most delightful idea. Why not visit me in Miami Beach this next winter? Isn't that when your season slows at the boutique?"

"Hmm…my sales do calm quite a lot. Oh, Gabriella, what a splendid idea. I would dearly love to come see you and your beach. I accept your kind invitation, and I do so relish the thought of a Florida vacation.

"Marvelous and I'll have the opportunity to repay your kindness. We must get our calendars out tomorrow and choose dates."

They traveled the rest of the short distance in companionable silence until Petunia steered her white, vintage British sedan into the gravel parking lot where a large barn with a purple neon sign flashed "The Jamboree." Music blared, and folks were coming and going dressed in Western finery.

Petunia glanced at Gabby. Her mouth hung open, and her head bobbed like apples floating in a barrel at Halloween. Petunia turned away to hide a grin. "Here we are, Gabriella. Now before you say a single word, you must make me a promise."

"Dear Pet, I've never—"

"Shhh. Promise me you will go along, and I'll promise you that tonight will be memorable, and maybe for you—"

Petunia's plea was interrupted by someone tapping on the car window. She pushed a button, releasing the window. "Petunia honey, I thought that looked like you sitting pretty as you please in this fancy sedan of yours."

"Hi, Fred. How nice to see you this evening." Petunia's good manners telegraphed a message for Gabby.

"My goodness, introduce me to this beautiful belle sitting next to you." Fred shoved his hand out to a shocked Gabby.

"Umm, Gabriella, I want you to meet the best Texas two-stepper in this area. Fred Holcomb, this is my new friend, Gabriella Cummings."

"Pleased to meet you, ma'am. Think I'll claim you first." Fred's grin was as wide as the brim of his hat.

"Excuse me?" Gabby huffed, staring aghast at the man's red checked shirt resembling some table cloth from a picnic. "Petunia, whatever is this man going on about?" Gabby said, ignoring Fred's dangling hand.

"Listen, Fred, why don't we catch up with you inside? I'm sort of in the middle of introducing Gabriella to the Jamboree," Petunia suggested, trying to temper the moment's high emotion.

"Sure thing, honey." Fred pulled his arm back and straightened up. He tipped his hat once again to both ladies and turned to greet another friend.

"Petunia, where are we?" Panic had settled in Gabby's throat.

"We are where some happy times are made two nights a week. Let's hurry. Promise now you'll go along. Trust me." Petunia pressed.

"Very well. Promise, but surely you can see I'm not attired…" Gabby stopped, seeing Petunia shifting in her seat.

Petunia grabbed two large shopping bags from the back seat. "Inside these bags are our skirts, blouses, and the rest we need to change us into dancers."

Gabby peered into the bag. "Dear me, is that a crinoline poking out?"

"It is. Come with me. We'll change inside." Petunia chuckled, opening the car door.

Gabby followed. "Well, at least, you picked my most flattering colors." An unexpected giggle escaped Gabby's lips. She covered her mouth, embarrassed to show girlish excitement at her age. Something surely was in Divine's water to have her acting so…agreeable.

Chapter 22

Lacey sat on her kitchen stool, turning her mind to wonder where Aunt Gabby might be at eleven o'clock. She'd enjoyed a fun evening with Stardust friends at Detective Dagger's, but now she was tired and wanting her bed and half-finished romance novel. Just as her concern notched up to the point of calling Gabby's cell phone, Petunia's headlights shone through the living room window. She heard voices long before the front door opened, and two dancers Lacey barely recognized failed at their attempts to step over the threshold together. The scene looked like two women from an opry house had arrived at her door.

Gales of laughter erupted as Gabby's crinoline billowing purple skirt flew up, covering her flushed face.

"My goodness, aren't we full of ourselves?" Gabby exclaimed, trying to catch her breath and tame her skirt.

"I quite agree. You go first." Petunia stepped back, allowing the lavender taffeta petticoat the respect it demanded.

Both women noticed Lacey's shocked face at the same moment, and true to her name, Gabby responded first. "Lacey precious, aren't I simply divine in Divine?" Gabby giggled and hiccupped, looking back at Petunia for agreement.

Petunia nodded, delighting in Lacey's reaction. "I fear your aunt may have overdone herself a tad in the Jamboree's punch bowl."

"I'm inclined to agree," Lacey said, wishing she could record Gabby's performance to share with her cousins.

"Lacey, Lacey, Lacey," her aunt interrupted in a sing-song voice. "They called the drink ambrosia, and Fred kept taking me back to that heavenly nectar after each dance. Petunia, I should have brought a sample home for our Lacey, Lacey, Lacey." Another hiccup followed.

"Aunt Gabby, I do believe you're a touch tipsy. Better have a seat on the sofa." Lacey didn't try to hide her amusement any longer.

Petunia watched, feeling relief that Lacey was taking her aunt's condition in stride. "Lacey, I'd like to explain. You see, I took Gabriella to the Jamboree for a night of—"

"Yes, simply a divine place, dear Niece," Gabby quickly interjected. "Is it warm? Where's my fan? I feel swoony."

"Maybe you'd be cooler if you go change into your nightgown," Lacey hid her mirth seeing Gabby sway toward her bedroom humming what sounded like a country music ballad.

"Petunia, I have no idea what transpired tonight, but it sure sounds like you two cut some kind of rug." Lacey gave a goodbye hug to the fruit punch abstainer and the new friend to Gabby.

"Yes, I think tonight went a long way to, let's say, loosening up Gabriella. I trust your evening was enjoyable?" Petunia stopped on the porch step.

"I had a wonderful evening with friends in Asheville, thanks. Drive safely those few blocks home."

Lacey turned out the lights on another day with Aunt Gabby but not before noting the day after tomorrow circled on the calendar for her aunt's departure. "Homestretch," she declared with enough verve to send Topaz scampering out the door.

Chapter 23

After breakfast, Old Mountain Cassie, sporting her red boots, loaded the truck's bed with the boxes of herbs. She'd drive the half hour to the shipper's and then…the lunch. Her day was mapped and timely. More she wouldn't allow to surface.

An hour later, the hostess asked, "How many in your party?" Her eyes mirrored disapproval at Cassie's attire.

"There will be two, and I'd like to sit on the veranda. Weather is invitin' me out there." Cassie's voice echoed her character's strength.

"Excellent choice. Follow me, please." The willowy blonde with way too much perfume led a sniffing Cassie outside.

Olive green umbrellas shaded distressed wood tables and chairs that were set with lemon yellow napkins and stoneware. Daisies stood proudly in clear vases centered on each table. Tucked in the corner, three men and their instruments were making some of the sweetest-sounding bluegrass music a body ever heard.

Cassie settled into the cushioned chair, closing her eyes so that her ears could appreciate the sounds of the banjo, fiddle, and Jews harp. The voices joined in pure harmony.

"You don't ever want them to stop," a deep baritone voice stated a fact.

"Not until this minute." Cassie opened her eyes to see her old beau smiling that special smile just for her. Branson leaned down and planted a kiss on the top of her head before claiming the chair next to hers.

"Will you marry me, Cass?"

"Stop it, you ole coot. Must you propose every time we meet up?" Cassie asked in mock seriousness.

"Well, one of these days you just might surprise me with a yes." His white hair looked freshly trimmed, and his blue eyes danced in merriment. A tan button-down shirt and navy khakis dressed him dapper.

The two sat making a stark contrast in style, but their hearts had joined many years past. They met when time allowed for sharing precious moments and their lives.

"Still waiting for my answer, honey."

"You'd skedaddle faster than Lickety Split if I ever said yes." Cassie teased.

"Yeah, I'd skedaddle, all right, you irksome woman, to get you right to the preacher. What do you have to say about that, turtledove?"

"I say pick up that menu and order us somethin' fine. Here comes our waitress." Cassie turned her attention back to the music or, at least, pretended to. Blast the man. He could still send her ole heart a racin'. Blast him again and his silver tongue. Wasn't she too old for this nonsense? Branson's voice brought her attention back.

"We'll have chicken and dumplings with a spring salad. It's your specialty, right?" he asked the waitress.

"Yes, sir. I'm sure you both will enjoy that choice." The waitress picked up the menus and disappeared.

"So, good-looking, we've got some catching up to do. I'll tell you all about my trip to a Greek Isle just perfect for us as a honeymoon, and you can fill me in on your newest Seeker."

Cassie's mouth flew open in surprise. "Branson, you've done it again. Gone and read my mind before I said a word about my Seeker. Not sure how you do it, but…ah, never mind. I plan to still enjoy the tellin' part, so there."

Her beau tapped his temple. "I've got powers," he said, grinning.

"Me too," she came back, matching his grin. Her expression grew serious. Cassie leaned closer to Branson and whispered, "I've been waitin' a long spell for this one. Enough said."

Branson paused to sip his ale the waitress had delivered, absorbing Cassie's words. "This is one encounter that I sense may just alter things for you in a marvelous way." He changed back to his light patter. "Ready to hear about my introduction to the Greek gods? Met a few goddesses, but they didn't hold a candle to you."

"Hush that and start your tellin'. You know how much I enjoy pretendin' I'm travelin' with you." Cassie relaxed, taking in Branson's fascinating stories and experiences, while a small secret ember glowed inside of her, wishing she'd been there in his company, seeing the ruins of temples and tasting the Greek's delicious victuals.

"There you have my winter interlude among the gods," he concluded, sitting back in his chair. "It's your turn now. Don't hold anything back 'cause I've got plenty of time for you…always have…always will." His Aegean blue eyes settled affectionately on Cassie's face.

The spell was broken when the waitress brought their apple dumplings with warm caramel sauce, along with steaming mugs of chicory coffee.

Cassie spent the next half hour sharing with Branson news about her work, which always brought forth fresh gratitude for her many blessings. She elected to omit almost all details about Lacey, preferring to share more if she felt directed.

Chapter 24

LACEY SAT AT HER DESK, frowning over the dwindling balance in her checking account. She prided herself on living fully but frugally, ever striving to grow her nest egg for the day she was shown her life's work. Truth, she felt more concerned about her lack of direction toward finding work. She couldn't bear the idea of having to leave Divine for a job. Job. The word offered no joy. She didn't want just another job, but what did she want? Lacey acknowledged a deep yearning to discover her hidden talents like Old Mountain Cassie, Serene, and others had, but that's as far as her thoughts had taken her. Was God even listening to her prayers for guidance? If so, the answers hadn't found her.

Gabby's chiming cell phone broke Lacey's confused thoughts. She heard her aunt's groggy hello from the kitchen.

"What did you just say, Bob? Please repeat your words once more, but do turn off that infernal drill or whatever is making that awful noise. My head is splitting."

Lacey heard nothing, assuming her aunt was listening to someone else talk for a change.

"Delays caused by what?" Gabby asked. "Well, if it can't be helped, of course, dear Bob, I will simply have to extend my visit. I cannot abide chaos. Keep me posted and do not rush this job. I want and pay for perfection. Yes, well, good-bye."

Lacey stood in total and complete disbelief. Her aunt wasn't leaving as planned, but she, Lacey, might. Serene. She'd call Serene. Where was her box of tissues? She felt a big cry coming on.

"Lacey darling girl, there you are." Gabby entered the den.

"Good morning, Aunt Gabby. I hope you're feeling well." Lacey inquired, trying to keep her voice cheerful.

"Well, except for a mild fruit-punch headache, I seem to be… quite chipper. Listen to my wonderful news. It appears that I can extend my visit with you a little longer."

"Really?" Lacey managed to get out. Her throat felt dry, and her eyes stung with more unshed tears. Buckets of them.

"Yes. Yes. My condo isn't completed. There's some back order with my cabinets. Plus, Bob's lead carpenter's, whatever that means, wife had a baby. Naturally, the man needed time off."

"Naturally," Lacey replied, sinking with her spirits into the chair.

"I know how lonely you must be living alone, and, well, I can spare you the sadness of my departure awhile longer," Gabby explained, feeling a gigantic dose of pride at her unselfishness shown to her niece.

"You're too kind. I really don't—"

"Tut-tut. I'm gratified to bring cheerfulness to your days in this holler of a—"

"Aunt Gabby, just how many more cheerful days can I expect with you here?" Lacey asked, clenching her jaw, dreading the reply of another week.

"Oh, dearest, that's the best part. The cabinets are still on the ship somewhere in the Pacific Ocean, so that means I can be a comfort to you for at least another four weeks." Gabby threw her arms in the air to celebrate and headed to the kitchen.

"Four weeks. Four long, uninterrupted weeks. Four blocks of seven days. Four—"

"Are you talking to me, precious?"

"More weeks." Lacey stopped her chant to respond. "Just counting my blessings, Aunt Gabby." Her hand reached for the phone and dialed Serene, only to hear her friend's voice say to leave a message.

"Four more weeks," Lacey said and hung up.

She escaped to her soaking tub, which never failed to soothe her spirit, but there may not be enough earth time to soak up this news.

Collected on the outside, Lacey now dressed in jeans and a turquoise knit top and went in search of her guest turned boarder. She found a note propped next to some fresh cut flowers from her garden's late blooms. By the size of the bouquet, it looked like Gabby had stripped every crimson tulip that had the courage to come up with the plucking aunt afoot.

Breathe, Lacey. Breathe. Gabby means well, she told herself. Taking a calming breath, she opened her front door to see three lone tulips standing. Lacey closed the door, repeating, "Only flowers. Only flowers," as she returned to read the note.

Dear Niece,
Petunia and I are off to the nursery—the flower kind, of course. I'm devoting this entire week to your pitiful gardens and beds. They need my loving touch and expert attention. Go on about your day. We'll sup tonight. Kisses.
Aunt Gabby

Lacey took the garden shears and went to clip the remaining tulips. "I can spare you Gabby's hoe." Great, now she was mumbling to flowers. She added them to the bouquet waiting inside. She fretted, wondering what her aunt might plant in her front yard beds. Probably some loathsome cactus that prospers in the mountains. Where had her quiet existence gone, and would she ever get it back?

Lacey encouraged her mind to escape to the kitchen and do some early prep for dinner. She placed salmon steaks in a citrus marinade and made a Bibb salad with dried cherries and almonds. She'd put the finishing touches on the meal later that evening but for now—errands; blessed errands waited to distract her.

Somehow, she'd have to make peace with Gabby's visit extended into infinity and the upcoming pillage to her poor flower beds. At least, this week, Gabby meddling would be confined to the dirt.

Lacey greeted Divine's folks as she went about slowly ticking off stops on her shopping list. Everyone liked to say to newcomers rushing around them, "Slow down, you're on Divine time now." Lacey wondered if her aunt had felt the time shift yet. No doubt she would with her extended stay. Lacey smiled, savoring her aunt's coming indoctrination. No one was immune to Divine's enchantments, not even Gabriella Cummings.

Lacey noticed Serene's open sign and took that as an invitation to share the news of the day. Clients of Serene's were exiting as Lacey, a smile plastered on her face, slipped by them, making a beeline for her best friend. She stood in front of Serene's desk, silent.

"Big smile. No, wait, let me see. That's an artificial big smile." Serene looked closer at her friend, taking in all the body language, and there was plenty—arms folded, fist clenched, hair piled cockeyed on top of her head, and, the final proof…wearing only one earring.

Lacey ventured over to the coffeepot and poured a cup. "Did you get my message?" She tipped the sugar container and let it pour.

"I saw that you called. I'd planned on ringing you after my clients left." Serene took the sugar away and pointed to the pair of chairs in the corner. "Sit and spin your yarn, kiddo."

"Four more weeks," Lacey said, commencing the babbling. "Four, count them, four… straight weeks." Lacey held up four fingers. "She's going to stay the live long month."

"Wow! Can we move past counting time and to the reason?"

"Her cabinets, it seems, won't hop on a faster boat."

"Ship." Serene corrected.

"Fine, ship. Honest to Pete, these cabinets must be on the Mayflower. Why me? I've lost my job, my quiet time off from a stress-filled job to figure out what I'm going to do, and…and today I lost my flower beds to Aunt Gabby, who, might I add, thinks she's saving me from severe loneliness and my garden from gross neglect." Lacey's smile cracked, and the pent-up tears broke through.

"Go ahead and cry, honey. That loopy smile had me plenty worried." Serene handed her the box of tissues. "You'll be okay now. Just let it all out." Serene reached over and turned her sign to read closed.

Lacey released her big cry. Drained, she sniffed a few more times, gaining her composure. "What will I do with her? Help me figure this out. I can't ask her to leave. She's my only aunt." Tears threatened to return for an encore.

Serene jumped in. "Okay, let me think here." She paced.

"You'd better come up with something fast. She's dedicated a week to redoing my front yard, and I suspect she'll be done a whole lot sooner. I refuse to think about what awful exotic plants are going to end up in my beds."

"Maybe you'll like—"

"I can see the cactus now. Jane Ann's going to have everyone in Divine coming by to see my horticulture experiment." Lacey snagged another tissue.

"Stay in the present moment with me. I think I've got a blossoming idea."

"Ha. Very funny. In my hour of desperation, you make jokes."

"Listen." Serene laughed, growing more enthusiastic about her plan.

Lacey settled down and took a sip of her tepid brew.

"Isn't Petunia's assistant taking time off for some six-week class? Do you remember hearing that? I do."

"I don't know, but why?"

"Well, if she's not going to work, maybe our Gabby could take over for her part time."

"My aunt? Work? You're kidding me."

"We'd present the idea differently, of course. Make her feel vital to—"

"Petunia does have her under a spell…a powerful one judging by last evening's escapades," Lacey said, taking to Serene's scheme.

"It's worth a try, don't you think? If we don't try this, then—"

"Four…four more—"

"No, no. Don't start that up again. You were doing so well."

Lacey quieted, seeing Serene move toward the telephone.

"Want me to call Petunia? Move your head up and down. That's a good girl." Serene chuckled.

Lacey kept nodding while she watched Serene call Petunia's shop.

"Petunia, hey, it's Serene. Hope you're having a good day. Listen, can I put you on speaker phone? I have Lacey here, and we have a spectacular idea to propose."

"Sure. Hello, Lacey." Petunia's tone was always friendly.

"Hi, Petunia. Umm, are you alone?" Lacey asked.

"Quite so. Tell me, girls, what can I do for you?"

Lacey whispered, "Serene, you pitch this crazy plotting, please."

Serene gave a thumbs-up. "Got a question. Petunia, isn't your part-time girl taking time off?"

"Why, yes, she's starting her potter's class the end of the week. It's some intensive. Oh, never mind the details, why do you, girls, ask?"

"Well, Lacey just told me Gabby is extending her stay another month."

Lacey laid her head down on Serene's desk, hearing the words spoken by someone else.

"Really? How wonderful for us. I've grown quite attached to Gabriella."

"Yes, she has that effect. Here's the thought, what about having Gabby help you at the boutique for the next few weeks?" Serene explained, making her case.

Lacey's fingers started massaging her temples. She wondered what the highest blood pressure reading ever recorded in the Guinness Book was and if hers might top it. Her attention returned to hear Serene's next sentence.

"I bet Gabby would just love to be around all those lovely fashions and lend a hand to help her new friend. Her days would be filled with purpose, and she wouldn't be bored."

Serene and Lacey waited anxiously for Petunia to hurry and absorb the plan. They looked at each other expectantly with crossed fingers held high.

Too much silence worried Lacey. "I doubt she'd let you pay her a cent," Lacey threw out with desperation coloring her words.

Serene rolled her eyes.

"I'm thinking, girls. This is a most interesting…what shall we call it? A proposition of sorts? Tell me, does Gabriella know of this…proposition?" Petunia asked, amusement tingeing her voice.

"Not exactly. Serene just came up with the scheme…I mean proposition a moment ago, but I think we can present this in a way that she'd be delighted," Lacey offered, angry at her slip.

"I can certainly use the assistance, but—"

Lacey recognized Petunia's hesitation and jumped back in, "Petunia, please, please help me. You've been so very kind spending time with my aunt, and I so appreciate what you've done. I'm desperate to find Aunt Gabby something to occupy her time." Lacey felt her hopes disappearing like her tulips and hyacinths had that morning.

"I'm just not sure she'd enjoy all the—"

Serene quickly interrupted, fearing Lacey's number babbling might return. "Petunia, we all recognize Aunt Gabby is high maintenance, but she adores and is impressed with your shop. It's us you'll be doing the favor for."

"Well, all right, if you two really feel my little shop can be of some help to a bored Gabriella."

"And don't forget you'll be helping me too. I've got to devote my time to contemplating my next career choice. I won't feel guilty leaving Aunt Gabby to explore options and such," Lacey explained, wanting to seal this deal.

"Yes, I suppose I understand. Okay then, so I'll leave this to you, two big plotters, to sell Gabriella this new…um, outfit shall I say? I'll ring her once you say she's agreed, and only then will I pull my 'Help Wanted' sign from the display window." Petunia finished, growing more entertained. She'd enjoyed the girl's pitch.

"Don't worry. Serene and I will be talking to her this evening. Thank you so, so much. You have no idea—"

"No problem," Petunia interjected. "Goodness, here comes Gabriella in the door. Bye, girls."

Serene and Lacey heard the phone connection end.

"Phase one of our battle plan completed—with success, I might add. Now, on to phase two." Serene scooted back in her chair.

Lacey threw up her hand and executed a smart salute to her friend. "You're the best tactical general in this girl's Navy. I just might survive this latest onslaught to my serenity."

"Good. Let's go celebrate. This calls for a brew, and I'm buying." Serene stood.

"Aye, aye, General Serene."

"Umm, Lacey, remind me to explain the branches of the military and the appropriate responses after we've had our first round."

"Affirmative," Lacey replied and added another salute.

Serene's hand returned a smart salute. "Good to have you back, Sergeant. You had me a tad worried."

The two friends entered Paulie's Pizza Palace and headed toward an empty table near the small bar area. Paulie only served wine and beer, sending the message he wasn't interested in attracting any serious drinkers.

The waitress came over to take their order. "Hey there, Serene, listen, Paulie's gone to the bank and print shop. Should be back in an hour. What ya having?" The petite brunette placed a napkin on the table.

Serene's face colored. "Thanks. I'll have one of your dark imported ales."

Lacey sensed the timing still not right to prod Serene about the obvious something with Paulie. "I'll try what the general here is having."

The waitress frowned, not understanding the title, shrugged, and wrote the order down.

Serene and Lacey passed the next half hour planning phase two. Serene promised to have this little skirmish won by the end of dinner. Lacey was counting on their persuasion to close out her long day with some sort of triumph. Any triumph.

Chapter 25

A LAUGHING PETUNIA AND GABBY walked into Paulie's for their own celebration.

Petunia spotted the younger women first and motioned to Gabriella to look over in the far corner. "What do you think? Should we have a bit of fun?"

"By all means. We can't ignore this perfect opportunity for a lark, now can we? I'm right behind you. Lead on," Gabby encouraged.

"May we join you, girls?" Petunia asked the two surprised faces.

"Of course," Lacey answered, moving her chair to make room.

"Fancy meeting you here," Serene added, realizing their chance had come to execute Operation Occupy Gabby.

"Hello, dear girls. I'll just squeeze in here," Aunt Gabby said, easing up on the high stool.

"Gabriella stopped unexpectedly to say hello and tell me all about her plans for your flower beds, Lacey," Petunia offered by way of explaining.

"Really?" Lacey acknowledged, already dreading hearing the names of some new species of cactus that thrives in the Appalachian Mountains.

"Lacey, darling girl, you're going to be positively enchanted by the selections I've made," Gabby gushed.

"And I'll bet no one in Divine will have anything as…as unique as me. Though you really shouldn't trouble yourself."

Serene listened, waiting for an opening to launch her volley.

"Of course, I must agree there will be enormous labor, but I've found a boy at the nursery who's agreed to do my bidding. Isn't that marvelous?"

"But the cost to you, Aunt Gabby," Lacey said, not wanting her aunt to waste money.

"It's a pittance, child. After all, I see how desperately you've needed me to come and take over, let us say, the upkeep of your diminutive cottage. And isn't it delightful that I've been given this extra time to devote to such a project?"

"Quite so, Gabriella." Petunia rushed to agree, bringing her attention back to the conversation and support of the joke.

Aunt Gabby was nobody's fool. She read the concern on her niece's face when she offered earlier to bring some order to that patchwork-looking front yard. Every time she passed by those flower beds, it reminded her of that horrid quilt on her bed.

Thanks to Petunia's fine sense of humor, Gabby had enjoyed many laughs during her sojourn. So, when Petunia suggested a bit of teasing fun, the now less serious Gabby readily agreed. Petunia watched her new friend set up the joke. She felt happy that both women, in the end, would be rewarded in their games.

"The nursery offered exquisite choices and themes, but I think I've settled on the exact one that's simply ideal for your yard." Gabby glanced at the younger women's expressions and saw that she'd successfully captured their full attention.

A worried frown settled between Lacey's eyes. "A theme?" she croaked.

Serene handed her a glass of water. "Don't keep us in suspense, Aunt Gabby."

"Oh, very well, if you insist. I'd considered having the work done and making the new look a grand surprise," explained Gabby.

"Actually, I think it's better if you show Lacey. That way she can enjoy the anticipation of her new gardens," Petunia said, warming to the tease.

Gabby reached inside her handbag, pulling out some folded pages. "Here's my inspiration. I found this design in the latest gardening magazine." She placed the torn-out glossy pages carefully on the table facing Lacey. "Perfectly splendid Feng Shui, don't you think?"

Lacey stared at the Japanese-inspired garden with funny-shaped bonsais, orange pagodas, and snarling red dragons crouching beside plants, ready to attack. "Wow. There's so much…umm…"

"Yard art," finished Serene. She sat transfixed, gazing at the photos.

"You know, the colors reminded me of that hideous quilt," said Gabby. She couldn't resist the comparison. She looked over at Petunia, who was battling to keep a straight face.

"Aunt Gabby, I can see how you might be pulled to the Asian influence, but are you sure this particular design is suitable for my small plot?"

"Ah, Lacey, I think the look offers, shall we say, interest?" Petunia chimed in.

A perceptive Serene took in the body language of the two conspirators. She decided to sit back and enjoy the morsel of silliness.

"Well, how about this idea? Maybe you could experiment with this interesting look in my backyard garden first," Lacey suggested diplomatically, trying to keep the desperation out of her voice. Her eyes pleaded to Serene for support.

Gabby reached across the table and flipped each page over. "Petunia, I think we need to let Lacey and Serene in on our little lark."

Petunia smiled and nodded in agreement.

"There now, dear one, lay your eyes on these pictures. I think this design will be more pleasing to your cottage's face."

Lacey looked at the photographs of the most endearing English garden. The cottage in the picture even resembled her place. "Aunt Gabby, I adore this design. Shame on you for playing such a trick," Lacey said, finally able to relax now that she knew her front yard wouldn't be turned into some Asian yard art debacle.

Serene turned back to the first pages of the Asian garden gone wrong and read the title, "How Not to Design Your Asian Oasis."

The four women burst into laughter, causing the waitress to come running to their table, fearing she'd broken Paulie's cardinal rule and let them get soused on beer and wine coolers.

Moments later, a more composed Petunia looked at her watch. "Goodness me, I must dash. The delivery truck is making a late drop for me. I must do a brisk walk back to the shop."

"I'll ring you later, Petunia," Gabby promised.

Serene and Lacey both waved bye while still engrossed over the English garden pictures. Gabby sat quietly.

Lacey glanced up, noting the change in Gabby. Her aunt having too much free time to think needed to be avoided. She kicked Serene under the table, hoping to bring her attention back to the mission.

"Poor Petunia works way too hard. Don't you think?" Serene said, back on track. She kicked Lacey back to signal the operation had begun.

"She does, and we need to help her with this latest problem. She urgently needs someone to fill in while her sales associate is away, but you know how particular Petunia is with staff," Lacey said, fortifying their battle plan.

"I don't know of anyone that I could recommend possessing style and flair." Serene acted frustrated. She took another sip of her ale, waiting for Lacey to respond.

"Me either, and the sales consulting position would only be a few short weeks. I suppose I could offer since I'm not working," Lacey said, firing the final volley.

Gabby's eyes opened wide as she rushed to intervene. "You assist Petunia? Darling Niece, that would never do. Why I'm the best suited for such an endeavor. After all, Petunia is my friend too. I simply can't allow her to be in such a lurch when my talents are being wasted while I sit and pluck flowers in Divine." Gabby touched her hair, adjusting into her prim pose.

"Gabby, what a splendid idea," Serene answered, giving Lacey a subtle victory sign.

"Why ever didn't we think of you before? You're positively perfect," Lacey added.

"Quite so. Listen, girls, please excuse me. I must hurry over to the boutique immediately. I can't let dear Petunia be frantic another second trying to locate someone living in this hootenanny with style and flair. You must agree?"

"Yes, go, Aunt Gabby. We'll catch up with you later," Lacey said.

Gabby gathered her purse and stood, tossing a twenty-dollar bill on the table. "Don't worry. I'm quite capable of supervising the gardeners while offering my refinement to Petunia," she stated, assuring them as she headed out the door, already lost in her planning.

Both younger women watched the door close behind Gabby before speaking.

"Serene, you're the best admiral in this whole woman's Air Force." Lacey saluted and released her arm into the chest of a surprised Paulie.

"Yous girls seem mighty loud with your 'clocutions' this evening." Paulie chuckled, rubbing his sternum. "Gotta an arm there, Lace."

"Oh, Paulie, forgive me. I didn't see you. Are you okay?"

"No problem. No problem. Hi, Serene." Paulie winked.

"Listen, I'd better get going myself. I've some telephone calls to make." Lacey already felt like a third wheel. She wondered when Serene would own up to being smitten with Paulie. "Thank you so much for coming to my rescue yet again. You're aces." Lacey gave a hug to her friend.

"You're welcome. I'm still going to explain the military to you. If I'm going to be the general, I need proper addressing, Sergeant Jordan. She's a mess with that," she added, never taking her eyes from Paulie.

"Aye, aye, General," Lacey replied. She gave Paulie's arm a squeeze as she passed.

"Hear that, Paulie? Ridiculous." Serene shook her head.

Lacey didn't catch his response. Her mind had moved to waiting chores before her aunt returned home. Operation Occupy Gabby bought her some needed peace. She admitted she still lacked the help to find her own true purpose. She'd just have to pray harder.

Chapter 26

THE NEXT WEEK HAD PASSED easy enough for Cassie as she and The Lessons waited for the next Lacey encounter. She'd stayed close to her land, putting her attentions on the vegetable and flower gardens. She enjoyed no shortage of visitors, but none of them human. All of God's creatures had a place in her heart, some more than others. Fur and feathers were always welcome.

Cassie sensed a visitor's presence approaching her. She stood, dusting off her khaki overalls and abandoning her garden gloves to the fence post. The wise woman walked toward a path, opening to her meadow and butterfly garden. She acknowledged their bright colors flittering around, lifting her spirits like she was one of the free to frolic.

That was the vision that greeted Lacey as she came into the clearing. Old Mountain Cassie, surrounded by butterflies, raised her hand in greeting.

"Oh my! I never expected the path to bring me here," Lacey sang out as she approached Cassie.

"I'm so pleased to see your face, Missy," Cassie said. "You've found my place, and I'm bettin' there's a good story of how you did it that needs telling."

Lacey's heart soared with Cassie's warm welcome. "That would be a winning bet to place, Cassie." Lacey laughed. I hope I'm not intruding on your peace here. I swear I never dreamed that I'd end up at your home when I discovered this new path."

The butterflies were including Lacey in their dance. A cobalt blue one landed on Lacey's arm, with wings opening and closing to show off its vibrant colors.

"Quite a welcome I'd say." Old Mountain Cassie pointed to a second golden butterfly resting on Lacey's shoulder.

"They're incredible. Such a color show." Lacey acknowledged. Her eyes glanced around, taking in Cassie's homestead. Funny how everything was exactly how she'd envisioned, and yet there was something quite enchanting about it all. Lacey's body felt a slight tingling, like a friendly current singing through her very being.

Cassie witnessed her niece's reactions and recognized Lacey was getting her first taste of being on an energy ley. They existed in the mountains scattered over the land with purpose. Yes, she had a lot of teaching to do and some listening too.

"Why don't you go sit in that swing, and I'll bring us a cup of tea?" Cassie pointed to the swing nestled in a perennial flower garden. A stone path guided the way, allowing for time to appreciate the blossoms.

"How enchanting all this feels," Lacey said in a low tone. "If you're sure it's no trouble, I'd love to pass some time in that swing." Lacey didn't wait for Cassie's reply but headed toward the seat.

Lacey slowly released herself to the swing's rhythm as her worries evaporated with the passing clouds overhead. Her mind hummed with a rare nothingness. New sensations filled voids within her body.

Old Mountain Cassie approached her niece, showing off the two new teacups holding a custom brew. She stood quietly, waiting for the swing to pause.

Lacey's eyes opened. She patted the seat next to her and, with the other hand, accepted the cup. What lovely floral cups. She looked into Cassie's eyes and felt an unusual connection.

A pleased Old Mountain Cassie sat down and, without a word, set a different rhythm for them. The older woman's foot pushed the earth with intention. She sipped her tea with a renewed vitality. Her special Seeker had finally arrived.

"Mmm, this tea packs a little zing," Cassie said, breaking the silence.

"I agree about the zing, and yet I feel so energized and relaxed at the same time.

"It's the land here," Cassie said, taking pleasure in the butterfly's freedom of expression.

Lacey sipped more of the tea. "This is yummy. Is there some kind of fruit in it?"

"Blackberries. Very good taster you have." Cassie nodded.

"Tell me about this place and what you meant and why I feel a connection of some kind."

"That *connection* word suits. Before I speak on this, why don't you first tell me about how you came to be here this day? If I'm not mistaken, you set out on this path awhile back."

"You're right," Lacey said, surprised and taken aback at Old Mountain Cassie's cryptic words. Lacey knew exactly what Cassie meant. Even though she didn't understand why she felt the pull to meet the woman of the woods, she knew the desire was real…palpable, unrelenting.

"Anytime you're ready. Just start the tellin'. No need to siphon out any of what your mind tells you to either."

"Do you have one of those siphoning kind of minds too, Cassie?" Lacey chuckled.

"Used to. Sent it packin', I did." Cassie shifted her back against the swing's arm, turning to face her Seeker.

Lacey glanced into the woods, remembering the first time she'd heard of Divine and Old Mountain Cassie's name. She guessed that was a good starting place. "I moved to Divine about two years ago, wanting to escape the stress of living in New York City. You see, I had already lost my parents. Oh, sure, I had Aunt Gabby and my two cousins, but we didn't communicate regularly. You know we were all involved in our own lives like so many people nowadays. Family is an afterthought except for holidays. Also, I wasn't in a romantic relationship at that point in time, so that freed me as well to strike out." Lacey offered a smile. "Anyway, I wanted a change and saw no reason not to go for it. So, I applied for a gem buyer's position with a midsized company based out of Asheville. I believed that I could find happiness and my sense of belonging in some nearby small town. I trusted a job paying a lot less could support a simple lifestyle in this area. I can't explain why, but this move just felt right." Lacey paused and drank from her cup.

Cassie sat silent, nudging the swing's movement along. She nodded her head a few times to let Lacey know she was mulling over her words.

Lacey continued, "You probably didn't mean for me to go back quite so far in my story."

"You wanted me to know for a reason. I'm likin' to hear about your inner and outer doings. Go on."

"Well, I visited a few small towns that I'd identified on the map as a possible fit. However, when I drove down the main street of Divine, I felt and knew all in the same moment my search had ended. Except for a bit longer commute, I couldn't find one valid reason not to settle here. Well, maybe the lack of available single men." Lacey cracked a grin.

"I've told you already that your fellow will show up here directly. You just wait and see." Cassie cleared her throat. "Many tell a version of your story."

"That's what my friend, Serene, says…about a guy, I mean." Lacey rushed past the subject. "Anyway, speaking of Serene, she helped me find the perfect cottage in town. It had everything and more I'd envisioned. And how could I not adore the quaintness and specialness of Divine? I've gotten to know people here easily. They're friendly and caring like no place I've ever been. Anyway, at Charlie's Holsom Market, I was standing by a display of cling peaches when I first heard Charlie and some folks exchanging tales about someone called Old Mountain Cassie."

"Ha. No surprise to me. That Charlie's always spinnin' yarns." Cassie chuckled.

"He does tell some stretchers, but that day the talk sounded intriguing, so after the couple left, I asked Charlie to tell me more about you."

"What did the ole buffalo say?"

"Well, unfortunately for me, he was busy and so not too much but enough to capture my imagination. He made you sound so mysterious, no, not mysterious, more…"

"Eccentric?" Cassie supplied with a chuckle.

"No, no. More like a sage who happens to be a bit reclusive," Lacey finished.

"Reclusive may be a fit…of sorts." Cassie pushed the swing's tempo up a notch.

"So, I'd hear little snippets every now and then about a 'Cassie sighting' and always wish I'd been the one seeing you. I kept hoping that I'd meet you on a trail sometime."

"Yes?" Cassie liked the story fine so far.

"I can't really explain the pull, but I felt it was important for me to know you. Now you'll think I'm some kind of loon." Lacey turned a concerned face toward Cassie.

"Nope. Would you like for me to tell you who I think you are, Lacey?"

"Okay," Lacey replied, her voice hesitant.

"You're a Seeker."

"A Seeker? A Seeker." Lacey tried on the title and frowned at Cassie. "Maybe. That might explain…Yes, I am seeking…something." Lacey shrugged.

"Let me help you a bit with some of the tellin'." Cassie didn't wait for approval. "You and I have crossed paths. Yes, and for a good reason. Seems we are meant to spend time in each other's company. Might you agree to that possibility?"

"Oh yes, though I don't, for the life of me, know why, but yes, I agree being here feels right…necessary somehow."

"Good. Now how about I shut my mouth and let you finish tellin' me how you got to this very place today?"

Lacey returned her attention to Cassie's last question. She jumped ahead in her story. "Right now, I'm dealing with losing my job and Aunt Gabby's extended visit. Well, to put it bluntly, I needed some time away from her and the 'activities' she's taken on around my house. I escaped to the woods for a hike and some solace. Still, I confess that almost every hike in this area lately holds the hope of my own Cassie sighting." Lacey beamed a smile in Cassie's direction. I set out today, noticing right off a few animals and birds were accompanying me. This has been happening lately but not as intense as today. I knew there had to be some meaning to these encounters."

"Makin' friends with my neighbors, are you, Missy?" Cassie replied, mirroring her pleasure.

"I must be. Before, I met a friendly squirrel and cardinal who showed up at a time I needed companionship. I confess I've kept that encounter to myself."

"I bet for more than the obvious reason too. Not every day a girl meets congenial critters. So, who introduced themselves today?" Cassie gently prodded.

"I started out on the same trail that I'd met the others. I was lost in thought when this deer and her fawn stepped onto my path. I stopped to give them space to cross over."

"Tell me, did the mother have one ear kinda layin' over?"

"Why, yes, she did," Lacey answered, wondering.

"That's Daffodil and her new baby, Sassafras. She's a cutie, and Daffodil loves to show her off…a real proud mama."

Lacey grinned. "For some reason, this all sounds perfectly rational. By the time I get home later, well…I'm not so sure my mind will be agreeing," Lacey said, pleased and yet still questioning.

"Miss Lacey, don't you go thinkin' too hard about any of this. Just watch and observe without doin' an editorial. So then?" Cassie pressed.

"Well, the two deer waited for me to continue on, and they, like, walked alongside me. The fawn, Sassafras, kept nudging my hand to pet her." Lacey watched Cassie's reaction.

"Really, I swear."

Cassie nodded. "She's a little love."

"She is." Lacey smiled, remembering her soft velvet nose. "So anyway, then I see a narrow trail converging on the path I was on. There stands this incredible group of wild turkeys, rabbits, and, of all things, a snapping turtle. They all were doing their best to claim my full attention with their chorus and dance. Cassie, I've never seen such a show. This group is ready for Broadway."

Old Mountain Cassie's mouth opened, letting out a burst of laughter. "You're a wit," she exclaimed, finally catching her breath.

Lickety Split came over to offer wet kisses to each other before he went to howling and prancing around the swing, adding his touch to the story.

"Guess he's auditionin' for a part too," Cassie added.

"Clearly." Lacey grinned, continuing her story. "Anyway, I sensed the trail they were so animated about meant I should go that way. I'm so glad that I did because the wildflowers and birds were incredible with colors as vibrant as the feathers on a peacock." Lacey hesitated, her eyes taking their fill of Cassie's charmed property.

Cassie watched, waiting again for her Seeker to collect new feelings.

"You have the same vibrancy here. I feel like I'm in the presence of a rainbow of magic seeing all the flowers bursting with color."

"Thank you. Your words sound real pretty to my ears. I confess a grand fondness for all colors myself."

"Yes, everything, not only looks, but feels enchanting. I don't understand any of this, but I believe you do. The forest creatures and finding the narrow path are what brought me to you this day." Confusion whirled around Lacey, but there was no denying where she sat and with who.

Cassie nodded and gave the swing more encouragement with her boot.

Lacey grew more pensive, having finished her recounting and tea. She sat as her mind peppered her with doubt and questions.

"You're lost in those pesky thoughts, aren't you?"

"How did you know?" Lacey returned to the present.

"We have plenty of time for some talkin' on that subject if you want. Why don't you tell me about your aunt?"

"Well, for starters, she's my dad's sister and quite a pistol." Lacey spent the next few minutes giving Cassie a snapshot of life with Aunt Gabby.

Cassie relished the stories and comedy enveloping Lacey as she told of her attempts to adapt to her relative's ways. And Lacey found that the telling brought her an unexpected release of the tension that had followed her to Cassie's.

"So, while my aunt means well, she's taken over the cottage's every empty space," she finished. "I had to get outside to breathe."

That place of awareness could be the bridge she needed to begin Lacey's introduction to The Three Lessons…if Lacey was willin'. She'd have to do a little probing. "Isn't it good you know where to go for your air?"

"True, but I've always sought to be with nature when I needed balance. And do I ever need some balance." Lacey released a heavy sigh.

"We have that nature love in common. We surely do." Old Mountain Cassie leaned over to take the stick offered by Lickety.

She threw it across the meadow at a distance that astounded Lacey. "Quite an arm you got there, Cassie."

"Nah. Just the breeze helpin' me give that dog an extra run." Cassie gave a grin. "You've wondered why you felt so connected here?"

"Yes, and I've fulfilled my part by sharing my tale of how I ended up in Divine, my life here, including today's discovery of your place. I think I'll shut my yap and listen to you. Something tells me I'm in for a remarkable sharing." Lacey reached over and squeezed the mountain woman's hand. She let go quickly, hoping she hadn't overstepped. Lacey settled into the swing cross-legged, allowing Cassie to set the pace of the swinging and whatever words were to come.

Cassie appreciated the open and friendly gesture. "Well, actually, Missy, I'd welcome a little participation here and there, but for now, I want to tell you right off that you're not my first Seeker to show up here, but you're my most special one, and I'll tell you why by and by. Your words tell me you've a yearnin' for learnin'." Cassie chuckled.

"You are so right. I do have a yearning to learn how to discover where my joy is hiding. Does that still make me a Seeker?" Lacey laughed, but the idea of seeking had rooted.

"Sounds like the makings of a Seeker to me. Do you want to explore findin' that joy? I've been known to share that secret map.

You interested? If not, we will keep enjoyin' our visit, but if yes, I'll ask for the answer to my question and then two promises from you. Ponder a spell if you need." Cassie paused to give Lacey a moment to take in her proposal.

"Wow. I'm really intrigued now." Lacey felt an unfamiliar excitement bubbling up inside. She'd believed the talk about Cassie having special wisdom, and it had landed her here.

Cassie gave her familiar nod, touching her chin down slowly. "Then, Missy, I'm gonna explain a bit more. First, I'm here to teach Seekers how they can tap into having an amazin' life. You see, God wants us all to discover our special gifts and use them for good. It's why we're here on this ole earth. And He wants to shower blessings on us, but we must help in our way. Here's what I say to my Seekers—find your passion, know your joy."

"'Find your passion, know your joy.' Hmmm I like that," Lacey replied.

"Trouble is, most folks can't seem to figure out how to light on their gifts. They stumble around in the dark, searchin' and lost. It's kinda like when Lickety chases his fool tail in circles, never going anywhere until he stops long enough to see what he's been missin'… what he really wants, and it's not his blame tail."

"Like me over the years, just marking time working at jobs that don't really satisfy me?" Lacey understood.

"Yes, ma'am, and that somethin' inside of you kept askin' for more to fill that hole. Losin' your job jostled you to pay attention to that emptiness. And now you're weary and ready for help. God and those on the Other Side answered your prayers…your call… and introduced you and me. Would you agree that's some kind of amazin' so far?"

"I'll say, Cassie, from hearing about you at Charlie's Market to sitting here facing you, it is incredible. And I crave to hear more. You're a natural teacher." Lacey felt charmed by Cassie's manner of explaining things.

"Well then, I best shift a bit of my sharin' ways. Speed things up since you are feelin' ready to explore a fresh way to live your sweet life. It's probably good if I first define a Seeker for you. Let's be sure you fit the name and want to answer the callin'. Cassie gathered her words. "A Seeker's qualities are a sincere and powerful yearnin' to live in joy, to discover their special gifts meant to serve others, and most important of all, grow into havin' a deep inner relationship with God. That's my short definition."

Lacey nodded while questions buzzed in her head.

"When Seekers are brought to me, I have somethin' powerful to share called The Three Lessons. They're ancient teachings that hold the secret to havin' that God-blessed wonderful life. So, Lacey, it's time for me to ask that question…are you that Seeker?"

A stunned Lacey looked into the wise eyes of Old Mountain Cassie. Lacey had hungered the last years to find the purpose and meaning in her life but never knew how. Incredibly, the door was being opened to her by this mountain sage she'd been drawn to. Lacey turned to a waiting Cassie. "Yes, I am that Seeker."

Cassie slapped her knee, pleased. "Guess that makes you my new learner. Okay, Missy, next I'm goin' to need those two promises from you." Cassie paused. waiting for her words to come. "One, I need you to trust whatever I tell you is truth. God and time will prove it so. Two, you aren't to share with anyone the teachings until God directs you to. Can you make those two promises?"

"I can and will promise you, Cassie." Lacey felt long-dormant anticipation awaken as she made the pledge.

Cassie offered an inviting smile. "Well then, we've got us an arrangement. Now I best add a bit of personal chat here about how it is with me. See, I'm supposed to be here on this blessed land in solitude mostly. It's been my path, me and my herbs and my Seekers that are sent to me. Simple. And just like you, my Seekers find me with God's direction, and each one of them joins me in honorin' the sacredness of our relationship. Do you understand my meanin'?"

"I do, Cassie, and I can easily make another promise to you. I already cherish finding you and your gifts. This arrangement is between us and God. Promise." A tear slipped down Lacey's face. "I give you the promises and my eternal gratitude too."

Cassie reached over and wiped the tear from Lacey's cheek. "You sit a few moments and collect yourself while I take these comely cups back to the cabin. Here's an exercise of sorts. See if you can ignore those doubtin' thoughts that are sure to come callin' bout what you're doin' here."

"Ignore my thoughts. Ha. I'll give it a go," Lacey answered more to herself than her teacher.

Cassie rose and walked toward the house. She didn't look back at her Seeker. She didn't need to. Lacey would soon learn where to draw for help.

Chapter 27

LACEY CLOSED HER EYES AS Cassie had directed seconds before. No surprise her thoughts returned sabotaging her serenity within seconds, just as expected. On and on, her mind chattered, telling her she was wasting time with such foolish exercises. Be sensible. Act sensible. Think sensible. She felt intense frustration that she couldn't shut down the incessant prattling.

"Be rude to those thoughts," Cassie's voice instructed. She'd returned.

"How?" Lacey asked with a faint voice and eyes still closed. No surprise that Cassie knew her mind was in control. "I need to ask you something else that is puzzling me. Does everyone's mind call the tune or just mine? Thoughts follow me to bed and wake me in the morning. They chase me all day and…"

"You are a questionin' type Seeker, Missy. Very good to be one of those. And because you've shown me this already, I'm feelin' this is the near perfect time to invite you to meet Lesson One. The answer of how to be rude to those thoughts is waitin' in The Lesson."

"You want to begin teaching me The Three Lessons now? How can I be ready so soon? Am I ready?" Lacey's voiced climbed in octaves, along with her worry.

"Of course you are. Otherwise, you wouldn't have shown your face here seekin' me. Before I introduce you, I need you to understand the teachings are powerful on their own and many books have been written on each one. But there's a problem. An important step somehow got left out along the way."

Lacey's frown lines appeared, making her words unnecessary to Cassie.

"Don't you fret. God's given me and others that key for our teaching." Cassie treasured The Three Lessons and their gifts.

"Okay, but I have another question." Lacey cut a grin Cassie's way. "Yeah, questions I never seem to have a shortage of. Anyway, I'm wondering, will I be taught here at your place?" She was still trying to absorb what was unfolding before her.

"Yes, ma'am. And you can expect some potent sprinklings to happen right here on my land. I'll be enhancin' the teachings, you might say." Cassie enjoyed the mystical parts that always came for new Seekers. That added extra spice to The Lessons, for her and a Seeker.

Lacey could only laugh, not even trying to grasp Cassie's meaning. She expected time would reveal what a sprinkling was. "Now you've got me thinking I've landed on charmed ground or something."

"Just about," Cassie replied, humor coloring her words. "Let's get back to your question of how you can be rude to those thoughts that run you plumb ragged every moment of every day."

Lacey got in a comfortable cross-legged position. "Guess I'm ready for…The Lessons."

Cassie pulled a wooden chair over and sat down, facing Lacey. The breeze quieted. The squirrels stopped scampering. The birds' chirping ceased. The creatures grew silent as if waiting on Cassie's words. She noted the shift and began, "Lesson One wants you to know that most thoughts are not your friends. You see, Missy, the mind acts like a freight train out of control, always takin' you somewhere. Seldom pulls into a station to let a body rest. Get my meanin'?"

"I think so. I can tell you that just described my mind. The freight train mind…yes, I have that kind." Lacey's fascination with Cassie's teachings grew.

"You said something about your mind telling you what to think and do pretty much all the livelong day. But take this notion inside, you've given your mind that control, and it likes it just fine too. It likes bossin' you around." Cassie leaned forward. "Lesson One asks you to fashion a new kind of workin' partnership."

Lacey listened to the words, trying to grasp the meaning. She didn't want to interrupt Cassie with more of her inane questions.

Cassie continued, "Know what the mind is? Nothin' but a churner...might even say a recycler."

"Well, I gotta say my mind excels at churning, but a recycler?" Lacey questioned.

"See it this way. You're always listenin' to the talkin' because it's the voice that's been guidin' your whole life. It's the only voice you know and trust. True?" Cassie asked.

"Actually, yes, but is it wrong to trust what my head tells me? I don't know any other way." Lacey admitted.

"You tell me the answer after we delve some more." Cassie chuckled. "Here's a notion that will drop your jaw. Your mind's voice is limited. You see, Missy, it can only draw information stored in that brain." Cassie tapped her own head. "Hear this part. Your mind can only tell you things you've learned from others—teachers, friends, the internet, television. Your mind's nothin' more than a recycler of thoughts that you've made truth. Understand?"

"I do. The thoughts are limited in scope by what I already know," replied Lacey.

"Very good, Missy. Would you agree that...kind of knowin' isn't nearly enough to serve us most days? We often need inner help and guidance that the mind fails at givin' us."

"Wow! So that's how it is. I'm just going to write a few things." Lacey pulled her journal and a pen from her jacket's pocket and wrote with an accepting smile adorning her face.

"Yes, ma'am, and there's more. Write this one down. As you've likely experienced in life, there are many times your mind doesn't have the answers you seek, but another voice does. And I'd say it's past time for you to connect and give that other voice... voice." Cassie grinned and relaxed back in her chair, treasuring The Lesson's message. "I'm wonderin' if you'd like to meet a voice that will never disappoint or lead you astray. One that will always have the right answers. One that you can trust to guide you to joy and your heart's desire."

"Sure, I'd love to have that voice in my head. Who wouldn't but..." Lacey wondered where Cassie was taking her.

"Then, Lacey, it's time to meet your…Spirit Self. The voice that is connected straight to God, where all Divine instruction originates. It's the part of you that knows your every need and wants you to have it too. And if you're puzzlin' how you can tell if your Spirit Self's voice is the one you're hearing, that's easy. It's the voice bringin' fresh insights and answers your mind doesn't have." Cassie knew she was pouring a lot on her new Seeker, but the gal was plenty bright.

"My Spirit Self. Okay, I sort of grasp what you mean. Just know that I've tried countless times to get in touch with my spirit without much success. I confess that until today, I didn't believe God had been much listening to my prayers. They'd gone unanswered for a long time. But hey, I'm willing to try. No, I'm more than willing. I'm a Seeker now. I seek to know my Spirit Self. I'm hoping you can show me how to get in touch."

Cassie kept to her lesson plan. "Let's start by celebratin' you've seen God's hand around my place here. The kindly critters, the charmed posies, all is His majesty. Take this truth in."

"All right. It's in and recorded, but I don't know what to do with it." Lacey laid her pen down.

"Well, that brings us to the next point…the connectin' part. How do you connect, is what I expect you'd be wonderin'. Am I right?" Cassie waited.

"Yes, I have no clue how to connect to my spirit. Right now, I'm hoping mine is still around." Lacey smiled to hide her fear.

"Oh, your spirit is close by. Never you worry. The best way for early Seekers to connect with the Spirit Self is by meditating. See here, you gotta get quiet and still that mind of yours of all the jabberin' it wants to do so the spirit can step in. You know now the jabber is nothin' more than a distraction meant to keep the mind boss. And, Lacey, the mind doesn't want you to change things up, but you are sure fixin' to." Cassie gave a chuckle. "What's the sayin'? There's a new sheriff in town. Your Spirit Self is about to be that newly elected sheriff, and that mind of yours is about to get whopped." Cassie punctuated her words with a smack to her leg.

Lacey laughed. She felt affection blooming for the woman who'd devoted her life to helping others. Realizing her thoughts, kind though they may be, had her again, she turned back to a knowing Cassie. "Sorry. Busted again."

"Lacey, you must watch those thoughts like you would a coiled snake. With practice, your mind will chatter less, and the space between those thoughts will grow. And in that space, your Spirit Self will slip in and give you Divine direction. If you'd like, we can create you a meditation practice later on that will really give you a big helpin' of spirit talkin' time."

"That would be great to learn to meditate the proper way. And believe me, I look forward when my mind and spirit can change places. That can't come soon enough for when I need serious guidance and answers." Lacey smiled. "Until you can help me understand how to get centered, I will try meditating with a CD I bought the other day. Now I understand why that CD called to me. I'd never purchased something like that before. Crazy. Would practicing meditation using that be a good next step?" Lacey chuckled with the recollection.

"Not crazy. Directed, I'd say. Your plan sounds dandy. Remember, only when you rely on your Spirit Self can you finally attract all the wonderful blessings that God has been waitin' to shower on you. He has so many gifts meant just for you, and you likely have unsaid prayers for Him that will get answered in His way in His time. Trust this."

"I've got nothing to lose, Cassie, and I'm feeling pretty excited to move forward."

Cassie nodded, continuing, "Let me touch on meditation. I'm goin' to speak plainly now. Understand that praying is talking and meditating is listening. Two different things entirely. Again, I say, Lesson One wants you to search out your best way to get quiet so you get direction. And here's a way to view it that might help. I want you to see God as your wise Senior Partner and your spirit as the young Junior Partner. Kinda keeps things straight in your mind." Cassie's eyes sparkled. "Seekers know from Lesson One that listenin' is where you get Divine instructions…from the Senior Partner. And plenty of listenin' you want to do, Missy, startin' today."

"Hmm, Senior Partner. I like it. I understand that I must learn a way to be still and listen, and I will. It's that important to me, Cassie. This is a precious gift you're offering. When I get home, I plan to study these teachings before my mind starts tampering with me. I'm glad my journal has my notes." Lacey hoped she could remember Cassie's many other shared pearls. She could already string a lovely necklace using Cassie's pearls of enlightenment. "And should I always call on my spirit to journal with me."

"That's a fine plan and fine Seeker talk. Today's teachin' will be settling in you over time. Remember, be rude to those thoughts. Get quiet. Listen. Yep, plenty to ponder and more to learn. Just you wait for Lesson Two. It's a dandy too." Cassie shifted in her chair before her next words came. "Haven't we had a nice visit with Lesson One, which I call Meetin' Your Spirit Self?" Cassie chuckled.

Lacey grinned back. "I agree about the enjoyable visit and the lot to ponder. Whew! I can't even conjure a question right now or a thought. That's remarkable for me."

"What say we take a stroll? We'll invite our spirits to come along. Let's see if yours accepts." Cassie stood. She did a few twists to encourage her stiff joints to comply. "Ready, Missy?"

"A stroll sounds perfect. My fanny is a bit numb from the swing. Be warned, though, you already know my mind can be pretty stubborn and controlling." Lacey glanced at the notes in her journal before clipping it shut.

"Well then, we'll at least get the body moving toward something I want to show you."

Chapter 28

Lacey followed Cassie, sure that whatever the mountain woman had to show would only lead her to question more. Minutes ticked by before Lacey realized her doubting mind had claimed control once again. She glanced over at Cassie, sensing she was being observed.

"So, what did you miss seeing on our little stroll just now?" Cassie stopped and faced her student. Her eyes sparkled smartly.

"Everything," Lacey answered truthfully, feeling let down and disappointed in herself.

"Well, the good news here, Missy, is you can turn right back around and walk the path all over again. The bad news is you're already different than you were a few minutes ago, so now your experience will be different, won't it?" Cassis said making her point.

"Yes, and I feel so angry at myself. Guess I didn't act rude enough."

Cassie laughed inwardly. "You'll learn. Havin' the awareness of another way to be and a new voice to listen to are pretty big doins' for one day. Come on, I still have more to show you before we end our time together."

"I'd love to see anything you have to show, Cassie, but I'm excited about what I hope are many more times together." Lacey feared she might not be such a catch as a Seeker.

Cassie read her mind. "You're a willin' Seeker. More me and God can't ask."

Lacey stopped walking feeling a change as if benevolent energy was flowing in and around her. Everything around her grew brighter. She looked toward the gardens and witnessed the colors pulsing from the flowers, the trees, on every living thing. "What's happening? Cassie? Cassie, I'm seeing everything sparkling with a kind of… vitality."

"You do, huh?"

"Is this for real? I mean I hope this isn't the beginning of some crazy type of a migraine," Lacey quipped, using her trusty humor to disguise her disbelief. "I do sometimes have visual disturbances from the headaches."

Old Mountain Cassie remained silent, observing. She especially enjoyed nature's exuberance with her new Seekers. The special sprinklin' she'd prepared Lacey for earlier had begun.

Lacey approached a bed of roses. She bent down to look closer at the iridescent light touching each petal. "Incredible," she whispered to the blossom.

The flower seemed to sway with gentleness toward Lacey as if to say thank you for the attention. The petals, peach and golden shades, intensified their color show.

Lacey glanced over at Cassie. "Are you seeing this? Quick, please tell me yes."

Cassie broke her silence. "I sure am, Missy. Why don't you take a sniff?"

"It's okay?" Lacey's mind kicked in a warning.

"Release the hold that thought has on you. Instead, feel your spirit's energy wantin' to connect to the roses. Can you?" Cassie instructed with a patient voice. "Now, say the feeling that is coming to you."

"Joy. Pure joy," Lacey said with a reverence as the flower's fragrance spoke to her senses. "I'm smelling joy…feeling joy."

Cassie nodded and dipped her head down to take a sniff of a nearby bloom. "Know what I smell?" She knew this early introduction was having a profound effect on her student.

"I can't imagine," Lacey replied softly, still bent over the glistening bush.

"I smell calmness. Come over here, girl, and put your sniffer on this beauty." Cassie held the flower in one hand and beckoned her Seeker with the other.

Lacey moved the few steps, eyes wide and her lips slightly parted, ready to speak.

"Well?" Cassie's one word asked a lot.

"Extraordinary. Oh my gosh! I just felt a wave of total calmness wash over the joy. What's happening? This is all way too strange, Cassie." Her mind begged for control, while her body and spirit relaxed even more with each whiff.

"You tell me what's happening." Cassie encouraged.

"Me? Let's see…okay, for one thing, my mind is telling me this is plenty crazy and probably coming from that tea I drank earlier." Lacey turned her head to look at Cassie, fearing she had just offended the woman with her unfiltered response.

Old Mountain Cassie released the flower along with a loud cackle. "Ah, but tell me what your Spirit Self is sayin'. I much prefer to hear from that part of Lacey. Ask your spirit to step in, and it will," she instructed, growing serious again.

Lacey tried to put some distance from the rose garden and her mind. She walked over to where a gazing ball sat atop an old hollowed out three-foot-tall tree trunk. Lush ferns circled the tree, and with Lacey's attention directed at them, they too began to shimmer with life. At that moment, her Spirit Self's voice spoke to her. The voice sounded loving compared to her edgy mind's voice.

Believe and trust.

Cassie came closer. "Wanna tell me what you heard?"

Lacey didn't hesitate. "Believe and trust. I think my spirit just spoke to me," she replied, never taking her eyes off the gazing ball.

"I'd say so. And so, who has your best interest here? What voice is carin' and gentle with you like God? Your spirit or your mind?" Cassie asked, encouraging Lacey to seek the bigger truth.

"My spirit." The calmness remained. "I'm really starting to hate my mind. What a robber of serenity it is. Whew!" Lacey exhaled loudly. "You've got some place here."

Cassie touched her Seeker's shoulder. "Come on. I'll keep you company part of the way to your vehicle."

"Goodness, I've overstayed," Lacey exclaimed, looking at her watch and surprised at how much time had passed.

"You did no such thing, Missy. I've enjoyed our time, becomin' you teacher and, most of all, introducing you to Lesson One. And what do you call my place?"

"Enchanting," Lacey answered.

"Yep, my enchanting place. I like that word a bunch."

The two women approached a narrow footbridge crossing a small creek. Both stopped and leaned over the railing to observe the trout swimming in the clear waters.

Old Mountain Cassie broke the solitude. "Back to my enchanted place. I'd like to explain a bit more about the land's curious doings before we say good-bye. It's like this Lacey: There are energy grids runnin' around the earth. Some folks call them leys. These places get powerful inputs, which makes everything act kinda charmed. The leys are God's stage for our witnessin' of this enjoyment and empowerment." Cassie paused, wondering if her Seeker understood.

"Don't stop. I think I'm with you."

"Good. Okay then, so these leys give off certain kinds of energies to all who are around them and able to sense. Doesn't matter if you're a flower, a critter, a person. All react to the special energy in a divine way."

"So, are you telling me the flowers and foliage were experiencing joy?"

"Oh yes, Missy, and you know why?"

Lacey shook her head. She turned and leaned her back against the railing, her thoughts dancing wildly in her head.

"Because you and I were enjoyin' them, and in our en-joy-ing"—Cassie sounded out each syllable— "they felt joy."

Lacey could only stare at Cassie.

"And in their joy, the energy combined to produce an aroma mirroring back to us that feelin'."

"So, I smelled their joy in my enjoying them?" asked Lacey, trying to grasp the explanation.

"Yes, ma'am, that you did. The ley intensified the experience for us and the flowers. All the shimmerin' and colors pulsing came from the special energies flowin' from the ground and heavens. I'm going to tell you what the energy here really is…it's God's breath."

"God's breath. That's beautiful. Oh my, I'm trying super hard here to trust and believe what you've shared…what I've seen, but…"

"What's that pesky head of yours conjurin' up?" Cassie questioned, knowing full well the gal's mind was messing with her. She understood its wily ways.

"My mind is telling me that I had some kind of psychedelic tea trip," Lacey replied, not able to stop her words from flowing out.

"Phooey. That's an easy test. When you come again, I won't be hospitable one bit. No tea until you and my flowers have another greetin'. So there, tell your mind to hush up."

Lacey laughed. "Mind, hush up. Cassie's telling me some spiritual truths that you don't get. How'd I do?" She felt relieved the mountain woman had turned to levity as a response.

"Just fine." Cassie reached over and patted her pupil's arm.

"A promise is a promise," Lacey said, wanting Cassie to know she could trust her, even if her skeptical mind said otherwise. It was a lot to weigh and accept. For some reason, crazy as this whole energy ley thing sounded, Lacey intuitively agreed to go with Cassie's explanation.

"You thinkin' again?" Cassie knew she was in strong competition with Lacey's mind.

"Umm, yes. This time, it's that you just gave me this incredible experience and that I'm going to spare you and corral my questions until next time. Is that okay?"

"You can try, girl, but I won't be a bit surprised to hear you tell me that those thoughts corralled you…even before you get back to your vehicle. Be patient with yourself."

Lacey nodded, enjoying Cassie's wit. She gave Cassie a hug. Stepping back with her hope that the mountain woman hadn't become skittish by the gesture, she asked, "Cassie, when can I come for another, umm…"

"Lesson." She picked up a small branch that had fallen across the path. "Well, I expect you'll show up here when you're ready or when those questions won't leave you be." Cassie knew her eyes would be layin' on her niece before a week got crossed off her calendar. Seekers, once awakened, craved more insights to feed their starving spirits.

Lacey accepted the response. "Then I'll say goodbye until next time. Thank you for the gifts of today. All of them. I sense my life is already changing all because of being led to you. How could it not? I mean this place, and you are all so astonishing."

Cassie didn't bother to answer but offered a nod. She couldn't give a quick reply to thanks she couldn't claim for herself. One day, her Seeker would understand.

Chapter 29

Lacey pushed her foot hard on the SUV's gas pedal, encouraging speed. Her time reflecting could wait until she dealt with the outer world's demands. Aunt Gabby, no doubt, would be contemplating dinner. Lacey didn't want her aunt back in the kitchen after last night's debacle inflicted on her oven.

She doubted Charlie had enough oven cleaner to tackle lamb splatters baked on for an hour. Her aunt had insisted on making an elegant meal for them. Lacey's favorite chef's pan waited in the trash can for pickup, and the oven cleaning, well, that would need to wait for a day she missed her workout.

Relief washed over Lacey as she glimpsed Petunia entering her cottage with a giant pizza box clearly marked with Paulie's trademark.

"Bless your heart," Lacey hollered to the woman standing on her porch and waving the box.

"You're welcome. Paulie said for me not to open it until we all sat down together. He seemed unusually proud of our dinner." Petunia smiled, shrugging her shoulders.

Gabby opened the door, nodding to Lacey and giving Petunia a hug. "I'm famished. Table's waiting, ladies."

Petunia set the box in the center of the table and took a seat. "I'll second the hunger cry. I worked up a cowboy's cattle drive appetite pricing my new fashions."

"Dearest Pet, I told you to leave tagging for me to do." Gabby admonished her friend while pouring the green tea in everyone's glass.

"I did. There are two boxes left." Petunia placed the orange-flowered cloth napkin in her lap.

"Lacey child, I almost forgot. You had a telephone call from some woman wanting to discuss a position with Evers and James Jewelers. I wrote the information down and left it on your desk."

"Thanks. I'll be sure to call her tomorrow. Let's eat," Lacey said, wanting to short-circuit any questions about her lack of employment.

Petunia lifted the box lid and folded it back, exposing Paulie's creation.

The three seated at the table stared at the pizza. There sat a piping hot large pie divided into three distinct sections. There was no doubt who got what.

True to her name, Gabby spoke up first. "Why, I've never smelled such an enticing aroma coming from a pizza before. That's simply got to be my side." Her heavily ringed fingers reached in for a generous slice covered in baby shrimp and avocado.

Lacey and Petunia waited for their turn, smiling at Gabby's remarks.

Gabby went on, "You see, we Florida gals simply adore our seafood and avocados." She took a bite. "Absolutely sublime."

Petunia snagged her personal slice. "I couldn't agree more, Gabriella. Paulie knows my passion for BLTs. He's topped my side with smoked bacon, baby spinach, and chopped yellow tomatoes. Yum. This tastes incredible. Lacey, dig in and report." Petunia moved the box closer to the younger woman.

"What's yours, dear Niece?"

"Hmm, Paulie outdid himself for me too. I have a white pizza with some tasty slightly sweet sauce topped with…"

Gabby stopped eating and looked more closely at Lacey's slice. "Am I seeing rose petals? Impossible."

Petunia turned her attention toward Lacey's plate. "Looks like roses to me."

"Umm, yes, it appears I'm having a few flower petals, arugula, and brie cheese tonight." Lacey took her first bite, concerned Paulie might have pushed the pizza envelope a little too far this time.

"Well?" Petunia and Gabby asked in unison.

"Joy." Lacey closed her eyes, remembering Cassie's rose garden. The flavors came together in a most extraordinary way. Her taste buds danced happily, and her surprised spirit acknowledged the rose petals' significance from her afternoon at Cassie's.

The ladies' chatter gave Lacey's mind the opportunity to explore the mind-blowing coincidence of her day in the gardens with Cassie and her pizza's rose petal topping. How did Paulie create the ideal pie for her? Know what she would love to eat and sense when she didn't even know. The puzzling contemplations wouldn't leave her be. How did Serene possess the uncanny ability to put people with the right property with minimal effort or time wasted? She thought of Bud's dairy and how anything made from his cows' milk gave food or drink such an enjoyable taste. She took a sip of her tea. Boy, was she ever having some kind of mystifying day, and a lovely little voice inside of her told her this was only the beginning. Mind-blowing, oh yes, her mind had been blown onto a new course.

"Lacey, please join us in conversation. Whatever has Paulie done by feeding you flowers? Petunia, are they safe for her to eat?"

"Aunt Gabby, of course, they're safe. Sorry, I was lost in thought." Lacey realized the truth of her words and gave up trying to be rude to the thoughts, at least, while having an outrageous posy pizza topping her day.

"I'm sure Lacey's pie is unique just like her," Petunia added. "I saved room for dessert like you requested, Gabriella. Tell me, what confection did you prepare for us this evening?"

"Umm, Aunt, you didn't go near my stove again so soon, did you?" Lacey's head turned in the appliance's direction. She breathed a sigh of relief to see it still standing looking stainless, at least, on the outside.

"Quiet, Niece. I already apologized for that leg of lamb Charlie stuck me with. That animal clearly had been fed a high-fat diet. I've never had lamb catch fire inside an oven." Gabby sniffed and tilted her nose up a notch.

Petunia covered her mouth with the napkin, trying to contain her mirth.

"Whatever you say, Aunt Gabby." No point in reliving their smashing of the smoke detector into a gazillion pieces with the broom. "What's this, sweetie, you're contributing tonight?"

"Well, I suppose I'd better do a little confessing first. You see, I was on my way to Charlie's to pick up the ingredients for my famous praline cake when I happened to run into Jane Ann. That is the name of the lady who makes those muffins you all love, right?"

Lacey and Petunia nodded.

"She was unloading baked goods from her car in front of Charlie's Market."

"And?" Petunia and Lacey said in unison.

Gabby stood, adjusting her frilly, ruffled violet skirt, basking in the attention. She went to the refrigerator and pulled out an enormous coconut meringue pie.

"Some kind of luscious," Lacey exclaimed.

"My thoughts exactly." Petunia seconded.

Petunia moved the empty pizza box to make room on the table, while Lacey reached for the stacked dessert plates sitting on the side.

The doorbell chimed. Gabby left the pie and handed Lacey the knife. "I'll get that."

In walked Fred, Gabby's dance partner and prince, and JT, Petunia's on and off again boyfriend.

"Did we time this arrival right or not, Fred?" JT moved toward the pie.

"I'll say," responded Fred, dressed for a night of square dancing. His blue plaid shirt, leather vest, faded jeans, with fancy boots peeking out couldn't compete with the silver buckle the size of Petunia's slice of pie hanging from his belt.

"Gals, cut us a big slab. We're gonna need the energy later," JT said.

Fred chuckled and looked over at Lacey. "Hi, gal. Doing okay?"

"Hello, fellows. Nice surprise. Pull up a chair." Lacey couldn't help liking these two dessert-intruding rascals. She sat with her fork poised, still in disbelief her aunt had taken to square dancing. Divine sure could cast some powerful spells.

They were all teasing and anticipating the night of high stepping when Lacey heard yet another rap on her door. "Who else did you invite, Aunt Gabby? There's only one slice of pie left," Lacey stated before the door opened without anyone at the table's help.

"Hey, I saw the cars outside and figured there just had to be something I was missing."

Serene walked through the door and tossed her handbag on the sofa.

Lacey handed her an empty plate and fork. "If you'd waited another minute, Fred could tell you all about how he consumed two slabs of coconut meringue pie. Right?"

Fred gave a boyish grin and nodded. "Better grab that one fast, Serene."

Serene did as told. One bite went into her mouth within seconds. "Hmm…Jane Ann has found her calling, and I am ever so glad of it."

"Well, good thing I didn't try to pass this treat off as my creation. Seems everyone in Divine knows way too much about each other," Gabby announced to the crowd with a mood as light as Jane Ann's signature pie crust.

"True enough, and we've turned our attention to the new gal in town. Isn't that so JT?" Fred acted flirty around Gabby and seemed puzzled by his own behavior.

"Fiddle. I've heard enough. Petunia, let's freshen up and let our escorts show us if they can keep up on that dance floor." Gabby blushed.

The two older women disappeared, leaving Serene and Lacey to carry on the conversation. Lacey chose to listen as Serene discussed the county tax rates not being increased with the two men who happened to be running for town commissioners.

Minutes later, everyone made their good-byes, leaving Lacey to value the quiet that used to be a staple at her cottage. Her journal, which had been abandoned for months, would serve as her new confidante. She opened to a blank page and recorded more memories of the day with Cassie. Relaxing music played in the background. Propped up in bed, the words flowed from the pen to paper with ease. Her new study guide was being birthed.

Chapter 30

Lacey held the phone to her ear, already in shock at the words bubbling out of her.

"I truly appreciate the generous job offer as senior buyer with your impressive company, and I'll be sure to thank my friend at Stardust for recommending me. Yes, I promise to call if I have a change of heart."

She hung up the phone and swiveled in her desk chair to look out the window. The leaves did a brief swaying dance in the breeze. A male cardinal with his bright red feathers landed on the bird feeder and, in an instant, hopped to her windowsill. He proceeded to peck lightly on the glass, looking Lacey in the eye.

Nature friends were calling her again. Another cardinal? This was getting weirder by the day and yet on some level not at all. Lacey released a breath and let her mind go to work. She'd just turned down a fantastic job so that she could hang out with some sage in the woods and maybe get in touch with her spirit's voice…her real work…and know God. Dare she also acknowledge that she was living in a town with some highly unusual people and that she was hungering to be one of them? And the cherry on top of this concoction was Gabby showing up, adding…Lacey stopped, unable to identify exactly what real value Aunt Gabby was adding to her life, but today she realized there had been a shift in her aunt's demeanor, a pretty nice shift. Lacey also realized her mind had been trying to convince her to figure out everything. Some thoughts, as Cassie told her, just didn't serve a body good.

The cardinal tapped again and cocked his head as if to say pay attention to me.

Lacey shook her head at his persistence. She went over to the window and tapped back.

Could he be the cardinal from Cassie's woods? Her mind screamed impossible. Lacey focused on the attention-grabbing red bird. Awareness hit. Lacey's face beamed. "Bird, I get it. You're free to go now, and thanks for the invite."

"Dear girl, are you on the phone still?" Gabby peered into the den, hearing Lacey's voice.

"Umm, no. Just chatting with a visiting cardinal," Lacey responded, already regretting her words hastily spoken.

"Well, I hope he's giving you some advice on securing employment."

"Oh, he's rather advanced and is for sure showing me a…path," replied Lacey, feeling her mood suddenly buoyed.

"Well, I don't need a bird to tell me I'm late to Petunia's. Be home around nine. Not to worry, darling Niece," she called out, passing down the hall.

Gabby disappeared before Lacey had a chance to inquire what on earth her aunt might be doing until nine that evening. Oh well, since she obviously wasn't serious about applying for a job or adding to her money market account, she'd answer the call, growing louder with each passing minute.

Chapter 31

By early afternoon, the SUV transported Lacey toward her destination. She glanced through the vehicle's sunroof to see rain clouds gathering for a matinee. Lacey pulled into the now familiar spot and grabbed her waterproof jacket as the raindrops delivered on the sky's promise. Minutes later, she stepped onto the wooden porch and knocked on the planked door. She didn't know what her reception would be, but she knew her sincere desire was to be right where she stood.

The door swung open with Cassie's words flowing out to greet her in welcome. "Miss Lacey, come on in. We've been expectin' you." Cassie stood to the side holding a contented Chakra.

Lickety Split supported Cassie's words with a few extra sloppy licks to Lacey's outstretched hand holding a bone.

Lacey entered the large room, immediately awakening to the fact that she was for real, standing inside Old Mountain Cassie's place and that she'd been expected. Too bad she couldn't share this happening with Serene. Returning to the present, Lacey realized Cassie hadn't moved a step but simply waited, observing. "Hmm, I'm still working on this being rude business and finding that other kinder voice." She grinned.

"Glad to hear it." Cassie smiled, pleased her niece hadn't abandoned the teachings. "Pick a seat. I've got some good ones."

"Cassie, are you sure another visit this soon is all right? This isn't in character for me to just show my face at someone's door, but I've an explanation of sorts."

"Go on. Be a tellin' then."

"Well, I had this cardinal visit me. And since the only peculiar acting cardinal I've ever met lives near you, I felt like I'd been sort of…summoned."

"Rest easy. Your visit is most welcome and, like I told you, anticipated." Cassie claimed her rocker without waiting for her guest to sit.

Lacey didn't miss that Cassie hadn't responded about the cardinal but elected to stay mute and chose a wingback chair upholstered in an unusual gold-textured fabric. She allowed a moment to take in the surroundings. Cassie's love for wood, evidenced by the wide plank hewn pine floors and post and beam construction, set the mood. Rustic charm abounded but with touches of an old-world influence. The chairs and two sofas were done in rich colors of fall leaves and were ideally situated to take in the massive rock fireplace. The dining area and kitchen shared in the grand openness and boasted cathedral ceilings. An impressively crafted staircase nearby led up to a loft area and other rooms, Lacey guessed. Old Mountain Cassie's unique style came as a surprise but, Lacey thought, complemented the woman perfectly.

Cassie drew her Seeker back. "Do you like my place?"

"I do, very much, in fact. It's a perfect reflection of you and your love for nature. I adore the design, and there's so much interest created with harmony. I like the touches of the outside brought inside, the bittersweet held by the pewter vase, and that little, abandoned bird's nest with the porcelain robin's eggs are so sweet sitting on the glass table here. Lacey's fingers caressed the piece. And your library of leather-bound books on those shelves looks impressive. There's so much to take in and enjoy. I feel nurtured in this space. Sorry, I get carried away sometimes. Please forgive my rambling on and on. I must sound like some—"

Cassie jumped in, "I thank you for those pretty words. No need to apologize for sharing your feelings about something that spoke to your heart. Your mind just now tried to get in the way of what your spirit wanted me to hear is all. You understand my home. I like that about you, Missy." Cassie gave her characteristic nod and increased her rocking tempo.

"Umm, Cassie, I don't mean to sound blunt, but why am I here? I mean I felt led to show up, and there's no other place I want to be today, but my mind is really struggling. I need—"

Lacey didn't get to finish for Mother Nature interrupted her flow. Lightning cracked. Thunder snapped to attention.

Lickety joined with Chakra to crouch down at Cassie's feet. Old Mountain Cassie reached to comfort her critters while she pondered how best to answer her Seeker's question. The lightning show outside bought her time. The noisy voice of thunder echoed, stifling conversation. Rain poured from the heavens, cleansing the land and those who called it home.

Cassie waited for silence and gave her reply. "You're here, Missy, because I have the second lesson ready if you're willing. And haven't you been led here to learn about your gifts…special gifts? And it's The Three Lessons that hold the secrets for you.

Lacey frowned at the word secrets.

"Are you willin' to see our meetin' as your destiny and mine? For it is. I'm going to ask you to accept this as truth." Cassie's tone echoed her earnestness to teach.

"I will trust your words, as I promised." Lacey could make that easy pledge.

"Good grief. Where did I leave my manners? Would you like somethin' to sip on, or do you still have a worry with my brews?" Cassie asked, giving an impish smile. She was already moving toward the kitchen and her favorite teapot with painted daisies and matching teacups.

"I'm a taker of some tea. No worries…yet." Lacey teased.

Cassie brought out a tin of fancy dark chocolate truffles and removed a half dozen, placing them on a milk glass plate. "You're gonna take to these."

"I think I already have. May I?" With Cassie's approval, Lacey bit into the sweet.

"Might as well join you." Cassie's mouth closed around a large bite.

"Mmm," they said in unison.

"Now pick yourself out a tea if you feel obliged," Old Mountain Cassie invited, pointing to a myriad of jars lined up with green labels declaring the contents.

"Sure." Lacey glanced at the names, none of which was what she expected. No Chamomile, no Earl Grey, no English Breakfast. Her hand remained at her side; she was undecided.

The mountain woman watched, amused, not offering any explanation.

"Sublime, Feisty, Quiet Spirit, Creative Splendor. Cassie, dare I ask about these teas?" She'd stopped reading aloud anymore of the names.

"Nope. Just select the experience that suits your moment. And nothin' there makes for psychedelic flower experiences." Cassie gave a chuckle.

"I didn't really ever think it was the tea the other day." Lacey smiled back. "Okay, well then, how about Ultimate Understanding?" Lacey handed the jar over to her teacher.

"I'd say you picked perfect…for both of us."

A few minutes later, Cassie felt an inner nudge to begin her lesson plan while they enjoyed the refreshments and the effect of the tea. "We agreed you'd be my next Seeker and that I might act as your teacher of sorts. You made me promises that need not be spoken of again." Cassie paused.

"Yes, Cassie, to everything you just said." Lacey wanted to assure her she'd not forgotten. She wanted to hear more…was keen to hear anything this wise mountain woman would share.

"Seekers have talents usually unique to them. We are all born Seekers, you see, sent here to serve using our special gifts. And the gifts come into bein' when the time is best suited, and we are willin', of course. Kind of like the tomatoes ripenin' out on my vine that don't want to be tasted until they turn that flavorful red color. Understand me?"

Lacey nodded, feeling excited.

"I suspect somewhere inside you've always known you were a little different than others. Had somethin' unique going on inside. Am I right?"

Lacey sat, quietly taking in Cassie's message or trying to. "Maybe." Memories of being a young girl and seeing her first gemstones displayed in a jewelry store rushed forward. She remembered her mom trying on a gold ring encrusted with pear-shaped rubies. Lacey felt anger wash over her when she looked at the stones. She begged her mom to pick another ring, telling her the ring was mad. Embarrassed by her daughter's behavior, her mom dragged her out of the store, leaving the store owner's shocked face fixed on Lacey. Oh yes, she acted plenty different that day, and a few others if she were honest.

Cassie watched the past emotions play across her niece's lovely face. "Ah, a memory to support my words. I like it when a Seeker can draw up the past easy like. Want to tell me what showed up?" encouraged Cassie.

Without hesitation, Lacey relayed the story with the ruby ring and the impact the experience had on her that first time. "So, it's as if I have this kind of connection with gems. They have something to impart to the wearer, and I can often sense the emotion they hold. They're powerful, and I respect them…a lot." Lacey grew silent, not wanting to say more. She'd never shared this with anyone.

"I agree, Missy. They are full of energy freely given. Another day I can promise you we will talk on this subject a plenty. For now, the memory serves to remind you of that first awareness of your gift." Cassie took another sip of tea.

"I do fancy gems. I never tire of being with them." Lacey's eyes sparkled like a Brazilian aquamarine just thinking of the vast varieties of colorful stones. *Powerful tea*, she thought, taking another sip of Ultimate Understanding.

"I expect that's true for always. Tell me, girl, is that enough of my goin' on about you havin' a special ability? You've named it." Cassie grinned and waited.

"I suppose so. I don't exactly run up and down my street proclaiming this thing I have with gemstones," Lacey said, her humor returning.

The thunder rolled off in the distance, signaling the cleansing had moved on.

"Not yet anyways." Cassie added her dose of humor. "I have a proposal that I sat with this morning. If it suits, I'd like to speak it now."

"Cassie, something tells me this is exactly the time for a proposal. With all the extraordinary things happening to me lately, I can't exactly trot my unusual gemstone connection over to my friend, Serene, or, heaven forbid, my Aunt Gabby for fear they'd have me carted off to Miss Ella's Rest Home."

The older woman remained mute but understanding.

"I can't go yapping about all the animals and birds of late making me feel like we're all the bestest of buddies, or me finding Old Mountain Cassie or the flowers getting all shimmery over my appreciation of them…well, you get the picture. Oh, and by the way, I turned down a super diamond buyer's job this morning too." Lacey grabbed a breath. "And I need a job. And instead of putting on my lucky yellow suit and showing up for a token interview, I said, 'No thank you.' And what do I do instead? I come knocking on your door to eat truffles, drink some tea of understanding, and confess to my flair with gems. So yeah, I'd say that I'm ripe for a proposal since, clearly, I'm off my personal grid of logical behavior." Lacey sat back in her chair, appalled at her ranting monologue. She cast a sheepish look at Cassie, fearing how her words must have sounded. What if she blew her chance to be in this incredible woman's presence…to learn the secret to joy and prosperity? Where was this Spirit Self of hers hiding, anyway?

"I enjoyed that bit of soliloquy. Yes, ma'am, I did." Cassie rocked a few times quiet. "You trusted me to let those feelings and yes thoughts out. Makes my work easier too. Think I'll try doin' what you just did and see how your mind likes my answers." Old Mountain Cassie paused a tick, preparing for her next teaching.

Lacey's mood changed, releasing her to receive Cassie's next words. Cassie saw the shift in her Seeker. Satisfied, she began her own brand of teaching. "First, you did right turnin' down that job. You're ripe just like my big boy tomatoes out in my garden for discovering your real life's calling, and it ain't no diamond buyin' job, Missy. The job doesn't describe what you're sent here to do. Nope. Listen to me, you and I are going on an inner journey where you'll meet that calling, and I'm bettin' a whole lot more."

Lacey raised an eyebrow but kept silent.

Cassie saw the expression of doubt. She pushed on. "Set aside that worry. You can afford to do this for a short spell."

The younger woman shook her head, afraid to take a leap. Where was her faith? "I'm not sure I can…"

"Yes, you can, Missy. Your Aunt Gabby's arrival and help with runnin' your house are giving us the time to do the explorin' and learnin', see? She's been sent to help…in her way. See that," Cassie added, knowing her Seeker was paying the emotional price of having her aunt meddle, but the financial reward meant freedom.

Lacey let the words move around in her head. Slowly, the truth of Cassie's words took hold. How could Cassie know her aunt had insisted on paying the utility and food bills? Lacey had argued, but Gabby held firm, saying that was the least she could do after Lacey's gracious, extended welcome. Aunt Gabby didn't even see the new garden as a payback since she'd been the one wanting to do the project for her own pleasure. She understood better the role Gabby was playing. Gabby did bring value, and it took Cassie to illuminate this fact. "That's all true, Cassie, though I'm not ready to ask you how you know these things." Lacey sipped her tea while her mind tried to gain control, offering empty answers.

Cassie closed her eyes.

Lacey waited. She didn't mean to cast a pall over Cassie's proposal. She knew things were changing around her, and she intuitively sensed Old Mountain Cassie's making herself available was no accident. The pull to find Cassie and now to delve into whatever the sage had to share was more powerful than her doubts and fears circling her. Sitting in the room with Cassie felt epic and yet familiar in a strange way…like she belonged here. Lacey finished with her mug and placed it on the table and glanced at Cassie.

"Better now?" Cassie asked her student.

"For the moment," Lacey replied truthfully.

"That's all we work in, Missy, the moment, that is. I'm feelin' roused to continue on if you be willin'?"

"Yes, please."

"Let me say once again our time together will lead you to knowin' what your life's work and gifts have in common. Takin' another job will not bring you lastin' joy but discoverin' what you're meant to be doing will. This is a promise I can make."

Lacey listened and relaxed into the chair. She watched the mountain woman fold her hands in a contemplating manner. The room glowed with the light outside cascading through the stained-glass windows on one wall. The rainbow of colors played on the wood floor, capturing Lacey's attention but only for a moment

Lacey heard her cell phone chiming in her backpack. "Sorry, that's my phone."

"Do you want to answer?" Cassie hesitated. "It's fine by me."

"Maybe I'd better. Excuse me."

"You need to go," Cassie stated when Lacey returned.

"I am so sorry, but I do. I must make a quick trip to Asheville to sign some Stardust papers. Can we pick our meet times before I go?"

"Lacey, come whenever you feel called or just drop by every other day in the mornin' time. Your visits will be welcome."

"Okay, both work for me. We'll keep it loose. Cassie, I need to ask you something else and please don't be offended." Lacey wanted to know the answer before going any further in their arrangement.

Cassie stood ready to see her guest out. "You ask. Offended, I won't be."

"Well, you see, I can't allow you to give your time to be my spiritual advisor of sorts and not compensate you. I want to—"

Old Mountain Cassie interrupted the flow of words by giving Lacey a warm hug. "Now listen up, Missy, I don't charge my Seekers. Never have. That's not how this works. There are laws of abundance that work out the compensation part." Cassie gave a nod indicating she'd had the final say.

"For now, I'll go along with your wishes. Thank you, Cassie. I'm so awed to have this opportunity to grow and learn under your tutelage." Lacey opened the door, hating to leave and already anticipating the life-altering lessons she felt confident were coming her way.

"Appreciate all of that. Don't worry. Your lessons aren't goin' anywhere," Cassie stated, sensing her niece's hesitation to leave. "Oh, I almost forgot. This is for you." Cassie handed over a brown bag.

Lacey accepted the bag with her inquisitive nature, already wondering about the contents. "Do you want me to open it now or later?" she asked, having learned not to assume anything when it involved Cassie.

"Later suits since you need to run off. Remember, though, to watch those thoughts and let go of the job hunt for now. Trust." Cassie stood, hands on her hips and feet planted.

"Got it." Lacey gave her a grin. "Thanks for whatever is in this sack. My time with you has been so fantastic, just like you. God is blessing me," Lacey stated.

"And blessin' me too. So long, Missy." Cassie watched the young woman disappear into the woods. They hadn't gotten very far today, but the bag's contents would help move her Seeker along.

Chapter 32

The marathon trip to Stardust for Lacey to sign more exit papers had taken her from Cassie. Weary, she quietly closed her bedroom door. She could hear Aunt Gabby's gentle snores as she'd walked down the hall. Finally, she had some private time to give Cassie's offering. She took a couple of cleansing breaths and suspended all thoughts, even if for a moment.

She carefully opened the end of the bag, deciding not to look inside but instead just reach in. Her right hand captured something that felt furry-like. She pulled out a tiny squirrel knitted from different shades of gray yarn. Draped around him was another surprise—a fine gold wire fashioned into a choker with a pendant dangling.

Lacey's breath escaped along with one word: *incredible*. She turned the sack upside down. A note, written on paper decorated with herbs around the border, offered an explanation. Holding on to the squirrel and gold treasure, Lacey read the note aloud:

> *Lacey*
>
> *The squirrel is but one of God's creatures who brought you to me. I made him as a reminder of how you were led to the one true path. This piece of jewelry I also created special for you. It has a story that will be told at a later time. But for now, look into the stone's heart, for there you will find my promise.*
>
> *Cassie*

"My goodness, are you ever lovely." She took the handcrafted gold wire necklace from the squirrel's neck. She held the jewelry in her hand and looked closely at the gem for the first time.

She'd never seen a rainbow of colors in anything but an opal… until this moment. The stone's facets shimmered transparent hues of red, orange, yellow, green, blue, and purple. Impossible. Her beloved rainbow of colors. Exquisite. And as a gemologist, she could only wonder where it had formed.

A million questions fired in her brain as she attempted just to stay focused on the stone's unique beauty. What did Cassie mean about looking into the heart of the stone to find her promise? That last question took control of her mind. Her mind had captured her again. She crawled into bed, put the pendant under her pillow, and propped the squirrel on the nightstand.

Lacey spent the next hour replaying the last few weeks and trying in vain to make any sense of the events and experiences. Her mind had been having sport with her again, and this time, she realized, offered no answers. Cassie was right—it was just a big churning machine. Her hand reached under the pillow in the darkness and felt the stone's presence. This was no dream, but she felt sure tonight's dreams would be as vivid as the rainbow dressing Divine's sky after a summer rain. A myriad of questions stayed with her as she closed her eyes on another mind-boggling and confusing day.

Chapter 33

THE NEXT MORNING FOUND LACEY holding the pendant. She'd pulled the piece from the hiding place to study the stone in the morning light. She scurried over to a southern facing window where the gem's beauty shown best.

As an expert on gems, she knew that her eyes were probably gazing on an uncelebrated jewel. The trusted four Cs used to evaluate a stone's worth came to her aid—cut, color, clarity, and carat weight.

Her skill served in recognizing that the cut, color, and clarity were exceptional. Lacey had no reference point to determine the cost of this beauty. The mineral and earth's heat, which joined to form this original specimen, were unknown. Even with a gem scope and other tools relied upon by gemologists, she doubted her identification skills would provide her answers.

She'd be willing to bet Old Mountain Cassie was privy to the origin of this rare find. One thing for sure, Cassie didn't have a tea for the gazillion emotions washing over her this moment. She looked at the stone once more before placing it back under her pillow. Tomorrow morning's visit with Cassie couldn't come soon enough.

Lacey still had her day to…to what? The thought got interrupted by voices coming from the main part of the house. "Oh no." She fretted. "Aunt Gabby's at it again. I feel the vibe that more changes are in the air," she said to Topaz.

The cat meowed and disappeared under her bed.

"Smart Topaz," she replied as she padded down the hallway to hear her aunt giving instructions in her typical drill sergeant style.

"Now listen to me carefully, young men. I won't abide any mess, drops of paint, empty soda cans, anything of that sort. The only acceptable change my eyes care to see this evening are outside siding and trim being painted the new color in those waiting paint cans. Have I made myself clear?"

"Yes, ma'am. You can count on us to do you a real good job. We're glad to be earning the extra money for prom," said the tall lanky teenager dressed in worn jeans and a T-shirt advertising a well-known rock band.

The other boy remained mute, obviously a wise choice, Lacey thought.

"That's fine. I understand it's a teachers' workday, so the sun will tell you when to quit," Aunt Gabby informed. "Jeb, you and Larry may knock on the door for repast around noonish."

"Excuse me?" Larry found his voice. His handsome looks wouldn't help him with Gabby.

"She means to get a soda and some kind of sandwich, you dope," explained Jeb as he ushered his buddy out the door.

Lacey waited until the boys were outside before making her presence known. "Aunt, I just heard something about paint. What plans do you have for my cottage now?" Lacey felt a touch of panic rising.

"Darling girl, good morning to you. I meant my latest idea to be a surprise. Now that the gardens are simply resplendent, well…the cottage's face looked so shabby."

"Shabby?" Lacey didn't see her home that way at all. She'd planned to try and hose off the pollen later in the week, hoping to buy another year before painting. Her finances of late begged for any maintenance delays.

"Dear one, don't give this minor project of mine another thought. Remember, it's my way of earning my keep." Gabby whooshed by with a buttery croissant on a napkin, heading for a chair.

"But, Aunt Gabby, I've told you that's not necessary. What color?" Lacey's mind moved her onto the number one fear of some hideous house color like lavender. Gabby had already informed her weeks ago that ladies of a certain age loved purple.

"Color? Oh yes, the paint shade is the most relaxing…Excuse me. That's my cell phone ringing in my room." Gabby disappeared in a flash, taking the answer with her.

Lacey's eyebrows flew up as she saw the boys outside the window busy with ladders and paint cans. There was only one thing to do. She opened the front door. "Hi, guys. Listen, would you mind popping the lid on that paint can for me?"

"Hey, Miss Lacey, you wanna help?" offered Larry with a dose of teasing.

"Shut up. We're working for her. Here you go." Jeb opened the lid.

Lacey bent down and looked at the shade of warm taupe and smiled. She recognized immediately how the color would complement the cottage's rock. The vivid floral display in the gardens, along with the hemlocks and rhododendrons, set quite the welcoming scene. "Looks nice, guys. Do a careful job, and I just might throw in a tip."

"You bet, Miss Lacey," the teenagers said in unison.

Lacey heard Gabby still chatting away as she walked past her room heading for the solitude of her study. She froze, hearing the words, 'If it can't be helped.' Another extension of her aunt's visit seemed imminent. The stars were not aligning for her to enjoy a solitary existence in her prettily planted and soon-to-be-painted place.

Not bothering to analyze her feelings on Aunt Gabby's continued sojourn in Divine, Lacey fired up her computer. This morning, she meant to search out any information on that extraordinary gemstone hiding under her pillow. Some unknown yet benevolent feeling kept her moving forward trusting Cassie. She had no shortage of questions about the unusual occurrences, but she'd made peace that time would provide answers, as Cassie promised.

Gabby's keen and observing mind told her that her niece must have approved the paint color and project since the study's door remained closed. "So much to do," she said with a sigh that somehow felt quite invigorating until Topaz showed. Gabby eyed his entrance with warranted suspicion.

Topaz sat inside the door opening, glaring at Gabby. With a sneeze directed her way, a tuft of fur acting like tumbleweed attached to Gabby's pants leg.

With a grimace, she plucked the fur from her trousers and deposited it in the trash can. Last time he'd paid a call, her favorite lipstick had gone missing, and before that, her makeup sponges. "There's nothing in my room for a cat. And you'd better beware, mister. I have no doubt you're the thief of my scarlet color lipstick and everything else missing. Swishing that tail at me just confirms you're the culprit."

A perceptive Topaz sauntered back into the hall, answering his cold reception with a loud meow.

Aunt Gabby followed, shutting her bedroom door with extra verve before charting her course toward the front porch swing and her young painters. A best-selling romance novel provided some distraction, as did the bowl of fresh cherries. The gentle breeze added to her pleasure of being in Divine. *Such a quaint town*, she thought. "Wouldn't it be lovely if I…" She was interrupted by her two unsatisfactory new painters.

"Jeb, Larry, not like that…no, paint in one direction. Give me that brush," Gabby demanded once she reached the boys.

"You don't think this looks cool?" asked Larry.

"Cool? The only thing cool out here is the breeze. Like this," she instructed. Her arm moved up and down in long easy strokes. The paint smoothed out where the boys had done the inferior job.

They watched, clearly willing to please even Gabby. The day's money was already spent in their young minds.

"Okay. Now you do the same while I watch." The brush changed hands.

Both teenagers took their place doing exactly as Gabby had instructed. They paused for a dose of approval.

"Better. You may continue using the proper painting techniques." She returned to the porch, thinking again how much Lacey needed her now. Lucky for her niece, she'd arrived in the nick of time. The novel kept her company until noon.

Lacey hadn't been successful in identifying the stone's heritage. She grew to accept the distinct possibility that the gem hadn't been catalogued by the experts. She smiled, thinking how like Old Mountain Cassie to have yet another treasure besides the herbs possessing their own uniqueness to share. Incredible was starting to feel normal.

Lacey stood in front of the mirror, admiring the rainbow of colors playing off the gem's facets as she styled her hair. Her white blouse provided the perfect backdrop to show off the stone's coloration. She grabbed the hairspray to put the finishing touches on her carefree cut. Lacey spent the next couple of minutes applying pastel lip gloss, a touch of gray eyeshadow, and mascara to complete the fresh-faced natural look she preferred.

She decided to devote the rest of her day to errands in town and maybe a wash down of her porch furniture. And if left alone, another attempt at meditating. Satisfied that she looked ready for the public eye, Lacey took one more admiring peek at her necklace. Sunlight coming from the window caught the gem in a different light. She removed the choker and looked deeply into the stone's center. "What's this? I didn't see that before." She ran to get her jeweler's loop and moved closer to the window, capturing maximum light. She peered into the center of the stone, and a tiny gold star surrounded by the color spectrum stared back at her. "Who are you?" she whispered, not knowing if she meant the gemstone, Cassie, or both.

Immediately, the emotion of sheer joy filled her being. She held the stone tightly. The feeling washed over her again and again like the ocean waves coming to shore. What activated this emotion? How did a piece of gold that resembles a star get implanted? Was God's hand in this? And how did Old Mountain Cassie fit in with these occurrences? One thing was certain—she was intrigued and eager to learn more.

Joy, along with growing unanswered questions, accompanied Lacey outside. "See ya later, Aunt Gabby. I'm off to do a few errands. This is a most glorious day in Divine," she said, walking down the sidewalk toward her vehicle. Her thoughts always by her side.

Chapter 34

LACEY GREETED THE NEXT MORNING with excitement knowing today she'd see Old Mountain Cassie. She'd devoted time to journaling and trying to meditate but finally accepted she simply wasn't Cassie schooled enough to have success with hanging out with her Spirit Self. She'd need to grow some patience and more training.

Her thoughts veered to Serene's birthday gift, waiting on the table for wrapping. Lacey prided herself on early shopping and preparation and detested the self-inflicted stress caused by waiting until the last minute to accomplish tasks.

The telephone's ring interrupted her musings. "Hello," she responded while tucking away the package. She listened to Aunt Gabby's contractor identify himself and the reason for the call before asking him to hold the line.

"Aunt Gabby? Your contractor needs to speak with you about some cabinet hardware," Lacey called out.

"Cabinet hardware? Oh dear, I've been so caught up with my little refreshing project here at the cottage it slipped my mind," Gabby prattled, taking the cordless phone from her niece.

"Good morning, Mr. Roberts. I've been remiss," Gabby began her conversation.

Lacey waved, motioning she was leaving. She had just enough time to make it to Cassie's by ten. Delaying her departure to hear about decorative cabinet pulls would only make her late, not to mention visit unwanted Gabby stress.

Lacey stood for the second time at Cassie's planked front door. She touched the choker and pendant around her neck, waiting for Cassie's welcome. The butterflies flitted in the gardens, landing on colorful flowers and enhancing their beauty. Lickety Split's feet thundered up the porch steps to stand next to her, his tongue hanging from his effort to greet.

"Hey, Lick, what ya been up to? Hmm, I see something blue all over your muzzle and tongue."

Cassie opened the door in time to hear the last sentence. "Hey there, Missy. What's this about a blue…? Good grief, dog, have you been in my blueberries?"

"Ruff," Lickety answered, showing his berry-stained tongue.

Lacey stood amused at the scene unfolding.

"Get yourself down to the stream and clean up. I won't have you inside stainin' my rugs and pretties. Go on. Get." Cassie turned her attention back to her guest. "At least, he's heading in the right direction." Cassie shook her head. "Come on inside, Lacey. Been looking forward to your visit all morning."

"Me too, Cassie. Here's a hug and some heirloom tomatoes. I didn't know if your garden was producing any this season. Here's a brown bag lunch for us later." Lacey handed both sacks over.

"Mighty thoughtful, Missy. Cassie took a quick gander inside the bags as she walked them to her kitchen counter."

"Umm, is that Lickety barking?" Lacey asked, unsure.

"Yep. That's the bark when he's snagged an unsuspecting trout. He's a show-off," Cassie replied, shaking her head yet again at the dog's antics.

"Wow. He's fast and aptly named." Lacey gave a laugh.

"We'll just ignore his invitation for braggin' and have something cool to drink. We can either sit in or out. You decide whilst I make us each a glass of my blueberry lemon tea."

"That's easy. My choice is outside in your enchanting gardens," Lacey answered, already anticipating the pleasure and hope of another mystical experience in the land of Cassie.

"Well then, just head out there and pick a pleasin' place to sit. I'll join you in a jiffy.

Don't let Lickety try and entice you with any of his offerins'." The mountain woman teased.

"Raw trout is not on my sushi menu. Holler if you need any help," Lacey offered before closing the screen door.

Lacey took a stroll, taking in each garden's distinctive personality. Of course, the butterfly garden felt special and had memories deposited there. She walked over to another small area that she'd missed seeing on the previous visit.

Tucked off in a private corner sat a wishing well of sorts. Rhododendrons had hidden it from view as if to protect the well from accidental discovery. To the right of the wooden structure sat a pair of Adirondack chairs painted cherry red. Their arms had generous cup holders meant to encourage a relaxing sit. Large drooping sourwood trees offered shade and a breeze. The flowers were an interesting mix of deep purples and lavender. Lacey couldn't identify them by name, but their colors called to her spirit, and the wishing well intrigued her. She claimed the closest chair and the spot for her lesson with Cassie.

The mountain woman appeared a few minutes later, holding two frosted glasses with a leaf-patterned napkin wrapped around the base of each glass. "Here you go. I see that you discovered my wishin' place." Cassie acknowledged, settling into the adjoining empty chair.

"Yes, I'd not seen this garden before. Honestly, you have so many surprises out here. Thanks for the cold drink." Lacey set the glass in the holder. "And speaking of surprises, I want to thank you for the incredible necklace and, of course, the cute squirrel you made. Both are exceptional and unique just like their giver. The pendant and I have been enjoying getting to know each other. It's so beautiful and the stone…unusual." Lacey's petite fingers lifted the piece of jewelry up to show Cassie she was wearing it.

"You're very welcome. I thought the design suited you well. I expect with your knowledge of gems, you have questions bubblin' for me."

Lacey gave a nervous chuckle. "You could say that. I confess to spending time trying to identify this stone," Lacey supplied.

"And?"

"And I came up with zip. Nada. And somehow that didn't surprise me since the stone came from you." Lacey paused. "So please add to the lesson plan—tell Lacey about the meaning and origin of this breathtaking treasure that just so happens to look like there's a gold star in the gem's center."

"We'll make time for just that. I'll let you enjoy the wonderin' a bit longer." Cassie teased. She hid the real reason for waiting behind her lighthearted response. She'd have to build up to the meaning of the rainbow gem, but at least, she'd given Lacey a sampling to pique her curiosity.

"Agreed. I'll try and contain myself," Lacey said, meaning each word. "So, we're going to explore my life's path to sustainable joy, yes?"

"Yes, ma'am. After all, that's why you're here. Here with me and here on our good earth."

Cassie paused to sip her beverage.

"Don't ask me why, but I suspect today's going to bring another life-changing happening. That seems to be what I can count on with you, Cassie." Lacey smiled. "And so, you know, I've been fretting more about being unemployed. I can't help it. My mind lives to remind me constantly of this fact and Gabby too."

Cassie sensed a story behind the urgency. "You have something more to add?"

"I suppose I should just tell you. Aunt Gabby announced yesterday, that her next project will be securing me employment. This is so not good. The woman's a honey badger when she takes on a project, and I don't want to be her next project. No way."

"Well, maybe she'll wait—"

Lacey jumped with her reply. "I don't think so. The other day she asked me if my steering wheel could be moved to the right side, which tells me she's been talking to our postmaster." Lacey rolled her eyes. "Definitely not a good sign."

"Your aunt sounds mighty carin'," Old Mountain Cassie answered, clenching her jaw to hide her amusement at her niece's accounting.

"Caring is one way to describe her. Not my first choice of words. More like way too helpful and involved. She also inquired how I enjoyed working with hair. Hair! Seems Barbie's salon needs a shampoo girl for the season. What's next? Having me milk cows for Bud at Sweet Clover Dairy?"

"Can't see your likin' to fiddle with hair or cows." Cassie snickered. "Then we best not dawdle. Let's go explorin', Missy, and see what you discover to set things right."

Lacey perked up. "I'm past ready and willing."

Satisfied of that truth, Cassie continued, "First, I'd like for both of us to relax some. Let our worldly concerns flow away with that stream over yonder."

Lacey glanced in the stream's direction, allowing her ears to tune into the water's voice. She nodded.

"We'll build on Lesson One. You're gonna like this day a plenty. Okay then, let's close our eyes and relax a spell. Remember to watch those thoughts when they intrude on the stream's voice. Let them drift on by. Yes, just see them for the bother they are and pay them no never mind. That's good. Just observe and…listen." Cassie's eyes told her Lacey was already floating down easily, so she allowed her eyes to close and join her Seeker on an inner journey.

Lacey felt the relaxation settle her. She sensed a cooling outside her body as if a mist had been sprayed over her. The warm breeze intensified the sensation. She sat quietly listening to the water and letting her tactile experience unfold. The feeling of joy from wearing the stone blended with the other uplifting feelings. Lacey did what Cassie had asked and let the thoughts pass by like they were on a conveyor belt. Seems with proper instruction and magical location she could be rude after all. Oops, that was a thought sneaking in. She released its hold and relaxed more, heightening her awareness of how the stream's voice changed in pitch. Such a lovely sweet song to hear.

Old Mountain Cassie's voice interrupted, "Lacey, it's time to come back. Let your eyes focus on somethin' incredible right in front of you."

Lacey opened her eyes to see the most glorious indigo butterfly resting on her knee. His wings opened and closed with the rhythm of her breath.

"Keep your attention on the beautiful butterfly that's come to greet you in the outer world. He's a reminder that metamorphosis is possible within each of us. You can change too, just as he did from a caterpillar who lived life crawlin' to a butterfly that's free to fly and touch down by desire. What does flittin' and flyin' look like to your spirit? Go ahead and sit with that."

Lacey sat as still as the giant boulder nearby. She watched the butterfly invite more of the sun's warmth by turning his body to take full advantage of the rays. He acted like his own solar panel. Lacey adjusted her position to achieve the same results. She tried to imagine what flitting would look like for her as the butterfly took flight.

He didn't travel far before landing on the wishing well's metal roof.

Maybe she didn't need to venture far either. Yes, maybe the earth's gifts, like gems, can be enjoyed by enough folks, even in a small town like Divine. Maybe. Lacey rested in amazement of what had just been given to her on so many levels, perhaps by the Junior Partner and the Senior Partner. Here she sat in a wooden chair, listening to noisy water and observing a butterfly. None of this was out of the ordinary, but today with Cassie, it had become extraordinary. "I think Lesson One took." She spoke softly, glancing at Cassie.

"Sounds like you received somethin' to ponder on…maybe?"

"I think the teacher needs to take some credit here. You showed me a way to open to my spirit and receive insights that are all…" Lacey stopped trying to locate her word.

"Fresh?" the mountain woman offered.

"Fresh, yes. I like that. I had a most refreshing glimpse at a change that might be for me."

"Maybe you can take that home with you and build on it by repeatin' the meditation? Be sure and invite your Spirit Self, though."

"Cassie, don't you think this place and you are what allow me to tap into this…state? I mean sitting in my bedroom chair doesn't feel like the place to do any genuine connecting, and believe me, I've been trying to. It's not working for me. I'm frustrated 'cause I like things to happen quickly. And all I get for my effort is mindless chatter. I ache to develop a meditation practice. Truly I do."

Cassie sat gathering in her delight at her new Seeker's growing desire to learn. She was witnessing Lacey's commitment to the teachings. "Rest easy. I have just what you're needin' in this moment."

Chapter 35

Cassie waited for her Seeker to find calm. "I'd say your questions and frets about how to connect to your sweet spirit have done a real fine job of settin' up Lesson Two. I'm givin' you a star for being dedicated." Cassie plucked an imaginary one from the air and tossed it to Lacey.

"I've always had a fondness for stars, so I will take it and Lesson Two with appreciation. This time, I'm ready to build on these remarkable teachings." Lacey vowed.

Mountain Cassie tapped her index finger on the chair arm, waiting for the words to come. "You're right about needing a fittin' place for being with your spirit, and Lesson Two teaches this very thing."

"Anything that helps me recreate what I just experienced, I want," said Lacey.

"You shared a fret that your bedroom didn't feel much welcoming."

"No, it definitely hasn't worked out. I even tried listening to my meditation CD to drown out Aunt Gabby's singing her favorite aria each morning. And I'm being kind calling what came from that mouth singing."

Lickety Split surprised both women by letting out a howl that stretched into the next county. Both women gave the dog a standing ovation, along with their laughter.

"Guess that's Lick's version of an aria," Cassie remarked, taking a tissue to dab her eyes.

"I swear your dog understands every word we say. And, Lick, I gotta say your aria was way superior to Aunt Gabby's. Well done." Lacey patted the dog's head. "Sorry, Cassie, back to school."

"Let's see, where was I? Oh yes, we all need to have a favorite place where our spirit can connect with God and the heavenly beings. This place might not appear out of the ordinary to other's eyes, but it is to the one seekin' and findin'. You follow?" Cassie paused to re-plait her braid and give her Seeker ponder time.

"Do you mean that not all places are created equal to plug into God and the beings on the Other Side?" Lacey pulled out her journal and wrote a few sentences. "Do you mind if I continue to make notes?"

"Scribe all ya want, Missy. Hear it this way. Seekers, one and all, must find a spot that's sacred-like to them. What might that place look like? It could maybe be a nook in your cottage that has a private feelin', a dedicated room, or even a sizable empty closet. I've got one Seeker who discovered a corner of his barn felt real obliging." Oh, and I have an Air Force general who's always on the move. He figured out how to create a space with a large, folded cardboard box. As I recollect, he used it as some kinda partition. I'm tellin' the truth gal. Takes it with him all over the world. Truth. I have another Seeker who cobbled out a spot in her boathouse just perfect for connectin' away from her kids. Just needs to be private and feel suited to you. Understand me?"

"I do. I believe I can find my spot now that you've explained more." Lacey put down her pen. Cassie having a general for a Seeker surprised her. She wondered who else had crossed Cassie's path.

"Very good, Missy. Let's expand on why you need this spot. Your Spirit Self and God enjoy having a meetin' place, for it's here your special joining happens. Think of the space as a kind of conduit feedin' your spirit daily guidance. Also, your prayers and requests go out that same conduit. See it this way. There's transmittin' and receivin' happening in your special place. Keep that image." Cassey observed Lacey's frown settle between her eyes. "Lasso that worry. I've got more to share on this lesson. You're doin' just fine, Seeker."

"Well, that's a relief. I confess to still being back, mentally searching for some private real estate at my cottage." Lacey offered a weak smile.

"Don't let your mind fuss with you about this. Listen, I'm going to say this part again. You are lookin' for a niche that calls to your heart, and that is where the energy will flow to and fro between you, God, and the heavenly beings who love and care for you. This spot will be co-created by you and God. And it even has a special name." Cassie paused for effect. "Lesson Two calls it your Divinin' Portal, but I expect you can name it whatever you fancy."

"I love Divining Portal. That name really says it all, doesn't it, Cassie? I understand better where and why I need to create this sanctuary. I mean if I want to have this higher relationship with my spirit and God, it makes sense I need a dedicated place. A Divining Portal."

"That's right. Now let's chat about your Divinin' Portal's decoratin'."

"What decorating? I'm confused." Lacey grinned. She was enjoying this lesson. "How can I decorate a closet or an alcove?" *Ahh, my mind*, she thought, *back at it again*.

"Raise up that pen. I'm gonna share what's made some of my Seekers divinin' space satisfying." Cassie cut a grin.

"Satisfying?" Lacey treasured Cassie's special relationship with language.

"Hush, gal. You get my meanin' fine. Anyways, here's some ideas for your portal. Keep the ones you like, for that's your Spirit Self givin' the nod."

Cassie continued, "For starters, you might wanna have an altar with things your spirit feels belongs. A cross, maybe a votive. Some nice-smellin' incense. Maybe a crystal or geode. You're partial to gems after all. Oh, and a verse that has meanin' to you is nice too. Any spiritual readings that you take to, be sure to have blank sticky notes nearby to pen your prayer requests and such. I especially like havin' angel cards to draw each day. The angels give me meaningful and loving guidance if I but ask. By and by, we can chat more about your Divinin' Portal as you birth it. Just be sure the joy is around your creatin'. Watch for that feelin', and you'll know this special place is pleasin' to you and God. You gettin' this?" Cassie studied her Seeker's countenance.

"Actually, I'm absorbing this all surprisingly well. What else, Cassie?"

"Well, once you have your place set up nice, we can visit about developing a ritual of enterin' into your sacred place and openin' that conduit. That part is real powerful, and plenty of blessings will flow to you. Did you get all that down?" Cassie leaned over to try and see what Lacey had written.

"I sure did. I'm feeling excited to have my own Divining Portal and try making these miraculous connections. Cassie, the lessons have been incredible. I'm empty of words but brimming with desire to know my Spirit Self and God. Oh, and yes, the angels and Others. Wait, do you believe they will want to link up with me?" Lacey's doubt came begging for attention.

"Hear me, Missy, these teachings are ancient, proven, and God-given. They always deliver on the promise. Wanna know why?" Old Mountain Cassie's voice grew reflective.

"Forgive my lapsing into doubt, but do tell me why," Lacey pleaded.

"Because they're bound by the universal laws that govern all that there is and will be. They are God's holy laws that support you having your heart's desire. All that is asked of you is to apply The Three Lessons to prove the teachings' truth. And you understand the need for this portal is to allow your spirit to come forth and be with God in a direct kind of way." Cassie exhaled a long breath, observing Lacey. She took a sip of her now tepid drink, understanding well The Lessons needed time to settle into a Seeker. She knew the proof of their power would always be in the unexpected blessings. "I know I've given you a plenty to cotton on. Good stuff, though, Missy. Real good." Cassie gave her nod.

"Yes, there's so much to grasp, but at least, I have my notes and you to rely on. Cassie, my wish to have a richer relationship with God is growing steadily inside as you share more and more. I'm feeling pretty sad learning about the God relationship I've missed having for so many years." Lacey released a heavy sigh.

"Ah, but now is the right time, Missy. I want to finish this last part. You've been experiencin' things at what you call my enchanted place. Know this. God's hand is on these mystical doings. But enchanted places live more than on the leys and closets and barns." Cassie cut a grin. "You'll find them inside a labyrinth, inside a chapel, and so on. Tell me, have you ever walked a labyrinth?"

"No, but I've found them intriguing. Hey, there's one on a church property just outside Divine. Hmm." Lacey tapped her chin with the pen. Her mind flashed to driving by and seeing Serene walking it a few months back.

"Well, you might wanna set those two feet inside that labyrinth one of these days and see what messages you come out with. Labyrinths offer lots of insights. God loves to visit us inside them. I've enjoyed no shortage of counsel there. Might even create one on my land for Seekers and me." Cassie gave another nod, signaling she'd had her say.

"I will definitely go visit the one nearby. At least, Gabby won't be there." Lacey sighed.

"That's a funny, Missy. I believe we've given Lesson Two some good study, and you understand the steps to create a Divinin' Portal and the why. I will get my nudge when Lesson Three wants to keep company with us. For now, are you seein' The Lessons are buildin' on each other? Just do some digestin' of everything," suggested Cassie.

"Boy, I've got plenty to digest and some creating and decorating to accomplish, as you instructed. Good that I'm not working so I can be devoted." Lacey tucked her journal away in her jacket pocket.

"I'm agreein' to all that. You're doin' extra good, and remember you got a star today." Cassie gave a chuckle. "What say we enjoy a walk? I have a story about one of my Seekers you might take to, and I have somethin' else you might fancy to gander."

Chapter 36

The first few minutes of the walk, both women enjoyed the companionable silence of words not spoken. The forest creatures' voices were all that accompanied them on their amble. The sage pulled two fruit drinks from her knapsack, offering Lacey one.

Cassie punctured the quiet. "You know, Divinin' Portals can be big open places for some Seekers. Still, you'll hanker for a small spot for faithful communing. Anyway, now to share my story…one of my Seekers felt vibrant and alive only when she was on the beach. That gal had to see the ocean, the waves, the seagulls catch a fish; had to walk on the white sand to find her inspiration and answers. Her joy and service to others lived there. She could have sat in your chair back at my place till all the icebergs melted and not found her connection or path to joy."

"Really? She felt nothing here on your land? Lacey found that statement hard to grasp. Cassie's land was charmed. She wouldn't be surprised to see fairies dancing on the mosses.

"Oh, Missy, that Seeker's eyes showed her amazement and the wonders here all right, but when the time came for her to apply the teachings, the sea called her home to where her big portal waited. We managed to work together pretty well long distance."

"Interesting. And can you tell me what's she doing now?" Lacey asked, fascinated by Cassie's gifts being far reaching.

"Sure can. She paints her love of the sea. Her gift is alive in her watercolors. Folks naturally gravitate toward her gallery to take home a painting so that they can visit the sea whenever their spirits need refreshin'. Just by lookin' at the painting, their spirits connect with God. See how that Seeker's gift is doin' good? Lots of joy movin' around, wouldn't you say?"

Lacey paused to reflect. "Yes, and how wonderful the artist's gifts are blessing others in such a moving way. There's such a difference between just having a career or job and discovering and using my special gift that uplifts others in some way. I see that's my real work here. Knowing that is huge, Cassie, and life-changing." Lacey shook her head, taking in the realization of what she'd been missing in her life.

"Yes, ma'am. You're puttin' things together right nice. Next, I want to build a bit more on my 'sea Seeker' and back to the folks that buy her paintings. You see, those that resonate to the same divine sea voice find their way to anything that puts them in touch with the water's energy. Gazing at one of those paintings in a Divinin' Room might do the trick to open their conduit. Understand?" Cassie needed to be sure Lacey's grasped portals could be large too.

"I do. Mystic Rock Park might be a large portal for me." Lacey recalled meeting Old Mountain Cassie there and feeling an instant connection to God's majesty. She'd return soon with this new wisdom and see if she'd found another portal.

"Yes, ma'am, those sittin' rocks make a fine portal for me too. Here's the thing of it, when the call to grow in your gift is strong enough, you must go to the place that lets you connect daily. It's your Divine Portal. Choose any of them but choose one daily when you're able. Am I makin' sense?" Cassie didn't want to confuse or scatter Lacey too far this early into the learning."

"Oh, Cassie, you make more sense than anyone I've ever known. Listening to you makes life seem…astonishing, just as you and The Lessons promised." Lacey stopped to hug her guide.

"Let's walk some more and not go back to sit." Cassie smacked her bottom, grinning.

Lacey followed, admiring the blooming mountain laurels painting the forest landscape and the blessed peace accompanying them. Rarified air hovered on Cassie's land. "You must own a lot of property. How great to call an entire mountain your home."

"Yes, I'm surely blessed that God allows me to be the steward of this ground. My mom's ancestors settled here. We go way back with this land and its offerings," Cassie explained.

"The mountain sure has an interesting shape to it. I've never noticed that on any of my hikes." Lacey didn't take the opportunity to share her grandmother's people came from the area but rather let Cassie talk.

"I call it Gumdrop Mountain, but everyone else calls it Old Mountain," Cassie answered.

Lacey, at last, understood how Cassie came to be called Old Mountain Cassie. She smiled from the inside.

"Not surprisin' you've not seen her before. She hides between those higher peaks over yonder. I see them as protectors." Cassie pointed over to the mountains.

"They are. I see what you mean."

"Follow me. I hear some visitors."

The two women continued as three deer appeared fifty yards ahead on the trail.

Lickety Split, who'd been exceptionally quiet, took off in their direction.

"Dog, don't you be anything but mannerly to our neighbors," Cassie hollered after him.

The dog slowed to a trot and kept his bark to himself. He approached the deer and commenced licking the young fawn's face, who stood unmoving, seeming to enjoy the attention.

"What in the world?" Lacey asked.

"Oh, he likes the taste of their fur. They don't seem to mind his show of affection. Don't ask me why. Critters have some peculiar ways." Cassie smoothed the wet fur down on the fawn's head.

"He sure lives up to his name," Lacey added, watching his ministrations.

"Daily," Cassie agreed, chuckling.

Cassie pulled a handful of dried berries from her pocket. She offered each deer a taste. "Haven't seen your family in a spell. The little one is sure growin'," she told the parents.

Lacey stood back a few feet since she was the stranger in this menagerie. She loved watching Old Mountain Cassie interact with all of nature.

"This here is Miss Lacey. She's learnin' about herself and is real appreciative of our woods. Lacey, come on over here and say howdy."

Lacey walked quietly toward the group. She put out her hand for the deer to sniff. "Nice to meet you all."

"We have Suze, Sherwood, and the youngin is Surprise," Cassie said, finishing the introductions.

"Surprise?" asked a puzzled Lacey.

"Yep. Suze and I didn't think she'd be havin' any more youngins. She's getting up there like me, but here comes our Surprise early spring."

"Cassie, you're a riot. Someone needs to write a book about you. It'd be a bestseller. You're a national treasure and a whole lot more."

Lacey saw the structure up ahead but kept quiet, preferring to let Old Mountain Cassie address its presence first. She figured it had to be what Cassie wanted to show her. The birds' chirping increased with each step the women took.

"Here we are," Cassie announced. They were still a few yards away but close enough for her Seeker to take in the surroundings. "This is the place where my spirit's work is done. It's a big part of my life's purpose."

Lacey nodded, not interrupting.

"Tucked around here are my cleared spots for any herbs that fancy bein' outside. See, even they have preferences?" Cassie pointed in the direction of a small raised garden bed.

"You know something? I feel your presence here. This is incredible, Cassie." Lacey turned in a circle, taking everything in. The building's design appeared to be at one with the woods, like it belonged, had always belonged. She counted seven raised plots with all shades of lively green leaves carefully tended in rows, making their presence known. Little signs stood as sentinels on each row. Lacey assumed they must state the herb's names. "Cassie, you have no shortage of enchanting places around you. All of your gardens here look positively happy and thriving."

"Why, thank you kindly, Missy, for noticin'. I confess that I chat a good bit with all of my growin' things. They've always seemed to like my style of tending," Cassie added with a chuckle as she moved toward a plot that showed young plants. "This little family is some special strawberry mint I'm encouragin' along. You are looking real pretty today." Cassie leaned down and touched the leaves with her still slender fingers. She spied a few unwelcome intruders and quickly discarded the weeds.

"Yum, strawberry mint sounds tasty. I'd put mine in a tall glass of lemonade." Lacey walked over and took a sniff of a leaf Cassie pinched off for her.

"Go ahead and chew it. Your belly will thank you," Cassie instructed.

Lacey placed the sprig in her mouth. "You know I really do taste a fresh strawberry and peppermint. How did you create this?" Lacey absently touched the gemstone around her neck. The feeling of joy bubbled up again.

Cassie didn't miss the connection. "Well, let's just say I have a kind of partnership agreement. Want to see inside my plant shed?"

"You call this a shed?" Lacey asked, pointing at the building.

"When I first got serious with my life's callin', all I had here on this land was a run-down plant shed that my granny had used for her herb cultivating. I took after her, you see. We both got the growin' gift."

"What happened to the shed? I don't see it," Lacey said, wanting to hear more. She adored family stories. They were like treasured heirlooms to her.

"Well, tell the truth. We had a bad ice storm come through a few years after I'd come to settle in here. A big ole top out a white pine tree fell smackdown on my little shed."

"How awful," Lacey responded with her caring spirit. She felt a growing connection to Divine, and especially Cassie and her land.

"I thought so the first week after it happened. I worked to salvage my potted plants. Brought them to my cabin hopin' to encourage them to stay with me."

"What changed your mind?"

"Well, it's like this, I was sittin' in my 'special place' one night, meditating. An idea seed came and planted right into my head that I needed to quit piddlin' with my herbs and get serious with using my gifts. Well, things commenced happenin' to nudge me on to build another shed. Lots of things."

"And I just bet those 'things' would make a great story for me to hear one of these days," Lacey said, smiling.

"You'd be right. I've used my tale with Seekers to help them know me and God. Come on inside the shed." Cassie held open the door, showing her polite ways, even deep in the woods.

Lickety ran in front of Lacey, wanting to be the first to enter. He turned and barked, adding his brand of welcome.

"Dog, your manners need some work. You were supposed to let Miss Lacey go first," Cassie said, admonishing her companion.

"Lick, it's okay. I can understand your excitement to be here." Lacey looked around the large room Cassie led her to. "This is some shed, Cassie." She teased.

"It's my name for the structure. Haven't heard that it minds," Cassie said, breaking into a grin. "Now come over here, and I'll introduce you some more."

Lacey joined Cassie in front of the large glass windows facing what she'd bet was true south.

"These are my trusted herbs."

Lacey raised an eyebrow.

Cassie nodded, still with her grin in place. "Trusted because they've served me well over the years by showin' up from my collection of seeds wherever I plant them. Trusted," she repeated for emphasis.

"I see," Lacey replied, growing more serious. "St John's Wort, Milk Thistle, Echinacea." Lacey read aloud what the labels stated in front of each herb.

"Do you know them?"

"Well, I know the names and a little about two of them, but Milk Thistle is new for me."

"Two out of three is right impressive. Milk Thistle treats your liver nice when it needs a touch of extra care."

"You can't tell by the name. Sounds like something you'd use to flavor milk." Lacey grinned.

"Don't think it would add much to the dairy cow's offering. Over here are more plants that I'm cultivatin' for special customers whose needs are specific."

Lacey gazed at row after row of small containers all with plants at various stages of growth. Each one appeared to be growing with vitality. "They all look so full of energy, just like the ones outside."

"They must be to deliver their benefits in a pure way. For you see, whatever your body takes in becomes that very thing in a way. The energy of, let's say, that St. John goes into the brain and then sends a brand-new message that you're back in harmony and able to deal with life without the overreaction of the mind. After a period of time, hopefully short, your mind settles back down, realizin' it had lost sight of an important truth. Old St. John can be put back on the shelf and called on if there ever be a need to remind the mind of this again." She paused to judge Lacey's reaction. "Want to ask me somethin'?"

"You know I do. What's the truth?" Lacey held her breath, anticipating with excitement Cassie's next words.

"Why, it's the truth that has always been…will always be, and you'll be hearin' all about it in Lesson Three." Cassie couldn't help giving the teaser.

"I will look forward to delving into this truth more with you, Cassie." Lacey sensed there must be great power in this truth.

"Anyways, this is my plant room where I spend plenty of time being in my joy. Here's where the ideas for some of the teas you've been sippin' get birthed.

Lacey saw the gardening tools, sinks, and organic bags of nutrients sitting in bins. Everything was tidy and clean. "You sure keep the place ship shape. I mean you use dirt, and yet I see none except in the pots."

"Follow me. Lick, you stay put in your bed. You know you're not allowed in the dryin' room." Cassie nodded approval when he lay back down.

Cassie led her Seeker down a short hallway and opened a door into a darkened room with only a faint glow of light.

Lacey couldn't tell where the light source was, but there was a feeling of dry air moving around the space. She saw the racks lining all four walls and then another row down the center of the room that held the flowers. "Tell me about this space."

"This is the dryin' room, as you probably figured out. Some herbs like to be settled this way rather than remain fresh and used right away. These dryin' herbs become even better at bestowin' their gifts to us if they spend time here. This room is like their Divining Portal. They're changing in a way much like your teacher, the butterfly, you met earlier. Their energies get crystallized like and become extra potent. I appreciate them wishin' to spend more time on earth to help us. Don't you?" Cassie was indeed teaching.

"I suppose. I must confess I've never thought about herbs on that level, but somehow, I feel glad knowing this. Yes, I appreciate their unbelievable gifts even more now that you've shared this."

"Yes, ma'am." Cassie turned, leading the way back to the hall. "Here's the place where I do the packin' up for shippin'. My office is over yonder in that alcove. I try not to spend too much time in that space. Doesn't suit me having to cipher and such."

"A necessary evil to have to keep records and accounting, even when doing what you love. I'm not a fan of paperwork either. I'd much rather be sorting through a delivery of colorful sapphires to select the ideal one for a ring design."

"We got that in common, sounds like. There are a few more rooms that get used for different things as I see fit, but this gives you a gaggle at my shed here."

"Actually, this room is interesting in many ways." She stood still, taking everything in with her senses. "I love all of the colorful rolls of string for tying up the packages of herbs. And your labels are really unique." Lacey moved closer to the rolls of stickers. "Like this one for lavender. You framed the gold-embossed word with purple sprigs of the flower. Very clever and inviting."

"Thank you kindly. I can take some credit for that idea. Designed them myself and had my printer make them up. Look at this roll. What do ya think?" Cassie pulled off a label and handed it to Lacey.

She looked at the green teapot and the words "Joyous Tea" underneath it. The image and words were framed by a tiny border of leaves. "Ah, those marvelous teas aren't just enjoyed around your place, I see. Joyous Tea," Lacey read aloud and sighed. "I especially like your nature theme combined with the cute teapot. They're all charming in their own way." Lacey lightly touched roll after roll with sincere appreciation for Cassie's eye for detail. She couldn't help feeling a bit surprised at the attention Old Mountain Cassie gave to all aspects of her business. And yet, Cassie didn't really treat it as a business at all, more like a ministering maybe—no, even that didn't capture the spirit here at the shed. Lacey's mind released her from any more attempts to find a label for the expression of Cassie's special gift.

―

"Goodness girl, we didn't eat your lunch. Stay a few more minutes while I run inside and nab that sack and some more juice for us." Cassie moved toward her cabin.

"You're right. We did miss a meal, and I am starving...really starving. Go get those sandwiches." She laughed.

"Back in a jiffy. You relax."

Lacey sat down. Hopefully, she'd have success in coaxing Cassie to talk about the gem while they ate. That also had been forgotten. *So many insights to be gleaned from this mountain sage*, she thought. She couldn't help but worry and wonder how much more time Cassie would devote to her.

Old Mountain Cassie returned, carrying a wooden tray. "Hope you like a taste of apple cider."

"It's one of my favorites. Thank you," Lacey said, taking the glass.

"I had to stop myself from claiming a bite of one of these sandwiches. They look so invitin.' Here you go." Cassie handed a small plate to her Seeker.

"It's nice to share a meal with someone who enjoys eating." Lacey touched her pendant. "Umm, Cassie, is this a good time for you to tell me about this exquisite gemstone?" She lifted the stone up, smiling, wanting to send an encouraging vibe.

"Gracious me, I did promise to touch on that subject, didn't I? Well, let's see here. Let me think a moment on where to begin my tellin'. Yes, the middle, I believe, makes the most sense for us today." Cassie allowed a few beats to pass as she gauged her Seeker's desire for factual information versus the desire for the intuitive piece.

"Middle's good," Lacey said, wanting Cassie to continue and not change her mind.

"This stone's been in the family, so to say, a good while now. I've had it with me knowing there'd be a time to hand it on."

"Ah, Cassie, don't you want to give it to someone in your family? The stone is so beautiful and unique that I'd think—"

Cassie stopped Lacey from continuing. "The gem is right where it needs to be. You'll see the rightness in time. Yes, ma'am, you will." Cassie gave her nod.

Lacey's cell phone rang. "Oh, Cassie, please excuse me. I've been gone longer than planned, so I'd better take this."

"Do. Don't want a soul to be worryin' any."

Lacey answered her phone. "Hi, Aunt Gabby. Yes, I'm wrapping up now and should be home within the hour. Why?"

Cassie watched her Seeker's face grow red as her jar of chili peppers resting on her kitchen counter.

"You accepted a job for me? You're kidding, right? No, don't say another word. I'm coming home to try and undo this mess. Really, Aunt Gabby, we must talk about this well-meaning meddling. See you in a few minutes." Lacey returned the phone to her backpack.

"Sounds like your aunt is pretty determined to get you workin' soon."

Lacey took a sip of the cool cider, trying to reduce the flush she felt on her face. "She's gone too far this time in her meddling...too far. I can't believe it, but she's—and I quote— 'secured me gainful employment with Holcomb's Plumbing.'"

"Plumbin'? That's a stretch, even with your talents and brains." Cassie turned her head to hide her grin.

"I'll say. Seems my experience as a gem buyer translates into purchasing plumbing supplies." Lacey shrugged and lifted her arms in the air. "Honestly, I guess I'm lucky to only have one aunt to muck up my calm, peaceful life."

"You'll put things right soon enough, gal. You go on, and we'll pick up where we left off next visit," Cassie replied.

Lacey rose. "Thanks for today. I confess that I'm growing to prefer your world a lot more to the one waiting at home."

"My pleasure. And, Missy?"

"Yes?" Lacey answered, her mind already lost in thought about Gabby.

"Not all aunts meddle," Cassie added for her own satisfaction and to plant a seed to harvest in the future.

Lacey leaned in to hug Cassie good-bye. "Well, feel free to introduce me to one of those aunts sometime. I'd welcome the contrast to who's at my cottage hunkered down for gosh knows how many more weeks."

Cassie held up a hand to wave her niece off. She sure hoped Lacey meant those parting words 'cause she'd be trottin' herself out aunt-like pretty soon.

Chapter 37

"Aunt Gabby? Are you here? We need to talk." Lacey's voice sounded harsh, even to her angry ears.

"Coming, dear girl. Coming. I'm so encouraged now that I've found you this simply ideal job, and you won't have to leave Divine. It's so perfect. I know you'll be ever so pleased with me once you hear. Do sit and let me fill you in." Gabby materialized, claiming the comfortable chair.

Lacey sat down in the opposite chair. "Aunt Gabby, I do appreciate you always wanting to help me and doing things around the cottage, so many things, but going around job hunting is—"

"Please don't thank me. It's my pleasure to come to your rescue. I've watched you fret and worry, and, well, I simply had to intervene and get you out of this job funk, let us say."

Gabby's expression showed delight in her newest accomplishment.

"Aunt, please, I need you to listen and understand." Lacey wondered if she could offer Gabby's contractor a bonus if he'd hurry things, for it was just a matter of time before her aunt moved on to matchmaking. That was the only area of her life that Gabby hadn't ventured yet, and she wasn't that desperate for a man. "Aunt, I'm capable of finding a job. Really."

"I understand, darling one, but I can make things so much easier. And last night on the dance floor with Fred was the opportune time for me to present you. Of course, you know his son runs the business nowadays, but Fred took to my proposal right away."

"Proposal?" Whatever was her aunt babbling about? "Look, Aunt Gabby, I'm not in the least bit—"

"Why, yes, I did a barter, you might say. Isn't that what they call it?"

"What, did you tell Fred? Before I detail for you the new rules, I want to know how bad my situation is," said Lacey.

"You've taken everything all wrong. I've outdone myself, even to the point of personal sacrifice to help you. You need employment. You simply can't hike your best days away in some forest."

"What?" Lacey felt her blood pressure soaring to meet the jet stream.

"Oh, never mind about this woodsy thing you've got, listen to what good I've done for you." Gabby took a sniff, having secured Lacey's full attention on her next words. "You, my precious Niece, are to be the parts procurer three days a week at Holcomb's Plumbing, and the other two days you will be out in the field, I think Fred called it, bidding new septic tanks. Isn't this just perfect?" Gabby struck a pose.

"Perfect? How can you think this—?"

"Silly you. Perfect because you can still be a buyer, only of plumbing things, and perfect because you get to be outdoors, just like you enjoy now. You know. Outside. Mother nature," Gabby waved her arm toward the outdoors while noticing her niece's face take on a peculiar expression.

"Field. Out in the field is not the same as hiking." At that moment, Lacey realized her life was a mess…a confusing mess.

Not happy at being interrupted, Gabby continued with her story. "And in return for Holcomb's taking you on to train, I've promised Fred that I will be his only dance partner. Just think of my little promise as but a small sacrifice to you, dear one. Oh, and you start Monday." Gabby settled back into the chair, pleased to share another example of her generosity.

Lacey tried to find some air to fill her lungs, but her mouth slammed tightly shut to override the scream waiting to escape. She remembered her trusty counting number exercise that had served her well over the last weeks, but she also knew there weren't enough numbers to count her back to sanity this time. Still, she had to try. Her voice returned within seconds, "Thirty-one, thirty-two, thirty-three—"

"Darling girl, whatever are you counting?" Gabby followed her niece's gaze to the ceiling and saw nothing unusual.

The doorbell chimed. Gabby jumped to answer. "Hello, Serene. Do come in, won't you?"

Gabby stepped aside.

"Hi, Gabby. Lacey around?" Serene saw her friend before Gabby could reply. She walked over to the sofa and looked down at Lacey.

"Fifty-one, fifty-two, fifty-three, fifty-four," Lacey said, continuing her self-prescribed therapy.

"Umm, Gabby, what's going on here?" Serene noticed Lacey's glazed-over expression.

"Well, I'm not quite sure. I was telling her my excellent news about securing the poor thing's employment at Holcomb's Plumbing, and she commenced this counting business, staring at the ceiling. Most unsettling."

"Seventy-seven, seventy-eight." Lacey felt proud at how focused she'd become.

"Lacey, Lacey, come on back. I'm here. We can fix this together," Serene whispered.

Lacey's eyes locked on Serene's, but she continued to count…a little slower. "Eighty-eight, eighty…"

"Come on. Let's go out on the porch. You can tell me about your day, and I'll tell you about my birthday plans." Serene pulled her friend to a standing position.

Gabby stepped aside to allow the two to pass. "Most perplexing. Could be hormonal," she offered to Serene.

"I don't think so, Gabby. Excuse us for a bit." Serene closed the screen door.

Lacey sat down in the swing.

Serene joined her and, with a push of her slender foot, set them in motion. "Okay, promise me you won't start counting again. I'm going to help get you out of what I suspect must be some awful plumbing job."

Lacey nodded, craving Cassie's wisdom now more than ever. "I refuse to order toilets and plungers. I'm not that desperate yet. How could Aunt Gaby think measuring for a septic tank suits me? Don't even get me started on this whole 'out in the field' business and what she thinks that means."

Serene pushed the swing a little faster to hurry Lacey along with her venting, her expression mirroring the humor of Gabby's latest escapade.

"Do I look like a woman that gets into faucets? Do I?"

"No, of course not." Serene managed to stifle a grin. "She's concerned about you not finding work. I have to admit I've wondered…"

Lacey's perfectly arched eyebrow raised.

Well, just the tiniest bit of wonder if you were really seriously looking. Tiny." Serene held up two fingers to illustrate. "See? Tiny."

"Look, I'm doing some inner work to discover what I truly feel led to do, and I don't need everyone worrying about me turning into some down and out lazy—"

"Whoa! Hang on. No one could ever think of you that way," Serene stated emphatically.

"Well, okay then. What am I going to do about this job that I'm to begin on Monday?" Lacey knew that feelings got hurt easily in a small town.

"Let's think. You don't have another job lined up by any chance, do you?"

Lacey frowned. "Didn't you hear what I just said? I'm doing—"

"Yes, yes, inner work. Lovely. Terrific," Serene rattled off. "You can't very well say that to a plumber now, can you?"

"No, of course not. I'll just call up Fred and tell him I've got something I'm working on. Thank him and all that."

"And if he asks you what? Your answer is?"

"That I'm working on getting his little honey, Gabby, back home to Florida by sundown," Lacey responded, letting sarcasm take over as her frustration escalated.

"Table Gabby's exit for the moment. How about you tell him you're going to help me for a couple of weeks?"

"Help you? Whatever could you need me to do?"

"My selling season is starting to really kick off. I could use you a few hours each week to take photos of my listings and do a little marketing project," Serene said, warming to her inspired idea.

"Really? You need some help? Not pity help?"

"I really do, and I'm betting by the time you complete that inner work project, you will have the path to your heart's desire."

"Hmm, I like the sound of all that," Lacey said, hope returning to her spirit.

"I'll pay you." Serene wanted to be fair. Having Lacey around would be a huge plus.

"You don't have to pay me, but if I should ever need your service, I expect to get the family rate." Lacey wondered where that idea came from.

"Deal. Shake." Serene offered her hand to Lacey.

"Deal." Lacey smiled and clasped her friend's hand. "Serene, you always show up when I need you and with answers too. You're wonderful…beyond wonderful."

"You're welcome. You know I was kind of worried seeing you in that state and counting catatonic like." Serene's mouth curled at the corners.

"That's my new form of aunt therapy. She never stops messing in my life, and I need her visit to be over soon. I love and care for her, of course, but Serene, I want my cottage back. I want my life back."

"I know. You've been gracious to allow her to stay. Everyone knows this. I do think your aunt has attached herself to Divine and is very happy here."

"Meaning I'm stuck with her?" Lacey asked, desperation replacing her happier mood.

"No, not exactly," Serene responded cryptically.

"You know something, and you're not telling me." Lacey turned to face her friend. She stopped the swing's movement. She lifted Serene's sunglasses and pushed them to the top of her head. "What's going on that I'm obviously missing?" Lacey looked at Serene straight on.

Brown eyes darted to a gold wristwatch. "Oh my, it's almost—"

"Never you mind the time on your watch. It's time you fess up. What do you mean 'not exactly'?" Lacey was like Lickety Split with a stick to be thrown. She wasn't giving up until her friend answered her growing concern. "Is Aunt Gabby planning on living with me permanently or something?" Lacey wailed.

"Shhh, not so loud. No, not living with you at all. See? No worries. Let's talk about my birthday plans. I have booked the theater for the evening." Serene talked faster, trying to engage Lacey in a new subject.

"Wait, just a Divine moment, what about the 'something' you didn't elaborate on?"

"That was your something, not mine. I've already told you she's not planning to live with you. After all, she's got a home, right?"

"Yes," Lacey said hesitantly, still feeling like she'd been outmaneuvered. So, I'm to assume you've told me everything I need to know?" Lacey gave her questioning one final try.

"Of course, now I'm going to pop inside and get Fred's telephone number. You can call him and then make peace with Gabby's latest meddling. Things will be hunky-dory."

Lacey was left wondering if she'd ever experienced hunky-dory?

Chapter 38

Lacey sat at the dining table, enjoying strawberry shortcake with a subdued Aunt Gabby. Since she'd squashed her aunt's attempt as a job recruiter, she tried to relax in the moment. No telling what project would claim her aunt next, but for tonight, there seemed to be a visage of peace in her valley.

"Tell me, Aunt Gabby, when will the condo renovations be completed? I know you spoke to your contractor earlier." Lacey asked, interrupting the heavy silence that had prevailed since she'd let her aunt overhear her conversation with Fred explaining Gabby had been a little too ambitious in accepting a job on her behalf.

"The condo? Oh yes, dear niece, I'm led to believe within the week." Gabby quickly shoved an uncharacteristic enormous piece of cake into her mouth.

Amused at the tactic to discourage any further condo talk, Lacey pressed on. "Guess that means your extended visit is coming to a close in a few days. Do you need any help with making plans for your return trip? Because I'd be happy to get online and see what flights are available?" Lacey loved her aunt dearly, but the thought of having the cottage to herself caused her spirit to soar. Of course, she'd welcome Gabby back for another visit way on down the road.

"Umm…no help required. I'm not planning on rushing back to Florida when the heat of summer is upon us down there. I simply can't abide the sultriness, you know, and besides, I'm inclined to admit to a growing fondness with our little Divine. Quite fond," she added before taking in another bite the size of the plum sitting in the basket centerpiece. Whipped cream from the dessert made a mustache above Gabby's upper lip, which added nothing to sweeten the words that had just left her mouth.

Lacey paused to gather her wits, feeling her brief interlude with calmness ebbing away. "Aunt, I don't think I'd exactly call your return a rush back. You've been with me for—"

"Oh yes, I see where your thoughts have taken you, precious," she quickly interjected.

"I don't mean to infer that I haven't enjoyed your visit or appreciated the improvements you've made, but—"

"I know how much you needed me, Lacey, and I'm ever so pleased to have come to your aid in your hour of need. Your dearly departed parents would expect me to look after you as I have tried to do over the last years. And since you've secured a job of sorts with Serene, I suppose I'm worry-free now and able to share my special news." Gabby looked at the amount of shortcake she'd devoured and frowned.

"News? You have more to tell me?" Lacey sat on her hands in case this latest tale might provoke an uncharacteristic reaction.

"Yes, I certainly do. Are you ready to hear my most thrilling adventure to date?" Gabby's voice notched up with her excitement. She clasped her hands with glee as her eyes danced like sparklers on the Fourth of July.

"Ready as ever." Lacey heard the quiver in her voice. Her aunt's animated state only escalated her concern. *This must be a doozy to get her this amped up*, she thought. Her night of peace and serenity had not lasted long before the next Gabby announcement came calling.

Gabby settled in her chair and took in a breath, building the suspense. "I've contracted to buy the Amethyst Inn."

"That darling Bed and Breakfast a few blocks away?" Lacey exclaimed in total surprise. "I didn't know it was for sale." Serene's earlier cryptic words came rushing back. *Of course, Serene's in on this*, Lacey surmised.

"The very one. Let me share how this was meant to be. This is just so fortuitous. So, I mentioned to Serene the other day how I simply hated to leave Divine. You already know how smitten I've become with the mountain life and my new friends."

Lacey nodded and took a sip of water to cool her inside.

"To continue, I asked Serene if she knew of any properties in town that might be a fit for someone of my taste." Gabby paused to observe her niece's reaction.

"Do go on, Aunt. Don't leave out a word." Lacey encouraged. She wanted plenty of ammunition to kill Serene if this meant Gabby was doing another renovation. "Go on, please."

"Delighted, I'm sure. I can already see how thrilled you are. So, where was I?" she asked, relishing the attention.

"Serene to the rescue," Lacey supplied with a heavy dose of sarcasm that no doubt Gabby missed.

"Yes, well, that Serene is really so clever. How does she do it? You see, I had my mind made up to purchase a darling cottage somewhere close to you so that we might continue our little meal sharing, etc. I wanted to surprise you, don't you know? But our Serene proposed a totally different direction that I must admit suits perfectly."

"The Amethyst Inn," Lacey answered, still hanging on to her mounting concern that her aunt's stay with her would surely be drawn out into infinity.

"Yes, and here's the perfect part. The adorable inn allows me to extend my hospitality and social graces to others visiting our Divine. I'm so needed here. Serene explained this all so well, something to the effect of how I can best use my talents. Yes, I think that's how she said it. Like I said before, she's such a clever girl, not to mention so helpful."

"Yes, Serene's good at helping." Lacey bit her tongue to avoid adding more that she might regret later.

"Serene said that owning a B&B provides me everything for happiness here. I'd have people to care for during their brief sojourns. I'll even have Jane Ann's delectable sweets to help with the breakfast menu, and I can keep the housekeeper, which frees me from the mundane tasks. And of course, I can remain close to you, which I know is so vital as a devoted aunt."

"Yes, most vital." Lacey couldn't ignore her mind's clamoring for attention. Her world went from one topsy-turvy moment to another.

How would she ever find balance? Well, at least, she made creating her meditation space a priority and had ordered the perfect little altar online. She'd even found and dedicated a place in her den for her Divining Portal. Hearing Gabby's voice a pitch higher in excitement brought Lacey back.

"Also, there's the monetary gain to my savings, which is a bonus I can't ignore. And I'd get to remain in Divine doing my part to help our little village prosper. Yes, Serene convinced me the inn is ideal, and upon touring the place, I quickly agreed. The place so needs my touch."

"Wait, so you have a deal?" Lacey asked, admiring Serene's speed to solve problems.

"My, yes, I certainly do. I'm closing next week. Serene is handling every detail. No need for me to tarry once I make up my mind."

"Guess not." *No tarrying evident with this arrangement*, Lacey thought. *Still trying to take in the news, though*. She rallied, giving Gabby's hand a squeeze to show her support while anticipating her boarder remaining weeks longer.

"Now you must listen to this last piece of news, for I know it will take the smile from your face, dear one." Gabby covered her niece's hand with her free one. "I must move into the inn first thing tomorrow so that I can have the current proprietress show me the ropes, so to say. I know this is awfully abrupt and upsetting for you." Gabby frowned, showing distress.

Lacey's joy returned in spades. "Aunt Gabby, I admit this is all happening very fast indeed, but I'm so happy for you. How could I ever allow myself to be anything but encouraging and supportive of this new enterprise? Truly, I'm totally fine and understand your need to spend time right away at the Amethyst Inn." Lacey gave a genuine smile, realizing her friend had achieved the impossible yet again.

Serene had given Gabby a way to make Divine her home and be surrounded by people that cared for her. Lacey had picked up enough in conversation with her aunt to know her Miami friends were what she called surface friends, whereas the smallness of Divine cultivated deeper relationships faster because people depended on each other in a more day-to-day way. And Serene's blessed work meant Gabby would be sleeping blocks away by tomorrow evening. Paulie's new word, *jubilation*, came to her mind. "Aunt Gabby, this is just the best news. I'll have you close by and a beautiful inn to visit."

"You are such a dream to take my departure so well. I'm leaving you a few projects that I'd planned to do, but you'll be able to carry on, won't you? After all, I'll be close by and can run over to check out and approve things."

"I'll manage," Lacey said, hiding her mirth.

"Please promise me you won't neglect my bedroom once you start earning a proper income? You simply must mute that color scheme. I've lost count of the aspirins I've swallowed since my arrival. Why, just last week, Charlie rang up another bottle for me inquiring, the dear man he is, about the source of my suffering so." Gabby looked up, her eyes dancing with merriment.

"Aunt Gabby, I promise I'll make that room a priority," Lacey said, amused.

Topaz sauntered by without glaring at Gabby. A first. Even the cat sensed a positive vibe in the air.

"I've more," offered Gabby.

"More? I'm not sure I can take in more news." Lacey tensed yet again. The reaction had become a reflex.

"Yes, you know how close Petunia and I've become?"

Lacey nodded. She held out a finger with whipped cream for Topaz to lick.

"Well, of course, I shared my news with her this afternoon while you were away. I'd promised to work at the boutique another two weeks, but now with me becoming an innkeeper, I had to let her know."

"I'm sure Petunia was thrilled and understanding of your need to devote time to the inn," Lacey offered.

"Yes, she's such a dear—"

"Aunt Gabby, sorry to interrupt, but what will you do now with your condo? You've spent all of this time, money and energy, to get it exactly the way you wanted."

"That's the more I was getting ready to share. You must listen to how I've achieved my perfection yet again. Petunia and I are going to close our establishments January through March each year to winter at my Florida place. I've oodles of room, and best of all, she's simply elated with my idea." Gabby paused to think. "Dearest, can you manage three months without me? It will fly by. You'll see."

Lacey smiled. "Not a problem, Aunt Gabby. I adore your winter plan. Truly it's the best of all worlds for you and Petunia."

"I think so too. Your cousins can certainly make use of the condo the rest of the year. You know how they like their little getaways. Everything is just so sublime." Gabby beamed with a renewed sense of life. "Goodness, that must be Fred's truck pulling in."

Lacey grabbed the phone before Fred's truck had departed from the curb with Gabby.

Serene answered on the first ring. "Serene here."

"I'm buying you a Percolator Coffee House gift card, and I just wanted you to know."

"I never turn down gifts, especially coffee ones. Should I ask why?"

"Aunt Gabby just filled me in on her news, and I've just one question."

"Which is?"

"Why in the name of all that's sane didn't you propose she buy the Amethyst Inn weeks ago? You could have spared me untold stress," Lacey chided her best friend.

"Because your gratitude wouldn't have been the magnitude it is now."

"I'm so happy to have my cottage to myself after tomorrow that I'm going to let your first remark slide."

"Excuse me, Lacey. Be right there," Serene hollered.

"You've got company? I should let you go. Wait a minute. Who's there?" Lacey goaded, not really needing an answer.

"Yes, yes, and not tellin'. Talk to you tomorrow."

Lacey turned and caught sight of a new addition perched on her end table. A photo of Aunt Gabby posed in the cottage garden stared back. She chuckled at her aunt's latest tactic to imprint a piece of herself with Lacey.

Chapter 39

Lacey spent the next morning helping her aunt pack her belongings in the same suitcases that brought Gabby to her door. It seemed her aunt had enjoyed shopping more than she imagined. Lacey eyed the stack of apparel on the bed and the overflowing luggage, which was unable to accept another item, even a scarf.

"Aunt Gabby, I think I've got some empty cartons in the utility room. We're going to need at least three to get all of your additional things over to the Amethyst Inn," Lacey stated, pointing to the piles staring back at them.

"Just wrap them up in that hideous quilt, dear girl. I will dispose of that rag myself for you." Gabby threatened with her voice just a tiny bit serious. She really did detest the vile thing.

Lacey shot her aunt a look, only to see the teasing wink delivered by Gabby. "Aha! Funny jab." They were both in excellent spirits, embracing this happy turn of events.

"The FDA needs to put a warning on that coverlet. I swear I'll report its existence if you don't promise me—"

"I promise already. Gosh, I feel the beginning of a headache with this chatter about my —"

"See, it's affecting you now spending time in here. You've no idea how I've suffered in this room and how I have tried to keep silent." Gabby put her hand to her brow.

With that, both women erupted into laughter. This was Gabby's way of acknowledging how dreadful her behavior those early days with Lacey had been. They'd both done considerable mellowing, but the essence of each remained intact. They were strong-principled women from different eras.

"Lacey, I know that I can be a tad trying, but also know I love you dearly, Niece, and I thank you for tolerating me. I've tried to compensate you in my own little way. Being here in Divine with you has shown me that I still have some life in me after all and that I'm capable of changing my view of the world a little bit too."

"Aunt Gabby, you're so welcome. I'm glad Divine has brought you happiness. It'll be grand having you share in my life, so I must thank you back for what you've given to me." Tears stung her eyes. Lacey never dreamed that she'd be capable of uttering such words to her aunt and mean every one.

Gabby turned to dab her own eyes with a tissue. She cleared her throat and moved to the dresser. "Very well, fetch me one of those cardboard boxes. I suppose my fine things can ride a few blocks in such conditions," she added.

Topaz entered Gabby's room, offered a loud meow, and settled on top of Gabby's suitcase as if to stamp his approval on her departure.

"Get out of here, you loathsome creature. Give me my last minutes here without depositing your fur on my personal things. And whilst you're about, return my makeup sponges and brushes you've been pilfering, you wretched beast."

Lacey entered the bedroom with boxes. "You'll miss each other," Lacey interjected. "Maybe you'd like a mouser for the inn."

"Don't you dare give that idea another millisecond of thought."

Lacey grinned back. She lifted Topaz to the window seat and carried the suitcases outside to her SUV.

Chapter 40

Lacey showed up at Old Mountain Cassie's earlier than she was expected. She felt like a young college student who'd just declared a major that would hopefully carry her into a fulfilling life. Did she believe this inner voice who spoke to her about promise when applying The Three Lessons? Was God's hand touching her in some profound way through Cassie? And why now? Cassie interrupted the musings of her intellectual self.

"Mornin', Miss Lacey. You caught me tendin' some early okra," Cassie explained, appearing at Lacey's side. "Do you like fried okra?" Old Mountain Cassie smiled to add to her welcome. Her dirt-smudged overalls showed she'd gotten to her garden early.

"Morning back, Cassie. I'm early. As for the okra offer, I'm afraid okra and I haven't been successful at making friends."

"I admit okra's charm can be a might skittish. I've got some cukes that might agree to pickin' if you'd like some of them."

"I'm a taker," said Lacey, feeling joy once again in the mountain woman's presence. She adored Cassie's endearing manner of speech. She wondered about Cassie's level of education but dismissed the thought, recognizing the mischief it was meant to cause.

"Well, okay then. It'll make those cukes happy to sit on a new plate in town."

Lacey relished Cassie's energy and take on life, even a vegetable's life. "Here, I brought lunch." Lacey handed a small cooler to Cassie.

"Ah, you didn't need to bring us lunch again, but I accept. Mighty curious, what's in this?"

"Assorted cheeses, fruits, also spinach and sundried tomato Spelt bread. Doesn't that sound tasty?"

"What do you say we eat early this time? I can taste that bread already," Cassie said, smacking her lips.

Old Mountain Cassie sauntered to the nearby garden and picked a few cucumbers while Lacey tagged behind. "Go ahead and put these in your backpack."

"Thanks. I almost forgot the best part of lunch. Dessert is dark rum chocolate torte."

"Whoeeeeee," sang out Cassie. "I feel good and spoiled."

"Exactly my thoughts when I stood drooling over the bakery sweets display. So, what are we going to be doing today, if you don't mind my asking?"

Cassie liked that her Seeker felt excitement and wonder. "We'll get to that lesson when we're led, but don't you have news about your aunt? Not long ago, you tore out of here like the roadrunner. Satisfy my nosy nature, if you don't mind." Old Mountain Cassie returned to her favorite chair by the wishing well.

Lacey wasted no time detailing to Cassie how she maneuvered herself out of a plumbing job and, more, Gabby's big news about buying the inn. "You're all caught up on the latest doings at my cottage. Never humdrum anymore," added Lacey.

Cassie noticed her niece's frustration seemed to be evaporating in the recounting. She'd just garnered the information needed for fine-tuning the day's teaching. She only had to wait for a sign given to her by those souls crossed over to proceed. It would come.

Cassie turned to face her Seeker directly. "Things sound chipper between you two now. Breathing space is powerful and important among family folk. Now I'm itchin' to ask, have you found a place for your divinin'?" Cassie wanted to punctuate the importance of Lacey's joining with God and the Others so The Lessons could soon start delivering on their promise.

"I absolutely have been most intentional on that assignment. Bet you'll be pleased to hear I ordered a small altar and a floor cushion that will be just perfect. I've got a Japanese screen left to me by my parents that I already placed in a corner of my den. That's going to be my Divining Place. I'm eager to be with God and the ones on the Other Side whenever they are sent my way."

"Your divinin' space will be pouring lots of joy on you. You're settin' things in motion. Just you wait."

Lacey continued, "I found a shop in a nearby town that caters to spiritual practice. Thought I'd see if my Spirit Self bonds with anything there. What's next for us today?"

Cassie's spirit felt the urge to begin the teaching. Time to bring another dosin' of wisdom to her Seeker. "How about we try buildin' on your accomplishments? Would you be open to me floatin' some 'freshies' by you?"

"Freshies?" responded Lacey.

"That's what I like to call new notions."

Lacey got comfortable in the chair, ignoring her tight muscles. She positioned her hands to rest gently in her lap and took in some clean mountain air.

Old Mountain Cassie noted the desired change come to her practicing Seeker. "Well done. Now, let's see about getting you a bit further on your inner journey and watch what freshie shows up. Take a look around you again and find your pretty spot. Take your time," Cassie reminded.

Lacey's eyes cast a gentle glance at her surroundings, not sure what made for a 'pretty spot' when so much of Cassie's land looked like a light-filled Monet painting. She noticed the sun's ray shining on an area a few yards away with singular brightness. Lacey turned her gaze fully in that direction.

The mountain sage nodded again, pleased her Seeker could tune into the light shifts meant to draw her in. She waited, saying nothing. Words became incidental and unappreciated. Cassie sensed a happening, the one she'd been cued to expect from her Guides.

Lacey felt her body revving to an unusual higher frequency as if she was tuning a radio from an AM station with all its static to a more clear-sounding FM station. A pleasant tingling moved through her as the light danced around a trio of camellias. A shimmer of silver particles began to shape into an image. Lacey breathed deeper in an attempt to relax her mind, fighting to engage her with its typical sabotaging chatter.

Seconds ceased to count as Lacey became fully focused on the visual experience unfolding. The particles continued slowly to fill in the shape of a person. Lacey's mind raced to explain. She ignored its rant, telling her to stop the imaginings. Her rudeness to the thoughts intensified as the silhouette grew. She didn't care if she was losing it. Her body felt more enlivened than any time in her life.

The image shimmered, growing in energy vibration until a woman's face appeared. The rest of the body filled in as if someone was pouring liquid into a mold. The image stood beaming a smile toward Lacey, waiting for recognition. Short blond curls framed a woman's face, and the body was draped in an iridescent violet robe.

Cassie remained quiet, eyes darting from the figure to her niece.

Lacey watched as the woman raised a hand to show Lacey an object. In that moment, Lacey knew without a doubt that she was staring at her departed grandmother. "Nene," she called the name she'd given to her grandmother as a toddler. Tears puddled in her eyes.

Her grandmother held up the cherished ragdoll that had once been hers and later "loved out" by Lacey.

A stunned Lacey acknowledged the remembrance of the shared dolly by having her fingers shape the four letters to spell out the doll's name…Cass. Cass, short for Cassandra…Cassie? Confusion danced in Lacey's mind.

Memories refreshed her love for Nene. Even though they'd shared only a few years together, Nene had crammed a lot of love into her granddaughter before she'd left her long illness behind. Love that Lacey carried with her each day. Love that had gone into molding her into the woman she was this day. Her Nene. Here right now. Impossible. Unbelievable.

The light around her grandmother flickered as Nene's left arm gestured in Cassie's direction, signaling an introduction.

Lacey glanced quickly at Cassie and witnessed a personal exchange between the two women. Did they know each other?

Nene's past had never been spoken of to her, but then she was only nine when her grandmother had passed. Maybe it was common for Cassie to have this type of spiritual experience, and so they were simply acknowledging this phenomenon. No, no. There's got to be more. The shared names...

Nene turned her attention back to Lacey.

Lacey whispered, "I love you, my Nene," and clasped her hands to her heart.

Violet took one final look at her cherished granddaughter. Her smile angelic, she blew Lacey a kiss good-bye.

Lacey felt the kiss touch her cheek. She blinked to clear her vision, and the three camellias stood alone. Lacey sat quietly with the myriad of thoughts and feelings coming into her consciousness. Where did she begin to process this whole experience...or anything else that had been happening since losing her job? She'd just spent precious moments in the presence of her departed grandmother. Hadn't she?

Chapter 41

Lacey's questions bubbled inside of her. "Oh my. I need some help here. Cassie, I have lots of puzzle pieces, and I trust they fit together somehow. I mean, my grandmother just appeared here, and I don't understand how or why. I know people who have been visited by deceased loved ones, so I'm sorta accepting these things happen, but…"

"Listen, we need to put aside for the moment the blessin' of you seein' your grandmother. First, I need you to remember that much of what you experience on my land is due in part to that special energy, which is God's divine breath."

"The Divine's breath in Divine." Lacey's mind remained thankfully mute while her spirit quickened with the connection. "Yes, I've surely witnessed your place is…enchanted," Lacey said, drawing on her word to describe anything around Cassie.

"Yes, and that liveliness you observe in my plants, herbs, flowers, butterflies is thrivin' because of that specialness. I can tell you this is so, but I can't explain how it's so. It's God's creation. His work."

"You take it on faith then?" Lacey asked.

"Yes, I do, and I know other places on earth have the same Divine breath manifestin' up all kinds of amazement for those able to see. To see means your senses are calibrated to witness the majesty as I like to call it. You, Missy, are a Seeker awakenin' those senses. For you, this will become natural. Your body ratchets up to match the frequency of the plants and flowers showin' off, the animals feeling safe around you. But the most powerful connectin' of all happens with you and the gems. They speak your language, just as the herbs, fauna, and critters chatter to me." Cassie paused. "Still with me?"

Lacey managed a nod.

"Well, let's see, so my herbs, plants, and I have our special relationship…no more of a partnership. Yes, I like the sound of that better. We're workin' together to create teas and such to help others who don't have the awareness or ability to do it on their own. You see, they need the teas' help to be better, but better in different ways, I mean."

"Can you maybe give an example? I'm trying to grasp the concepts."

Cassie paused. "Take it like this. In my kitchen, I have my herbs all jarred up with labels sayin' what they're about. Right?"

"Yes." Lacey relaxed.

"And while you aren't adept at growin' herbs gifted with God's breath, you're able to know which jar has the tea your spirit is longin' for, yes?"

"Most times, I guess. And if not, someone seems to always show up in my life to reflect back how I'm being." Lacey smiled, thinking of Serene's and Paulie's gifts. She'd need to give more thought about them another day. Similarities were surfacing in her consciousness that somehow felt comforting and confounding.

"Aren't you ready to serve now too?"

"I think so, yes." Lacey caught Cassie's last sentence.

"Good. Takin' you to my plant shed was a means to get you that extra dose of understandin' needed for this very day. I'm going to speak more about me and my herbs. You already know I grow my herbs in service of others. Understand, Lacey, my job is to help the plants to grow and serve. My gifts are seeded there if you get my meanin'. I simply take the special seeds handed down to me by others in my family and, with God's blessin', tend and send them out to help. So, you see how I throw light upon my gifts and use them. You as a Seeker came in search of your own gifts. You were drawn to me and didn't much question that pull, just kept searchin' and hopin' for us to meet, right?"

"Yes, it's like I told you, I felt compelled to find you for some reason I didn't fully understand then. Now, I'm beginning to grasp the significance, and I suspect even this whole unique gift thing."

"Good. You arrived with the wonder of being led by inner desire, and of course, we can't forget God's critters helpin'." Cassie grinned. "You've had two life lessons. The first bein' you must have the desire to know God and your Spirit Self in a deeper way. The second lesson is you must garner the knowledge of how to enjoy this relationship with Him and His helpers by gettin' into a portal. You grow that understandin', and in a little more time, Lesson Three will ask for your attention. Got all that?"

"I think so. I've been living in my journal and meditating daily and, of course, praying. I'm truly and humbly seeking and want to have God active in my life."

Cassie nodded, indicating her approval. "What say we take us one of those lunch breaks and enjoy the victuals you brought? I expect you know I've more to share about your Nene, and I just might give you a hint about the potent Lesson Three comin' down the pike."

Chapter 42

THE SUN DECIDED TO WARM the day enough for the two women to seek a shady spot on Cassie's porch. The sunflower-yellow-painted wood swing called to Lacey while Cassie's cherished rocking chair invited her.

"After that tasty refreshin' lunch, think I'll jump back into a bit more explainin' and expandin'. You willin'?"

"To be honest, I'd welcome some explaining for sure." Lacey took a breath, preparing to enter the state of awe…again.

"I'm gonna say somethin' that might sound an alarm in your noggin. Just hear the words and try not to judge them." Cassie paused. "I knew you'd be comin' to see me."

Lacey's mouth gaped, while her mind struggled to take in Cassie's words.

"Stop that, Missy. Don't let your mind interfere by placin' fear and doubt in our way."

Lacey grabbed a breath. "Okay," she said with a short exhale. "I'm trying, Cassie, but this visit by Nene, along with other things, are adding up in my book to be pretty out of the ordinary. I mean, I can handle birds and squirrels coming on to me, but you saying you've been expecting me and my dead grandmother stopping by for a visit to your place…well…"

"You just relax and hold to that trust of Old Mountain Cassie like you promised. We still have some more astoundin' things to share. Plenty more."

Lacey obeyed and unclenched her hands. She ignored the thoughts racing around in her head, choosing instead to focus on the sage…who'd been waiting for her arrival.

"I knew you'd be comin' because I too get signs and visits every now and again. I saw what you saw a while ago, but here's the important part. I interpreted the experience differently. Bet you wanna know why."

"Why?"

"Because we each have a relationship with who showed up."

"We do?" Lacey's voice squeaked. She picked up a hand fan from the nearby table. "You have a relationship with my deceased grandmother?" Lacey questioned, coming back to the present.

"Yes, ma'am. I know your grandmother pretty well. She came to visit us today so that you might be acceptin' of what I have to reveal. Make ready, for I'm about to flabbergast you with a surprise that I sincerely hope will please you as much as it pleases me."

Lacey laid the fan next to her, noticing her hands trembling. She waited for Cassie's next words.

"Your grandmother…Violet…is my older sister." Cassie's mouth closed around the last word as if to seal the truth.

"What? No. Are you serious? Oh my gosh! How can that be?" Lacey shook her head in disbelief. She grew quiet, allowing her thoughts free rein. At the moment, she welcomed her mind's chatter. "I knew my mother's side of the family had some roots somewhere around this area." Lacey's mind worked to accept this revelation.

"We surely do enjoy some roots, Missy. Deep ones." Cassie looked forward to elaborating on their heritage down the road. She watched Lacey continue processing the news.

"And the doll named Cass added to my perplexity today. Yes, I see now clues had been dropped in my lap, but I really hadn't put them together because it seemed irrational to do so," Lacey said, recognizing the truth of her words. She paused as Cassie's bombshell washed over her again. "Wait a minute…holy smokes! Cassie, that makes you my—"

"Great aunt," Cassie finished, eyes glistening. "Can you handle another aunt?"

"You and I are related? Family?" Lacey asked, ignoring Cassie's question. She was hanging back, digesting the pronouncement one more time. "My grandmother came visiting to help prepare me for this revelation. I can't believe this. Maybe I'm dreaming, and I'll wake up with Topaz hungry and Aunt Gabby refusing to feed him like always."

"You're awakenin' all right, Niece, but not in the way you mean." Cassie hinted.

"Wait a minute, just how long have you known about me? I mean that I moved to Divine and all." Lacey tossed out the question, not sure she wanted the answer.

"Let's see, how should I answer you?" Cassie looked closely at Lacey's confused expression. "I've known of your existence since shortly after your birth. Families may be fractured, but news makes its way around nevertheless. As for when I found out you were livin' nearby? Well, that's my own funny like story." Cassie gave a chuckle.

"Tell me. You must tell me," Lacey exclaimed. "It's good to hear that I'm not the only one getting hit with shocks."

"Okay, well, a few months back, I happened to be in Mercer's Mercantile and overheard Frank tell his wife a special order for Lacey Jordan had come in. I stood there not believin' my ears, let me tell you. I felt plumb bowled over, but I knew God had the powers to accomplish much."

"Boy, can I relate. What did you think and do?"

"Oh, I got me some kind of clever. I saw your order on the counter, so I trotted over to Frank and asked who had the good taste to order such a fine pair of hikers."

"You're a riot, Cassie. Go on."

"Well, he told me a cute sassy thing with the prettiest aqua color eyes had moved here a while back." Cassie batted her matching ones toward her niece, grinning. "Of course, his wife filled in a lot of blanks by comin' over and talkin' about your job and all. I felt pretty sure my great-niece had found her way home and brought her own unique gift to be unwrapped too."

"Beyond belief," Lacey added. "And you didn't want to look me up…introduce yourself?"

"Sure I did, but then I was told in my Divinin' Portal that I best sit tight and let you find me. I already knew you had a talent that needed refinin' and that just maybe you would become my next Seeker. I waited to be led and guided, relying on my lessons like I've taught you to do." Cassie patted her niece's hand.

"I get your meaning, Cassie." Lacey laughed.

"Gal, you gotta know ever since you found me, I've been bustin' to tell you everything. Never had to work so hard to watch my yapper." Cassie's hands covered her mouth for effect.

"Hmm…so should I assume you've got more secrets tucked away that you can't divulge?" Lacey leaned over and gave a little tug to Cassie's cap to show her teasing.

"Who? Me?" Cassie flipped her braid over her shoulder, acting coy. "Look here, Niece, from this point forward, The Three Lessons will take you to understandin' God's ways of caring for us. Like I been sayin', we will be workin' the last one directly. Enough said." Cassie leaned back in her chair, catching sight of a hawk flying magnificently overhead.

"Cryptic but definitely comforting." Lacey couldn't help feeling like she'd journeyed into a wormhole.

Cassie took a breath, getting more direction. "What do you think about having me take a side trip and tell you more about Nene and our family? I have some family photos to share some other time. Anyways, kinda gives glue to our bondin' as aunt and niece."

"I'd love that, Cassie. Lacey pulled her sunglasses over her eyes and stretched out in the swing, ready to receive more."

Cassie spent the next hour detailing the family tree and explaining their family's gifts and talents.

"I understand so much more now, and especially this impulse that kept shooing me your way. And it's really cool how you've got the gift with the herbs from your father's side of the family and Violet, the special connection with gems coming from your mother's line, which, clearly, I've inherited. The difference is, I long to tune into the stone's frequency, develop a grand relationship with them, but never had anyone to show or support me…until now." Lacey beamed a smile as bright as the sun reflecting in the nearby stream.

"You're right about my sister and your mama too. Their free will took them on a path of not living fully in the creation. It was their choice. However, Violet's visit today served to show us both that by golly, she's workin' with her gifts from the Other Side to help you. Don't you reckon, Missy?"

"I'd reckon we've got some serious proof of that fact." The corner of Lacey's mouth turned up.

"Niece, I'm a might tuckered. I think we'll call today's accomplishments most satisfactory. Let's enjoy a saunter back to your vehicle. I will send you home anticipatin' that next lesson on how to live with time."

"Hmm, with time? Guess that's my hint, and anticipating I shall be." Lacey gave a lingering hug to the woman known to all as Old Mountain Cassie, but to Lacey now…as Aunt Cassie.

Chapter 43

SERENE SPENT THE NEXT MORNING helping Lacey get familiar with the office and detailing what she needed assistance with first. The two wasted no time finding their rhythm and assessing what tasks Lacey would enjoy most over the next couple of weeks.

"So, then after lunch, you can go snap some photos and take a few measurements for me of an interesting building here in town. Then you can organize the mail-out postcard project. That's where your creativity and love for all things color can soar," said Serene, feeling happy to have her friend to brainstorm ideas for the coming selling season.

Serene, if it's okay, I'd like to make my own list of to-dos before I leave," Lacey replied. "Actually, I've got a few design ideas for the postcards already rattling around in my head. It'll be fun." Lacey's felt glad to be productive once more. The bonus was helping her truly unselfish friend who'd done so much for her. Lacey counted another blessing. Her spiritual study time was illuminating what a wonderful Senior Partner she had working on her behalf. She kept wondering what Cassie's Lesson Three hint meant about living with time.

The building was to be a silent listing for the first week on the market. Serene would have the property for sale, but there would be no sign or advertisement declaring it. The seller had strict criteria on the way he wanted the listing handled and what type of enterprise he'd agree to occupy the space. According to Serene, his vision for Divine was that any new businesses must stay true to the town's heart and soul, and if someone had to ask what that meant, they weren't the one.

Lacey glanced at the address to be sure she was heading in the right direction. Serene had acted vague about the place when giving information about the listing particulars. *Oh well*, Lacey thought, *she's got her reasons. Real estate agents have to keep tight-lipped. All that confidential experience sure served Serene well when it came to chatting about Paulie.* Lacey chuckled to herself.

She spoke to a few of Divine's residents as she continued down the sidewalk. Lacey noticed traffic had picked up as the tourists and summer residents returned.

"Well, good morning, Ms. Lacey. Nice to see you decorating our little village's sidewalk this fine day," Mayor Morgan exclaimed, already working for re-election still a year out.

"Good to see you too, Mayor." Lacey kept walking. She didn't relish the idea of being grilled about what she might be up to with a camera dangling from her neck. She could keep a silent listing quiet too.

Spying Jane Ann unloading baked goods at Charlie's store entrance, Lacey quickly ducked inside Petunia's shop. *Serene must have a time navigating Divine's streets with her top secret real estate doings*, Lacey surmised.

Petunia looked up from totaling her sales tickets, offering a knowing grin. "Morning, Lacey. Just out of curiosity, who are you avoiding out there?"

"Jane Ann. Shhh." She placed her fingers to her lips, afraid an unseen customer might hear their exchange.

"A wise move. Glad that I was here for the rescue." Petunia shook her head, amused, as Lacey exited in safety.

Chapter 44

WHILE LACEY WAS DODGING A savvy and astute Jane Ann, Cassie was in the city catching up with her old beau again over another lunch. Today Branson had sweet-talked her into trying a Middle Eastern restaurant called Ali Kabob's. He'd surprised her at seven o'clock that morning with a phone call announcing a desire to lay eyes on her.

She'd congratulated herself in leaving the overalls in the closet and instead choosing a pair of black jeans, a pale blue blouse, and a printed vest. She wore smokey topaz earrings and a simple gold chain. All of this represented what she called her dressed-up look, and anyone in her acquaintance could count on one hand the times they'd seen her gussy up to look feminine. She'd done a fair job that morning convincing herself the extra effort on her appearance was to please her and had zip to do with seeing Branson's face, which was now smiling and locked on her a few yards away.

As usual, he'd chosen a table by the window. Cassie moseyed over to him. "You'd better not have lied to me about this place havin' taters and veggies," Cassie said as she bent down and rewarded him with a peck on the cheek.

"Ah, darling, it's good to hear that bossy voice again," Branson replied, looking up at the woman who would forever hold his heart.

"Bossy? I'll have you know I'm nowhere near bossy, you ole coot." Cassie took her seat before he could rise and do the gentlemanly act of assisting.

"You're right, Cass. I'll just say you have some strong preferences," Branson corrected.

Cassie cut him a wide grin. "Now you've got me pegged proper. Hand me that menu since you clearly plan to ogle me a bit." She reached over to snag the menu. No way were her readers coming out. She'd have to squint to find her vegetables.

"Yes, ma'am, ogling you is one of my favorite pastimes that I never seem to get enough of." He watched Cassie's discerning eyes narrow to make out the fare listed. He grinned, amused that her vanity still held her captive. "Umm, Cass?"

"What?" she answered, a tad too curtly even to her ears.

"Try turning the menu over." He reached across the table and gently righted the menu.

"That is better. I thought it must be written in Farsi or something." Cassie's dimples appeared to be mirroring her mood. The rascal had already bested her, and she'd not been in his company five minutes.

"How about trusting me to order? Here's the waiter now," Branson informed.

"Okay, if you promise no mutton meat."

"Promise, darling. I haven't forgotten your dislikes, not one of them." Branson reminded her with devilment in his expression.

"Ready, sir?" the tall, olive-skinned waiter asked with his heavy accent.

"My lady and I will have pungent potatoes, stuffed grape leaves, a green salad, and hummus with pita squares," Branson ordered, never taking his eyes from Cassie's.

"Very good, sir. And to drink?"

"I'd like hot tea," Cassie piped up.

"Tea for two," Branson quipped, handing the menu to the waiter.

"I don't think he got your little joke." Cassie laid her napkin in her lap.

"He's too young and probably new to our country to boot. Hey, have I told you how lovely you're looking this day? Tell me, darlin', did you go to that trouble for me?"

"Are you daft? Don't you know we women dress to please ourselves?" She met Branson's eyes.

"Well, that may be, but you've managed to please me also. You're still enticing as ever. When you going to give in and marry me, Cass?"

"The day you stay your fanny in Divine. Ha. There. You've got an answer. That should shut that Irish blarney."

The waiter returned with the tea and salads, which gave them both a moment to digest the words that hung in the air over them.

"Cassie?" Branson whispered with a question.

The quiet gentle way he spoke her name snapped Cassie's head to attention. "Branson?" The sassiness had evaporated, leaving her without her protective shield.

"Did you mean what you said or—"

"Or was I pullin' your leg that won't let you settle any place longer than the moon's phase?" The words meant to let them both off the hook by returning her sass to the conversation. "I wanna talk about where you've been and where you're goin'."

"All right, for now, I'll slip you a pass, but one day—and it won't be long—you and I are going to pick up right where we left off a moment ago. And that, Cassie my girl, you can put in your corncob pipe and smoke." His eyes signaled to Cassie that he meant business.

"Guess we still got it, huh?"

"I always thought so." Branson teased. He knew full well what Cassie meant. They'd had years of fun slinging idioms.

"Where's the gypsy blood called you? Start the tellin'. I don't have all day," Cassie tossed back.

Branson obliged the love of his life with a recounting of his last trip and even produced some photographs to embellish his stories of seeing the Aztec ruins and hearing the myths as they savored a delicious lunch. Cassie put in her bid for a return visit to Ali Kabob's, which served as her seal of approval.

"I have to admit I do enjoy your sharin' of faraway places. Makes me feel like I'm there when I close my eyes." Cassie sat back in her chair, relaxing.

"And I've told you to come with me anytime I'm holding a suitcase." Branson reminded her.

Cassie ignored the invitation. "Where to next?"

"Actually, I'm considering a cruise to Jamaica."

"Why? You've done that as I recall."

"Good memory, darlin' Cass. This cruise is more a reconnaissance mission," he replied, setting the hook. He knew Cassie couldn't help her curious nature.

"You, old coot, settin' me up like that. Who are you spying on and why?"

"Come with me, and you'll know." Branson reached over and covered Cassie's hand with his own. "You can spare a week from those herbs and potions." He pleaded. One day, she'd say yes. He felt it deep in his core, and that's why he kept showing up with invitations.

"Remember, I've got a Seeker, a most special one, so no, I can't set sail Mr. Columbus and reconnoiter diddley squat. Thanks, all the same." Cassie set her own hook with some satisfaction.

"Of course…a new Seeker. Come on. Let's get out of here. I've got someplace else to take you for a good time. Who knows, maybe it will even loosen that tongue of yours to tell me about this special Seeker."

"And you just might hanker to tell me about your detectin', gumshoe," Cassie fired back, holding her ground.

"Truce…truce." Branson closed the car door on Cassie, blocking her reply. He loved the woman, Lord help him, but one of these days, he may be forced to shanghai her out of Divine, even if it was only for a week. The idea had merit. He leaned over and kissed her forehead and then settled in the driver's seat.

Chapter 45

Lacey scanned the sidewalk for possible interrogators and was relieved to see the coast clear. She hurried around the corner, finding a surprise. She checked the building number. Yes, this was the store.

She entered with her spirit filling every cell with unexpected joy. "Hello, Allison." Heart pounding, she moved toward the young woman in her late twenties standing behind a counter.

Allison's faded jeans and work shirt testified to her labors, and her smile showed genuine friendliness. "Hey there, Lacey, this is a perfect timing for your visit. Come on in. Serene called and told me to expect you."

"Oh, good, sorry I'm a few minutes late. You know how hard it can be to walk down a sidewalk in Divine without delays," Lacey explained. She hadn't really gotten to know Allison that well despite their shared interests. She wondered why Allison had decided to leave Divine.

The younger woman must have read her thoughts. "I bet your mind is trying to figure out why in the world I'd want to move away from our town, especially since my business and I have always been blessed here?" Allison grabbed another empty box.

"Yes, I couldn't help wondering that exact thing, but really, I don't want to pry."

"Oh, I think I can trust you if Serene sent you to me. It's like this, I have an opportunity to do something really fun and different, and I couldn't be more excited." Allison clasped her hands together, showing gratitude to the heavens above.

"I hear that excitement in your voice, and I'm truly happy—"

"I'll tell you," Allison said, interrupting and moving closer to where Lacey stood. "I've contracted with a cruise ship to manage their premier jewelry store. You see, I've always had the wanderlust but never the pocketbook to allow it. Now I can see places I've only dreamed of and still use my jeweler skills and talents. Isn't that just so cool? Clearly, God's hand is on this opportunity."

"I agree. Allison, that's way cool and a lot synchronistic, I must say. Isn't it great when things fall into place?" Lacey felt happiness for the young woman discovering her path and prayed hers would be shown soon too.

Allison grew quiet and thoughtful staring at Lacey. "Speaking of synchronistic, I just had the most glorious idea pop into my head. Want to hear it? It concerns you."

"Me?" Lacey's voice raised an octave along with her pulse. She glanced around at the near empty display cases.

"Get ready for this. How about you buy the building? You make this place yours and craft your original jewelry pieces right here. You have the talent. It's perfect timing. Besides, Serene said you'd been laid off recently, and I'm vacating the end of the month. I've sold most all my inventory to the shop over in Highlands, so you can have what's left, like my workstation here, as my gift to you," Allison offered.

Lacey stood in the middle of the store, taking in Allison's proposal and generosity. Her Spirit Self grabbed hold of the hope. Could her devotion to her lessons already be gifting her with a path? Cassie had instructed her to pay attention to signs. This sign was looking like bright neon flashing her name, but how could she ever afford to buy the building, not to mention the expense of inventory? *Don't be foolish*, her mind quickly intervened. *How can you take such a risk? Get real and get a job, Lacey.*

"Lacey? Did I lose you, girlfriend?" Allison waved her hand in front of Lacey's face.

"Oh, sorry, my blasted mind took me on a short side trip."

"Ah, the mind. Don't you dare let it sabotage this idea, at least not yet," Allison instructed, showing her awareness of the mind's games.

Lacey gave a relieved smile. "Thanks for the reminder. I've been working on that exercise quite a bit lately. What were you saying again?"

"Actually, I was building on the idea of how you could make this place yours if you feel so inclined. I don't mean to pressure you in the least. I know Serene has someone out of town talking to her about the building."

"Really? So fast?"

"Yeah, it's some guy who wants to open a sign shop, and while not exactly what my uncle is envisioning, it doesn't violate my uncle's wishes. He's actually the owner. At any rate, somehow, I don't see a sign shop in here. Know what I mean?"

"I do understand the fitting part. Allison, I confess to loving your idea, but sadly, I don't see me financially able to purchase the building and start a new business." Lacey released a heavy sigh, her chastising mind picking up where it had left off.

"Listen, why don't you go over to the bank and speak with Elliot about a loan? He's super trustworthy and an excellent place to begin." Allison encouraged. She taped another box closed.

"Well, guess I could give it a try. No harm asking. Oh, Allison, you must know your shop has always captivated me with your south-facing bay window that's so inviting. There's such charm with your eclectic showcases and comfortable chairs. I'm sure your customers felt welcome here." Lacey held a box lid down while Allison sealed it.

"You're right about all of that and thank you. I will miss Divine something terrible, but hey, you can take the space and create the environment that reflects you. I know you can." Allison pointed to her heart. "I feel it here."

"I appreciate the vote and support." Lacey squeezed the young woman's hand.

"Why don't you do your measuring and take the photos? They'll be helpful later for you when you make your offer." Allison chuckled. "Listen, I've got to finish packing up some of the pieces in the back."

"No problem Allison. By all means continue with your packing." Lacey's thoughts shifted back to herself. Could that sly Serene be directing those special real estate brokering gifts her way?. "We'll see, Serene, if you're that good. We'll see," Lacey mumbled, trying to squash her growing excitement.

"Looks like you're done." Allison came over to where Lacey had taken the last reading on the tape.

"Yep, I think I have everything. Allison, thank you for sharing your idea and encouraging me to pursue this. I'm going to head over to the bank and see if I can catch Elliot before he goes to lunch. I'll be sure and tell Serene about our conversation. Is that okay by you?"

"Sounds super-duper to me. I'm here to help you in any way that I can. I'll even talk to my uncle and do a bit of cultivating, let's say. As I said, he's extremely particular about who gets to serve Divine. Oh, just one more thing, Lacey?" Allison walked over to Lacey.

"Yes?"

"I'm about to say something that I've never said, but it just popped into my head. I think it's meant for you."

"I'm listening."

"Take this one step and then wait, trusting the next one will show up." Allison shrugged.

"Got it and I understand." Lacey winked. "Be seeing you and big thanks again."

Lacey's feet carried her to the bank's entrance, while her mind scampered into the future. She realized as she stood outside the bank's large double glass doors her mind had hijacked her again. Lacey hoped she hadn't passed someone on the sidewalk without, at least, a hello.

She glanced down at her slacks and blouse with a frown. Not exactly business attire, but then Divine defined its own by a whole different set of rules. Lacey pushed through the door, trusting she was exactly where she needed to be, and her mind, well, it could go sit in the corner.

Lacey sat waiting outside Elliot's office for her turn, wondering what kind of crazy she'd become pondering a real estate loan. Her mind had come out of the corner.

Elliot approached. "Lacey? Is there something I might help you with today?"

Chapter 46

Branson pulled his black luxury sedan into a parking spot near the Arboretum's main building. "I thought you might enjoy visiting here this afternoon. The gardens, I understand, are in full bloom and glorious." His face shown genuine happiness to please the most incredible woman he'd ever known.

"Goodness me, you know how to turn a girl's head with flowers," Cassie responded, primping like a belle. "Are you up for a short hike on one of their nature trails later?" Cassie asked, returning to her natural state.

"That I am. Brought my hiking boots even. After all these years, I know my girl's likes pretty well."

"I'm goin' to ignore the 'my girl' chatter because you've scored a home run bringin' me here." Cassie teased. She reached for her tote bag and pulled out her hikers. "See? I'm a good Girl Scout. Always prepared."

"Well, get them on and let's go see some posies. By the way, there's also a show happening here today. Say you're my gal, and I'll escort you to that exhibit as well." Branson waved two tickets in front of Cassie's excited face as proof.

"I'll say I'm your fat mama if it means there's an exhibit inside that place," Cassie quipped. "Hurry up. Flowers are awaitin' me."

"Right behind you, Mama. Lead the way." How he loved Cassie's enthusiasm with nature. She glowed with vitality whenever she stood anywhere near flora and fauna.

Cassie gave a whoop when she spied the sign pointing to the orchid show. "Orchids! Did you know this was an orchid show? Of course, you did," Cassie answered her own question. She grabbed Bran's arm and pulled him down the hall.

"Slow down, my girl." He begged. "These orchids are here all day."

"Gracious me. Would you just look at this room full of beauty? I wonder if they'll have a Ghost Orchid on display. I've only seen pictures of them."

"Ghost Orchid you say?" Branson frowned at the name but didn't doubt Cassie's knowledge for a second.

"Yes, sir, that's their name. You know, Britain declared them extinct back in nineteen eighty-six, and lo and behold, there was a new sightin' of them over there in two thousand five. How about that?"

"Impressive, just like you with your smarts with flowers," Branson said, giving her the credit she deserved. The woman was mad for anything having a petal or a leaf. Branson looked over the list of orchids and their location on the information sheet handed out. His face broke into a grin. "Darlin', what's it worth if I trot you right over to see a Ghost Orchid?"

"Don't you tease me."

"What's it worth?" Branson waved the map.

"You, rascal, you're tryin' to take advantage of my inability to decipher maps and get my direction straight. Is there one here, really? Don't you dare mess with me." Cassie's dimples winked at her beau.

"Yes, ma'am, there most certainly is and just so happens a grand prize winner to boot. Give me a little kiss, and I'll have you gawking at that orchid in two shakes of a—"

Cassie stopped his word playing and flirting by standing up on her toes and planting a tender kiss on his lips. She felt color rise to her cheeks. "Shut your yap and get movin'. You've taken full advantage of my fondness for orchids today. A scoundrel, that's who you are, mister." Cassie latched on to Branson's arm, waiting to be led.

"Sticks and stones might break my bones, but names will never hurt me," Branson retorted, still engaged in their idiom game. He'd scored a proper kiss, and that would carry him for the afternoon. Over lunch he'd shared now that he was older, the lure of traveling the world felt a whole lot less enticing. Besides, he'd pretty much had his passport stamped in all the places his heart yearned for in the last decades.

Cassie gave him one of her "I caught you" squints. "How long are we gonna stand here while you're lost in those blasted thoughts? Which way now?"

Branson chose to ignore the reminder. "Let's see. Go left where that man in the tan shirt is holding the toddler's hand, and your delight will be waiting at the end of the aisle."

Cassie let go of his arm and, in a flash, positioned herself in front of the orchid she'd longed to see. Her appreciating eyes missed nothing of the blossom's beauty. "Really something," she murmured, in awe of the day's gifts to her.

Branson stood back, allowing her the solitude so necessary for her full enjoyment. He knew her ways and had an abiding respect for her talents. He was sorry she'd never accepted his proposal to add to her happiness. As long as he was standing on top of the grass, he vowed to keep pitching himself to the woman who claimed his heart so many years back. "Tell me, darlin', is that orchid as pretty as a picture or not?"

"Much more, Bran. Almost takes my breath plumb out of me. I could stand here all day communin' with this plant. I could, but then I'd miss paying my respects to all the other orchids that grew into this moment." Cassie backed away from the prize winner so that others could step forward.

"Well then, come on this way. I've got our route all figured out. If we turn this corner, we'll work our way backward to the beginning."

"Never did do things logically. No need to start now," Cassie gave a little chuckle as she followed him on the guided tour. "Tell me about this first row's show-offs."

Branson read to Cassie the history and other information written in the brochure that he felt would heighten her enjoyment of the exhibit. They spent the next hour weaving in and out of the rows. They declared a love for a different color of orchid and made a case for why their choice was superior to the others.

"Let's go. So happens I know the perfect trail for us. Won't be too hot either. Sun will be to our backs." This time, Cassie took the lead.

"Okay, I'm no chauvinist. You got the reins. I'm yours to do with as—"

"Hush up and drink the juice I just gave you," Cassie said, putting a stop to his flirting.

He opened his bottle cap and took a cool drink. "See how trainable I am?" He held up the bottle as proof.

"'Bout time you realized my teachin' skills. Just wait till I show off namin' the wildflowers for you."

They walked single file the few minutes it took to reach the trail Cassie had chosen. A short time later, Branson broke the tranquility; they'd each been enjoying outdoors away from the crowds.

He bent over and plucked a wild daisy growing along the edge of the path. "She loves me. She loves me not," he recited, pulling off one petal at a time. "She loves me. She loves me. She loves me." He teased, dropping three more petals.

"Shut up, you, and stop pickin' the flowers." Cassie, of course, knew he'd been working with a wildflower and not a planting. She hid her smile by turning away and doing the unexpected. She unbraided her long hair and let it fall down her back. Her heart felt as young as the fresh daisy Branson still clung to.

"She does love," he told the flower in a loud whisper meant for Cassie's ears. He threaded the stem through his shirt buttonhole. He didn't care if he looked silly sporting a daisy with only half the petals intact because each time Cass looked at him, she'd be reminded of his affection. "Yep, I agree. Flowers sure are powerful," he tossed over his shoulder, admiring her still lovely corn silk hair, which was now a silvery blond in the sunshine.

She glanced over at him to see what prompted his last remark. Seeing the daisy staring back, Cassie could only shake her head and cover her mouth with her hand to hide her expression of happiness. That man was never subtle in his messages or use of symbolism.

"Cassie, is there anything I can say that will convince you to take this trip with me? Anything at all? I'll buy you a truckload of those flowers and have them delivered tomorrow if you'll just agree for once." He closed the passenger door on her surprised face and left her with the moment to ponder his serious invitation.

She had her answer waiting when he joined her in the next seat. "I can't think of a thing that would entice me to set foot on a movin' deck, but thanks all the same." She patted his shoulder and then turned to look out the windshield at the male cardinal chirping his omen at her on the fence post. Her heart skipped a beat.

"You don't have a clue to the adventure you're missing with me, but I'll accept your no…at least for now." Branson maneuvered his vehicle smoothly through rush hour traffic, delivering Cassie to her waiting truck.

She glanced over at the man that had come in and out of her life for so many years and who somehow held her constant heart. "We had a good day. Enjoyable. Every moment," she said, delivering her thoughts in short bursts. Cassie saw the daisy still clinging to Branson's buttonhole.

He followed her eyes and, with a gentle hand, plucked the flower. He passed the posy over to her. "He loves you," he said softly.

"I know." Cassie leaned over and touched her lips to his. She slipped out and, with her straight back, walked to her truck, never looking back. She couldn't. The sound of the engine grew faint, telling her Branson had moved on…again.

Chapter 47

Elliot cleared files off the empty chair. "This is a nice surprise. I didn't expect to see you until the festival meeting tonight." Elliot motioned for Lacey to occupy the plaid wingback chair across from his desk.

"Gee, thanks for reminding me about the meeting." Lacey took a seat and pulled out her notebook and pen.

"Don't know if we'll ever agree on this summer's festival theme, but tonight's gathering should be plenty entertaining." Elliot smiled, already anticipating the lighthearted banter sure to make an appearance. Divine's folks were unique but with caring spirits. "So, what brings you to the loan side of the bank? I hope there isn't a problem with our servicing your cottage's loan?" Elliot asked, frowning.

"No, nothing of the sort. Actually, this idea is only a few minutes old, so forgive my spontaneity and lack of preparedness too." Lacey took a breath.

"Of course, and you've succeeded in piquing my curiosity. Please do continue." Elliot's friendly manner grew serious.

"Well, I'm helping Serene for a couple of weeks with some real estate marketing project. This is all confidential, right?" Lacey needed to be sure before proceeding.

"You have my word."

"Good. So, I've been measuring and photographing the Gold Nugget for what Serene calls a silent listing until she puts the "For Sale" sign out next week."

"Sorry to hear Allison is closing. I'd always assumed her business carried her nicely, especially with her Uncle Branson owning the building. Come to think of it, I don't know what I'll do for my wife's birthday gift. Allison always helped me select something that pleased the pants off her. Pardon. Didn't mean that the way it sounded." Elliot turned crimson.

"That's okay, Elliot. I get it, and if you can help me, maybe I can help you back." Lacey grinned.

Elliot cleared his throat, trying to reclaim his banker persona. "Do you know if her business had taken a downturn?"

"I don't think that's really the reason for closing. She stated an opportunity to travel and work at the same time was offered to her. At any rate, she's thrilled and ready to start a new life adventure." Lacey glanced at her watch, worrying Serene might come looking for her if she didn't wrap this meeting up soon.

"And you fit into this where?"

"Well, Allison knew my background in the jewelry industry and that I'm looking for a fresh opportunity. You know how word travels the streets of Divine."

Elliot nodded, smiling. "I've heard you'd lost your job. Sorry, Lacey."

Lacey waved her hand, signaling she'd moved on. "Thanks, Elliot. So anyway, Allison throws me this idea that I should explore buying the building and opening my own jewelry boutique. I must admit the plan immediately grabbed my heart, so I made a beeline, whatever that means, down to see you. I want to explore if I have any hope of taking Allison's brainstorm and making it my reality." Lacey sat back in the chair, waiting while Elliot stared off, considering her words.

"Actually, I like the proposal of seeing you become Divine's newest entrepreneur."

"I hear a 'but' hanging in the air," Lacey replied, tensing with her fears. Cassie wouldn't approve of her thoughts. She quickly relaxed her fists, ignoring her traitorous mind.

"There's always a 'but' at a bank, especially nowadays. So here it is, you need a sizable down payment whenever you do commercial deals, and you'll need to formulate a business plan for the bank directors to review. Are you up for the challenge?"

"I think so as long as I've some sort of guideline to use, but how much is sizable?"

"Sizable is usually around twenty percent of the purchase price for a bank-held loan. Do you know the numbers yet?"

"Not yet, but Serene I'm sure does. I guess my next step is to determine if I can come up with the down payment, right?"

"That's correct, and Lacey we're particular about that twenty percent coming from you and not another loan. The board would accept the monies being gifted to you as long as there was no expectation of repayment. Is that clear?" Elliot placed his pen down on his desk, having concluded his note taking on their conversation.

"Yes, I understand everything you've shared. Unfortunately, I don't have anyone in my life willing to shell out some hefty sum and call it a gift. Guess I will go consider my options." Lacey made an effort to summon a smile.

"Absolutely. Go see what Serene can tell you. She knows the owner's mind. I'll be here whenever you're ready to take the next step. Take this loan application with you and a guide to what we want in a business plan." Elliot rose and extended his hand.

Lacey stood and took the envelope. "Thank you so much for taking the time to counsel me. I don't know if I'm supposed to do this, but I do know I want to try...more with each passing minute."

"Desire is a major ingredient for success. Go stir that pot."

Lacey smiled at Elliot's attempt to show respect for her endeavors. Guess I will see you again in a few hours."

Elliot nodded, waving, as he returned to his ringing phone.

Lacey tried desperately to ignore the thoughts flooding her with what a waste of time this whole exercise would prove to be and how she didn't have any business starting a business. She chuckled at her mind's attempt at humor meant to lure her into the lair. "Be rude to the chatter," she chanted, trying in vain to focus on the sidewalk cracks under her moving feet.

That didn't work. She gave a heavy sigh and kept walking, offering a token wave to Jane Ann, making the rounds across the street with her dog in tow.

Another sabotaging voice asked her if she honestly thought Allison's uncle would see her as a viable buyer for his building? Well, at least, she didn't have long to wait to find out if Serene thought her qualified. She'd call that a good first step.

Lacey opened the real estate's office door minutes later. "I'm back. Did you miss me?"

"Where have you been? I was getting worried that you'd tripped over the tape measure and were sprawled out on the floor or something." Serene moved closer, relieving Lacey of the camera.

"Actually, I had an unexpected stop to make after I finished." Lacey emptied her arms of the notebook, tape measure, and handbag onto the reception desk.

"Well, sure, that's fine. No problem," Serene said, turning back to her office. "Wait a minute." She stopped and returned to Lacey, looking again at her face. "I recognize that expression. You've been up to something. Yes, you have," said Serene, grinning.

"Maybe." Lacey hesitated and rolled her eyes. "I hate it when you read me like this," Lacey groaned, no longer trying to conceal her excitement.

"You forget my job is to read people, and right now, I'm hungry and nosy. Let's go—"

"Hi ya, ladies. Paulie's back again. I brought yous lunch." He entered, holding up two cardboard containers. I'm known for my exemplary service, eh, Serene?" asked Paulie, working his new word for the day.

"Yeah, Paulie, you're right about that. Great service is you." Serene winked, walking over to take the containers.

"Paulie, you're the best. What did you make us, you darling man?" Lacey lifted the lid.

"Yous funny, Lacey. Nothing fancy like. Just some extra nice hoagies. You enjoy this roasted veggie sandwich. This one here is yours, Serene. Meatball." Paulie opened the other container and held it under Serene's nose. "Take a whiff. Seeing yous both all happy like is all I wanted. I gotta be going. Can't leave the palace to those goofballs I've got working today," Paulie answered, clearly joking about his loyal employees. They were all extended family to the generous Paulie.

"Bye, Paulie, and thanks again," both ladies echoed as the door closed.

"Isn't he a sweetie?" Lacey couldn't resist a little fishing.

"Yes, he is. Now tell me what you've been up to while we devour our lunch. Oh, goody. Look, here's a cannoli. Did you get one?" Serene pushed the dessert wistfully to the right. Her waistline had been expanding lately, thanks to Paulie's cooking.

"No, I didn't get a cannoli. Let's see. I have a giant Italian wedding cookie. Maybe I got your sweetie by mistake," Lacey said, raising her brow for effect.

"Not mine. Very funny. Enough dessert talk. Back to you and don't stall. Tell me before someone else interrupts us."

"Okay, okay. So, I measure and all. No problem. Allison was there packing the contents of a few displays. We got to talking, and she told me her wonderful news, and then suddenly, she springs this idea on me." Lacey took another bite.

"Don't you dare take a bite when the best part is yet to come. Swallow and talk to me."

Lacey rolled her eyes. "Well, her bright idea was for me to consider opening a jewelry shop right there. She explained her uncle owned the building and had given you instructions on the kind of business he'd be willing to contract with." Lacey went in for another bite, trying to gauge Serene's reaction.

Serene sat quietly chewing. She motioned with her hand for Lacey to continue.

"All right, so I told her the idea actually excited me, but I didn't know if I could make it happen financially for starters. I figured talking to you and Elliot might be a good first step." Lacey put her sandwich down. "Are you going to say anything or just sit there stuffing your face?"

"I'm going to keep stuffing my face until I've heard everything. Keep talking. There's more for me to digest than this hero here." Serene joked.

"Fine. So, I decided to stop by the bank on my way back here and see if by chance Elliot was free, which incredibly he was. He explained for starters I would need to have twenty percent to put down and a business plan for the board to review with my loan application." Lacey noticed Serene had stopped eating and instead sat engrossed. "Look, I really need your help, okay? And let me add, I also suspect you set me up with this encounter days ago with your happy chatty 'Oh, Lacey, come work for me and help me with my projects…' yadda, yadda." Lacey pointed her index finger at Serene.

"Me? Set you up? As I recall, you were the one who insisted on bartering your services for mine. Little did I know you'd be collecting your first day on the job," Serene bantered back. She couldn't be happier that Lacey had taken the bait. Meant to be, she hoped.

"I did? I did. Wow! Aren't I savvy?" Lacey preened.

"I'd say so." Serene eyed the cannoli and the other half of the sandwich.

"Serene, just this once, I'm going to let you think that I'm buying your pretending not to have orchestrated this whole plan. Know why?"

"Because I'm your closest friend and ally? Because I know what's best, or maybe it's my agent skills extraordinaire that you've grown to appreciate?"

"There's all of that, but no, I've recently grown to understand a bigger picture and purpose in our lives is weaving in and out daily. I believe I'm being directed. Truly." Lacey grew pensive, digesting what she'd just stated aloud. She'd spoken her own "freshic." Aunt Cassie would be pleased. She turned her attention back to Serene. "I know that I'm being shown my path to joy," Lacey stated again with more conviction.

"And, dear friend, on that we can agree. Chasing what you're passionate about brings joy." Serene's knowing matched her friend's. "Let's celebrate your epiphany with dessert." Serene's cannoli toasted Lacey's cookie.

"My stars and garters, this is good. If you don't snag him, I swear I will." Lacey teased, lightening the mood.

"You ought to taste mine." She ignored the threat. "So, would you like for me to fill you in on the major details of this listing before it becomes public?"

"You know I would. Hang on while I get my notebook."

"Write this down. Price is firm at three hundred thousand, no terms, quick close, and owner approval of the type of business. Here's the info sheet on the square footage estimate, taxes, insurance, etc. I'll calculate the exact footage from your measurements to verify. This info is what you'll need to get started in running numbers and such."

"I'll need, like, sixty grand just to put down for a loan. I don't think that will leave me enough to buy inventory, displays, and whatever else will make my list by nightfall. Oh, Serene, I don't see how I can swing this. I didn't expect the price to be so much."

"I know that's a lot of money to come up with in cash, but the building is actually priced way under the tax value. Branson is more of a philanthropist when it comes to his Divine holdings. This is a steal of a deal as we agents say."

"Really?"

"Really. You may not realize, but there's a small apartment upstairs that can be finished off. That's not been calculated by me in the price either again at Branson's request. He insisted that I allow him to set the price despite my telling him I could get him much more. Highly unusual, I must say, but hey, he's the boss." Serene shrugged, smiling.

Lacey's disappointment mirrored in her face. "This sounds like a really great investment opportunity. Only God could bring this gift to me."

"I totally agree, Lacey. This is pretty incredible in timing and offering."

"I guess I may be over my head here, but I'm still going to run the numbers and all later." Her mind jumped in, saying, *I told you so...I told you so* in a singsong voice. She sat lost listening, not even arguing this time.

Serene registered her friend's downtrodden expression but refused to support it. "Listen, Lacey, you absolutely should do some figuring. This is an enormous opportunity, so don't you dare give up at this point. Do you want to turn your back on God's offer? Promise me you will take the next step? Let me see a smile too."

"Okay, promise." Lacey forced a smile.

"And we'll talk again tomorrow and see what we can come up with. Sound good?" Serene moved toward the front entrance.

"Sounds good. You know that you're incredible?"

"I know. Some days it's hard to be humble." She chuckled, closing the door. Lacey was applying her lessons. Today she'd put them to use and tapped into the Law of Attraction.

Chapter 48

Relaxed on her porch, Cassie allowed the quietness of the early evening to gentle her spirit. The book rested on her lap but, somehow, she didn't feel the pull to get lost in another's story. Tonight, she'd wait for the early stars to show her the way into her own story, which was still unfolding by the grace of God.

Old Mountain Cassie rocked watching the change to the night shift as more creatures showed up for duty. A bat whizzed by, beginning his early hunt for insects. Tree frogs tuned their voices, preparing to announce the coming darkness. Crickets joined in, adding their distinctive chorus to evening's song. Cassie breathed deeply, saying good-bye to the day shift and freely appreciating what night-life brought to her spirit. Her right foot touched down on the porch's plank floor, encouraging the rocker's rhythm to one more subdued.

Cassie detached from her body's doings, opening to a higher consciousness. Some of her greatest insights got imparted in this state. She welcomed the guidance…needed the guidance. Cassie was the first to admit too much thinking took her off track more times than not. Today with Branson had sent her to the rocker unsettled, and at her age, the feeling was most unwelcome.

After all these years, why did his invitation and proclamations tempt her? Her spirit's inner and outer work had always held her focus; it was the way. She'd never considered deviating from her calling…never thought she could share her life and still honor the commitment made so long ago to God and her Guides. Yet somehow, others seemed capable of having love and work co-exist just fine.

Why was she feeling a push to keep company with a man this late in her life? She laughed off hormones as the culprit, yet she couldn't help but grow more introspective, replaying his words. Something quickened inside, opening up the possibility for a loving companion. *Silly fool*, she admonished herself, having allowed such thoughts to take her on a ride.

Cassie relaxed more, seeking the altered state of nonbeing where the true divine wisdom and guidance waited.

Chapter 49

Lacey sat deliberating over her own struggles. She wished that she could spend this evening at Cassie's getting direction on how to process the day's twists and turns. Until tomorrow came, she had a festival meeting to distract her.

Her spirit lightened, thinking how impossible Divine made it to be unsocial, except if you happened to be Old Mountain Cassie. Well, that wasn't exactly fair, for she suspected Cassie was selectively social. Yes, highly selective, but Lacey understood the need for that choice. Time spent with Cassie had enlightened and enlivened her own purpose for selective solitude. Teachings seemed to be attracted more to silence somehow.

A glance at the clock told Lacey it was time to add her two cents about Festival Divine. Too bad she couldn't be a store owner planning the festival from that perspective.

Whoa! That negative thought slipped right in on her. She hadn't determined all was lost on that front yet, but yes, she had to admit things didn't look all that promising. She'd read the message on Serene's and Elliot's faces, or at least, she "thought" she had.

So far, she'd not been successful in stifling her creative self from laying out the store with displays and selecting an inviting color scheme, activities she relished. Good grief, she didn't have an inkling of what kind of gems or designs she'd fill the shop with, much less how she'd find time to create the pieces. Lacey chuckled at how many carts she'd lined up before the horses.

The large meeting room was lit with the energy of people, while the recessed lights settled for second place. The discussion on the festival theme was well underway when Lacey took her seat.

"Now, Charlie, you remember last year how you struggled to keep pickling cukes in stock once the women announced there would be a judging of bread and butter pickles," the mayor stated.

"Mayor Morgan is right, Charlie, I couldn't get near my telephone to confirm our weekly poker game's location for Mrs. Mercer calling the ladies trying to barter extra pickling cucumbers," Frank Mercer grumbled.

"You never win a plug nickel at that poker game no ways, so hush up," Mable Mercer declared, which caused the room to burst into guffaws.

Charlie came to life over in the corner. "Listen up, everyone, if you'll give me notice, I promise to order in enough of whatever the women deem this year's judging to be on," he said, not wanting to miss an opportunity for extra business at the grocery.

Heads bobbed in approval and appreciation.

"Okay then, let's vote it. Everyone in favor of another canning contest, say aye," said the mayor, instructing the group.

The ayes rang out strong, and Lacey added her voice to the group. She waved to Barbie and Serene sitting together and admired the hairstylist's afternoon handiwork on her best friend. "Cute cut," she mouthed to the two and gave a thumbs-up.

They each sent a smile her way.

Lacey made a mental note to make an appointment soon and see what Barbie could do for her mop. She turned her attention back to the meeting.

"Let's get some committees formed, folks," Mayor Morgan interjected, trying to get everyone back on track.

Within ten minutes, Lacey had been tapped, followed by plenty of encouragement to head up the decorating committee. With any luck, she'd be able to recruit Gabby to help her. She'd need her aunt or anyone with a beating heart, especially if she could pull off the feat of starting her own business. Everyone knew she wasn't working, meaning she had plenty of time to devote to the festival. Her name went up on the dry erase board, making it official.

Barbie must have read Lacey's mind from across the room. "Hey, Lacey, the kids and I are happy to help decorate."

"Thanks, Barbie, and I accept. Tell your kids ice cream cones on me each day they volunteer," Lacey answered back.

"Hey, Lacey, count me in too." Bud's working farmhands waved to her from across the room. Lacey always thought Bud had the kindest eyes she'd ever seen, and his personality complimented that caring spirit with his dairy cows.

"Gotcha down, Bud. Be warned, everyone, I'm making a list of names of any who want to help. Don't be shy," said Lacey, holding up her notebook.

"We all love you, Lacey, and wouldn't dream of welching," Elliot sang out with a chuckle.

"Thanks, Elliot. Does that mean I can add your name?" asked Lacey, teasing.

"You sure can," said Louisa, his wife. "Try and teach him how to use a hammer before you send him home, will you, Lacey?"

More laughter erupted because all in Divine knew Elliot's talents were at the bank and not with anything tool like.

"Yeah, Elliot, you be careful holding that hammer. I still tear up each time I think of you having to cut a toe hole in a perfectly good pair of dress shoes that you'd just bought from me. Ruined those loafers and all because you went and dropped that blasted hammer on your big toe," said Frank Mercer, punching a snickering Charlie in the ribs.

"Hey, if you all remember, it was me he woke up at midnight for a house call," said Doc Andy. "A throbbing toe. Geez, I've had women hold off delivering their babies till daylight out of consideration."

Elliot's face turned crimson. "Shut up, you guys. I've got what you call a low pain threshold. I'll have y'all know that toe still talks to me."

The room broke into another round of laughter as Elliot flexed his foot in the air for added flair.

"Okay, okay, let's get back to committee forming." Mayor Morgan pleaded, wiping tears from his cheeks. "I need someone to handle getting the word out. Call it advertising or whatever. Who wants to run their mouth for Divine?"

Lacey sat back and enjoyed watching the friendly residents helping to celebrate their love for Divine's special day. No one slacked. If anything, they were guilty of overextending themselves in time, money, and energy. A special place to call home, Lacey acknowledged once again, and now two aunts were living right here. Crazy.

The meeting ended with the festival's theme agreed upon, Ice Cream Churn. Bud and Sweet Clover Dairy would sponsor the day, and the merchant's association would add their financial support.

Lacey entered her den and collapsed into her desk chair. She accepted the midnight oil would be burning brightly on her endeavors. The light of day may, however, cast a shadow, but until then, she vowed to work on writing an impressive proposal for the bank's directors.

Chapter 50

LACEY AWAKENED WITH MORE QUESTIONS than answers. Were there no aspects of her life that felt secure and within her grasp to understand? She sat with that latest question. Uncertainty grabbed hold, and her mind seemed to have conjured up enough inner turmoil to carry her through twenty lifetimes.

She took one last sip of her latest favorite coffee, chocolate truffle, appreciative that, at least, turmoil wasn't swirling in her cup of java. She might be flirting with becoming a sarcastic cynic this morning if there was such a combo of character traits. Lacey released her ponytail, shaking her head to try and clear her mind. Ha. Clear her mind, as if that was possible. She'd managed to lose sight of The Lessons. A glance in her mirror showed an unaccomplished Seeker would be knocking on Cassie's door soon.

"Lacey, come inside. Still feels damp from last evenin's rain."

"Hi, Aunt Cassie." She felt genuine happiness calling this wisdom-filled woman Aunt.

"Boy, I like my new name a heap," Cassie preened. "Let's sit over in those real comfortable chairs with the extra plump cushions."

"Sure thing." Lacey settled. "Before we get into more teachings, I have a question that's been following me around. Actually, I have lots of questions, as you can imagine, but this one's easy."

"I will take an easy one." Cassie grinned.

"I was wondering if you know or ever knew Aunt Gabby? I've not said a word to her, or anyone for that matter, about my discovering another aunt." Lacey's dimples, identical to the ones belonging to the woman sitting next to her, appeared.

"Well, let me think. We've never met, but I did hear her spoken about a few times by the family. As you know, Violet didn't expend much energy keepin' in touch with us. A few letters conveyin' big news was all we had to look forward to over the years. Gabby was mentioned favorably, as I recall," Cassie concluded.

"So, there's a good chance Aunt Gabby doesn't know much about you or your side of the family?" said Lacey, not sure how to handle Cassie's introduction to Gabby.

"Knowing my sister's desire to avoid anything extraordinary, I'd wager my favorite bed pillow and feel pretty sure my head would be on it tonight that she doesn't." Cassie gave a little chuckle, expecting the reason behind the question was coming.

"Then how might I share your existence in my life with Gabby?" Lacey felt growing anxiety around this sharing.

"Would you mind if I make a recommendation?"

"Please." Lacey's face grew serious.

"Why don't you trust God and the Guides to give you that direction at the proper time? After all, I'm hidden away here and not likely to pose a problem for you. See here, Niece, it's not just your aunt that will learn of our blood connection, but it's all of Divine."

Lacey's face registered surprise, telling both women this truth hadn't occurred to her. She didn't want to bring unwelcome attention to Cassie. Lacey massaged her temples, feeling the first pangs of a migraine threatening. These headaches were becoming a real barometer of her mind's ongoing campaign not to relinquish control. Lately, nothing in her life was stagnant or ordinary. "Oh my gosh! You're right. This changes everything for both of us, doesn't it, Aunt Cassie?"

"That it will, Missy. Why don't we let go of the frettin' and trust God to handle things? I can promise you that I'm not frettin' over this one tinker," said Cassie, already knowing that trusting to be the highest and best next step. God delighted when she gave him her daily concerns. And Cassie liked God happy with her.

"The concept of turning things over is still novel, but with all these new happenings in my life—and that's a really broad sweeping statement of late—I'm for your trust plan." Lacey relaxed back in the chair and closed her eyes.

"Your head messin' with you?"

"Unfortunately, yes." Lacey squinted to block out the morning sunlight coming through the group of windows facing her.

"Got just the thing. Hang on a minute." Cassie disappeared into the kitchen, humming.

Lacey heard a utensil stirring something in a glass.

Cassie held up a goblet with a cloudy liquid still swirling. "Drink this down, and I'll guarantee your migraine will be a memory in less than thirty minutes."

Lacey took the glass and sniffed. "Smells okay, but what's the potion?" She couldn't resist chiding her aunt, and it did help lighten her mood.

"Hmph. Course, it smells fine. It is willow bark with a pinch of valerian," Cassie supplied, adding her dose of sass.

"Willow bark is…you've told me. I can't remember."

"Aspirin, Missy. Now drink it all." Cassie felt gladness whenever she could witness her herbs giving goodness.

Lacey held up the glass and drank to her fate, keeping quiet her skepticism that she'd be pain-free soon. Her migraines liked to come for extended visits.

"You rest, and I'll go outside and do some tendin' in the gardens. Come join me when the pain high-tails it. Won't be long. You'll see."

Lacey nodded and closed her eyes, settling into the chair. "Thanks, Aunt Cassie," she mumbled, grateful to have a gifted healer for an aunt.

Old Mountain Cassie closed the front door with a soft touch. She'd taken a dose of her own medicine just before Lacey arrived. She'd slept the night away in the porch rocker and awakened that morning a touch stove-up. Cassie clung to her puzzlement of finding a blanket covering her. A mystery was laid on her literally and figuratively. "Hocus pocus isn't in my vocabulary," she told Lickety Split, who was walking next to her. Guess she'd practice what she preached, trusting the mystery of who'd come callin' would be solved in due course…she hoped.

Chapter 51

Lacey awakened in a half hour and acknowledged she'd been sleep-deprived from the long hours working on her plan the night before. Dismissing the upcoming bank meeting from her mind, she stood and stretched, feeling renewed and completely pain-free.

The mountain woman watched her niece's approach. She placed the spade in the bucket and dusted off her overalls. "See, now I can accept that thank-you."

"Make it a huge relieved thank-you. That bark is some terrific stuff. I don't even feel like I had a migraine. I'm a walking testament to your healing talents." Lacey added, more for herself to hear, marveling again at Cassie's gift with herbs.

Cassie stood smiling and gave one of her approving nods.

"Since I feel human again, can we please and thank you get to Lesson Three today?" Lacey wanted to build on what she'd learned and put it into practice. She sensed there was a missing piece needed to amplify her connection with God and the Other Side, and maybe then things in her life would jell.

"Ahh, you're wantin' that lesson, are you? Well, let's see if your spirit and God agree in a while." Cassie liked that her niece's spirit felt hungry. "For now, do you have anything to share before I invite you to have another uncommon kinda day?"

"Actually, I do have something to share, but if it's all the same to you, I'd like to save my news until later? It sort of has me agitated and well…" Her fingers absently reached up to touch the gemstone pendant always around her neck. Joy returned, trumping the negative thoughts seemingly ever on the periphery of her mind.

Cassie noted the unconscious gesture and the gem's strength imparted to her niece. Lacey's mood had shifted. "News can wait. Let's get you some schoolin'. Why don't we head on over to that wishin' well? You've an affinity for that well ever since you laid eyes on the structure, and with good reason, as you're about to find out." Cassie enjoyed her Seekers, discovering that things were not always as they seemed. The well was a favorite and likely for as many reasons as there were Seekers still to come.

Moments later, Cassie and Lacey scooted the two wooden benches together to form an L shape facing the structure. Lacey made no attempt to analyze why this juxtaposition was needed. She trusted and waited for Cassie's next request as she eyed the intricate design of the wishing well's rectangular sides. Funny she'd never noticed the carvings.

Lacey watched Cassie busily position some pots of clover on one side of the bench.

Cassie's attention to detail broke, noting Lacey's questioning gaze. "Looks bafflin', huh? I'm just doing my teachin' sprinklings." Cassie snickered.

"So far, I'd say yes."

"You can expect your Spirit Self to meet that un-baffling need. Take a seat. I'm gonna tell you about how that wishin' well came as a gift to me when I first claimed this land for my upbringin'." Cassie cast an appreciative gaze at the structure.

"Upbringing? Do you mean as a young girl you came here because I thought—"

"Quiet yourself, gal. Sometimes my words carry two meanings. Sometimes more," Cassie stated abruptly.

Lacey covered her mouth with one hand, eyes smiling to let her aunt know she'd mind her manners and not interrupt.

Seeing the endearing gesture, Cassie relaxed, reminding herself Lacey had only begun her journey. She'd been given quite a bit to absorb in a short time too. She guessed her sore muscles had her ornery. Cassie took in a cleansing breath. "Good girl." Cassie cracked a grin. "Ignore my crotchety disposition. My age is showin' a tad today. To answer your question, upbringin' has other meanings."

"I did my real growin' right out here amongst God's creation. This place is where my gifts blossomed right along with my flowers and herbs. And that ole wishin' well showed me how knowledge of the inner and outer world could be brought up to me. Not down, as you would expect. No, much of what I needed came up through me. Still does when I'm behavin' like a grounded earth gal." Cassie shrugged. "Upbringin'."

Lacey's head tilted, showing she was pondering her aunt's words. She gave the go-ahead.

The corner of Cassie's mouth twitched. Her niece had decided to be mute for a spell, but the dimple signaled Lacey's good spirits remained intact. Cassie propped her feet on her pail. "You see, the thing needed attention, much like me. You name it, that wishin' well needed it. I'm talkin' about having to replace all the wood and roof shingles." Cassie looked fondly at the structure and gave a little chuckle.

"And you?" The story had captured Lacey's full attention.

"I needed shorin' up too. Or rather my body, mind, and spirit did. Here I sat on the side of a mountain, young, alone, and without my clarity of purpose. All I had was the awareness of my gift to grow livin' things well and the land given to me to prove it. Me and this well went to work…on each other." Cassie grinned, clearly enjoying the memory. She poured some lemonade from a waiting thermos perched on a nearby carved tree stump table. She handed a small cup of the liquid to Lacey. "Here you go. Let's wet our whistles."

Lacey took the paper cup and drank the contents in one long gulp. "Thanks. I didn't realize how thirsty I'd become."

"Willow bark does that to a body." Cassie drank her refreshment from the thermos's cup as she collected her thoughts.

Lacey repositioned herself and stretched out on the bench, eager to hear more.

"So, each mornin' I'd rise and hurry out here actin' like a carpenter. I'd nail up boards, turn around to get another nail, only to have the blasted piece of wood hanging cockeyed. I expect my body became the first part of me to prosper by the wishin' well's attention. Yes, ma'am, got me into pretty good shape in a few weeks. And the well taught…showed me what it wanted its body to look like as mine got more refined. The day I brought home some reclaimed carved teak wood and commenced nailin' them to the sides was the day the boards held to perfection."

Lacey glanced at the carved sides, still not able to make out the design or shapes. She did appreciate the beauty and uniqueness of the wood.

"I came to understand the existence of a grand plan, even for that ole wishin' well. I figured I must have one too. So, by and by, I kept enhancin' the structure, getting fitter each day. When I'd completed the labor of birthing a right handsome wishin' well, I remember standin' back to admire its beauty, and I confess, my own self's." Cassie's face colored.

Lacey felt a rush of pleasure for that young girl's accomplishments so many years ago. Clearly, the memory held a special place in her aunt's heart. She pulled a peppermint from her pocket and leaned over to place the candy on Cassie's knee.

"Thanks. I confess I've never tasted a candy that I didn't fancy… well, except horehound. Vile tastin' things." Cassie gave a little shiver.

"Hmm, I've never heard of horehound, but the name's certainly no turn-on," Lacey added, unwrapping her mint. "I'm totally engrossed in your story and want to hear more."

Old Mountain Cassie gathered her thoughts. "Well, like I said, me and that wishin' well had developed a right nice shape, but that was only our outer shell if you know what I mean?"

"I do now, thanks to you."

"I recall that I still felt lost and empty. My mind loved to remind me of that daily, which only made those feelings grow. Oh, and how they grew. Like my squash vines over yonder tryin' to take over the tomatoes." Cassie paused for Lacey to look at the garden. "One day, I'd put the last coat of sealant on the teak. I remember admirin' how pretty each side of the well looked all richly varnished when somethin' made me look down at the ground. Know what I saw?" Cassie asked, making sure her Seeker's thoughts hadn't wandered.

"Tell me. I could never guess." She sensed the best was yet to unfold.

"I saw a bunch of clovers that had sprung up."

Lacey frowned, her mind telling her, *So what, clover. Big deal.* Her spirit said, *Not so fast. This is, after all, Old Mountain Cassie's clover.*

Cassie shook her finger at her Seeker, knowing full well Lacey's thoughts had intruded.

"I know. Be rude. What about the clover?" Lacey prompted.

"Well, they were sittin' there pretty as you please all green and lush except for one strikin' difference." She paused, building Lacey's anticipation. "Every single one of them were four leafers. Every one."

"Impossible," Lacey voiced her doubts without hesitation.

Cassie grinned at her niece's response. "That's what I said as I knelt down, running my fingers through the green carpet of them. Then I realized my mind was the culprit tellin' me lies…tryin' to convince me my eyes lied. I remember those pesky thoughts told me I must be daft. On and on my mind chattered. I tell you, I got worked over real good that day. I recollect at one point agreein' with my mind, and then I'd look down at those four leaves holdin' to the stem, starin' back at me by the hundreds. Kept provin' my mind lied just by their very existence."

"That's some story. I can see how that might boggle your mind." Lacey's attention held.

"Yep. That was the day I got the big lesson that my mind is not my friend. It wants control all the time to spin yarns, threaten my joy. And I'm willin' to bet your mind has been workin' overtime on you for a long spell. Isn't that so?"

"Yeah," Lacey's voice responded before her mind could filter and defend its position, "but—"

"No buts. The first answer is the truth. The second is your mind messin'. Good you didn't pause to answer me." Cassie nodded to emphasize the importance of her words.

"Actually, I now understand what that means. So, you accepted the impossible?" Lacey asked, returning to the story, hungry for more insights.

"I did, but only until that evenin' in bed. My mind decided to plant the seed that those clovers were a hallucination or some such thing and that come mornin' they'd be gone provin' the point. Well, I remember grabbin' the flashlight I kept on my night table and startin' to trudge out to the wishin' well to see for myself if they were in the ground. You see, I hadn't replaced the roof yet, so the well's base stood wide open, so to say. Understand?"

Lacey nodded. "What did you find?"

"Not at all what I expected. Instead, I see this beam of light cascadin' down from the sky. Yep, I sure did, Missy. I stood there gawkin' at the sight from my front porch, not dare budgin'. Call me transfixed. I think that's the word."

"Sure is." Lacey felt fascinated at how Cassie chose unexpected words to hold her listeners. "So, you were transfixed?"

"Yep, and a good word for me that night." Cassie returned to the memory.

"Where did the light come from?" Lacey stopped, remembering her Seeker manners.

This time, Cassie ignored the interruption. "The light grew brighter and brighter. In a matter of seconds, this ball of intense golden brilliance descended from the sky smack into the wishin' well's opening. Guess it was good I hadn't fastened a roof on the thing." Cassie paused to recoil her braid and secure it with a pin, giving her Seeker time to appreciate the awe of that night.

Lacey claimed a gulp of air and unwrapped another mint. This delay gave her mind ample time to crash into her consciousness with some fresh babbling meant to cast doubt on her aunt's accounting. Lacey chose to ignore the thoughts because her desire to believe and trust were stronger. "Wow! How extraordinary."

"And then some, Niece. And then some," Cassie replied, returning to her memories. "I must have been glued to my porch floor for a long spell waitin'. I don't know what I expected. I mean, tell me what else from the heavens could top that show."

Lacey shook her head, not able to offer up an answer but getting Cassie's meaning.

"Guess at some point I realized the darkness had moved back in, and my flashlight's dead batteries no longer supported me bein' outside. Funny…I didn't feel the least bit obliged to check out that wishin' well's new addition, and I sure as blazes didn't give those clovers another care. No, ma'am. They could have been ten leafers, but this Cassie chose to go back inside and let my mind have at me. Fact is, I welcomed the company."

"I can see why."

"You know, I'd heard tell from my granny that Old Mountain here had some specialness, but she'd not done an exemplary job preparin' me." Cassie paused to adjust her position.

Lacey's head shot up when she heard Paulie's new word, *exemplary*, come out of her aunt's mouth for a second time. No coincidences, she thought again. There must be a connection there, but Cassie's voice brought her back to the present.

"Course energy leys and such weren't words used back then. Guess *specialness* covered things in granny's opinion, or maybe she feared I'd not stay and settle here if she did much elaboratin'. She'd been right too," Cassie added with amusement dancing in her eyes.

Lacey rested her chin in her hand, waiting. What a teaching and dose of sprinklings this was turning out to be.

"I recollect goin' to bed prayin' for a whopper rainstorm to come spend a week with me. Anything to keep me from goin' outside for a spell. Not that I felt afraid exactly, just confounded," Cassie explained with a shrug.

"If that had happened to me, I'd be checking into the closest hotel in the noisiest city I could find," Lacey countered.

"Hidin' out, huh?" Cassie chuckled.

"Way out." Lacey emphasized'

"Nah, I just needed some processin' time. Know what happened next?"

Lacey shook her head.

"God answered me with a gully washer that lasted three straight days. I do recall takin' my biggest umbrella and goin' out the next afternoon to see if those clovers were gone or, at least, beat down from the rain."

"And?" Lacey asked.

"And not only were they standin' up tall and proud like sentinels, they'd gone and doubled in size."

"What?" Lacey struggled to make sense of it all.

"Yep. Truth told. In fact, that's some of them in the clay pot parked next to you, Missy."

Lacey turned and hung her head down, peering into the pot. "Holy smokes! They're all fours. This is crazy. How can they still be around after all these years?"

"They keep on duplicatin' year after year. Decades now. They don't freeze. They thrive in every season. They confound me. I planted these clovers in this red clay pot to use for my teachin,' but they actually reside in a big area all around the wishin' well. Good genes, huh?" Cassie grinned.

"That's an understatement," Lacey replied, gently touching the cool, soft leaves.

"Wanna hear more?"

"Are you kidding? There's more?"

"Yep. I continued refurbishin' the well's structure. Put a new metal roof on it all by myself I did. Course, I've replaced that a couple of times since then, but I admit feelin' proud of that particular accomplishment."

Lacey nodded in agreement, impressed that her aunt had done the job alone.

"I worked beside those clovers that entire summer. One day, I woke up wonderin' how deep that well might be and if there was any water in it. I'd avoided any probing since the night of that energy ball, as I came to call the thing seen fit to enter my well."

"Energy ball. Interesting name," Lacey answered.

"It is that. Anyway, I bought a new bucket with a long rope and decided to drop the pail down as far as I could that same afternoon." Cassie stood up.

"What are you doing?" Lacey asked, afraid her aunt was calling it a day.

"Come on over, and I'll show you."

They walked side by side in silence the few feet to the well.

Cassie turned the hand crank and slowly lowered the oddly shaped bucket. The bottom had a trap door of sorts. She didn't utter a single word, just kept turning the crank, dropping the bucket lower.

Lacey released any expectations and watched.

Old Mountain Cassie changed direction and began cranking even slower, her breath labored. The bucket cleared the opening with a sparkling liquid dripping down its sides.

Lacey had never seen water glisten with such energy. She waited for Cassie to explain.

"Take a gander inside my bucket."

Lacey leaned over slowly and looked. "Is that what I think it is?"

"Yes, ma'am. Say it."

"I'm staring at a smattering of tiny gold nuggets settled in the bottom of a wooden bucket, which were just brought up by my newly discovered aunt, on land that has some mystical doings, and… and…I've gotta sit back down."

Old Mountain Cassie reached into the bucket and pulled out a nugget. She handed it to a now reclining Lacey. "Here you go. Proof you can take home."

Lacey wrapped her fingers around the pea-sized shiny rock. Surreal came closest to describing her encounters with Old Mountain Cassie. She heard her voice respond, "And I guess next you'll be telling me about some type of rainbow to go with the pot of gold down in that well?" She began fanning herself with her free hand.

Cassie didn't miss the change of tone. She expected and understood her niece's high emotions. "Actually, I thought I'd save that rainbow tellin' for later down your seekin' path." The mountain woman tied the rope off, allowing the bucket to dangle and dry out.

Lacey laughed but kept the hand fan going.

"Well, I suppose a smidgen more about my clovers still needs telling." Cassie sat down next to the clay pot. She plucked a single clover and twirled it between her thumb and index finger like a parasol. Her eyes closed.

Lacey wondered what her aunt was about but sensed time would march forward, bringing the answer soon enough. She cherished the moment to compose herself and prepare for…the unimaginable. She pushed herself into a seated position on the bench.

Cassie's eyes opened and smiled kindly at her niece. "These clovers bring answers, provide guidance, affirm choices, and such. All four-leaf clovers can do this for us." Cassie held up the vibrant green parasol, turning it ever so slowly as she gauged Lacey's reaction.

Sensible Lacey had a question. "I'm confused. How can a four-leaf clover be so smart?"

"I need you to really hear and take in what I'm about to say. No filterin', okay?"

Lacey grew serious and nodded her agreement.

"These clovers are full of energy because God's breath is on them. These green shoots are devoted. They provide a means to connect with more of the universe's laws, and yes, even put them to use. The clovers are aids."

Lacey's doubt crept back in. "I can accept the clovers have God's breath as you said on them, but a clover as an aid? Really?"

"Yep, really. Are you ready to hear this last piece of 'glory' around the wishin' well?"

"Glory? Sure, tell me about the glory. I'm already on sensory overload." Lacey studied the gold nugget.

Cassie felt the familiar shift inside, signaling her words would now flow from a higher place…her Spirit Self and God were communing. "The clover provides help to the glory of the person in possession of it. You pick one from the Bouquet of Glory, as I call any of the places where a four leafer resides, hold it up close to your heart askin', for example, for some understandin.' It's important to keep the clover with you while the guidin' laws gather to provide answers. God's breath inspired the four leafers to become special messengers, and their energies remind us of what we came here knowin' but are asleep to most times."

"And that is?" Lacey interjected.

"That we're never alone here in our living. That the Other Side works tirelessly to walk with us on our charted journey. The clovers are a reminder of that by enlivenin' the forces to come to our aid. They are a 'something' to hold on to as proof of this truth." Cassie took in a breath. She'd just delivered some high insights and a Seeker's tool to use.

Lacey could only stare at the woman next to her so full of wisdom and love for God's creation.

Cassie waited for her niece to process the teaching. "Care to hear what I like to do with my special picked clovers?"

"Okay," replied Lacey, hoping to be able to absorb more mystical wisdom.

"I save them, put them between wax paper, and mark what message or answer came from that particular one. I'll hold onto it until I have peace around me with whatever I'd been wrestlin' with. Might be a decision weighin' heavy on my heart, or even a direction to take with my work. Does that make sense? Are my words connectin' with your spirit yet?"

"Maybe." Lacey forgot and returned to thinking. She knew how to reason with her head. She'd had lots of years to hone that skill. "Let's say I have this question about some decision, and I'm not clear yet on what the right choice might be. Following me?"

"Yes ma'am, I'm followin' you just fine."

Lacey smiled, pleased her aunt was open to her exploring. "You're saying all I do is seek out in nature a four-leaf clover, hold it with my question until an answer is shown?"

"You got it. And the fours will show themselves when you have a need of one. The clover sets the intention in motion. When you look at it, you're reminded of the universe's ability to do what you perceive to be the impossible. My thrivin' crop of all fours symbolizes this pretty well, wouldn't you agree, Missy?" Cassie broke a grin.

"Oh yeah, I can agree to that being an excellent example of the impossible," Lacey replied, shaking her head.

"And those clovers shouldn't be existin' together?" Cassie prodded.

"Shouldn't be," Lacey parroted back, still pondering the impossibility of all four-leaf clovers residing there for years, undisturbed by nature or human.

"And yet here they are spendin' the day with us, even teachin' anyone who takes the time to look down and get out of themselves long enough to truly see with new eyes…to understand with a pure spirit that—"

"The impossible is possible," Lacey supplied with a bright smile lighting her from within.

"Well said, Missy. The impossible is possible when God's breath is touchin' down. Now, is there ever a time when that couldn't be?" asked Old Mountain Cassie.

"No?" answered Lacey, feeling unsure.

"No," said Cassie with a strong voice. "No," she said again, driving her message home. "Here take this." She reached over, depositing something in Lacey's outstretched hand.

"What is…a little envelope?" Lacey looked at it, confusion dressing her face once again.

"Reach down and pick yourself a four leafer. That waxed envelope will keep the clover green and intact. It'll remind you that the impossible is possible whenever doubt creeps up on you, and it will." Cassie nodded, watching her niece slip the now protected clover into her pocket.

"Something tells me I'll be pulling that symbol of power out a good bit over the next few weeks." Lacey's eyes traveled to the wishing well. The question that had been waiting inside of Lacey came forth.

Cassie watched, expecting to be asked what all her Seekers wanted to know after today's special sprinkling. Lacey had experienced a big helping of the mystical world that awaits everyone who connects with God and their Spirit Self.

"Aunt Cassie?"

"Yes, Niece."

"How do you explain those gold nuggets getting into the well? And…what are you doing with them? I know it's probably none of my business, but you've got to agree that this whole wishing well story is…pretty fantastic."

Cassie took a moment to get direction for how best to respond. "My head tells me there must be a rich gold vein down there, and that missile of a hot rock…a meteor…busted things up, and those nuggets are a means of income should I ever need to sell them to keep myself cared for, if you get my meanin'."

Lacey held the piece of gold and peered at the rugged shape, admiring the characteristics of the shiny metal, not to mention the allure. "I can understand the logic of the mind, but what does your spirit tell you?"

"Sharp Niece, I have here seekin', for that voice is the only one matterin' to me." Cassie closed her eyes and breathed in the warm mountain air. "My Spirit Self tells me the golden orb was sent from the heavens to guide me how to teach the impossible, and that's exactly what I've done with those nuggets and the clovers too. Teach the power of the impossible, provin' our mind is not the friend we've always assumed it to be. The mind tells big whoppers. Don't ya know by now?" Cassie gave a chuckle.

Cassie continued, "That knowin' sets you free for even greater examples of what your mind says is impossible. Pretty soon, you'll quit listenin' and trustin' that chatter when you know there's a bigger truth. That's when your spirit will turn you toward amazement. There you'll find the eternal truths."

"Wow is all I have for me to say." Lacey had been writing her aunt's words as she knew the understanding would need time for processing. And then she'd be asking questions in her Divining Portal."

Cassie nodded. "So anyways, since amazement is more a feelin' this day than a thought, if you travel inward with that feelin', you'll uncover some powerful truths. Your truths. Special ones just for you."

"And do I still travel by meditation?"

"Like I've told you, best vehicle I know to get you where the truth and guidance lives. We've been workin' on your roadmap all along. You see this now. To discover your gifts and life's work, you've got to travel out of your mind. You've taken a few trips that have been enjoyable and helpful, haven't you?"

"Oh yes, Cassie. They've been a lot more than just helpful and enjoyable."

Cassie smiled, pleased. "Lacey, you're goin' home with somethin' real in your heart and in your pocket. Remember this, that hunk of gold cannot be destroyed. Neither can you…the spirit you. Not ever." Cassie sat back, having delivered the one message she'd been tapped time and time again to teach. "Seek first to know your Spirit Self, and there you will find God waitin.' Any questions moving around inside?"

"You're kidding me, right?" Lacey laughed. "I've got scads of questions, but I also trust that I've been shown where to plug into for those answers."

"Then I say we need to be tastin' my victuals and not any lessons until we're hungry for them. Plan on comin' back first thing tomorrow so I can share Lesson Three. After a night of savorin' today, you'll be ripe for more." Cassie gave a little cackle.

"I trust you, Aunt Cassie, to know when to feed me." Lacey laughed.

"Listen to this, Missy. I've made our family's recipe vegetable soup. Picked the fixins' from my garden. I baked cornbread muffins to chase that soup down. You a taker?"

"You need to ask?" Lacey followed her aunt with Lickety Split on her heels. Cassie was right. She was overflowing with teachings and needed time to digest. Probably a lifetime…or more.

Chapter 52

THE NEXT MORNING, CASSIE'S FIREPLACE offered the last bit of warmth to both women as they settled into the gold brocade cushioned chairs, teacups in hand. Old Mountain Cassie had risen early, anticipating her niece's wish to hear this last imparting.

Not squandering precious time, Cassie jumped in, "Tell me, is your journal helpin' you get accustomed to this new way of bein' in this world? Havin' any success you want to share yet?"

"Yes, the journaling and studying my notes from our sessions are adding clarity and meaning, but, Aunt Cassie, is it normal? I mean, have your other Seekers accepted the unusual things that happened to them without letting their minds sabotage the work? Because when I start thinking about what all has transpired over this short time I've been with you…well, I feel like you're my fairy godmother with a super active wand. By the way, where's my prince? Do you have him stashed?" Lacey paused, trying to find words to explain, not feeling her comparison was spot on. "Seriously, you know what I'm trying to say?" Lacey grew quiet.

Cassie let out a laugh. "I understand you just fine. It's not every day you run across an Old Mountain Cassie type who turns out to be your great aunt and who helps conjure up a visit with your grandmother who crossed over, tells you all matter of tales like gold nuggets residin' in a wishin' well while she teaches spirit lessons. Let's not forget my tea brewin' talents, just to name a few experiences. Think I've touched on the big ones, but it's really The Three Lessons that are center stage, and the rest act as backdrops or is it props?" Cassie shrugged and turned to face Lacey.

Lacey chuckled. "First, I hear you about the teachings being the real precious jewel, for they most certainly are."

"I've got your answer. Let's mosey outside. Sun's been shinin' pretty here all mornin', and I think Lickety would enjoy some time at the stream. We've not been payin' him attention. See that pitiful dog lyin' by the door sulkin'?" Cassie pointed, watching his tail wag.

Lacey moved toward the dog with her hand out.

Lickety Split rose and touched the doorknob with his paw and looked back at the approaching women, offering his distinctive grin.

Cassie opened the door, watching Lick bolt outside. "No fishin'," she hollered behind him. Let's go sit by the wishin' well again. I'm partial to the spot. I'll just grab the thermos of infused mountain spring water if we need to wet our whistles. You need anything else?"

"Nope. I've got my journal and pen, so I'm peachy." Lacey followed the keeper of her next insights outside.

Cassie claimed a breath before beginning. "Your spirit recognizes truths and always tries to settle your mind. You're here on this earth to accomplish…to evolve…to love…to serve…to grow closer to God. Ah, but the mind wants control and doesn't like one bit this new path you're on. Aren't you witnessin' this more and more?"

"Yes." Lacey had come to understand how she'd been dominated by so much senseless thinking.

"All of my Seekers, all of them, Lacey, feel and experience their lessons very similar like. You've been called to learn a new way to be. This learnin' has been charted…by you before comin' into this life. Big doings usually are charted, don't you know? And I can promise you that everything is exactly as it needs to be. Exactly, Missy. You just keep takin' with a glad heart the gifts being brought to you, okay?"

"Okay," Lacey answered, her voice showing some hesitation.

"You thinkin'?"

"Yeah, I confess, but maybe this kind of thinking isn't too bad." Lacey grinned.

"That may be true. Not all thinkin' is bad, as you've come to understand. You can't not think and ponder things. Just be watchin' those thoughts that lead you astray and remember their source was first outside of you. Let me hear what's lyin' on that mind?"

"I'm thinking about how we have such abundance in our world. I've been shown that by you. And yet I always seem to be focused on the scarcity. So many of us think there's never enough. We're always worried about getting our fair share. We've lost our way to this higher knowledge you've been teaching." Lacey gave a heavy shrug.

"Tell me more." Cassie encouraged.

"Take watches for example. It's like we really need just one reliable watch. After all, we can only wear one at a time, but society puts emphasis on acquiring more to show off, to have a backup, to go with a new outfit. Never enough. And then look at our love affair with food. Buy large amounts. Eat super-sized meals. I mean, we act like a famine is imminent," said Lacey, her voice full of pent-up emotion. She cast a quick glance toward her teacher, measuring Cassie's reaction to her rant. The sage's face gave nothing away.

"Yes, ma'am, I can see why you'd say all of those things." Cassie waited, knowing her words weren't needed just yet.

"Right now, I'm shifting my beliefs to allow for a whole new way to live an awakened life. And believe me, it's all pretty exciting and wonderful, but my controlling self 'reminds' me that at any moment, the abundance can and will be taken. See? Scarcity back again for an encore, even while I try to grow enlightened." Lacey released a frustrated sigh.

"Okay, let's you and me spend an extra moment or two delvin' into this subject. And I haven't forgotten you still have news to share that I suspect has somethin' to do with your present upheaval."

"You're right, and I believe you've just tapped into another core issue for me. I would so appreciate a special dose of your wisdom here." Lacey's two clenched fists rested in her lap. She made a point to relax, opening them with her exhaled breath. Her eyes returned to Cassie's face.

Cassie stepped right into Lacey's emotional water. "You're afraid."

Lacey frowned, hearing the words spoken so forthrightly.

"Yep, you're afraid," stated Cassie, marching on. "That rascal fear has paid you an unexpected and most unwelcome visit. I'm thinkin' somethin' pretty special and life-changin' has come callin', and you're lettin' thoughts distract you with their stories…old stories, Missy." She paused to allow the message to settle on her Seeker. Cassie called this tart talk.

She could sense Lacey had accepted what had been said, and so she continued, "I have a different kind of gold nugget to share with you this day." Cassie paused for effect. "Not only are you afraid of the newness, but you're also afraid of the sameness."

Lacey started to protest, but Cassie resumed.

"Yes, that's truth, Niece. There your fanny sits on the fence straddlin' the doubt and fear, which, if you recall, your bothersome mind conjured up for you. It's all the mind can do when threatened."

Mouth agape, Lacey stared.

"Well, let me tell you once more that the gifts you're discoverin' can't be taken away. Not ever. Even by your mind tellin' you different. They belong to you. They're your treasure given by God. Hear me?" Cassie's countenance radiated her purity of purpose.

A solemn nod was Lacey's answer.

Cassie persisted. "Once awakened by The Three Lessons, the spirit takes over as it should. You work with The Lessons in the way that suits you. And you know what else? God supports your doin' exactly that when it's done for the higher good. This discovery of yours is all about figurin' out the how in the Now. Did you hear what I just said? For it's the precious gift of Lesson Three."

"I heard but not sure I get it," Lacey replied.

"Missy, to get Lesson Three, you must meet me somewhere," Old Mountain Cassie instructed.

Lacey glanced around, wondering if there was another garden or trail she'd be introduced to. "Where do I need to go, Aunt Cassie?"

Well, it's the only place God wants any of us to be…the Now. The present. No other place will do. Plenty of smart folks have been tellin' us this for ages, but we were missin' some pieces to have it work. I will explain better in a bit. First, let your ears hear this. Did you know now is where all spiritual doings happen? Yes, ma'am, no other place." Cassie nodded.

Lacey tapped her pen against her cheek, reflecting. "I suppose that's true, but I never really thought that way."

"Ya know, I've a particular fondness for Ralph Waldo Emerson. He and I see things pretty near the same. You ever kept company with his words?" asked Cassie.

Lacey's face registered surprise that her aunt had read Emerson. "Only a little in college lit courses."

"Hmm…well, I'm feelin' led to call on Mr. Emerson to attend to your teachin'. You see, he had quite an attachment to bein' in the Now. He said, 'With the past, I have nothing to do; nor with the future. I live now.'" Cassie waited.

"I'm following." Lacey's journal's blank page stared back. She didn't know what to record.

"Here's The Lesson's teachin'. Everything you seek…want…need…waits in the Now. Answers don't live in the past, nor in the unhappened future. No, it's only in the present moment you or any of us can ask God for guidance and receive it. You must stay awake in the Now, ever listenin' and watchin' for your answers. You ask, what should you do next? Only in the Now will you be shown. Thinkin' about the past or ponderin' into the future won't get you what you seek. Emerson just told you this. Understand?" Cassie quieted, watching Lacey write. She turned her attention to Lickety, offering his stick. Her arm released it to the breeze.

Lacey paused looking to Cassie. "So, I need to try and stay focused in the Now as I go about my day so that I won't miss guidance or gifts?"

"That's right, Missy. And the bonus is when you live in the Now, you will begin to think and act differently too." Cassie smiled.

"Tell me if I get this. The past and future can't know my answers. It's just the mind's way of trying to stay in control and rehash what's stored in its intelligence. But if I'm awake in the moment, then God's able to reach me with solutions. The past is over, and the future hasn't happened, so how dumb of me to waste energy there. Geez. I must watch my thoughts and ensure they are acting in the present moment with me. Yes, this is a super important lesson, Cassie."

"You did real fine takin' that inside. I like the way you said it better than me." Cassie laughed. I believe it's time for you to have the secret to havin' the amazin' life you long for. Are you ready for this last part?"

"I'm gratefully ready." Lacey squeezed her aunt's hand.

"The secret to livin' in amazement is you must integrate The Three Lessons, for they depend on each other to deliver on the promise. You see, the Spirit Self, the Now, and the Divinin' Portal together connect you to God and the Others. These are the missin' pieces most folks don't know about that I mentioned a few minutes ago. You gotta be always integratin' The Three Lessons. They live and thrive for each other and you. That's the secret to having the life up until now that you only dreamed about. It's time in the Now to claim your many blessings."

"Aunt Cassie, may I offer a prayer of praise and gratitude in this present moment?" Lacey knelt by her aunt's chair and asked her spirit's voice to find God.

Chapter 53

AFTER LACEY'S PRAYER, THE TWO women craved a different kind of nourishment. The porch found them enjoying fruit bowls with fresh berries and peaches and warm pecan muffins. Cassie served what she called toastin' wine to celebrate Lacey's meeting all The Three Lessons.

"What say we return back to our benches by the wishin' well?" Cassie chuckled, noting her niece's raised brow. "I want to do a bit of polishin' with you."

"Polishing? I don't know if I'm up for more—"

"Ah, come on with me in the Now. See what other gifts might be for you." Cassie and Lickety headed for their spot, trusting their Seeker was following.

―

"First, Niece, I want you to understand that these experiences you've been witnessin' have been gifted to you. Know why?"

"I might have a tiny inkling, but I prefer to hear the answer from you if you don't mind."

Cassie smiled. "So that your very reason and purpose can be shown to you. For it's God's breath on you and your actions that have filled you with wonder. You've been bathed daily with and in those feelins' so that you can discover the pure passion in your callin'. Remember what I told you early on? Find your passion. Know your joy. And there's God's breath."

"God's breath on me too? How beautiful that sounds." Lacey sighed.

"I agree." Cassie glowed in her own joy from God's breath.

"Cassie, you and The Three Lessons have led me to embrace my calling…my purpose for being. It's the gems and me here to help others, and I recognize that God's breath has literally blown blessings my way so often, but I didn't recognize them," Lacey said with a sigh. Then she added, "But I do now."

"I hear ya, but don't be surprised if your thoughts still mess with you. They always will, but in time, they will become more helpful and less interfering. What say you tell me that news I've been slap bustin' to hear?"

"I understand. Let's see. Well, it happened the other day when Serene sent me out to measure a building in town," Lacey spent the next minutes detailing the events and ending with her arduous nights spent trying to determine how she could ever afford to buy the building and open her shop. She acknowledged the chance to have her own shop had come in the Now and how fortunate she'd been paying attention.

"Goodness me, but God certainly seems to be working extra hard on this store blessing. Let me see if I've got this all set in my noggin."

"Please ask me anything." Lacey tried to remain composed, but her excitement in sharing her news had taken control despite her doubts in accomplishing this new dream. Her fingers absently reached to touch the pendant around her neck.

"You've been shown the perfect place for your gifts to be put to use, but you don't have enough funds to make it happen?" Old Mountain Cassie summed, getting to the heart of Lacey's perceived problem.

"Pretty much. Nor do I have access or a clue as to what kind of gems I'd even want to use to create my designs. You see, I want my pieces to…well, speak to others like your teas and herbs do. I feel the call to create beautiful jewelry to evoke joy and healing for others, or whatever the pieces are called to do. I'm open to what manifests." Lacey paused to gather her words. "The desire is alive inside of me, but it's like I'm being blocked from seeing what this would look like in the future." Lacey took a breath and then released it slowly but kept her returning doubts.

"And Miss Lacey, can you tell me again where you're looking for these blocked answers?" Cassie waited.

"Well, for starters, I'm looking ahead to tomorrow afternoon and whether I should drop the papers to Elliot, and then I—"

"Missy, you've left the present moment already. See how easy we slip unaware into the past or future? You're lookin' in the wrong time." Cassie patted her niece's hand.

"I'm not a very quick study on living in the Now." Lacey felt defeated.

"Hush up. You're doing fine. You're still a learnin' Seeker. We will build more on that foundation. You bring your frets and confusion back here tomorrow. We will do more integratin' and such."

"In the meantime, I will practice integrating with my Spirit Self, in my Divining Portal, in the Now. How's that sound?" Lacey went to hug her aunt.

Cassie laughed and accepted the hug. "That'll work."

Chapter 54

LACEY'S GROWING DOUBT AND SADNESS of acquiring a shop accompanied her to the coffee brewer the following morning. Even Serene's "trust the process" pep talk the night before hadn't lifted the dark cloud or Gabby's drop by showing off the fancy room keys she'd had fashioned for Amethyst Inn. Lacey tried escaping to her Divining Portal before bed, but her mind went along, demanding she focus on the potential financial problems looming if she attempted such a scheme. She'd promised Cassie to bring her growing list of frets this morning but wondered what further teachings her aunt could possibly have to offer. Yep, she was a Doubting Lacey this day.

Lacey and her aunt journeyed back to the benches by the wishing well. Each had enjoyed a few minutes in meditative silence.

Cassie broke the spell. "Well, I guess this is as good a time as any for you to pick up that bound notebook hangin' on the bench's arm." Cassie pointed to the book.

Lacey straightened, reaching for the addition of a notebook. She looked at her aunt questioningly. She felt anticipation rise with her hopes in gaining another piece to her life's puzzle. "Now what?" Lacey held the bound book.

Cassie bided her time until Lacey appeared more settled but still drenched in doubt. "Ever read the Bible?"

Lacey's head shot up at the unexpected question. "Actually, yes, I've started reading it regularly."

Old Mountain Cassie nodded, pleased with the response. "I fancy Proverbs. A lot of good teachin' in that book. Bet you didn't know old Proverbs has a powerful message that's been waitin' for you?"

"No, I didn't know that. So, what does Proverbs have for me?" Lacey attempted a grin.

"Oh, not too terribly much. Just another key of how to awaken fully. The Now that I've been teachin' you has all the answers you will ever seek. Every single one." Cassie didn't miss a beat. "And the peculiar part is that truth has been tucked away pretty as you please in old Proverbs 2: 9-10 for a very long time, waiting to enlighten generation after generation."

"My interest is piqued, Aunt Cassie, and I admit feeling needy today."

"Good enough. I'm going to say the words as they're written in my *Living Bible*, but I expect you'll want to read them later for yourself." She bid the words forward.

"He shows how to distinguish right from wrong, how to find the right decision every time. For wisdom and truth will enter the very center of your being, filling your life with joy."

Cassie read the verses again, giving the words the reverence they deserved.

Tears pooled in Lacey's eyes as the words found a new home. She sat unmoving, absorbing the strength of the teaching.

"But remember, as Lesson Three teaches, as simple as this truth seems, putting it into being is not easy. Your mind will try every trick to keep you out of the Now. Even though your mind has been cooperatin' and interested these last minutes, it will test your mettle again and again. See that as proof you're awake." Cassie gave a knowing smile. "Never forget what you need to do."

"I know. Be rude to my negative thoughts, and I am becoming ruder and ruder, especially during meditation. I've got a ways to go, but I will not be thwarted in developing more rudeness." Lacey's mouth turned up.

"Good to hear that determination. Clear that path for your guidance to get through. Pull those weeds daily to keep the path open and easy to walk. Do that and you'll always have a beautiful pathway leading to fresh blessings. More than you can imagine. Another promise."

"Aunt Cassie, I will strive to be a devoted gardener as much like you as I'm able to master in this lifetime. I'm going to aspire to that lofty goal and keep our family's special talents alive," declared Lacey, making a silent and solemn commitment to God and herself.

"What pleasin' words to my ears. Listen to your teacher and aunt and don't you be frettin' anymore about your work. You know how to find the answers to the question about your new adventure? You simply turn to God and ask to be shown."

"Right. And then I wait in the Now for the answer to appear."

"Yes, only in the Now, and the Now includes?"

"Whatever state I happen to be in in the present moment is now," Lacey supplied, feeling her confidence soar, finally grasping what Cassie had been nurturing within her.

"And you take a dose of patience each morning knowing the answers bear fruit in their own time, but they'll always come if you're watchin'. Always." Cassie let her words settle.

"That special book tied to the bench wants some of your time. It came with us before, but today is the better day. I'm going to leave you with this last assignment to complete. You'll be doin' some unusual writin', so enjoy." Cassie winked. "No need to seek me out to say bye. I'll be up at the plant shed." Cassie stood, her eyes searching for Lickety.

Lacey opened her mouth to object. "I can't be done already…I mean—"

"Oh, Missy, we'll still be having our visits and fine-tunin' of you. Don't you worry. I'm sensing that things are about to get mighty busy for you, and I'm right here to help as your aunt and your teacher. Don't go forgettin' we're family." Old Mountain Cassie leaned down and kissed her niece's forehead.

Lacey released a breath. "That's good to hear 'cause I was afraid. Geez, I see what you mean. Blasted thoughts had me fretting again."

"Ahh, but not for long this time." Cassie moved away. "Take the time in Now to savor the sweet taste of what you're about to do. Stop by in a day or so and bring your news. I'll be waitin' with the perfect tea." She turned, whistling for Lickety Split.

Lacey watched the pair disappear down the path. She closed her eyes and said a prayer of gratitude. It was the easiest prayer she'd ever said.

The cardinal perched on the wishing well's roof sang out. The squirrel, who'd been sitting quietly under Lacey's bench, scampered away. They'd fulfilled their calling. Others would come to watch over her. They always had.

Chapter 55

Lacey opened the book to the first page, having released all expectations. The words lit the page.

Seek no more. Blessings are flowing upon you for the rest of your earth life journey. You've been guided to this very spot to place inside the book a record of your appreciation so that God might activate all laws in your favor. Your destination will be made clear as these laws unfold. You've been chosen by your Heavenly Guides to witness and then share this ancient truth. Begin by recording your known gifts. Don't delay. Now is the time. Your time. Take up the writing instrument and use it constructively.

Lacey read the instructions once more, noting the uniqueness of the pen. Each color in the spectrum glowed from the instrument. The pen appeared to have a life of its own; glittering in the sunlight with expectation directed at her. She clicked the writing implement and hoped her brain would follow suit, for she knew not where to start. She'd had a lifetime to appreciate her love for gems, and most especially she appreciated being led to Cassie, who'd been the most recent instrument of guidance to understanding her gifts. And of course, the Law of Attraction and the Law of Abundance had been a part of this greater gift.

She remembered Cassie's emphasis on ignoring her mind's negative dictates and chuckled. Her brain was not the source for her appreciating or for tapping into, but her spirit certainly was there waiting as the higher choice. She recognized the brain served as a vehicle to take her where she needed to go for this connecting, and nothing more.

Lacey took a cleansing breath and, with her long exhale, emptied her mind. A tranquil stillness held her in the moment as the pen began to move of its own free will across the page.

A shocked and surprised Lacey read as she wrote, not knowing what the next words appearing on the page would be.

Sentences filled the pages, bringing her to the present moment of her life's recording. Her time on earth had been a series of events and encounters building to this very moment. In what she'd perceived as randomness had really been Divine Order. Recording appreciation illumined this.

Lacey sat quietly, waiting, with her stilled pen. She recalled her lessons: ask and you shall receive. "Okay, I suppose I've completed journaling my personal appreciation. What next?" she asked aloud in her new Now state.

The wind answered by blowing the book's pages ahead to another entry where words waited to be read.

Lacey glanced down at a peach-colored page. Colorful bumble bees and dragonflies bordered the paper.

What do you wonder? Here in the Now is your opportunity to receive the answer.

Lacey watched the butterflies flit and flutter in the flower garden while she sat pondering her wonder. Lots of questions surfaced, but, somehow, they all seemed so tepid…so ordinary compared to this moment's experience.

Her spirit came to her rescue, thirsty to receive forgotten truths from the higher plane. She wrote:

I wonder, how is it possible for God to really know and care for me?

Seconds slipped by, suspending Lacey's awareness of her surroundings. All that mattered was a growing concern that the pen didn't have an answer. Realizing her mind's disrupting ways had snuck back in, she took a cleansing breath and turned her focus to the Now and to valuing the pen's indescribable beauty and strange powers.

Her hand quivered. The pen took off with verve to provide the answer, which only added to her wonder.

Because God resides in and with you, thereby always caring for each of your needs, you can never be alone. You cannot be separated. You cannot cease to be. God is part of you, and you are part of God. The God that is: All-knowing. All-caring. All-loving.

The pen stilled. Lacey felt the silence as the words on the page began to fade. Had she imagined the pen wrote a reply? No. Definitely and a resoundingly no. This was yet another strange and life-changing encounter to add to the growing list of experiences deemed impossible.

She closed her eyes, trying to imprint the words on her heart. Doubt crept in. How could God be in her? She'd never considered this possibility. All her life, Lacey thought of God as a deity outside overseeing, orchestrating, doling out punishment when needed. And yet if God indeed resided inside of her, then by golly, God surely could and would know and care for her. But where in her exactly? And of course, that meant that God dwelled in everything, not just her. Yes, dwelling in and out, both. How? Her mind begged to question. How indeed?

Lacey felt the breeze return. She sensed the strong "intention for attention." Again, the pages in the book advanced stopping at another place where violet paper with stars and moons orbiting around the edges waited for her pen. She held the pen in place as her eyes gazed down to the words flowing across the page.

Doubt not the impossible, for there lies the chamber door to truth. Hold to your passage key.

Lacey read the words again. Her mind responded, asking, *Where is the passage to the truth?* She didn't have a clue what this…Yes! The passage key was meant to unlock the door to Now. This secret had been brought to her repeatedly, but she'd always been in her head, ignoring the signs. She saw at once her own Divine Plan. She finally understood now that her worries about having her own shop served merely as a distraction. With God inside of her and Cassie's teachings, Lacey felt she'd crossed the threshold into the chamber of knowing. Worries served only those who remained on the other side of the door.

Old Mountain Cassie had spent her life showing Seekers the way to discover their gifts. She was right about the truths being simple but difficult to grasp and hold to. These incredible experiences served as steps to reach this higher vibration of living. "Thanks for being so patient, God. And I plan to hang onto the key and pray The Three Lessons live inside me."

Chapter 56

That evening, Cassie and her beloved "traveling" rocker kept company out on the porch, taking in the cool mountain air blowing into the valley. The stars shone silvery against the sky's cerulean canopy. Lightning bugs blinked, adding more color to the inky darkness. The breeze stilled in preparation for the quietness Cassie needed to collect her words. On she rocked, nodding every now and again until satisfied with her instructions, and then she reached for the phone.

"Evenin', Branson. How am I findin' you?" Cassie asked, offering a dose of polite sweetness.

"Well, sugar, I'd say this surprise call is finding me pleased as punch. How say you?"

"Me? Oh, I'm Jim Dandy," she replied, scoring an idiom point. "Enjoyed a most special day with my most special Seeker." She set the bait, hoping the old trout would bite.

"Glad to hear it. Are you calling because you miss me? Maybe?"

"Course I miss your company, but actually, I need a kindness this particular evening. Are you of a kindly mood?" Cassie added a dash of feminine charm to her voice.

"Gal, you've got wiles a plenty. You know you do, and I feel them working on me clear over here in the city. So yes, I'm feeling especially kindly right this minute. Let me hear what you're needing, but be warned, I'm inclined to ask for some kindness back." Branson chuckled, already counting on some bargaining chips to play.

"Oh, I've got your kindness already picked out. Don't go troublin' yourself on that account."

"Darling, you get on with your asking, and we'll settle up once I know what's in that pretty head of yours."

"You still own that buildin' in town where your niece has her little jewelry store, don't you?" Cassie asked, easing her way along.

"Yes, ma'am. She's closing it, though, and going to have an adventure, she tells me. Kinda taking after her favorite uncle, you might say."

"Yes, I'd heard that about the closin' and that you'd like to maybe find a buyer for the building."

"That's one plan I'm leaning toward. Had a few sniffers already, but I'm particular about what I want to go in my building. You know it belonged to my father. Good memories. One comes to mind if you know what I'm referring to, Sugar." Branson laughed.

"Yeah, you buzzard, I remember that day just fine. No need to trot it back out." Cassie sniffed.

Branson ignored her. "Yep, Cassie's first kiss. Stole it right next to the plows."

"Hush up and listen." Cassie interrupted the laughter coming her way.

Branson quieted. "I'm listening."

"Well, my special Seeker just so happens to have discovered her gifts lie with gems and is ready to open her own shop. You see, she's plenty experienced and had been a top gem buyer for a company over where you live until a cutback in staff recently left her without a job. Of course, I see it as a good thing." Cassie paused, giving Branson a chance to respond.

"Go on, Cass." Branson's voice grew serious.

"Well, she visited your niece's store the other day and is convinced the place is pretty near perfect except for one tiny problem that might turn up." She took a breath before hitting him with the real pitch.

"And would I be correct to think I'm to be the solution to this tiny problem?"

"You would and should," Cassie stated, feeling more convinced herself having heard the words spoken aloud.

"Keep talking, woman. Get to the meat 'cause I'm looking forward to my dessert." He reclined back in his leather desk chair and grabbed a pad and pen to make notes about Cassie's coming proposal.

"The only dessert you're…oh, never mind." He'd just baited her. "My Seeker is findin' a bank loan, not to her liking."

"Cassieee…" Branson said, stretching out her name.

"Okay, fine. The bank may not find the loan to their likin' either, but that's because they've gotten—"

"Forget the bank. Get to my part." Branson pleaded.

"I think you should be her bank and hold the mortgage. I mean, you don't really need the money all at once, do you?" Cassie didn't give him a chance to reply. "You'd have a nice tidy income for your generous heart."

"Wait, did I just hear a genuine compliment coming from your lips?"

Cassie sighed. "Close enough." Her sassy tongue intruded. She quickly checked her clipped tone. "Why, yes, sir, a real nice compliment. As I was explainin', you'd benefit havin' the income and a fine gal as your buyer."

"How fine? I'm asking, how can you vouch for this lady only just knowing her a short time? I'd need references, a business plan to look over and, of course, some money down—"

"Hold on a minute, my recommendation isn't good enough?" Cassie's back stiffened as her jaw clenched.

"Darlin', this is business. I'm willin' to listen to your proposal because I'm a besotted old fool, but I'm also a man who tends his investments as carefully as you do those plants of yours. Fair enough?" Branson grabbed his amortization sheet, relishing his newly elevated position with Cassie. "Well?"

"Fair enough…I suppose." Cassie couldn't argue against sound judgment. She'd have to trust him with some of her secrets starting with Lacey being her great niece. And a great niece she'd turned out to be too. She'd already developed a powerful love for the gal.

Thirty minutes later, it was Branson who confessed to covering her with the blanket while she slept in her porch rocker. Cassie smiled for having that mystery solved but more because he'd come callin'. Best of all, they'd struck a deal, one that surprised, and even pleased her. Trust Branson to come collecting his first installment of kindness the next weekend. Cassie blushed, remembering him calling a kiss from her his favorite dessert. She might convince herself to buy a new lipstick—a pretty red one to go with her sassy boots.

She hollered Lickety Split inside, turning off the lights as she made her way to bed. Tonight, she'd probably end up dreamin' about that old coot instead of getting instructions from the Guides. Men were certainly distractions, but then again, they sure could cause a female to enjoy a little extra mirror time. Cassie pinched her cheeks and brushed her long fine hair free from the braids before bidding her antique vanity mirror good night.

Chapter 57

Serene closed the front door and returned to sit on the sofa. "I'm wiped, sister. This has been my most favorite birthday ever. I think renting the theatre for my party was a big hit. Everyone seemed to enjoy the movie, too.

"It sure was a hit, and I can honestly say that I've gotten every drop of joy out this day," Lacey responded truthfully.

"Hmmm…I'll give you a pass on elaborating on those drops 'cause I want to open my gift. Bring it hither. I'm ready."

Lacey claimed the bag from the table and handed it off to her friend. "Here you go. I suppose I've tormented you long enough."

"This wee box? Hint, if you please, and make it easy. Don't leave me feeling like some dullard."

"Okay, a pity hint said simply. Here goes…shiny metal is your clue. Reminds your spirit of all that's true." Lacey felt surprised that the hint seemed to roll off her tongue.

Serene looked at her friend and saw the light pulse around Lacey. "This gift has your energy deposited through it. This may sound crazy, but I see and feel the connection."

Lacey stared, mouth agape. There were many layers of awareness in her friend that she was coming to recognize.

"You've made me something extremely special out of…yes, my guess is gold. How am I doing this time?" Serene asked softly.

"Fantastic! How did you know all of that? Serene?"

"I suspect we've shared the same teacher."

Lacey's eyes widened. No coincidences, Cassie had told her, and no shortage of synchronistic twists and turns. Another astonishing one had just been confirmed. Her old life had been replaced by this vibrant existence all residing in the Now. Unthinkable had replaced thinkable, and her weary mind was learning to take a backseat. She realized Serene sat waiting on her to say something. "Go ahead. Open the lid." Lacey smiled.

Serene had unwrapped the gift but had gone no further, wishing for them both to have a moment to treasure this new connection. She was sure that Old Mountain Cassie had another Seeker…the woman sitting next to her. Serene's fingers trembled as the energy transferred from the piece to her. She recognized and understood her dear friend's special gift was for both of them.

Lacey's wish for a shop would surely manifest. That's how the Law of Attraction and Guides operated. Serene had her own experience under Old Mountain Cassie's tutelage proving this. She'd suspected Lacey's unrelenting attraction to anything Cassie meant she was a gifted Seeker. Incredible and wonderful Divine had attracted another rare one. Serene knew her friend was waiting expectantly for some response. "Lacey…Lacey, words aren't flowing, but some pretty extraordinary energy is. This piece…well, it's radiant. It's just become my most prized jewelry treasure. Tell me." Serene looked into her friend's shining eyes and knew Lacey understood.

"Oh, Serene, you sat there staring at the bracelet, not uttering a word, and making me feel the bracelet had failed us both but in a different way." Lacey released a pent-up breath and beamed a smile back.

"Tell me…please." Serene touched the gold-wire-wrapped bracelet, reverently appreciating the vivid emerald cabochon woven into the intricate design.

"Shall I tell you how the piece came to be?" Lacey asked, careful not to give away her promise to Aunt Cassie.

"If that's what you want to share, absolutely. Tell me the bracelet's story then."

"Hmm, how to begin? I've always loved gems and jewelry, but then you know this part, of course." Lacey smiled. "My hesitation came from my worry that I didn't have the ability to create special pieces. My design classes from school were a long time ago, but I kept some of my equipment and jewelry findings."

"That's pretty cool."

"Oh yes, that's an understatement. Let me just sum it up by saying I've had some incredible encounters that supported my exploring jewelry design with a glad heart. The bracelet gracing your wrist is my very first piece. Guess that makes you my tester of sorts.

"Well, lucky me to be the chosen one.

"My turn. This bracelet has an energy that I sense. A powerful, good energy and I suspect that it's coming from your time with creating it, along with the gem's power. Lacey, you do have an extraordinary gift that I can promise you will intensify as you develop. And know that I'm here supporting that development, okay?" Serene squeezed her friend's hand.

"Very okay. Sounds to me like I have a kindred spirit on my journey and we share more that can be spoken of."

"Yes, so true. So, next step is a place for you to keep creating these bonny beauties." A wise Serene leaned over and gave Lacey a warm hug.

"That's my most sincere hope." Lacey rose, preparing to leave. "I see Elliot tomorrow to learn whether I qualify or not."

"Things will work out one way or another. Trust." Serene held up her arm, showing off the bracelet. "Anyone having this natural gift has many pieces waiting to be birthed."

Chapter 58

Lacey entered the bank's door, offering a relaxed smile to a waiting Elliot who was dressed in a navy suit and a loud tie, clearly a gift from some patron.

"Come in. Take a seat, Lacey. Didn't we all have a great time at Serene's party last night?" Elliot wanted to set a friendly tone to ease his next words.

"We sure did. Divine's like no other place. I'm blessed to call it home. Elliot, why don't we get right to the point of our meeting?" Lacey's voice maintained the friendliness she felt for this kind man no matter the outcome.

"Right. Well, Lacey, the directors met. I sure regret having to tell you this. The board felt with the current economy, they'd need another twenty thousand to make you the loan" Elliot sucked in a breath and continued, "They're very impressed with your business plan and of course you, but—"

"But it's a numbers game like you told me before, and emotions can't be a factor," said Lacey, finishing for him.

"Well…yes. I'm sure sorry. I wanted to bring you better news."

"Thanks, Elliot. I know you did."

"Have you come up with some alternative financing? I'd like to see you become one of Divine's merchants. You'd be a darn good asset to our town, and me and some other guys are going to be counting on your help with the wives' birthday and Christmas gifts." He grinned.

"And I'd be happy to create something special for Louisa. As for other financing, unfortunately, nothing has presented that is viable to me."

"Promise me you won't despair on the plan just yet. Think on it some more."

"Ah, thinking…not my ally of late," Lacey responded sagely.

"Excuse me?" Elliot asked, confused.

"Nothing. Never mind. A reflective moment." Lacey smiled. She rose, extending her hand. "Thanks again, Elliot, for your efforts on my behalf. I know you did your best for me."

"I did, Lacey. Look, maybe I could make a couple of calls to other banks for you—"

"No, don't trouble. I sense I'm going to need a different approach if I'm to be successful. And I promise not to despair just yet," Lacey added, realizing she didn't feel thwarted one bit—not by Elliot's news or her mind's chatter. She had her lessons to pull from now and God as Senior Partner.

"Good, good. Keep me posted and give a call if I can help in any other way."

"I will. See ya later." Lacey waved to Jane Ann, entering the bank.

Lacey stood outside the bank's entrance, focused on the Now moment waiting for inner direction. She felt the pull from Old Mountain Cassie and the nudge of the energy-filled leys. She'd promised Cassie she'd drop by, and now appeared to be the perfect time before her thoughts made her a prisoner of defeat. Maybe she could meditate there in the midst of the leys; surely that rarified environment would help bring her clarity. Satisfied with the plan, she got behind the wheel and turned the vehicle toward the forest.

Lacey caught sight of a rainbow touching Aunt Cassie's mountain as she stepped out of her SUV. *An excellent time for a pot of gold to find me*, she mused, slipping into her hiking boots. She twisted her hair into a top knot before proceeding down the now familiar trail.

A friendly squirrel scampered over to greet her. The little fellow managed to keep her company, forcing back her fretful thoughts. As Lacey veered toward Cassie's cabin, the red cardinal appeared at her side, chirping and flapping his wings to distract her. Lickety's ears caught the bird's announcement, and he ran toward the commotion.

"Well, hey there, Lick. I was just coming for a visit." Lacey reached down to give the dog a pat.

He barked and turned in circles, showing Cassie's note wrapped around his collar.

"What's this?" Lacey folded the paper, after reading the instructions. "I understand this greeting excitement of yours now. Guess I need to alter my course to the plant shed, huh?" Lacey addressed the menagerie around her. Her weary mind had given up offering explanations for how Cassie seemed to know when a Seeker would be calling.

The cardinal sang out and flew off in the shed's direction, leaving the dog and squirrel to follow, along with Lacey. Lick walked by her side, licking her hand every few yards until the building came into view.

Chapter 59

THE MOUNTAIN WOMAN STOOD WEARING her trademark overalls and a happy face. "See, your guide did his job. Come on inside. Expect you need a hand washing," said Cassie with a loud chuckle as she patted her dog's head.

Lacey laughed. I've never known a dog to lick a person to a destination before. He's something, this fellow." She leaned down and rubbed an ear. "I confess I tested him a few times to measure his loyalty and commitment to the task."

"How'd he do?" Cassie asked, giving her canine an affectionate glance.

"You'd be proud. Whenever I moved off the trail, he'd stop and wait for me to return to that spot. He gave the sweetest little cries to entice me back. He's the most remarkable dog I've ever known."

Lickety Split barked his agreement before going in search of his water bowl. Clearly, he felt dehydrated from all his ministrations to Lacey.

Cassie watched him take long drinks. "Yep, he came that way. Come on inside and keep me company whilst I tidy the counters. We can take a short hike after I feed you some freshly baked blond brownies."

"I can't say no to any of those offerings." Lacey followed her aunt to the sunny room, noticing the herbs sealed in bags ready for boxing. "Let me help so I can get a tasty treat sooner." Lacey grabbed a roll of paper towels and white vinegar cleaner and went to work.

"How'd you know, Missy, that was my next step?" Cassie asked, watching Lacey wipe down the stainless top.

"Gosh, I didn't stop to think. I guess I just…" Lacey paused from her task and saw her aunt's expression.

"You're intuiting, Missy. Understand me?" Cassie's gaze penetrated past the controlling mind of her niece.

"Is that what this new behavior is called?" Lacey finished cleaning and joined Cassie at the door.

Cassie noted the pendant around Lacey's neck before flicking off the light switch and grabbing her lunch sack. "Follow me to a spot I think you'll find most agreeable."

The two women set an easy stride down the trail, chatting about nothing in particular, saving the real talk for when they stopped. A lush green meadow opened that could use up a day in the savoring.

Lacey spoke first. "Yet another enchanting place! I suppose this is still on your property?"

"Yes, ma'am. Pretty spot to sit and spin a spell, don't you agree?"

"Spin a spell? Hmm...there's got to be a double meaning tucked in between those words." Lacey's thoughts surfaced, sabotaging her light mood by recalling Elliot's words. Cassie's voice brought her attention back to the clearing where they stood.

"Getting harder to slip anything past my graduatin' Seeker. Here, taste."

Lacey took the napkin holding a large blond brownie that Cassie had slipped out of her pack. The first fingers of real disappointment in her meeting with Elliot wrapped around her heart as her real fingers wrapped around the brownie. Her body betrayed her by following the negative thought and tightening her stomach instead of enjoying the first bite of Cassie's sweet.

She took another bite, lost in sadness.

"Lacey? Stop that! Come back to me in this moment. This is where your answers are waitin' to help you."

Lacey stared at her aunt, amazed she'd read her so quickly.

"I see on your face the meetin' didn't support the path to your passion," observed Cassie. She took another bite of her brownie, watching her niece's reaction.

"Aunt Cassie, you are so right. I'm feeling so disheartened, and my mind is telling me to give up despite my attempts to be rude. The thoughts have trespassed on my lovely time with you. I'm so sorry."

"No need to apologize to me, but I would welcome hearin' what Elliot said."

"Well, he told me the directors weren't comfortable loaning unless I can produce another twenty thousand, which I can't. No way."

"Tell me this, have you, deep down inside, let your mind convince you that all is lost, or have you chosen to wait in the present for your next step to be shown? Remember Proverb's teaching:"

"He shows how to distinguish right from wrong, how to find the right decision every time. For wisdom and truth will enter the very center of your being, filling your life with joy."

"I slipped," Lacey answered softly. She tucked the verse into her heart this time for safe keeping.

Cassie continued, "Well then, Niece, step away from the emotions that claimed you a moment ago and tell me who you've been since walkin' out of Elliot's office. Call her back if she's the awakened one that I've been keepin' company with of late." Cassie sat down on a large boulder with a dose of patience to wait for Lacey to figure things out.

Lacey walked over to another large rock that had a flat surface. She planted her bottom down and posed the question to herself. "Who have I been?" she whispered. Her eyes closed, hoping the truth came to her rescue.

The Lacey who had learned to trust in higher guidance emerged in full glory, reminding her that a slip of a few minutes into negative thinking only counted if she remained there, comfortable in her old patterns. And of course, the past solace of wallowing had been absent this time. Instead, a hunger to be true to her gifts brought her to this moment of wanting to remain fully awake, and so she forgave herself.

Lacey drew on the teachings, allowing her Spirit Self to be in control, to keep returning to the Now no matter how many times it took, and to spend time in her special space where God and her

Guides would be waiting to empower and infuse her. Those were The Lessons. Cassie had been right in saying the practice was far from easy.

Lacey felt certain she'd been drawn to Divine to develop her gifts. She believed in a plan for everyone. Old Mountain Cassie had been waiting to guide her to the greater truths…the life-changing truths. Once glimpsed, God's spiritual laws added the critical layer of proof to her discernment. She'd read about the Laws of Attraction and Abundance and saw the role they could play in answering her inner desires.

She knew without question that she had abilities with gemstones to create what others needed for their own spiritual advancement, just as Cassie had special gifts around herbs and Serene real estate sales. And she bet her last bite of brownie that others had been called to Divine to tap into their own uniqueness. She expected more would follow in time, but for this day, this moment, Lacey sat in perfect bliss, waiting to be shown her next step of how to create jewelry with divine design. She grabbed a cleansing breath of mountain air, releasing any lingering doubt with an exhale. Her eyes found Cassie's face and, with it, her fragile inner peace.

Chapter 60

TIME TO EXPLAIN HER LAPSE to a still but watchful Cassie. "Call it a momentary loss of signal," she offered, informing Cassie she was back and with her sense of humor that she'd come to rely on more and more to keep her spirit engaged.

"Well, Niece, whatever those words were about, I'm gonna take them to mean my student is ready to learn firsthand how God is always caring about our happiness. You open to another taste of amazement? It'll be better than the brownies, I can tell you that. This may be the most whoppin' proof you've had since we met." Cassie gave a nod for extra emphasis.

"Are you serious? You've got more to share?" Lacey moved to sit next to her aunt.

"You really took a fancy to that buildin' in town and still do feel pretty sure that's where you visualize your shop wants to be?"

"Yes, absolutely. The energy embraced me immediately when I entered," Lacey responded, puzzled.

"Then hold on to your knickers cause a bloomin' blessing landed in our lap this time."

"Excuse me?"

"Shhh...just listen. So happens my old beau by the name of Branson owns that property." Cassie grinned.

"Your beau? Why, Aunt Cassie—"

"Hush, no need to take a side trip on that subject," she said, blushing. "Let me continue. I got a prod to call him last evenin' and see what kind of bargain I might strike. See how God orchestrates?"

Lacey gave a nod, releasing Cassie's hand so that she could turn and face her aunt.

"Steady yourself. I'm about to dose you with a happy shocker. You can call that buildin' yours and some pleasin' purchase terms, if, of course, you're obliging. And, gal, you'd better be because the old coot has me cookin' him dinner, and only God knows what new plans might be stirrin' in that head of his." Cassie looked into the woods, wondering…hoping.

"Oh my—"

"Yes, and here's the paper where I wrote things out all clear like for you. Look her over while I celebrate with another blondie." Cassie took a generous bite while watching a deer couple waiting to visit her at the edge of the clearing.

"My gosh, this all looks a hundred times better than what I'd worked on with Elliot. You both even thought of a lower mortgage payment until I get established. However, did you get him to agree to such a low interest rate?" Lacey noted the tightness around Cassie's mouth. "Oh no, what else did you agree to?"

Cassie straightened her back. "I gotta take a trip…a blasted… cruise of all things." There. She'd finally been able to speak the words aloud. She could tell Lacey was close to havin' the vapors again, so she finished the telling. "His niece is the one you met who's closin' her store, and oh, Branson's uneasy about her decision to take on such a venture. He wants to see for himself that she's settled and happy workin' on that boat." Cassie paused.

"I see." Lacey waited for her aunt to give some sign of how she was coping with such a promise.

"Niece, I must be feelin' some kind of powerful love for you to agree to such nonsense. Yes, ma'am, a powerful love." Cassie cracked an elfish grin.

Lacey bit her tongue to keep from adding Cassie just might feel a "powerful love" for her old beau too. How funny to think of her aunt with a man. She chose instead to respond with appreciative words. "Cassie, you are wonderful…the best…the most unselfish… the most cunning…the—"

"That's it. Keep going. I'm gonna need a heap more praisin' to get me on that boat."

"Ship," Lacey corrected.

Cassie cocked a disapproving eyebrow.

Lacey quickly continued on, "Let me add the smartest…the most gifted herbalist…the most generous and loving. Aunt Cassie, I do love you so. You and God make an awesome team at making impossible dreams come true." Lacey wrapped her arms around the older woman's neck, and this time mutual love wrapped them both.

Chapter 61

LATER SITTING ON A BOULDER, both women's discussion moved to the particulars of the purchase agreement when another worry came calling on Lacey.

"Cassie, I need so much for the shop ... inventory for starters. Oh, and supplies, displays and ..."

"Whoa, Missy, take a breath. Slow that pony down a mite." Cassie was savoring each moment unfolding with divine purpose. In time, Lacey would reflect on this day with a big helping of awe and wonder. Until the jade box got handed over, Cassie needed to keep Lacey focused. "Lacey?" She saw her niece counting something on her fingers. "Lacey!"

"Yes? I'm here really in the moment, counting how many showcases I can fit in the shop. You know, actually what if I didn't do the typical look of a jewelry store?"

"Well, I suppose—"

"You see, I want to create an environment that speaks to our spirits. Aunt Cassie, that's my destiny. I know it. Oh no!"

"Now what?" asked a startled Cassie. The girl was wearing her out. She grinned.

"I simply must have gold wire to craft my designs, but more importantly, I have to find beautiful and incredible gems. You know, ones that are distinctive, unique?" Lacey tried to communicate her inner vision and desires to Cassie.

"There are plenty of pretty stones, but unique is a tall order I'd be thinkin'," Cassie added with a twinkle in her eye.

"You're right, of course. Still, I can't settle for any old ruby or amethyst. I want to specialize in a stone that isn't all over the marketplace…yes, a stone that has spirit…a stone like this one." Lacey's slender fingers reached up, touching the special rainbow gem Cassie had given to her.

"That one's plenty unique, all right. And I can vouch for its spiritual enhancing qualities."

Lacey smiled in agreement. "But even if I could locate gems with extraordinary energy, the price would be prohibitive for me to have in inventory." She dropped her head. Her creative juices were running into a dry creek bed, it seemed.

"I think you just said you couldn't afford to buy gems that are special, even if you could lay hands on them? Did I understand you right, Missy?" Cassie kept her twinkle.

Lacey was only half-listening. Instead, she'd taken note of the change on her aunt's face. "Right," she mumbled, watching Cassie rise.

"Come on. Bring all those frets and worries with you, if you want to waste a perfectly peaceful walk back to my place. Or if you dare, leave the care. Trust your desires and needs to be answered in the Now. I'm gonna speak clear like. Keep asking. Keep appreciating. Keep aspiring. That's my kind of insurance."

Lacey laughed, appreciating yet another Cassie insight. "You're right. I think appreciating is what I'll take back on our walk. I'll start by saying I so appreciate you and what you got Branson to agree to and…"

"And my brownies?"

"Most certainly the brownies." Lacey chuckled, enjoying their banter and thinking Cassie's brownies tasted exactly the same as Serene's.

Cassie tossed her braid over one shoulder in a saucy manner. "And did I happen to tell you these old bones of mine have to set sail as a part of this barter?"

Lacey chuckled. "Yes, you know that you did. And because of your great sacrifice, I'll tell you what I'm going to do for you."

"This I gotta hear. Watch these tree roots along this part of the trail. They throw you down and give you a close look of the ground without givin' a body any warning."

"Watching, thanks. Okay, listen to this, I'm going to take you shopping for some new outfits to wear on your cruise. My treat. How's that sound?" Lacey grew serious again. "I mean, it's the least I can do for an aunt who's devoted such immense time, energy, and caring…Aunt Cassie, there really aren't enough gratitude words—"

Old Mountain Cassie stopped her niece, not needing that kind of praise. "I don't take to fancy duds. Never have. But…" Cassie grinned. "But I might consider takin' a look at…oh, what do you call them? Sundresses?" Cassie winked. "Do red boots and sundresses keep company?"

"Hmm. Let me get back to you on that fashion question."

Chapter 62

"Care for a frosty glass of mint lemonade?" Cassie moved to open her screen door.

"Sounds reviving. Need some help?" Lacey's manners answered before her body could object.

"Just come in and sit."

Old Mountain Cassie took the pitcher out of the refrigerator and set two daisy-patterned glasses on a bamboo tray. She flashed back to Branson's words and their day at the Arboretum when he plucked the daisy's petals. "The old fox," she mumbled under her breath. He'd got her good on last night's bartering, getting her to agree to board a boat…ship…whatever the name of the fool thing, she was committed. It had been a long time since they'd kept that kind of company.

Cassie placed the tray with glasses on the table next to the waiting jade box. Funny how she'd grown attached to its recent presence after so many years of being hidden away. She reached for the exquisite rectangle of jadeite.

What ya got there, Aunt?"

"Oh, somethin' that's been waitin' on you for a heap of years." She turned and carried the box toward the screen door. "Bring our drinks to the porch."

"Waiting on me?" Lacey asked, puzzled, as she came up behind her aunt. By now, she'd learned she could count on one thing with Cassie…the unexpected.

Lacey and her curiosity settled in a cushioned rocker.

Cassie enjoyed her niece's confused expression. "Feelin' about ready for the icin' on your cake? Frostin' is the last thing you do to a cake, ya know."

"I suppose this means we're done with my lessons for real?" A dose of melancholy found Lacey.

"Yes, handin' over this box settles my commitment. You've learned how to live a blessed life in this world…moment by moment. You've been shown your true path. Time's right to use your gifts with gems and help others awaken. Niece, you've a grand life unfoldin' in service, always servin' God and the higher good.

"I hear your words, Aunt Cassie. I do. I'm just not sure I'm ready to be turned out." Lacey smiled gently, but fear shone in her eyes.

"I have questions for you. Do you believe…do you trust what you've been told? What you've been shown?

"Again, I say yes to all those questions. And I realize I'm acting all clingy."

Cassie chuckled but said nothing.

"I understand my lessons. I'm witnessing firsthand how God, my Senior Partner, can work with me. I've for sure experienced the real connection we have with the Other Side. I'm trying to stay awake and integrate these teachings into my daily life." Lacey paused.

"Sounds like a graduatin' Seeker to me. You've got the tools, Niece. Use them. Make things meaningful for you and others. Your hands and heart are primed and ready. Time you invited your head to join in. It still has an important support role to play. Honor that. Here's one of my freshies for you—head, heart, and hands equal harmony. I call that my special elixir recipe. It's a new one. You like it?" Cassie grinned.

"Aunt Cassie, you are the most precious jewel I'll ever know. The special elixir recipe. See, that was another lesson I needed? You can't call me done."

"Now listen up here, Lacey, my recipe addition is nothin' more than cake decoratin'. You're done. Toothpick's clean. Let go of those fears this minute circlin' your head. That active mind of yours will come to play a supportin' role once you abandon doubt and worry."

"Toothpick's clean, huh?" questioned Lacey.

"As a whistle."

"Cassie, you promised, though, that we'd still have plenty of times to fine-tune me and all." Lacey needed assurance one more time.

"My truck needs tunin' every now and again. We do too. How about we help each other stay tuned?" Cassie offered.

"Deal!" Lacey's relief washed over her as Cassie leaned in to shake her hand.

"Good. Now about that icing. I've been hankerin' all day to do this." Cassie placed the jade box in Lacey's lap. She sat back, waiting for her niece to respond.

"You know, I've noticed the box in your living room before. Sort of called to me whenever I came inside. Guess maybe it's because of the vibrant inlaid jade. "So, what am I to do next?"

"Well, I must admit I expected you to like this box but not for the reason you said. Wanna know why?" Cassie's eyes brightened, promising much more.

Lacey's hands gripped the rocker's arms. "Okay, I'm ready. Tell me."

"This jade box belonged to…your Grandmother Violet."

Lacey's mouth dropped open. "My grandmother? Nene?"

"Yes, ma'am. You know that Violet was older than me when she left with Morton to marry? Anyways, she gave me that box restin' in your lap. Put me in charge of its safekeepin', I guess you'd say. Told me to give it to her granddaughter one day should she ever have one. And one day is today. It's all yours. Belongs to no other."

Lacey gazed at the box, bereft of words and thoughts.

Old Mountain Cassie kept rocking. "Missy, if you're tired of starin' at that box, open that lid and add another extra, extra special moment to your collection." Cassie felt pleased that Violet had given her a gift too. Being able to watch Lacey's sure-to-be-surprised face was her icing.

Lacey nodded and lifted the jade lid, peering inside at the contents. An envelope that had yellowed from age stared back. She delicately removed the contents and placed the box on the side table. Cassie tipped her head to encourage Lacey to break the purple wax seal.

Lacey closed her eyes, pulling the papers from the envelope and another tiny envelope that held something solid. Lacey unfolded the letter, noting the date was likely when Violet left home in the carriage with Morton. Lacey read aloud.

> *Dearest Granddaughter,*
>
> *I know not if our destinies meant us to meet, but I do know that I love the hope of your being immensely. If you are holding this letter, it means you've been spending time with my baby sister, Cassandra. I asked her to safeguard my inherited box for you when I left our family home.*
>
> *By now, I expect that you've discovered the women of our family have been given certain gifts to use for good. As I grew up, something inside caused me to ignore my gift. I didn't want to be bothered to use it, you see. I wanted to have fun, marry, and live an ordinary life. I chose that heavily traveled path. Time will tell me if I've wronged.*
>
> *I do suspect I haven't acted wisely, but alas, I'm committed and strong-willed, I'm told. What I'm bestowing on you is the gift I never unwrapped or allowed any daughter I might have to unwrap. The gift to feel the vibrations from gemstones surely resides now within you. I trust my sister has helped you understand this is your path to sustaining joy.*
>
> *So, dear one, today must surely be your graduation, like others that have come before you. This day, you begin anew by using your special gifts to help others. Gems are powerful. Let them teach you how to apply their powers. But first, you must meet the gems you have an affinity with. And that, precious granddaughter, is the "piece of peace" I leave in your hands now. You need look no further.*
>
> *Your loving grandmother,*
> *Violet*

Lacey removed the remaining papers from the envelope, unfolding them carefully. The writing on the heavier paper reminded her of calligraphy. Shock hit her as she read the document. A flush gave her skin a rosy glow that only intensified as the words sank in.

"What? Not possible! Cassie, this…this…is a…deed to a gem mine right here on Old Mountain." Lacey couldn't breathe. She wouldn't breathe until she opened the tiny envelope.

"Don't you go gettin' swoony on me, Missy. Go on. Open that last blessin.'" Cassie had to admit she was having some trouble taking in air herself.

Lacey's fingers shook as she emptied the envelope's contents into her hand. She peered down at the face of a second rainbow gem matching the pendant hanging from her neck. Could this be? *Impossible*, her mind answered without hesitation, but the teaching of Cassie and Violet said otherwise.

She'd been bequeathed a mine of the unknown rainbow gemstones. Lacey gave the rocker a workout as her poor mind tried to catch up with the joy filling her spirit. She'd had the chamber door open. She'd been given a way to share her gifts with others, and it all happened in the Now, as Cassie had been promising. Further proof wasn't needed of The Three Lessons value.

Lacey realized that seeking the uncommon path to meet Old Mountain Cassie had led her right to the rainbow and her own divine pot of gold. Lacey felt the smile form around her heart before it broke through to her face. "You know, Aunt Cassie, we have riches far greater than a wishing well with gold nuggets or this glorious gem I'm holding. We have the priceless treasure of knowing how to live with God in the Now where everything we need is waiting." Lacey beamed her joy.

"And speakin' that truth, Missy, earns you the Divine Diploma."

Epilogue

The Christmas Season

To an outsider arriving in Divine, the scene looked like a picture straight from a Charles Dickens Christmas. The festive season was upon the village, bringing a fresh offering of snow and holiday spirit. The white powder covered the streets and, while not inviting to vehicles, did welcome the half dozen leased horse-drawn sleighs and drivers in black top hats that the town's business owners had voted to employ. This extra piece of nostalgia was meant to grow Divine's coffers while offering a safer means to transport folks around the town's slippery streets.

Lacey smiled at the magical scene playing outside her shop's window. With the help of Divine providence, her two aunts, and friends, she'd managed to get Divine Gems, the town's only unique jewelry shop, opened just in time to celebrate the holiday season.

She finished putting the tray of custom-made gemstone rings into the showcase pausing a moment to take in her shop's still evolving spirit. Cassie had given her two words meant to inspire, as she brought her dream to life… "nature's enchantments." Those powerful words had remained with her as she designed and decorated the inside, and especially while she crafted her enchanting jewelry in the backroom studio.

Lacey took in the décor surrounding her, appreciating how the gold walls painted the color bliss seemed to glow with the natural light pouring through the large bay window. The high beadboard ceiling she'd left distressed, large geodes, and wood carvings of critters were scattered in a few places to help capture the nature's enchantment theme.

Her jewelry pieces rested on velvet in three antique walnut showcases that had lived life in a turn-of-the-century candy store, according to Aunt Gabby, who had snagged them at a dear price and declared them meant for the shop. Lacey loved the addition of the upholstered moss green stools in front of each showcase, which gave her customers a place to relax and enjoy their time spent with the rainbow gems she'd named Divine's.

In the corner, a brass table held a brewer of hot tea with a special blend created by Aunt Cassie that guaranteed to enliven each customer with only one sip. A tray of Jane Ann's freshly baked gingerbread cookies iced with lemon buttercream rested next to the napkins and brown mugs. Delectable offerings were carefully chosen daily to please the body's palate, the décor to settle and quiet the mind, and the gems once embraced to impart what the spirit needed.

The gems' presence in the shop had an immediate energizing effect on everyone who entered, even if they spent only a short time surrounded by their influence. She'd been working like one of Santa's elves to get a few dozen jewelry pieces finished while staying true to her vision of using only cut and faceted gems from her mine. Lacey had come to learn that the stones carried more meaning and power for the wearer than there were stars in the galaxy. They were a source of infinite good.

Lacey continued to be a loyal and devoted student of Cassie's teachings. The Lessons and God's breath touched her every moment with blessings and guidance. She felt immeasurable gratitude for having had the life-altering encounter with Old Mountain Cassie. The joy of what her life's purpose was bringing to her had only intensified with the passing of time.

Of course, she'd enjoyed a steady stream of customers, each bringing through her door a need, a desire that she with God's grace had been able to meet. Even kind, sweet Elliot had taken on the job of spreading the word around to Divine's men that Lacey had the "perfect pretty" for their wives.

The scene continued out the shop's window with Paulie tucking a tartan throw around Serene's legs before signaling the sleigh's driver to proceed up the street. Lacey glimpsed Jane Ann with Charlie holding Rascal's lead as they walked toward his market. And to see Bud from Sweet Clover Dairy slip in the Percolator Coffee House's door right behind Barbie meant something else was brewing in there besides coffee. "Love is surely in the air," she said, grinning at Topaz who sauntered by. The cat preferred to spend his days in the shop now that Gabby no longer was at the cottage to provide a venue for his mischief.

The door chimed, bringing Lacey's attention to the day's first customer. "Good morning, Mayor. What brings you out and about so early?"

Mayor Morgan yanked off his hat and gloves, his face flushed a deep red, his breathing labored. "Lacey, you've got to save me. I just heard my wife on the phone with Mable Mercer telling her she would put me in the doghouse for sure and nail my normally swinging door shut if I forgot our anniversary this morning. I don't have much time here. She'll be calling me to brunch soon." He grabbed a breath, making his way to Lacey with unusual speed for the portly man.

Lacey hid a grin with her hand knowing that his wife kept him on a tight leash. "So, I'm assuming you forgot today was your anniversary?"

"Yep, I did, but honestly, I don't know why I can't remember the dang day. The woman loves to remind me often enough how she was the best Christmas gift I ever got in this life." Mayor Morgan scratched his head, thinking about his dilemma.

"What have you done so far, and how can I help save you?" Lacey beamed him a wide smile, hoping to calm the worried man.

"For starters, I've just slipped out of the house, leaving the shower running and the bathroom door locked so Mildred wouldn't get wise to me being gone. No, don't ask me how I plan to get back in there. I haven't worked that part out just yet, but I need a special gift for her that will impress the woman enough to let me sleep in my bed tonight and not on that frilly overstuffed sofa she just bought. I really need something extra special, Lacey, and speedy."

"A special gift? Hmmm…"

The mayor jumped back in, "Elliot and some of the other fellows have bragged to me that you have a knack for helping us men find jewelry that puts some spell on our women, making them feel all 'sappy happy.' I need one of those pieces in the worst possible way. What ya got to show me? Quick, pull out something from this case." The mayor sat down on the stool, glancing at his wristwatch.

"Since you're in a terrible hurry, I won't waste time responding to the 'sappy happy' comment. I'll save that for another time." Lacey chuckled. "Relax and let me have a few seconds to get a clear sense of what jewelry style Mildred would connect with. The ideal piece spoke to Lacey as she pulled out the tray of pins. "This one should do nicely. Your wife wears a lot of scarves, and this ornate floral design with the center cut oval stone would be perfect on a scarf." She handed the piece to the mayor.

He gave it a cursory glance but then paused before handing it back to Lacey. The stone captured his eye. "Why, this is incredible! I've never seen a gem with all these colors flashing." He continued to gaze into the stone's heart. "This is perfect for my Mildred," he said in a now calm and uncharacteristically loving voice.

Lacey smiled, appreciating the gem's powers at work. "I think so too. Give me a moment to wrap it, and we can settle the bill later." Lacey put the pin in a Divine Gems box with a multicolored ribbon atop and handed it to the jubilant mayor. "Happy Anniversary. And, Mayor, something tells me Mildred is going to feel a lot more than 'sappy happy' very soon. Good luck getting back in the house," Lacey hollered to his retreating back.

"Thanks, Lacey…for everything." He opened the door and stood aside as a younger man entered. "If you're in the doghouse with the wife, you've come to the right place."

"No wife. For me, it's an older sister."

"Well, good luck." In a rush, the mayor let the door slam, setting the electronic bell to ring like an alarm.

Startled by the noise, Lacey turned away from her gift-wrapping station to come face-to-face with a man whose smile set her aglow, but it was his discerning eyes, the color of warm cognac, that drew her in. Her breath caught. She dropped the box of bows and quickly kneeled to gather them, still not having spoken a single word of greeting.

"Let me give you a hand before I beg your help in choosing a present for my impossible-to-please sister. My name's Sam, and I've just moved to Divine." He dropped down next to her, throwing some of the bows into the box.

"Thanks. I'm Lacey," she replied, amazed that she could form three words. Her heart did some crazy flip-flop. Whatever was wrong with her? And for heaven's sake, why was the doorbell still chiming?

Old Mountain Cassie stood outside Lacey's shop window with Lickety Split by her side. She rubbed the dog's ears absently while nodding her head at what she saw happening inside. "About time her fella showed up, and looks like we've got us another new Seeker."

About the Author

As an author, Tonya's both sensitive and moved by the effect that inspirational narratives can have on people. Those observations illuminate why her prose often conveys powerful spiritual messages, which invite reflection and exploration by her readers.

When Tonya moved to the mountains, she found fresh writing ideas waiting. From her favorite porch rocker, gazing out at a tranquil lake, the irresistible character of Old Mountain Cassie came calling, bringing the nudge to scribe her story.

She is enthusiastic about crafting beguiling characters, dashes of snappy humor, and engaging dialogue, which leaves her fingerprint on each page.

Tonya seeks quiet at undiscovered coffeehouses, cherishes walks on secluded beaches, and always, always takes "the road less traveled" (F. Scott Peck).

Both her fiction and nonfiction stories have been published in numerous anthologies, e-magazines, local press, and literary magazines. She chooses to write using different pen surnames for each genre but remains true to her given name…Tonya.

She invites readers to visit www.tonyawrites.com.

CPSIA information can be obtained
at www.ICGtesting.com
Printed in the USA
LVHW09s0117160918
590266LV00001B/124/P